WHEN THE CRITICS READ

Something

Happened

THIS IS WHAT HAPPENED!

———o———

"Joseph Heller has discovered and possessed new territories of the imagination, and he has produced a major work of fiction, one that is as distinctive of its kind as *Catch-22*, but more ambitious and profound, a brilliant commentary on American life that must surely be considered as the most important novel in at least a decade!"

—John W. Aldridge
in *Saturday Review/World*

"Endlessly fascinating . . . Maintains Heller in the first rank of American writers . . . The vision we get is one of chilling recognition. What is revealed is not really the hero at all, but ourselves. Me. You. Them."

—William Kennedy
in *The New Republic*

The Literary Happening

"*Catch-22* became the novel of the '60s. Now Heller has provided the novel of and from the '70s . . . In his first book Heller took on the military system. This time he's undoing the American Dream."

—Larry Swindell
in the *Philadelphia Inquirer*

"A major literary event!"

—Eliot Fremont-Smith
in *New York Magazine*

"Magnificent . . . powerful . . . an extraordinary novel . . . the most talked-out book of the year . . . a true novel of our times."

—*Publishers Weekly*

of the Decade!

"Riveting . . . with a brilliant and exquisitely prepared-for shock ending that makes everything fall into place . . . you have to take it seriously!"
—Mary Ellin Barrett
in *Cosmopolitan*

"It keeps the reader transfixed!"
—*Los Angeles Times*

"It will be read and read and read!"
—*Kirkus Reviews*

MORE PRAISE FOR

SOMETHING HAPPENED

"Convincing and compelling!"

—Rust Hills
in *Esquire*

"The satisfying successor to *Catch-22*!"

—*Baltimore Sun*

"Do you dare allow a book to bruise you like a kicked apple? If so, you will—no, you must—read Joseph Heller's *Something Happened*!"

—*Cincinnati Enquirer*

Something Happened

Joseph Heller

BALLANTINE BOOKS • NEW YORK

A portion of this book first appeared in *Esquire*.

Library of Congress Catalog Card Number: 74-8550

ISBN 0-345-27538-1

This edition published by arrangement with Alfred A. Knopf, Inc.

Manufactured in the United States of America

First Ballantine Books Edition: September 1975
Ninth Printing: November 1977

Something Happened

I get the willies

I get the willies when I see closed doors. Even at work, where I am doing so well now, the sight of a closed door is sometimes enough to make me dread that something horrible is happening behind it, something that is going to affect me adversely; if I am tired and dejected from a night of lies or booze or sex or just plain nerves and insomnia, I can almost smell the disaster mounting invisibly and flooding out toward me through the frosted glass panes. My hands may perspire, and my voice may come out strange. I wonder why.

Something must have happened to me sometime.

Maybe it was the day I came home unexpectedly with a fever and a sore throat and caught my father in bed with my mother that left me with my fear of doors, my fear of opening doors and my suspicion of closed ones. Or maybe it was the knowledge that we were poor, which came to me late in childhood, that made me the way I am. Or the day my father died and left me feeling guilty and ashamed—because I thought I was the only little boy in the whole world then who had no father. Or maybe it was the realization, which came to me early, that I would never have broad shoulders and huge biceps, or be good enough, tall enough, strong enough, or brave enough to become an All-American football player or champion prizefighter, the sad, discouraging realization that no matter what it was in life I ever tried to do, there would

1

always be somebody close by who would be able to do it much better. Or maybe it was the day I did open another door and saw my big sister standing naked, drying herself on the white-tile floor of the bathroom. She yelled at me, even though she knew she had left the door unlocked and that I had stumbled in on her by accident. I was scared.

I remember also, with amusement now, because it happened so long ago, the hot summer day I wandered into the old wooden coal shed behind our red-brick apartment building and found my big brother lying on the floor with Billy Foster's skinny kid sister, who was only my own age and even in the same class I was at school. I had gone to the shed to hammer the wheels and axles from a broken baby carriage I had picked up near a garbage can and use them on a wagon I wanted to make out of a cantaloupe crate and a long plank. I heard a faint, frantic stirring the moment I entered the dark place and felt as though I had stepped on something live. I was startled and smelled dust. I smiled with relief when I saw it was my brother lying on the floor with someone in the sooty shadows filling a far corner. I felt safe again. I said:

"Hi, Eddie. Is that you, Eddie? What are you doing, Eddie?"

And he shouted:

"Get the hell out of here, you little son of a bitch!" And hurled a lump of coal.

I ducked away with a soft moan, tears filling my eyes, and fled for my life. I bolted outside into the steaming, bright sunlight in front of my house, where I scuttled back and forth helplessly on the sidewalk, wondering what in the world I had done to make my big brother so angry with me that he would swear at me like that and hurl a heavy lump of coal. I couldn't decide whether to run away or wait; I felt too guilty to escape and almost too frightened to stay and take the punishment I knew I deserved—although I didn't know for what. Powerless to decide, I hung and quivered there on the sidewalk in front of my house until the enormous wooden door of the old shed finally creaked open toward me and they both came out slowly from the yawning blackness behind. My brother walked in back of her with a smug look. He smiled when he saw me and made me feel better. It was only after I saw him smile that I noticed the girl in front of him was Billy Foster's tall and skinny kid sister, who was very good in penmanship at school but could never get more than a seventy on a spelling, geography, or arithmetic test, even though she always tried to cheat. I was surprised to see them together; it had not entered my mind that he even knew her. She walked with her eyes down and pretended not to see me. They approached slowly. Everything took a long time. She was angry and said nothing. I was silent too. My brother winked at me over her head and gave an exaggerated tug to the top of his pants. He walked with a swagger I had never seen before and knew at once I did not like. It made me uneasy to see him so different. But I was so grateful for his wink that I began wiggling with happiness and excitement and began giggling at him almost uncontrollably. I was giddy with relief and started jabbering. I said:

"Hi, Eddie. What was happening in there, Eddie? Did something happen?"

And he laughed and answered: "Oh, yeah, something happened, all right. Didn't something happen, Geraldine?" And, smirking, nudged her playfully on the arm with his elbow.

Geraldine pulled away from him with a quick, cross smile of annoyance and moved past bot' of us without looking up. When she was gone, my brother said:

"Don't tell Mom."

He knew I wouldn't if he asked me not to.

Later, when I began to visualize and dwell upon (I still do fantasize and dwell upon that episode when I look back, and I look back more and more often now) the many wet, scratchy, intense, intimate things that probably *had* happened on the floor of that coal shed that day, I was amazed and almost marve'ed out loud at the idea of my big brother joined in sex with Billy Foster's skinny kid sister, who was even a few months younger than I was and had big teeth and was not even pretty.

3

There was so much more I wanted to find out then about him and her on the floor of that shed, but I was never bold enough to ask, even though my brother was normally a mild, helpful person who was very good to me while he was alive.

Today, there are so many things I *don't* want to find out. I'd really rather not know, for example (even though my wife and I feel obliged to probe), exactly what kind of games are played at the parties my teenage daughter goes to, or what kind of cigarettes are smoked, or what color pills or capsules are sniffed or swallowed. When police cars collect, I don't want to know why, although I'm glad they've arrived and hope they've come in time to do what they've been called to do. When an ambulance comes, I'd rather not know for whom. And when children drown, choke, or are killed by automobiles or trains, I don't want to know which children they are, because I'm always afraid they might turn out to be mine.

I have a similar aversion to hospitals and the same misgivings and distaste for people I know who fall ill. I never make hospital visits if I can avoid them, because there's always the risk I might open the door of the private or semiprivate room and come upon some awful sight for which I could not have prepared myself. (I'll never forget my shock in a hospital room the first time I saw a rubber tube running down inside somebody through a nostril still stained with blood. It was tan, that tube, and semitransparent.) When friends, relatives, and business acquaintances are stricken with heart attacks now, I never call the hospital or hospital room to find out how they are, because there's always the danger I might find out they are dead. I try not to talk to their wives and children until I've first checked with somebody else who *has* talked to them and can give me the assurance I want that everything is no worse than before. This sometimes strains relationships (even with my wife, who is always asking everybody how they are and running to hospitals with gifts to visit people who are there), but I don't care. I just don't want to talk to people whose husband or father or wife or mother or child may be dying, even though the dying person himself might be someone I feel deeply attached to. I never want to find out that anybody I know is dead.

One time, though (ha, ha), after someone I knew did die, I braced myself, screwed up my valor, and, feigning ignorance, telephoned the hospital that same day to inquire about his condition. I was curious: I wanted to see what it would feel like to hear the hospital tell me that someone I knew was dead. I wondered how it was done; I was preoccupied and even titillated by this problem of technique. Would they decide he had died, passed away, succumbed, was deceased, or perhaps even had expired? (Like a magazine subscription or an old library card?) The woman on the telephone at the hospital surprised me. She said:

"Mr. _____ is no longer listed as a patient."

It took nerve to make that telephone call, it took *all* my nerve. And I was trembling like a leaf when I hung up. Certainly, my heart was pounding with great joy and excitement at my narrow escape, for I had fancied from my very first syllable, from the first digit I dialed, that the woman at the hospital knew exactly what I was up to—that she could see me right through the telephone connection and could see right into my mind—and would say so. She didn't. She just said what she was instructed to say and let me escape scot-free. (Was it a recorded announcement?) And I have never forgotten that tactful procedure:

"Mr. _____ is no longer listed as a patient."

Mr. _____ was dead. He was no longer among the living. Mr. _____ was no longer listed as a patient, and I had to go to his funeral three days later.

I hate funerals—I hate funerals passionately because there is always something morbid about them—and I do my best to avoid going to any (especially my own, ha, ha). At funerals I do have to attend, I try not to speak to anyone; I merely press palms and look overcome. Occasionally, I mumble something inaudible, and I always lower my eyes, the way I

5

see people do in movies. I don't trust myself to do more. Since I don't know what to say when somebody dies, I'm afraid that anything I do say will be wrong. I really don't trust myself anymore in any tight situation whose outcome I can't control or predict. I'm not even happy changing a fuse or an electric light bulb.

Something did happen to me somewhere that robbed me of confidence and courage and left me with a fear of discovery and change and a positive dread of everything unknown that may occur. I dislike anything unexpected. If furniture is rearranged even slightly (even in my office) without my prior knowledge it is like receiving a blow in the face or a stab in the back. I dislike everything sudden. I am angered and hurt by surprises of every sort; even those surprises that are organized to bring me pleasure always end with a leaden aftertaste of sorrow and self-pity, a sensation that I have been planned against and exploited for somebody else's delight, that a secret has been kept from me, that a conspiracy has succeeded from which I was excluded. (I am not the easiest person to live with.) I loathe conflict (with everyone but the members of my household). There are many small, day-to-day conflicts with which I am simply unable to cope any longer without great agony and humiliation: a disagreement with a repairman who is cheating me out of service or a small amount of money, or a conversation of complaint with one of those blankly elusive people who work in the business offices of telephone companies. (I would sooner let myself be cheated.) Or the time the mice got into the apartment before I became a minor executive with my company and began earning enough money to move out of the city into my own home in Connecticut (which I hate).

I didn't know what to do about those mice. I never saw them. Only the cleaning woman did, or said she did, and one time my wife thought she did, and one time my wife's mother was almost sure she did. After a while the mice just disappeared. They went away. They stopped coming out. I'm not even sure they were really there. We stopped talking about them and they seemed to be gone, and it was just as though

6

they had never been there at all. They were baby mice (according to all responsible accounts) and must have squeezed their way in through the small squares in the grille covering the radiator. I didn't mind the mice too much, as long as I didn't have to see or hear them, although I would often catch myself listening for them and occasionally believe I did hear them. But they gave my wife the creeps and kept her in a constant state of fright. She wanted me to do something about them.

So every night I had to set traps for them. And every morning, while my wife and children watched fearfully over my shoulder, I had to open each of the closet and cupboard doors, peer behind each of the sofas and beds and corner armchairs, to see what new and ugly surprise was lying in wait for me to help launch that particular day. Even no surprise was a shocking surprise. It bothered me to have my family standing around staring at me in such grave absorption and suspense, because two of my children are high-strung and insecure to begin with and were already scared enough. My other boy has brain damage and doesn't know anything. And I wasn't so sure even then that I liked my family well enough as a group to want them pressing upon me so closely in such a tense and personal situation.

I never knew what I would find when I opened the doors to inspect my traps or looked behind the furniture, stove, or refrigerator. I was afraid I would catch the mice and find them dead in the traps and have to dispose of them. I was afraid that I wouldn't catch the mice, and that I would have to go through the same repulsive ritual of setting and inspecting the traps night after night and morning after morning for God knows how long. What I dreaded most of all, though, was that I would open a door in the kitchen and find a live mouse crouching in a dark corner that would hesitate only long enough for me to spy it and then come bounding out past me beneath the thick, rolled-up magazine I always gripped in my sweating fist as a weapon. Oh, God, if that ever happened. If that ever happened, I knew I would have to make myself hit it as hard as I could. I knew I would

7

have to force myself to swing at it with all my strength and try to bludgeon the poor thing to death with one solid blow, and I knew I would fail and only cripple it. Then, as it lay there before me still struggling on its smashed and broken legs, although I would not want to, I knew I would have to raise the heavy magazine and club it again, and then again, and perhaps then again, until I had killed it completely.

The possibility of finding a live mouse behind every door I opened each morning filled me with nausea and made me tremble. It was not that I was afraid of the mouse itself (I'm not that silly), but if I ever did find one, I knew I would have to do something about it.

The office
in which I work

In the office in which I work there are five people
of whom I am afraid. Each of these five people is
afraid of four people (excluding overlaps), for a total
of twenty, and each of these twenty people is afraid
of six people, making a total of one hundred and
twenty people who are feared by at least one person.
Each of these one hundred and twenty people is afraid
of the other one hundred and nineteen, and all of
these one hundred and forty-five people are afraid
of the twelve men at the top who helped found and
build the company and now own and direct it.

All these twelve men are elderly now and drained
by time and success of energy and ambition. Many
have spent their whole lives here. They seem friendly,
slow, and content when I come upon them in the
halls (they seem dead) and are always courteous
and mute when they ride with others in the public
elevators. They no longer work hard. They hold meetings, make promotions, and allow their names to be
used on announcements that are prepared and issued
by somebody else. Nobody is sure anymore who really
runs the company (not even the people who are cred-
ited with running it), but the company does run.
Sometimes these twelve men at the top work for the
government for a little while. They don't seem interested in doing much more. Two of them know what I
do and recognize me, because I have helped them in
the past, and they have been kind enough to remember

me, although not, I'm sure, by name. They inevitably smile when they see me and say: "How are you?" (I inevitably nod and respond: "Fine.") Since I have little contact with these twelve men at the top and see them seldom, I am not really afraid of them. But most of the people I am afraid of in the company are.

Just about everybody in the company is afraid of somebody else in the company, and I sometimes think I am a cowering boy back in the automobile casualty insurance company for which I used to work very long ago, sorting and filing automobile accident reports after Mrs. Yerger was placed in charge of the file room and kept threatening daily to fire us all. She was a positive, large woman of overbearing confidence and nasty amiability who never doubted the wisdom of her biases. A witty older girl named Virginia sat under a big Western Union clock in that office and traded dirty jokes with me ("My name's Virginia—Virgin for short, but not for long, ha, ha."); she was peppy and direct, always laughing and teasing (with me, anyway), and I was too young and dumb then to see that she wasn't just joking. (Good God—she used to ask me to get a room for us somewhere, and I didn't even know how! She was extremely pretty, I think now, although I'm not sure I thought so then, but I did like her, and she got me hot. Her father had killed himself a few years before.) Much went on there in that company too that I didn't know about. (Virginia herself had told me that one of the married claims adjusters had taken her out in his car one night, turned insistent, and threatened to rape her or put her out near a cemetery, until she pretended to start to cry.) I was afraid to open doors in that company too, I remember, even when I had been sent for by one of the lawyers or adjusters to bring in an important file or a sandwich. I was never sure whether to knock or walk right in, to tap deferentially or rap loudly enough to be heard at once and command admission. Either way, I would often encounter expressions of annoyance and impatience (or feel I did. I had arrived too soon or arrived too late).

Mrs. Yerger bullied us all. In a little while, nearly all of the file clerks quit, a few of the older ones

10

to go into the army or navy, the rest of us for better jobs. I left for a better job that turned out to be worse. It took nerve to give notice I was quitting, and it always has. (I rehearsed my resignation speech for days, building up the courage to deliver it, and formulated earnest, self-righteous answers to accusing questions about my reasons for leaving that neither Mrs. Yerger nor anyone else even bothered to ask.) I have this thing about authority, about walking right up to it and looking it squarely in the eye, about speaking right out to it bravely and defiantly, even when I know I am right and safe. (I can never make myself believe I *am* safe.) I just don't trust it.

That was my first job after graduating (or being graduated *from*) high school. I was seventeen then—that "older," witty, flirting girl under the Western Union clock, Virginia, was only twenty-one (too young now by at least a year or two, even for me)—and in every job I've had since, I've always been afraid I was about to be fired. Actually, I have never been fired from a job; instead, I receive generous raises and rapid promotions, because I am usually very alert (at the beginning) and grasp things quickly. But this feeling of failure, this depressing sense of imminent catastrophe and public shame, persists even here, where I do good work steadily and try to make no enemies. It's just that I find it impossible to know exactly what is going on behind the closed doors of all the offices on all the floors occupied by all the people in this and all the other companies in the whole world who might say or do something, intentionally or circumstantially, that could bring me to ruin. I even torture myself at times with the ominous speculation that the CIA, FBI, or Internal Revenue Service has been investigating me surreptitiously for years and is about to close in and arrest me, for no other reason than that I have some secret liberal sympathies and usually vote Democratic.

I have a feeling that someone nearby is soon going to find out something about me that will mean the end, although I can't imagine what that something is.

11

In the normal course of a business day, I fear Green and Green fears me. I am afraid of Jack Green because my department is part of his department and Jack Green is my boss; Green is afraid of me because most of the work in my department is done for the Sales Department, which is more important than his department, and I am much closer to Andy Kagle and the other people in the Sales Department than he is.

Green distrusts me fitfully. He makes it clear to me every now and then that he wishes to see everything coming out of my department before it is shown to other departments. I know he does not really mean this: he is too busy with his own work to pay that much attention to all of mine, and I will bypass him on most of our assignments rather than take up his time and delay their delivery to people who have (or think they have) an immediate need for them. Most of the work we do in my department is, in the long run, trivial. But Green always grows alarmed when someone from another department praises something that has come from my department. He turns scarlet with rage and embarrassment if he has not seen or heard of it. (He is no less splenetic if he *has* seen it and fails to remember it.)

The men in the Sales Department like me (or pretend to). They don't like Green. He knows this. They complain about him to me and make uncomplimentary remarks, and he knows this too. He pretends he doesn't. He feigns indifference, since he doesn't really like the men in the Sales Department. I don't really like them, either (but I pretend I do). Generally, Green makes no effort to get along with the men in the Sales Department and is pointedly aloof and disdainful. He worries, though, about the enmity he creates there. Green worries painfully that someday soon the Corporate-Operations Department will take my department away from his department and give it to the Sales Department. Green has been worrying about this for eighteen years.

In my department, there are six people who are afraid of me, and one small secretary who is afraid of all of us. I have one other person working for me who is not afraid of anyone, not even me, and I would fire him quickly, but I'm afraid of him.

The thought occurs to me often that there must be mail clerks, office boys and girls, stock boys, messengers, and assistants of all kinds and ages who are afraid of *everyone* in the company; and there in one typist in our department who is going crazy slowly and has all of *us* afraid of *her*.

Her name is Martha. Our biggest fear is that she will go crazy on a weekday between nine and five. We hope she'll go crazy on a weekend, when we aren't with her. We should get her out of the company now, while there is still time. But we won't. Somebody should fire her; nobody will. Even Green, who actually enjoys firing people, recoils from the responsibility of making the move that might bring about her shattering collapse, although he cannot stand her, detests the way she looks, and is infuriated by every reminder that she still exists in his department. (It was he who hired her after a cursory interview, on a strong recommendation of the woman in the Personnel Department who is in charge of finding typists and sending them up.) Like the rest of us, he tries to pretend she isn't there.

We watch her and wait, and pussyfoot past, and wonder to ourselves how much more time must elapse before she comes on schedule to that last, decisive second in which she finally does go insane—shrieking or numb, clawing wildly or serene, comprehending intelligently that she has now gone mad and must therefore be taken away, or terrified, ignorant, and confused.

Oddly, she is much happier at her job than the rest of us. Her mind wanders from her work to more satisfying places, and she smiles and whispers contentedly to herself as she gazes out over her typewriter roller at the blank wall only a foot or two in ·front of her face, forgetting what or where she is and the page she is supposed to be copying. We walk away

13

from her if we can, or turn our backs and try not to notice. We each hope somebody else will do or say something to make her stop smiling and chatting to herself each time she starts. When we cannot, in all decency, delay any longer doing it ourselves, we bring her back to our office and her work with gentle reminders that contain no implication of criticism or reproach. We feel she would be surprised and distraught if she knew what she was doing and that she was probably going mad. Other times she is unbearably nervous, unbearable to watch and be with. Everyone is very careful with her and very considerate. Green has complained about her often to the head of Personnel, who does not want to fire her either and has contacted her family in Iowa. Her mother has married again and doesn't want her back. Martha has bad skin. Everyone resents her and wishes she would go away.

The company is benevolent. The people, for the most part, are nice, and the atmosphere, for the most part, is convivial. The decor of the offices, particularly in the reception rooms and anterooms, is bright and colorful. There is lots of orange and lots of sea green. There are lots of office parties. We get all legal holidays off and take three days off with pay whenever we need them. We have many three- and four-day weekends. (I can't face these long weekends anymore and don't know how I survive them. I may have to take up skiing.)

Every two weeks we are paid with machine-processed checks manufactured out of stiff paper (they are not thick enough to be called cardboard) that are patterned precisely with neat, rectangular holes and words of formal, official warning in small, black, block letters that the checks must not be spindled, torn, defaced, stapled, or mutilated in any other way. (They must only be cashed.) If not for these words, it would never occur to me to do anything else with my check but deposit it. Now, though, I am occasionally intrigued. What would happen, I speculate gloomily every two weeks or so as I tear open the blank, buff

14

pay envelope and stare dully at the holes and numbers and words on my punched-card paycheck as though hoping disappointedly for some large, unrectifiable mistake in my favor, if I did spindle, fold, tear, deface, staple, and mutilate it? (It's my paycheck, isn't it? Or is it?) What would happen if, deliberately, calmly, with malice aforethought and obvious premeditation, I disobeyed?

I know what would happen: nothing. Nothing would happen. And the knowledge depresses me. Some girl downstairs I never saw before (probably with a bad skin also) would simply touch a few keys on some kind of steel key punch that would set things right again, and it would be as though I had not disobeyed at all. My act of rebellion would be absorbed like rain on an ocean and leave no trace. I would not cause a ripple.

I suppose it is just about impossible for someone like me to rebel anymore and produce any kind of lasting effect. I have lost the power to upset things that I had as a child; I can no longer change my environment or even disturb it seriously. They would simply fire and forget me as soon as I tried. They would file me away. That's what will happen to Martha the typist when she finally goes crazy. She'll be fired and forgotten. She'll be filed away. She'll be given sick pay, vacation pay, and severance pay. She'll be given money from the pension fund and money from the profit-sharing fund, and then all traces of her will be hidden safely out of sight inside some old green cabinet for dead records in another room on another floor or in a dusty warehouse somewhere that nobody visits more than once or twice a year and few people in the company even know exists; not unlike the old green cabinets of dead records in all those accident folders in the storage room on the floor below the main offices of the automobile casualty insurance company for which I used to work when I was just a kid. When she goes crazy, her case will be closed.

I had never imagined so many dead records as I saw in that storage room (and there were thousands and thousands of even deader records at the warehouse I had to go to once or twice a year when a question

15

arose concerning a record that had been dead a really long time). I remember them accurately, I remember the garish look of the data in grotesquely blue ink on the outside of each folder: a number, a name, an address, a date, and an abbreviated indication of whether the accident involved damage to property only (PD) or damage to people (PI, for personal injury). Often, I would bring sandwiches from home (baloney, cooked chopped meat with lots of ketchup, or tuna fish or canned salmon and tomato) and eat them in the storage room downstairs on my lunch hour, and if I ate there alone, I would read the New York *Mirror* (a newspaper now also dead) and then try to entertain myself by going through some old accident folders picked from the file cabinets at random. I was searching for action, tragedy, the high drama of detective work and courtroom suspense, but it was no use. They were dead. None of the names or appraisals or medical statements or investigations or eyewitness reports brought anything back to life. (The *Mirror* was better, and even its up-to-the-minute true stories of family and national misfortunes read just like the comic strips.) What impressed me most was the sheer immensity of all those dead records, the abounding quantity of all those drab old sagging cardboard file cabinets rising like joined, ageless towers from the floor almost to the ceiling, that vast, unending sequence of unconnected accidents that had been happening to people and cars long before I came to work there, were happening then, and are happening still.

There was a girl in that company too who went crazy while I was there. She was filed away. And in the company I worked for before this one, there was a man, a middle-minor executive, who went crazy and jumped out of a hotel window and killed himself; he left a note saying he was sorry he was jumping out of the hotel window and killing himself, that he would have shot himself instead but didn't know how to obtain a gun or use one. He was picked up off the ground by the police (probably) and filed away.

I think that maybe in every company today there

is always at least one person who is going crazy slowly.

The company is having another banner year. It continues to grow, and in many respects we are the leader in the field. According to our latest Annual Report, it is bigger and better this year than it was last year.

We have twenty-nine offices now, twelve in this country, two in Canada, four in Latin America, and eleven overseas. We used to have one in Cuba, but that was lost. We average three suicides a year; two men, usually on the middle-executive level, kill themselves every twelve months, almost always by gunshot, and one girl, usually unmarried, separated, or divorced, who generally does the job with sleeping pills. Salaries are high, vacations are long.

People in the company like to live well and are unusually susceptible to nervous breakdowns. They have good tastes and enjoy high standards of living. We are well-educated and far above average in abilities and intelligence. Everybody spends. Nobody saves. Nervous breakdowns are more difficult to keep track of than suicides because they are harder to recognize and easier to hush up. (A suicide, after all, is a suicide: there's something final about it. It's the last thing a person does. But who knows with certainty when a person is breaking down?) But nervous breakdowns do occur regularly in all age and occupational groups and among all kinds of people—thin people and fat people, tall people and short people, good people and bad people. In the few years I have been in charge of my department, one girl and one man here have each been out for extended absences because they broke down. Both have been fixed and are now back working for me, and not many people outside my department know why they were gone. (One of them, the man, hasn't been fixed too well, I think, and will probably break down again soon. He is already turning into a problem again, with me and with everyone else he talks to. He talks too much.)

17

In an average year, four people I know about in the company will die of natural causes and two-and-a-half more (two men one year, three the next) will go on sick leave for ailments that will eventually turn out to be cancer. Approximately two people will be killed in accidents every year, one in an auto, the other by fire or drowning. Nobody in the company has yet been killed in an airplane crash, and this is highly mysterious to me, for we travel a lot by air to visit other offices or call on customers, prospects, and suppliers in other cities and countries. When regular, full-time employees do go on sick leave, they are usually paid their full salary for as long as the illness lasts (even though it may last a lifetime. Ha, ha), for the company excels in this matter of employee benefits. Everybody is divorced (not me, though). Everyone drinks and takes two hours or more for lunch. The men all flirt. The women all respond, except for a few who are very religious or very dull, or a few very young ones who are out in the world for the first time and don't understand yet how things are.

Most of us like working here, even though we are afraid, and do not long to leave for jobs with other companies. We make money and have fun. We read books and go to plays. And somehow the time passes.

This fiscal period, I am flirting with Jane. Jane is new in the Art Department and not quite sure whether I mean it or not. She is just a few years out of college, where she majored in fine arts, and still finds things in the city daring, sophisticated, and intellectual. She goes to the movies a lot. She has not, I think, slept with a married man yet.

Jane is assistant head of the Art Department in Green's department. There are only three people in the Art Department. She has, like the rest of us, much time in which to brood and fantasize and make personal phone calls and kid around with whoever in the company (me) wants to kid around with her. She has a tall, slim figure that's pretty good and a clogged

18

duct in one eye that makes it dribble with tears. She wears loose lamb's-wool sweaters that hug the long points of her small breasts beautifully. (Often, my fingertips would love to hug and roll those same long points of her small breasts just as beautifully, but I know from practice that my desire would not remain with her breasts for long. They make a convenient starting place.) Her good figure, prominent nipples, and clogged tear duct give me an easy opening for suggestive wisecracks that cover the same ground as those I used to exchange with that older girl Virginia under the big Western Union clock in the automobile casualty insurance company (the company is still in business after all these years, at the same place, and probably the clock too is still there, running, although the office building is now slated to come down), except that now I am the older, more experienced (and more jaded) one and can control and direct things pretty much the way I choose. I have the feeling now that I can do whatever I want to with Jane, especially on days when she's had two vodka martinis for lunch instead of one (I, personally, hate vodka martinis and mistrust the mettle of people who drink them) or three whiskey sours instead of two. I could, if I wished, take her out for *three* vodka martinis after work one day and then up to Red Parker's apartment nearby, and the rest, I'd bet, would be as easy as pie (and possibly no more thrilling). I can make Jane laugh whenever I want to, and this, I know, can be worth more than half the game if I decide I seriously do want to play, but *I'm* not sure either whether I mean it or not.

Probably, I should be ashamed of myself, because she's only a decent young girl of twenty-four. Possibly I should be proud of myself, because she is, after all, a decent and very attractive young girl of only twenty-four whom I can probably lay whenever I want to. (I have her scheduled vaguely somewhere ahead, probably in the weeks before the convention, when I will be using everybody in the Art Department a great deal.) I don't really know how I am supposed to feel. I do know that girls in their early twenties are easy and sweet. (Girls in their late twenties are

19

easier but sad, and that isn't so sweet.) They are easy, I think, because they are sweet, and they are sweet, I think, because they are dumb.

On days when *I've* had two martinis for lunch, Jane's breasts and legs can drive me almost wild as she parks her slender ass against the wall of one of the narrow corridors in the back offices near the Art Department when I stop to kid with her. Jane smiles a lot and is very innocent (she thinks I'm a very nice man, for example), although she is not, of course, without some sex experience, about which she boasts laughingly when I taunt her with being a virgin and denies laughingly when I taunt her with being a whore. I make teasing, rather mechanical and juvenile jokes (I've made them all before to other girls and ladies in one variation or another) about her eye or sweater or the good or bad life I pretend she is leading as I lean down almost slavering toward the front of her skirt (I don't know how she can bear me in these disgusting moments—but she can) and gaze lecherously over the long stretch of her thighs underneath, even though I know already I would probably find her legs a little thin when I had her undressed and would probably describe her as a bit too skinny if I ever spoke about her afterward to anyone.

I think I really do like Jane a lot. She is cheerful, open, trusting, optimistic—and I don't meet many of *those* anymore. Till now, I've decided to do nothing with her except continue the lascivious banter between us that tickles and amuses and encourages us both. Maybe her face and her figure are a little too good. I used to like girls who were tall and heavy, and slightly coarse, and maybe I still do, but I seem to be doing most of my sleeping these days with girls who are slim and pretty and mostly young. My wife is tall and slim and used to be very pretty when she was young.

The people in the company who are most afraid of most people are the salesmen. They live and work under pressure that is extraordinary. (I would not be able to stand it.) When things are bad, they are

20

worse for the salesmen; when things are good, they are not much better.

They are always on trial, always on the verge of failure, collectively and individually. They strain, even the most secure and self-assured of them, to look good on paper; and there is much paper for them to look good on. Each week, for example, a record of the sales results of the preceding week for each sales office and for the Sales Department as a whole for each division of the company is kept and compared to the sales results for the corresponding week of the year before; the figures are photocopied on the latest photocopying machines and distributed throughout the company to all the people and departments whose work is related to selling. In addition to this, the sales record for each sales office for each quarter of each year for each division of the company and for the company as a whole is tabulated and compared to the sales record for the corresponding quarter of the year before; along with this, cumulative quarterly sales totals are also kept, and all these quarterly sales totals are photocopied and distributed too. In addition to this, quarterly and cumulative sales totals are compared with quarterly and cumulative sales totals* (*estimated) of other companies in the same field, and these figures are photocopied and distributed too. The figures are tabulated in stacks and layers of parallel lines and columns for snap comparisons and judgments by anyone whose eyes fall upon them. The result of all this photocopying and distributing is that there is almost continuous public scrutiny and discussion throughout the company of how well or poorly the salesmen in each sales office of each division of the company are doing at any given time.

When salesmen are doing well, there is pressure upon them to begin doing better, for fear they may start doing worse. When they are doing poorly, they are doing terribly. When a salesman lands a large order or brings in an important new account, his elation is brief, for there is danger he might lose that large order or important new account to a salesman from a competing company (or from a competing division

21

of this company, which shows how complex and orderly the company has become) the next time around. It might even be canceled before it is filled, in which case no one is certain if anything was gained or lost. So there is crisis and alarm even in their triumphs.

Nevertheless, the salesmen love their work and would not choose any other kind. They are a vigorous, fun-loving bunch when they are not suffering abdominal cramps or brooding miserably about the future; on the other hand, they often turn cranky without warning and complain and bicker a lot. Some sulk, some bully; some bully and then sulk. All of them drink heavily until they get hepatitis or heart attacks or are warned away from heavy drinking for some other reason, and all of them, sooner or later, begin to feel they are being picked on and blamed unfairly. Each of them can name at least one superior in the company who he feels has a grudge against him and is determined to wreck his career.

The salesmen work hard and earn big salaries, with large personal expense accounts that they squander generously on other people in and out of the company, including me. They own good houses in good communities and play good games of golf on good private golf courses. The company encourages this. The company, in fact, will pay for their country club membership and all charges they incur there, if the club they get into is a good one. The company seeks and rewards salesmen who make a good impression on the golf course.

Unmarried men are not wanted in the Sales Department, not even widowers, for the company has learned from experience that it is difficult and dangerous for unmarried salesmen to mix socially with prominent executives and their wives or participate with them in responsible civic affairs. (Too many of the wives of these prominent and very successful men are no more satisfied with their marital situation than are their husbands.) If a salesman's wife dies and he is not ready to remarry, he is usually moved into an administrative position after several months of mourning. Bachelors are never hired for the sales force, and salesmen who get divorced, or whose wives

22

die, know they had better remarry or begin looking ahead toward a different job.

(Red Parker has been a widower too long and is getting into trouble for that and for his excessive drinking. He is having too good a time.)

Strangely enough, the salesmen, who are aggressive, egotistical, and individualistic by nature, react very well to the constant pressure and rigid supervision to which they are subjected. They are stimulated and motivated by discipline and direction. They thrive on explicit guidance toward clear objectives. (This may be one reason golf appeals to them.) For the most part, they are cheerful, confident, and gregarious when they are not irritable, anxious, and depressed. There must be something in the makeup of a man that enables him not only to *be* a salesman, but to *want* to be one. Ours actually *enjoy* selling, although there seem to be many among them who suffer from colitis, hernia, hemorrhoids, and chronic diarrhea (I have one hemorrhoid, and that one comes and goes as it pleases and is no bother to me at all, now that I've been to a doctor and made sure it isn't cancer), not to mention the frequent breakdowns from tension and overwork that occur in the Sales Department as well as in other departments, and the occasional suicide that pops up among the salesmen about once every two years.

The salesmen are proud of their position and of the status and importance they enjoy within the company, for the function of my department, and of most other departments, is to help the salesmen sell. The company exists to sell. That's the reason we were hired, and the reason we are paid.

The people in the company who are least afraid are the few in our small Market Research Department, who believe in nothing and are concerned with collecting, organizing, interpreting, and reorganizing statistical information about the public, the market, the country, and the world. For one thing, their salaries are small, and they know they will not have much trouble finding jobs paying just as little in other companies if they lose their jobs here. Their budget, too, is small, for they are no longer permitted to undertake large projects.

Most of the information we use now is obtained free from trade associations, the U.S. Census Bureau, the Department of Commerce, the U.S. Chamber of Commerce, the National Association of Manufacturers, and the Pentagon, and there is no way of knowing anymore whether the information on which we base our own information for distribution is true or false. But that doesn't seem to matter; all that does matter is that the information come from a reputable source. People in the Market Research Department are never held to blame for conditions they discover outside the company that place us at a competitive disadvantage. What is, is—and they are not expected to change reality, but merely to find it if they can and suggest ingenious ways of disguising it. To a great extent, that is the nature of my own work, and all of us under Green work closely with the Sales Department and the Public Relations Department in converting whole truths into half truths and half truths into whole ones.

I am very good with these techniques of deception, although I am not always able anymore to deceive myself (if I were, I would not know that, would I? Ha, ha). In fact, I am continually astonished by people in the company who do fall victim to their own (our own) propaganda. There are so many now who actually believe that what we do is really important. This happens not only to salesmen, who repeat their various sales pitches aloud so often they acquire the logic and authority of a mumbo-jumbo creed, but to the shrewd, capable executives in top management, who have access to all data ought to know better. It happens to people on my own level and lower. It happens to just about everybody in the company who graduated from a good business school with honors: these are uniformly the most competent and conscientious people in the company, and also the most gullible and naïve. Every time we launch a new advertising campaign, for example, people inside the

24

company are the first ones to be taken in by it. Every time we introduce a new product, or an old product with a different cover, color, and name that we present as new, people inside the company are the first to rush to buy it—even when it's no good.

When salesmen and company spokesmen begin believing their own arguments, the result is not always bad, for they develop an outlook of loyalty, zeal, and conviction that is often remarkably persuasive in itself. It produces that kind of dedication and fanaticism that makes good citizens and good employees. When it happens to a person in my own department, however, the result can be disastrous, for he begins relying too heavily on what he now thinks is the truth and loses his talent for devising good lies. He is no longer convincing. It's exactly what happened to Holloway, the man in my own department who broke down (and is probably going to break down again soon).

"But it's true, don't you see?" he would argue softly to the salesmen, the secretaries, and even to me, with a knowing and indulgent smile, as though what he was saying ought to have been as obvious to everyone as it was to him. "We *are* the best." (The point he missed is that it didn't matter whether it was true or not; what mattered was what people *thought* was true.)

He is beginning to smile and argue that way again and to spend more time talking to us than we want to spend listening to him. My own wish when he is buttonholing me or bending the ear of someone else in my department is that he would hurry up and have his nervous breakdown already, if he is going to have one anyway, and get it—and himself—out of the way. He is the only one who talks to Martha, our typist who is going crazy, and she is the only one who listens to him without restlessness and irritation. She listens to him with great intensity because she is paying no attention to him at all.

Everyone grew impatient with him. And he lost his power to understand (as he is losing this power again) why the salesmen, who would come to him for solid proof to support their exaggerations and misrepresentations, turned skeptical, began to avoid him, and refused to depend on him any longer or even take him to lunch. He actually expected them to get by with only the "truth."

It's a wise person, I guess, who knows he's dumb, and an honest person who knows he's a liar. And it's a dumb person, I guess, who's convinced he is wise, I conclude to myself (wisely), as we wise grown-ups here at the company go gliding in and out all day long, scaring each other at our desks and cubicles and water coolers and trying to evade the people who frighten us. We come to work, have lunch, and go home. We goose-step in and goose-step out, change our partners and wander all about, sashay around for a pat on the head, and promenade home till we all drop dead. Really, I ask myself every now and then, depending on how well or poorly things are going with Green at the office or at home with my wife, or with my retarded son, or with my other son, or my daughter, or the colored maid, or the nurse for my retarded son, is this *all* there is for me to do? Is this really the *most* I can get from the few years left in this one life of mine?

And the answer I get, of course, is always . . . *Yes!*

Because I have my job, draw my pay, get my laughs, and seem to be able to get one girl or another to go to bed with me just about every time I want; because I am envied and looked up to by neighbors and coworkers with smaller salaries, less personality, drab wives; and because I really do seem to have everything I want, although I often wish I were working for someone other than Green, who likes me and likes my work but wouldn't let me make a speech at the company convention in Puerto Rico last year, or at the company convention in Florida the year before—and who knows I hate him for that and will probably never forgive him or ever forget it.

(I have dreams, unpleasant dreams, that relate, I think, to my wanting to speak at a company convention, and they are always dreams that involve bitter frustration and humiliation and insurmountable difficulty in getting from one location to another.)

Green now thinks I am conspiring to undermine him. He is wrong. For one thing, I don't have the initiative; for another, I don't have the nerve; and for still another thing, I guess I really like and admire Green in many respects (even though I also hate and resent him in many others), and I know I am probably safer working for him than I would be working for anyone else—even for Andy Kagle in the Sales Department if they did decide to move me and my department from Green's department to Kagle's department.

In many ways and on many occasions Green and I are friends and allies and do helpful, sometimes considerate things for each other. Often, I protect and defend him when he is late or forgetful with work of his own, and I frequently give him credit for good work from my department that he does not deserve. But I never tell him I do this; and I never let him know when I hear anything favorable about him. I enjoy seeing Green apprehensive. I'm pleased he distrusts me (it does wonders for my self-esteem), and I do no more than necessary to reassure him.

And I am the best friend he has here.

So I scare Green, and Green scares White, and White scares Black, and Black scares Brown and Green, and Brown scares me and Green and Andy Kagle, and all of this is absolutely true, because Horace White really is afraid of conversation with Jack Green, and Johnny Brown, who bulldozes everyone around him with his strong shoulders, practical mind, and tough, outspoken mouth, is afraid of Lester Black, who protects him.

I know it's true, because I worked this whole color wheel out one dull, wet afternoon on one of those organizational charts I am always constructing when I grow bored with my work. I am currently occupied (as one of my private projects) with trying to organize a self-sufficient community out of people in the company whose names are the same as occupations, tools, or natural resources, for we have many Millers, Bakers, Taylors, Carpenters, Fields, Farmers, Hammers,

Nichols (puns are permitted in my Utopia, else how could we get by?), and Butchers listed in the internal telephone directory; possibly we'd be a much better organization if all of us were doing the kind of work our names suggest, although I'm not sure where I'd fit in snugly there, either, because my name means nothing that I know of and I don't know where it came from.

Digging out valuable information of no importance distracts and amuses me. There are eleven Greens in the company (counting Greenes), eight Whites, four Browns, and four Blacks. There is one Slocum . . . me. For a while, there were two Slocums; there was a Mary Slocum in our Chicago office, a short, sexy piece just out of secretarial school with a wiggling ass and a nice big bust, but she quit to get married and was soon pregnant and disappeared. Here and there in the company colored men, Negroes, in immaculate white or blue shirts and very firmly knotted ties are starting to appear; none are important yet, and nobody knows positively why they have come here or what they really want. All of us (almost all of us) are ostentatiously polite to them and pretend to see no difference. In private, the salesmen make jokes about them.

("Know what they said about the first Negro astronaut?"

"What?"

"The jig is up.")

I am bored with my work very often now. Everything routine that comes in I pass along to somebody else. This makes my boredom worse. It's a real problem to decide whether it's more boring to do something boring than to pass along everything boring that comes in to somebody else and then have nothing to do at all.

Actually, I enjoy my work when the assignments are large and urgent and somewhat frightening and will come to the attention of many people. I get scared, and am unable to sleep at night, but I usually perform at my best under this stimulating kind of pressure and enjoy my job the most. I handle all of these impor-

28

tant projects myself, and I rejoice with tremendous pride and vanity in the compliments I receive when I do them well (as I always do). But between such peaks of challenge and elation there is monotony and despair. (And I find, too, that once I've succeeded in impressing somebody, I'm not much excited about impressing that same person again; there is a large, emotional letdown after I survive each crisis, a kind of empty, tragic disappointment, and last year's threat, opportunity, and inspiration are often this year's inescapable tedium. I frequently feel I'm being taken advantage of merely because I'm asked to do the work I'm paid to do.)

On days when I'm especially melancholy, I begin constructing tables of organization from standpoints of plain malevolence, dividing, subdividing, and classifying people in the company on the basis of envy, hope, fear, ambition, frustration, rivalry, hatred, or disappointment. I call these charts my Happiness Charts. These exercises in malice never fail to boost my spirits—but only for a while. I rank pretty high when the company is analyzed this way, because I'm not envious or disappointed, and I have no expectations. At the very top, of course, are those people, mostly young and without dependents, to whom the company is not yet an institution of any sacred merit (or even an institution especially worth preserving) but still only a place to work, and who regard their present association with it as something temporary. To them, it's all just a job, from president to porter, and pretty much the same job at that. I put these people at the top because if you asked any one of them if he would choose to spend the rest of his life working for the company, he would give you a resounding *No!*, regardless of what inducements were offered. I was that high once. If you asked me that same question today, I would also give you a resounding *No!* and add:

"I think I'd rather die now."

But I am making no plans to leave.

I have the feeling now that there is no place left for me to go.

Near the very bottom of my Happiness Charts I put those people who are striving so hard to get to the top. I am better off (or think I am) than they because, first, I have no enemies or rivals (that I know of) and am almost convinced I can hold my job here for as long as I want to and, second, because there is no other job in the company I want that I can realistically hope to get. I wouldn't want Green's job; I couldn't handle it if I had it and would be afraid to take it if it were offered. There is too much to do. I'm glad it won't be (I'm sure it won't be).

I am one of those many people, therefore, most of whom are much older than I, who are without ambition already and have no hope, although I do want to continue receiving my raise in salary each year, and a good cash bonus at Christmastime, and I do want very much to be allowed to take my place on the rostrum at the next company convention in Puerto Rico (if it will be Puerto Rico again this year), along with the rest of the managers in Green's department and make my three-minute report to the company of the work we have done in my department and the projects we are planning for the year ahead.

It was downright humiliating to be the only one of Green's managers left out. The omission was conspicuous, the rebuff intentionally public, and for the following four days, while others had a great, robust time golfing and boozing it up, I was the object of expressions of pity and solemn, perfunctory commiseration from many people I hate and wanted to hit or scream at. It was jealousy and pure, petty spite that made Green decide abruptly to push me off the schedule after we were already in Puerto Rico and the convention had gotten off to such a promising start, and after I had worked so long and nervously (I even rehearsed at home just about every night—to the wonder and consternation of my family) on my speech for the three-minute segment of the program allotted to me and had prepared a very good and witty demonstration of eighteen color slides.

"Stop sulking," Green commanded me curtly, wearing that smile of breezy and complacent innocence he likes to affect when he knows he is cutting deep. "You're a rotten speaker anyway, and you'll probably be much happier working the slide machines and movie projectors and seeing that the slides of the others don't get all mixed up."

"I want to do it, Jack," I told him, trying to keep my voice strong and steady. (What I really wanted to do was burst into tears, and I was afraid I would.) "I've never made a speech at a convention before."

"And you aren't going to make one now."

"This is a good talk I've got here."

"It's dull and self-conscious and of no interest to anyone."

"I've prepared some fine slides."

"You aren't going to use them," he told me.

"You did the same thing to me in Florida last year."

"And I may do it again to you next year."

"It isn't fair."

"It probably isn't."

I waited. He added nothing. He is so much better at this sort of ego-baiting than I am. It was my turn to speak, and he had left me nothing to say.

"Well," I offered, shrugging and looking away.

"I don't care if it's fair or not," he continued then. "We're discussing an important company convention, not a college commencement exercise. I've got to use what little time they give us on the program as effectively as possible."

"It's only three minutes," I begged.

"I can use those three minutes better than you can." He laughed suddenly, in the friendliest, most inoffensive fashion, as though nothing of consequence had just happened, letting me know in that arrogantly firm and rude manner of his that the argument was over. "You must understand, Bob," he bantered (while I thought he might actually throw an arm around my shoulder. He never touches me), "that this ambition of yours to make a little speech is nothing more than a shallow, middle-class vanity. I'm as shallow as you are, and as middle class as the best of them. So I'm going to take your three minutes away

31

from you and cover you and your department in my own speech."

You bastard, I thought. "You're the boss," I said.

"That's right," he retorted coldly. "I am. And you've already received more than enough attention here for an employee of mine. I want to make certain that nobody in this company gets the idea you're working for Andy Kagle and not for me. Or that you're doing a better job in your position than I'm doing in mine. Do you get what I mean?"

I certainly did, then. Green was reasserting his ownership of me publicly by demonstrating his right to treat me with contempt. And in his own long (rather self-conscious and pedantic) speech to the convention, he "covered" me and my department in a single aside:

"And Bob Slocum and his people will help, when you feel you really need them, provided your requests are not unreasonable."

And that was all, even though the two projects I had prepared for the coming year were the real high spots of the whole convention. Everyone was enthusiastic about them, even executives from other divisions of the company, who were there as guests and observers: several asked to meet me and expressed the wish for work of similar kind and quality in their own areas of the company. I could have had a grand, triumphant time that week if not for Green (Green's?) kicking me off the schedule. The salesmen, who would have to use these projects in connection with their own work, congratulated me over and over again and never stopped slapping my back as they drank their whiskey in the evening and their Bloody Marys at breakfast in the morning (although some were already implying that they would want to discuss some modifications with me for their own purposes when the convention was over and we were back in New York). And even Arthur Baron, who is boss of us all in this division, drifted over to me on the terrace of the hotel during one of the twilight cocktail parties to tell me that both my projects were the best of their kind he had ever seen and would probably be very useful.

Arthur Baron, who is tactful and soft-spoken, addressed his comments to Green, who was standing beside me on the terrace because he does not like to be seen standing alone. (I was Green's roosting place for the moment, while he took his bearings; and I knew he would walk from me to someone more important as soon as he spied an opportunity. At crowded social or business gatherings, Green never leaves one person unless he has someone else to move to.) Green laughed quickly and gave all credit for the work to me; then he promptly diminished its importance by declaring he had not even seen any of it until that same afternoon (which was not true, since his criticism and suggestions all through the previous ten weeks had helped enormously, and nothing had been included without his inspection and approval.) Green went on to observe, with another pleasant laugh, that the excellent response to something prepared by me without his knowledge or assistance all went to prove what a superb administrator he was. (All I was able to get in to Arthur Baron was a mumbled:

"Thanks. I'm glad.")

"The only legitimate goal of a good administrator," Green continued affably, smiling directly at Arthur Baron and excluding me from his attention entirely, "is to make himself superfluous as quickly as possible, and then have no work of his own to do until he's promoted to vice-president or retires. Don't you agree?"

Arthur Baron chuckled softly in reply and said nothing. He turned from Green to me, squeezed my shoulder, and moved away. Green beamed hopefully after him, then turned somber and began to worry (I guessed) that his hint to Arthur Baron about a vice-presidency had been too broad. He was already regretting it. Green knows he often pushes too hard—even at the exact moment he is pushing too hard—but he simply cannot control himself. (He is out of his own control.)

(I am in it.) I am dependent on Green. It was Green who hired and promoted me and Green who recommends me for the generous raises and good cash bonuses I receive each year.

"You were a third-rate assistant when you came to work for me," he likes to joke when we are getting along comfortably with each other, "and I turned you into a third-rate manager."

I am grateful to Green for promoting me, even though he makes fun of me often and hurts my feelings.

Green is a clever tactician with long experience at office politics. He is a talented, articulate, intelligent man of fifty-six and has been with the company more than thirty years. He was a young man when he came here; he will soon be old. He has longed from the beginning to become a vice-president and now knows that he will never succeed.

He continues to yearn, and he continues to strive and scheme, sometimes cunningly, other times desperately, abjectly, ineptly, because he can neither admit nor deny to himself for very long that he has already failed. Green fawns compulsively and labors clumsily to curry favor in every contact he has with someone in top management or someone near top management. He knows he does this and is ashamed and remorseful afterward for having demeaned himself in vain; he is willing to demean himself, but not in vain. Often, he will turn perverse afterward and deliberately offend somebody important in order to restore what dignity and self-respect he feels he has lost as a man. He is a baby.

Green is a clever tactician at office politics whose major mistake has always been to overestimate the value of office politics in getting ahead. He has refused to recognize that promotion to high place in the company has invariably been based on certain abilities and accomplishments. He has never really understood why so many people of less intelligence, taste, knowledge, and imagination have gone so much further than he has and *have* become vice-presidents. He does not see that they work hard continuously and that they believe in the company, that they do well and meticulously whatever they are asked to do, that they do *everything* they are asked to do, and that they do *only* what they are asked to do—and that this is what the company wants. Green will not grant that these people are all luminously well-qualified for the higher positions into which they are moved.

At least they *appear* to be well-qualified for their new positions at the time the promotions are made. Periodically, errors occur: forecasts miscarry and people fail; a man tires, weakens in will, or buckles under new responsibilities at the office or new problems at home and ceases to operate as anticipated, and we have another minor malfunction in Personnel. We have another nervous breakdown or another executive (the envy of rivals and subordinates) who resigns (in quiet disgrace) for a job with another company or is pushed aside to allow someone else to move through or retires early or puts a bullet through his head. Periodically, I would imagine, we have single instances of all: a man breaks down, is pushed aside, resigns or retires, and then puts a bullet through his head, although I am unable to think of anyone offhand who has succeeded in traversing this full gamut of defeat. The company survives all mishaps.

While other men in high position work hard and believe in the company, Green worries hard and still tries to believe in himself. He has a vacillating infatuation for Mildred, a young, divorced girl in his department who helps coordinate production, and he surprises her often in the office, or at the banks of elevators, by kissing her suddenly and noisily on the mouth, always though with a flippant, loud remark to denote indifference and only, I suspect, when someone else is there to see. Other times he will stride past her without notice or make some terse criticism of her work or the appearance of her desk, humbling and wounding her cruelly without provocation. And she, of course, adores him in return and is scared stiff. That is, I think, the way Green wants all people to feel about him, adoring and scared stiff.

He is, I think, as big a coward as I am; yet, he is the only person in the company with enough courage to behave badly. I envy that: I am cordial and considerate to many people I detest (I am cordial and con-

35

siderate to just about *everybody,* I think, except former girl friends and the members of my family); I trade jokes convivially with several salesmen who annoy the hell out of me and make me waste much of my time with their frantic and contradictory requests; I get drunk with others who bore and irritate me and join them at orgiastic parties with secretaries, waitresses, salesgirls, housewives, nurses, models from Oklahoma, and airline stewardesses from Pennsylvania and Texas; I have two men in my department I'd like to fire and one girl, and there are days when I would truly like to be rid of them all; but I try not to show how I feel, and I'll probably never do anything about any of them, except keep hoping sullenly that they'll disappear on their own; I'm glad that Martha, our crazy typist, isn't going crazy in my department, because I know that I wouldn't have the nerve or competence to do anything about her before she finally falls apart; there's a fellow executive in the Merchandising Department I have lunch with once or twice a month who I sincerely wish would drop dead. (Once a year we have him to dinner, always with a lot of other people, and once each spring he has us to lunch on his God-damned boat.) I know so many people I want to be mean to, but I just don't have the character.

Green, on the other hand, is notorious for being frank and unkind (he is frank, I suspect, *just* to be unkind). He would rather make a bad impression than no impression. He tries extremely hard to be inconsiderate to people on his own level and lower. He creates tension, terror, and uneasiness in an organization that values harmony, dreads disagreements, conceals failure, and disguises conflict and personal dislike. He is aggressive and defensive. He attacks others and is sorry for himself.

People in the company, for example, do their best to minimize friction (we are encouraged to revolve around each other eight hours a day like self-lubricating ball bearings, careful not to jar or scrape) and to avoid quarreling with each other openly. It is considered much better form to wage our battles sneakily behind each other's back than to confront each other directly with any semblance of complaint. (The secret attack can be denied, lied about, or reduced in significance, but the open dispute is witnessed and has to be dealt with by somebody who finds the whole situation deplorable.) We are all on a congenial, first-name basis, especially with people we loathe (the more we loathe them, the more congenial we try to be), and our wives and children are always inquired about familiarly by their first names, even by people who have never met them or met them only once. The right to this pose of comfortable intimacy does not extend downward to secretaries, typists, or mail boys, or more than two levels upward through the executive hierarchy. I can call Jack Green Jack and Andy Kagle Andy and even Arthur Baron Art, but I would not call anyone higher than Arthur Baron anything but mister. That would be not only dangerous but rude, and I am always hesitant about being rude (to anyone but the members of my family), even when it isn't dangerous. Even Jane in the Art Department still calls me Mr. Slocum respectfully when we meet (sometimes by telephone appointment when I am feeling especially frivolous) and kid around in one of the back corridors, and Jane and I have gone pretty far with each other by now in conversation. I used to encourage the girls I was after to call me by my first name, but I've learned from experience that it's always better, and safer, and more effective, to preserve the distinction between executive and subordinate, employer and employee, even in bed. (*Especially* in bed.)

People in the company are almost never fired; if they grow inadequate or obsolete ahead of schedule, they are encouraged to retire early or are eased aside into hollow, insignificant, newly created positions with fake functions and no authority, where they are sheepish and unhappy for as long as they remain; nearly always, they must occupy a small and less convenient office, sometimes one with another person already in it; or, if they are still young, they are simply encouraged directly (though with courtesy) to find better jobs with other companies and then resign. Even the wide-awake young branch manager with the

37

brilliant future who got drunk and sick one afternoon and threw up into the hotel swimming pool during the company convention in Florida two years ago wasn't fired, although everyone knew he would not be permitted to remain. He knew it, too. Probably nothing was ever said to him. But he knew it. And four weeks after the convention ended, he found a better job with another company and resigned.

Green, on the other hand, does fire people, at least two or three people every year, and makes no secret of it; in fact, he makes it a point to let everyone know immediately after he *has* fired someone. Often, he will fire someone for no better reason than to cause discussion about himself or to wake the rest of us up for a while. Most of us who won't ever amount to anything really big here, including Green, do tend to sink into lethargy and coast along sluggishly on the energy and new ideas that helped us make it safely through the year before. That's one of the reasons we won't ever amount to anything much. Most of the men who do make it toward the top are persistent hard workers if they are nothing else (and they are frequently nothing else. Ha, ha).

Sometimes the people Green fires are people he likes personally whose work is good enough (that may, in fact, be just the reason he does fire them—that he has no reason). Then he will grow compassionate and become seriously concerned with their plight (as though he were not the one who created it). He will begin an earnest effort to find other jobs for them somewhere else in the company. He is usually not successful, for his zest for catty advantage quickly replaces his original (and uncharacteristic) good intention, and his approach turns malicious and self-defeating.

"He'd be perfect for you," is one method Green likes to use in recommending someone in his department to someone who is the head of another department. "He just isn't good enough for me."

Once he has made this point in enough places, he soon forgets about the people he has fired, and they go away.

He is charming (ha, ha). At the important company

38

planning sessions that are held out of town every three months at some luxurious resort hotel or plush country club with a well-known golf course, division and department heads (I am told) normally do not argue or complain or express dissatisfaction aloud with each other's work or viewpoint. But Green does: Green criticizes, ridicules, and disparages impatiently, and he always protests vehemently against any cuts in his own budget or any new curtailments of his activities. Then he is sorry. Green rocks the boat impetuously, and is fearful afterward that he is going to sink. He is better read than most people in the company and affects a suave, intellectual superiority that makes even Arthur Baron slightly uncomfortable and makes Andy Kagle and everyone else in the Sales Department feel crude and graceless. (I am much better educated than Green is and, I think, more intelligent, but he is glib and forward, and I am not.) News of Green's repartee and audacious bad behavior at these planning sessions (Green does not even play golf) usually trickles down to us (mainly through Green himself) and we are often proud to be working for him; but I know he is tormented each time by the fear that this time he has at last gone too far. Green worries that none of the important people in the company really like him, and he's right; he is wrong, though, when he surmises it is only because they envy him. (He really isn't likable.) And then there are the many other worries that I know assail Green because the company is large and mainly Protestant.

Green, for example, is afraid of Phillip Reeves, a timid, underpaid young employee in Green's own department, and this amuses me greatly because I know that Phillip Reeves, who is Protestant, English, and went to Yale, is afraid of Green; each complains to me about the other. Reeves confides in me because he thinks I am capable, honest, and unpretentious; he knows I drink and lie and whore around a lot, and he therefore feels he can trust me.

"I'm absolutely terrified every time I have to go into his office," Reeves complains to me about Green. "He'll make some sarcastic remark as soon as I walk in, and I won't be able to think of a single intelligent thing to say in reply. I freeze. It's as though I'm paralyzed and struck dumb. It's all I can do to nod or shake my head or mumble answers to his questions, and I stand there almost speechless with an idiotic smile on my face while he goes on and on making caustic remarks. I can't say that I blame him. Afterwards I hate myself for being so stupid and tongue-tied."

"I'm absolutely terrified every time I have to speak to him in my office," Green complains to me about Phillip Reeves. "It's those good manners of his, I guess, and that vulgar good breeding. I can cope with good manners and I can cope with good breeding, but I can't cope with good manners *and* good breeding. They throw me off stride, and it's like listening to some total, idiotic stranger running off at the mouth as I hear what I'm saying and realize what I'm doing. I'll make some innocent joke to him when he walks in, just to try to put us both at ease, and he'll just draw to a stop and stare back at me with that icy, superior smile frozen on his face. I can't get a response out of him. I become so rattled that I begin making one asinine remark after another in an effort to be friendly, but he just stands there in supercilious contempt and waits for me to finish. He must despise me by now, and I can't say that I blame him. God knows he does nothing to put *me* at ease, I can tell you that. Afterwards, I hate myself for being so stupid and weak. I wonder why I don't fire him. Because it would be an admission of defeat, that's why, even though his work *is* lousy."

I do not tell either of them about the other (although I do try to cheer Reeves up). Neither would believe me, and it would do no good. They've got the whammy on each other—it's as plain as that—and nothing can change the whammy that springs up between one person and another and usually lasts a lifetime.

Green's got the whammy on me.

"I think they've decided to fire *me*," Green blurts out to me unexpectedly. "Kagle's the one they should get rid of, but I think that he and Horace White have finally persuaded them. Your pal. You hear things. Go find out from Kagle or Brown or someone else just what's going on. Or I'll fire *you*."

I don't think Green really intends to fire me (but I'm never that confident about it for very long. I'm not secure about it at all on days when I know he is in a bad mood and I see his door shut for long periods of time). I know Green likes me, although we are not close, and confides in me, and I know he likes my work and the way I run my department for him. And I know Green is afraid of Andy Kagle, who likes me also and might try to protect me, and of Arthur Baron, who also likes me (I think he likes me: Arthur Baron always treats everybody as though he likes them—him—even people I know he doesn't like, so how can one be sure?) and might not let Green fire me. Kagle has sworn, in fact, that he *would* protect me if Green ever decides he does want to get rid of me, and that he would take me right into his own department at a much higher salary, just to spite Green, so I seem to be perfectly safe, until I go to Kagle to find out what I can about Green and hear him say, as soon as I walk into his office:

"I think they've finally decided to fire me!"

And where would I be if that happened?

Andy Kagle, as head of our Sales Department, has a very powerful position with the company and is now afraid of losing it.

He may be right. His name is all wrong. (Half wrong. Andrew is all right, but Kagle?) So are his clothes. He shows poor judgment in colors and styles, as well as in fabrics, and his suits and coats and shirts do not fit him well enough. He moves to madras and paisley months after others have gone to linen or hopsack or returned to worsted and seersucker. He wears terrible brown shoes with *fleur-de-lis* perforations. He wears anklets (and I want to scream or kick him when I see his shin). Kagle is a stocky man of less than middle height and was born with a malformation of the hip and leg (which also doesn't help his image much); he walks with a slight limp.

Kagle has ability and experience, but they don't count anymore. What does count is that he has no tone. His manners are not good. He lacks wit (his wisecracks are bad, and so are the jokes he tells) and did not go to college, and he does not mix smoothly enough with people who did go to college. He knows he is awkward. He is not a hearty extrovert; he is a nervous extrovert, the worst kind (especially to other nervous extroverts), and so he may be doomed.

Kagle is one of those poor fellows who started at the bottom and worked his way up, and it shows. He is a self-made man and unable to hide it. He knows he doesn't fit, but he doesn't know when he doesn't or why, or how to alter himself so that he will fit in as well as he should. Gauche is what he is, and gauche is what he knows he is (although he is so gauche he doesn't even know what the word *gauche* means, but Green does, and so do I). He has a good record as head of sales, but that hardly matters. (Nothing damages us much anymore.) He thinks it counts. He really thinks that what he does is more important than what he is, but I know he's wrong and that the beautiful Countess Consuelo Crespi (if there is such a thing) will always matter more than Albert Einstein, Madame Curie, Thomas Alva Edison, Andy Kagle, and me.

Kagle is a church-going Lutheran with a strong anti-Catholic bias that he confides to me in smirking, bitter undertones when we are alone. He begins small meetings at which Catholic salesmen are present with joking references to the Pope in an effort to radiate an attitude of camaraderie. The jokes are bad, and nobody laughs. I have advised him to stop. He says he will. He doesn't. He seems compelled.

Kagle is not comfortable with people on his own level or higher. He tends to sweat on his forehead and upper lip, and to bubble in the corners of his mouth. He feels he doesn't belong with them. He is not much at ease with people who work for him. He tries to pass himself off as one of them. This is a gross (and gauche) mistake, for his salesmen and branch managers don't want him to identify with them. To them, he is management; and they know that they are nearly wholly at his mercy, with the exception of the several salesmen below him from very good families above him who do mingle smoothly with higher executives in the company who have *him* at *their* mercy, making him feel trapped and squeezed in between.

Kagle relies on Johnny Brown, whom he fears and distrusts, to keep the salesmen in line (to be the bad guy for him). And Brown does this job efficiently and with great relish. (Brown is related to Black, by his marriage to Black's niece.) Brown's success in scaring the salesmen merely strengthens Kagle's insecurity and weakens his sense of control. Kagle is convinced that Brown is after his job, but he lacks the courage to confront Brown, transfer him, or fire him. Kagle (wisely) avoids a showdown with Brown, who is blunt and belligerent with almost everybody, especially in the afternoon if he's been drinking at lunch. Kagle would rather go out of town on an unnecessary business trip than have a showdown here with anybody about anything, and he usually manufactures excuses for travel whenever his problems here or at home with his wife and children build toward a crisis he wants other people to settle. He hopes they'll be over by the time he returns, and they usually are.

With the exception of Brown (whom Kagle hates, fears, and distrusts, and can do nothing about), Kagle tries to like everyone who works for him and to have everyone like him. He is reluctant to discipline his salesmen or reprimand them, even when he (or Brown) catches them cheating on their expense accounts or lying about their sales calls or business trips. (Kagle lies about his own business trips and, like the rest of us, probably cheats at least a little on his expense accounts.) He is unwilling to get rid of people, even those who turn drunkard, like Red Parker, or useless in other ways. This is one of the criticisms heard about him frequently. (It is occasionally made against him by the same people other people want him to get rid of.) He won't, for example, retire Ed Phelps, who wants to hang on. ("I'd throw half those lying sons of bitches right out on their ass," Brown enjoys bragging out loud to me and Kagle about Kagle's sales force, as though challenging Kagle to do the same. "And I'd put the other half of those lazy bastards on notice.")

Kagle wants desperately to be popular with all the "lying sons of bitches" and "lazy bastards" who work for him, even the clerks, receptionists, and typists, and goes out of his way to make conversation with them; as a result, they despise him. The more they despise him, the better he tries to be to them; the better he is to them, the more they despise him. There are days when his despair is so heavy that he seems almost incapable of stirring from his office or allowing anyone (but me) in to see him. He keeps his door shut for long periods of time, skips lunch entirely rather than allow even his secretary to deliver it, and does everything he can by telephone.

Kagle is comfortable with me (even on his very bad days), and I am comfortable with him. Sometimes he sends for me just to have me confirm or deny rumors he has heard (or made up) and help dispel his anxieties and shame. I do not test or threaten him; I pose no problem; on the contrary, he knows I aid him (or try to) in handling the problems created by others. Kagle trusts me and knows he is safe with me. Kagle doesn't scare me any longer. (In fact, I feel that I could scare him whenever I chose to, that he is weak in relation to me and that I am strong in relation to him, and I have this hideous urge every now and then while he is confiding in me to shock him suddenly and send him reeling forever with some brutal, unexpected insult, or to kick his crippled leg. It's a weird mixture of injured rage and cruel loathing that starts to rise within me and has to be suppressed, and I don't know where it comes from or how long I will be able to master it.) Kagle has lost faith in himself; this could be damaging, for people here, like people everywhere, have little pity for failures, and no affection.

I have pity for Kagle (as though I have already delivered my insult or kicked him in his deformed leg viciously—I know it will happen sooner or later, the wish is sometimes so strong), as I have pity for myself. I am sorry for him because he is basically a decent person, if not especially dazzling or admirable. I do worry and sympathize with him often, because he has been good to me from the day I came to work here for Green, and is good to me still. He makes my job easier. He relies on my judgment, takes my word, and backs me up in disputes I have with his salesmen. Many of his salesmen, particularly the new ones, hold me in some kind of awe because they sense I operate under his protection. (A number of the old ones who are not doing well hold me to blame, I'm sure, for having helped bring them to ruin.) Invariably in these disagreements with his salesmen, I am right and they are wrong. I am patient, practical, rational, while they are emotional and insistent. It is easy for me to be practical and rational in these situations because I am not in the least bit endangered by the business problems that threaten *them*.

Kagle often comments jokingly to Arthur Baron and other important people, sometimes even in my presence, that I would be much better in Green's job than Green is; Kagle does this with a gleam of mischief if I am there, because I have begged him not to. I am not certain if Kagle really believes I would be better than Green or is merely making an amiable gesture that he thinks will honor me and get back to Green to irritate and concern him. Because Andy Kagle is good to me and doesn't scare me any longer, I despise him a little bit too.

I try my best to conceal it (although I am often surprised to discover a harder edge to my sarcasms and admonitions than I intended. There is something cankered and terrifying inside me that wishes to burst out and demolish him, lame and imperfect as he is). I try my best to help and protect him in just about every

45

way I can. I am the one who even offers regularly to carry censures and instructions from him to Johnny Brown that he shrinks from delivering himself, although I will never risk anything with Brown after lunch if I can possibly avoid it. Along with everyone else who knows Brown, I endeavor to steer clear of him after lunch (unless I need him on my side in an argument with someone else), when he is apt to be red-eyed and irritable with drink and in a contrary, bellicose mood. Brown in a bad temper with whiskey working inside him always gives the clear impression that he is eager for a fist fight. And there is no doubt that with his deep chest, sturdy shoulders, and thick, powerful hands. he can handle himself in one. And there is also no doubt that Brown is usually right.

The current (and recurrent) antagonism between Kagle and Brown is over call reports again. The salesmen are reluctant to fill out these small printed pink, blue, and white forms (pink for prospects, blue for active, and white for formerly active; that is, accounts that have lapsed and are therefore prospects again, though not necessarily lively ones) describing with some hope and detail the sales calls they have made (or allege they have made). The salesmen are reluctant to come to grips with any kind of paperwork more elaborate than writing out order forms; they especially hate to fill out their expense account reports and fall weeks, sometimes months, behind. The salesmen know beforehand that most of the information they will have to supply in their call reports will be false. Brown maintains that call reports are a waste of everybody's time, and he is reluctant to compel the salesmen to fill them out. Kagle is afraid of Brown, and he is reluctant to compel Brown to compel the salesmen to fill them out.

But Arthur Baron wants the call reports. Arthur Baron has no other way of keeping familiar with what the salesmen are up to (or say they are) and a no more reliable source of knowledge on which to base his own decisions and reports, even though he is certainly aware that most of the knowledge on which he bases his decisions and prepares his own reports is composed of lies.

I try to keep out of it and expel an air of innocence and sympathetic understanding to all concerned. I would rather sit here in my office writing, doodling, flirting on the telephone with Jane, or talking to a good girl named Penny I've known a long time, or classifying people in the company and constructing my Happiness Charts, than get mixed up in this one. I don't care about the call reports and don't have to. The matter is trivial; yet, it seems to be one of those trivial matters that might destroy a person or two, and I don't see how I can gain favor with one person in this situation without losing favor with another. So, prudently, I contrive to keep as far away from it as I can, although I *will* manage to mention every now and then to a salesman I happen to be with on some other business that Kagle, Brown, or Arthur Baron has been asking about his call reports and that it is extremely urgent they be handed in as soon as possible for prompt study and evaluation. (I don't manage to mention—and never would—that I think they're a waste of everybody's time but mine.)

In this and other small ways I do what I can to be of help to Kagle (and Brown) (and Arthur Baron). I give him advice and I bring him gossip and news and portents from other parts of the company that I think will be of value or concern to him.

"What do you hear?" he wants to know.

"About what?"

"You know."

"What do you mean?"

"Jesus Christ," he complains, "you used to be truthful with me. Now I can't even trust you, either."

"What are you talking about?"

"I hear that I'm out and Brown's in, and that you probably know all about it. I was tipped off in Denver."

"You're full of shit."

"I like your honesty."

"I like yours."

Kagle grins mechanically, sardonically, and moves with his slight limp across the carpet of his office to close the door. I smile back at him and settle smugly into his brown leather armchair. I always feel very secure and very superior when I'm sitting inside some-one's office with the door closed and other people, perhaps Kagle or Green or Brown, are doing all the worrying on the outside about what's going on inside. Kagle has a large, lush corner office in which he seems out of place. He looks nervous and tries to smile as he comes back and sits down behind his desk.

"Seriously, you hear everything," he says to me. "Haven't you heard anything?"

"About what?"

"About me."

"No."

"The grapevine says I'm finished. They're going to listen to Green and Horace White and get rid of me. Brown's got the job."

"Who told you that?"

"I can't name names. But I was tipped off by people in Denver who passed it along to me in strictest con-fidence. It's true. You can take my word for it."

"You're full of shit again."

"No, I'm not."

"There's nobody in our Denver office who would know something like that or tip you off about it if they did."

"Only about the Denver part. The rest is true."

"You tell terrible lies," I say. "You tell the worst lies of anybody in the whole business. I don't see how you ever made it as a salesman."

Kagle grins for an instant to acknowledge my humor and then turns glum again.

"Brown tells you things," he says. "Hasn't he given any hints?"

"No." I shake my head. (Everybody seems to think I know everything. "You know everything," Brown said to me. "What's going on?" "I didn't even know there was anything going on," I answered. Jane asked: "What's going on? Are they really getting rid of the whole Art Department?" "I wouldn't *let* them get rid of you, honey," I answered. "Even if I had to pay your salary myself.")

I shake my head again. "And it's probably not true. They'd never put Brown in. He fights with everybody."

48

"Then you *have* heard something," Kagle exclaims.

"No, I haven't."

"Who would they put in?"

"Nobody. Andy, why don't you stop all this horseshit and buckle down to your job if you're so really worried? If you're really so worried, why don't you start doing the things you're supposed to do?"

"What am I supposed to do?"

"The things you're supposed to do. Stop trying to be such a good guy to all the people who work for you. You ain't succeeding, and nobody wants you to be. You're a member of management now. Your sales force is your enemy, not your buddy, and you're supposed to be theirs and drive them like slaves. Brown is right."

"I don't like Brown."

"He knows his business. Make Ed Phelps retire."

"No."

"That's what Horace White wants you to do."

"Phelps is an old man now. He wants to stay."

"That's why you have to force him out."

"His son was divorced last year. His daughter-in-law just took his granddaughter away to Seattle. He might never see the little girl again."

"That's all very sad."

"How much does it cost the company to keep him on, even if he doesn't do anything?"

"Very little."

"Then why should I make him retire?"

(Kagle is right, here, and I like him enormously for his determination to let Phelps stay. Phelps is old and will soon be dead, anyway, or too sick to continue.)

"Because he's past the official retirement age. And Horace White wants you to."

"I don't like Horace White," Kagle observes softly, irrelevantly. "And he doesn't like me."

"He knows his business also," I point out.

"How can I tell it to Ed Phelps?" Kagle wants to know. "What could I say to him? Will you do it for me? It's not so easy, is it?"

"Get Brown to do it," I suggest.

"No."

"It's part of *your* job, not mine."

"But it's not so easy, is it?"

"That's why they pay you so much."

"I don't get so much," he digresses almost automatically, "what with taxes and all."

"Yes, you do. And stop traveling all the time. Nobody likes that. What the hell were you doing in Denver all this week when there's nothing going on there and you're supposed to be here organizing the next convention and working on your sales projections?"

"I've got Ed Phelps working on the convention."

"A lot he'll do."

"And my sales projections are always wrong."

"So what? At least they're done."

"What else?"

"Play more golf. Talk to Red Parker and buy a blue blazer. Buy better suits. Wear a jacket in the office and keep your shirt collar buttoned and your necktie up tight around your neck where it belongs. Jesus, look at you right now. You're supposed to be a distinguished white-collar executive."

"Don't take the name of the Lord in vain," he jokes.

"Don't you."

"I've got a good sales record," he argues.

"Have you got a good sports jacket," I demand.

"Jesus Christ, what does a good sports jacket matter?"

"More than your good sales record. Nobody wears jackets with round leather patches on the elbows to the office, unless it's on a weekend. Get black shoes for your blue and gray suits. And stop driving into the city in your station wagon."

"Okay," he gives in with a gloomy, chastised smile and exhales a long, low whistle of mock surprise and resignation. "You win." He gets up slowly and moves toward the coat rack in the corner of his office for his jacket. "I promise. I'll get a blue blazer."

It will be too big—I can see it in advance—and

hang over his shoulders and sag sloppily around his chest, and he will probably get his worsted blue blazer just about the time the rest of us have switched to mohair or shantung or back to madras, plaids, and seersucker. It is already too late for him, I suspect; I suspect it is no longer in his power (if it ever was in his power) to change himself to everyone's satisfaction. For the moment, though (while I am still with him), he makes an effort: he buttons his shirt collar, and slides tight to his neck the knot of his tie, and puts on his jacket. It is a terrible jacket of coarse, imitation tweed, with oval suede patches at the elbows.

"Better?" he wants to know.

"Not much."

"I'll throw out these brown shoes."

"That will help."

"How's Green treating you these days?" he asks casually.

"Pretty good," I reply. "Why?"

"If you were in my department," he offers with a cagey, more confident air, and the beginnings of a mischievous smile, "I would let you make as many speeches as you want to at the next convention. The salesmen are always very interested in the work you're doing for them and what you have to say."

"So long," I answer. "I'll see you around."

We both laugh, because we each know what the other wants and where the fears and sore spots are. Kagle knows I want to keep my job and be allowed to make a speech at the next company convention. (God dammit—it would be an honor and an act of recognition, even if it is only three minutes, and I've earned it and I want it, and that's all!) And I know that Kagle wants my help in defending himself against Green (and Brown) (and Black) (and White) (and Arthur Baron, as well).

"You'll let me know if you do hear anything, won't you?" he asks, as we walk to the door.

"Of course I will," I assure him.

"But don't ask questions," he cautions with a dark, moody snicker. "You might give them the idea."

We laugh.

51

And we are both still chuckling when Kagle opens the door of his office and we find my secretary outside talking to his secretary.

"Oh, Mr. Slocum," she sings out cheerily, because that is her way, and I wish I were rid of her. "Mr. Baron wants to see you right away."

Kagle pulls me to the side. "What does he want?" he asks with alarm.

"How should I know?"

"Go see him."

"What did you think I was going to do?"

"And come and tell me if he says anything about getting rid of me."

"Sure."

"You will, won't you?"

"Of course I will. For Christ sakes, Andy, can't you trust me?"

"Where are *you* going?" Green wants to know, as I pass him in the corridor on my way to Arthur Baron's office.

"Arthur Baron wants to see me."

Green skids to a stop with a horrified glare; and it's all I can do not to laugh in his face.

"What does he want with *you?*" Green wants to know.

"I haven't any idea."

"You'd better go see him."

"I thought of doing that."

"Don't be so God-damned sarcastic," Green snaps back at me angrily, and I lower my eyes, abashed and humbled by his vehemence. "I'm not even sure I trust *you,* either."

"I'm sorry, Jack," I mumble. "I didn't intend that to sound rude."

"You come see me as soon as you've finished talking to him," he orders. "I want to know what he says. I want to know if I'm being fired or not."

"What was Kagle talking to you about?" Brown asks when I bump into him.

"He wanted to know what you were up to while he was away in Denver."

"I was correcting his mistakes and protecting his

God-damned job, that was what I was up to," Brown retorts.

"That's just what I told him."

"You're a liar," Brown tells me pleasantly.

"Johnny, that's what they pay me for."

"But everybody knows it . . ."

"So?"

". . . so I guess it doesn't matter."

"A diplomat, Johnny. Not a liar."

"Yeah, a diplomat," Brown agrees with a gruff and hearty laugh. "You lying son of a bitch."

"I was just coming to see you," Jane says to me. "I want to show you this layout."

I stare brazenly at her tits. "I can see your layout." She starts to giggle and blush deliciously, but I turn serious. "Not now, Jane. I have to go see Arthur Baron."

"Oh, hello, Mr. Slocum," Arthur Baron's secretary says to me. "How are you?"

"You look fine today."

The door to Arthur Baron's office is closed, and I don't know how to cope with it, whether to turn the knob and go right in or knock diffidently and wait to be asked. But Arthur Baron's twenty-eight-year-old secretary, who is fond of me and having trouble with her husband (he's probably queer), nods encouragingly and motions me to go right through. I turn the knob gingerly and open the door. Arthur Baron sits alone at his desk and greets me with a smile. He rises and comes forward slowly to shake my hand. He is always very cordial to me (and everyone) and always very gentle and considerate. Yet I am always afraid of him. He's got the whammy on me, I guess (just as everyone I've ever worked for in my whole life has had the whammy on me), and I guess he always will.

"Hello, Bob," he says.

"Hi, Art."

"Come in." He closes the door noiselessly.

"Sure."

"How are you, Bob?"

"Fine, Art. You?"

"I want you to begin preparing yourself," he tells me, "to replace Andy Kagle."

"Kagle?" I ask.

"Yes."

"Not Green?"

"No." Arthur Baron smiles, knowledgeable and reassuring. "We don't really think you're ready for Green's job yet."

There is a polite irony here, for we both know that Kagle's job is bigger and more important than Green's, and that Green would be subordinate to Kagle if Kagle were of stronger character. The proposition stuns me, and for a few bewildered seconds I have absolutely no idea what to say or do or what expression to keep on my face. Arthur Baron watches me steadily and waits.

"I've never done any real selling," I say finally, very meekly.

"We won't want you to do any," he replies. "We want you to manage. You're loyal and intelligent and you've got good character and good work habits. You seem to have a good understanding of policy and strategy, and you get along well with all kinds of people. You're diplomatic. You're perceptive and sensitive, and you seem to be a good administrator. Is that enough to encourage you?"

"Kagle's a good man, Art," I say.

"He's a good salesman, Bob," Arthur replies, emphasizing the distinction. "And you'll probably be allowed to keep him on as a salesman if we decide to make the change and you decide you want to."

"I know I'd want to."

"We'll probably let you keep him as an assistant even, or as a consultant on special projects with people he'd be good with. But he hasn't been a good manager, and we don't think he's going to be able to get better. Kagle doesn't go along with the rest of us on too many things, and that's very important in his job. He lies a lot. Horace White wants me to get rid of him just because he does tell lies to us. He still travels too much, although I've told him I want him to spend more time here. He dresses terribly. He still wears brown shoes. That shouldn't count, I know, but it does count, and he ought to know that by now. He doesn't send in my call reports."

"Most of the stuff on the call reports isn't true."

"I know that. But I have to have them anyway for my own work."

"Brown is in charge of that," I have to point out.

"He doesn't control Brown."

"That isn't easy."

"He's afraid of him."

"So am I," I admit.

"And so am I," he admits. "But I would control him or get rid of him if he worked for me. Would you?"

"Brown is married to Black's niece."

"I wouldn't let that matter. We wouldn't let Black interfere if it came to doing something about Brown."

"Would you let me fire him?"

"If you decided you really wanted to, although we'd prefer to transfer him. Kagle could have had him fired, but by now Brown has a better grasp of specifics than he has. Kagle never wants to fire anybody, even the ones who are drunks or dishonest or useless in other ways. He won't fire Parker or retire Phelps, and he doesn't cooperate with Green. And he still discriminates in the people he hires, although he's been warned about that, too."

"It's a very big job," I say.

"We think you might be able to handle it."

"If I couldn't?"

"Let's not think about that now."

"I have to," I say with a grin.

He grins back sympathetically. "We'd find another good job for you somewhere else in the company if you found you wanted to stay here, unless you did something disgraceful or dishonest, and I'm sure that wouldn't happen. You don't have to decide now. This is just an idea of mine, and it's anything but definite, so please keep it secret. But we are trying to look ahead, and we'd like to know what we're going to do by convention time. So give it some serious thought, will you, and let me know if you would take it if we did decide to move Kagle out and give it to you. You don't have to take it if you don't want to—I promise you that—and you won't be penalized if you don't." He smiles again as he stands up and continues in a lighter tone. "You'll still get your raise this year and a good cash bonus. But we think you should. And you might just as well begin preparing yourself while you make up your mind."

"What should I do?"

"Keep close to Kagle and the salesmen and try to find out even more about everything that's happening. Decide what realistic goals to establish and what changes you would have to make to achieve them if we did put you in charge."

"I like Andy Kagle."

"So do I."

"He's been very good to me."

"It isn't your fault. We'd move him out anyway. He'll probably be happier working for you on special projects. Will you think about it?"

"Of course."

"Good. You'll keep this quiet, won't you?"

"Sure."

"Thank you, Bob."

"Thank you, Art."

"What did Arthur Baron want?" Green demands, the instant I'm out in the corridor.

"Nothing," I answer.

"Did he say anything?"

"No."

"Anything about me, I mean."

"No."

"Well, what did he say? He must have wanted to see you about something."

"He wants me to put some jokes in a speech his son has to make at school."

"Is that all?" Green snorts with contempt, satisfied. "I could do that," he sneers. "Better than you."

Up yours, I think in reply, because I know I could squash him to the ground and make him crawl like a caterpillar if I ever do find myself in Kagle's job. But he does believe me, doesn't he?

"What did Arthur Baron want?" Johnny Brown asks.

"He wants me to put some jokes in a speech his son has to make at school."

"You're still a liar."

"A diplomat, Johnny."

"But I'll find out."

"Should I start looking for another job?" asks Jane.

"I've got a job you can do, right here at hand."

"You're terrible, Mr. Slocum," she laughs, her color rising with embarrassment and pleasure. She is aglow, tempting. "You're worse than a boy."

"I'm better than a boy. Come into my office now and I'll show you. What boy that you go with has an office with a couch like mine and pills in the file cabinet?"

"I'd like to," she says (and for a second I am in terror that she will). "But Mr. Kagle is waiting for you there."

"What did Arthur Baron want?" Kagle asks as soon as I step inside my office and find him lurking anxiously in a corner there.

I close the door before I turn to look at him. He is shabby again, and I am dismayed and angry. The collar of his shirt is unbuttoned, and the knot of his tie is inches down. (For a moment, I have an impulse to seize his shirt front furiously in both fists and begin shaking some sense into him; and at exactly the same time, I have another impulse to kick him as hard as I can in the ankle or shin of his crippled leg.) His forehead is wet with beads of perspiration, and his mouth is glossy with a suggestion of spittle, and dry with the powdered white smudge of what was probably an antacid tablet.

"Nothing," I tell him.

"Didn't he say anything?"

57

"No. Nothing important."

"About me?"

"Not a word."

"You mean that?"

"I swear."

"Well, I'll be damned," Kagle marvels with relief. "What did he talk about? Tell me. He must have wanted to see you about something."

"He wants me to put some jokes in a speech his son has to make at school."

"Really?"

"Yeah."

"And he didn't say anything about me, anything at all?"

"No."

"Or the call reports or the trip to Denver?"

"No."

"Ha! In that case, I may be safe, you know. I might even make vice-president this year. What did he talk about?"

"Just his son. And the speech. And the jokes."

"I'm probably imagining the whole thing," he exclaims exultantly. "You know, maybe I can use those same jokes someday if one of *my* kids is ever asked to make a speech at school." He frowns, his face clouding suddenly with a distant distress. "Both my kids are no good," he reminds himself aloud abstractedly. "Especially the boy."

Kagle trusts me also. And I'm not so sure I want him to.

"Andy," I call out to him suddenly. "Why don't you play it safe? Why don't you behave? Why don't you start doing everything everybody wants you to do?"

He is startled. "Why?" he cries. "What's the matter?"

"To keep your job, that's why, if it's not too late. Why don't you start trying to go along? Stop telling lies to Horace White. Don't travel so much. Transfer Parker to another office if you can't get him to stop drinking and retire Ed Phelps."

"Did somebody say something?"

"No."

58

"Then how do you know all that?" he demands. "Who told you?"

"You did," I bark back at him with exasperation and disgust. "You've been telling me about all those things over and over again for months. So why don't you start doing something about them instead of worrying about them all the time and taking chances? Settle down, will you? Control Brown and cooperate with Green, and why don't you hire a Negro and a Jew?"

Kagle scowls grimly and broods in heavy silence for several seconds. I wait, wondering how much is sinking in.

"What would I do with a coon?" he asks finally, as though thinking aloud, his mind wandering.

"I don't know."

"I could use a Jew."

"Don't be too sure."

"We sell to Jews."

"They might not like it."

"But what would I do with a coon?"

"You would begin," I advise, "by finding something else to call him."

"Like what?"

"A Black. Call him a Black."

"That's funny."

"Yeah."

"I've always called them coons," Kagle says. "I was brought up to call niggers coons."

"I was brought up to call Negroes coons."

"What should I do?" he asks. "Tell me what to do."

"Grow up, Andy," I tell him earnestly, trying with all my heart now to help him. "You're a middle-aged man with two kids and a big job in a pretty big company. There's a lot that's expected of you. It's time to mature. It's time to take it seriously and start doing all the things you should be doing. You know what they are. You keep telling me what they are."

Kagle nods pensively. His brow furrows as he ponders my advice without any hint of levity. I am getting through to him. I watch him tensely as I wait for his reply. Kagle, you bastard, I want to scream at him desperately as he meditates solemnly, I am trying to help you. Say something wise. For once in your mixed-up life, come to an intelligent conclusion. It's almost as though he hears me, for he makes up his mind finally and his face brightens. He stares up at me with a slight smile and then, while I hang on his words hopefully, says:

"Let's go get laid."

The company has a policy about getting laid. It's okay.

And everybody seems to know that (although it's not spelled out in any of the personnel manuals). Talking about getting laid is even more okay than doing it, but doing it is okay too, although talking about getting laid with your own wife is never okay. (Imagine: "Boy, what a crazy bang I got from my wife last night!" That wouldn't be nice, not with gentlemen you associate with in business who might know her.) But getting laid with somebody else's wife is very okay, and so is talking about it, provided the husband is not with the company or somebody anybody knows and likes. The company is in favor of getting laid if it is done with a dash of élan, humor, vulgarity, and skill, without emotion, with girls who are young and pretty or women who are older and foreign or glamorous in some other way, without too much noise and with at least some token gesture toward discretion, and without scandal, notoriety, or any of the other serious complications of romance. Falling in love, for example, is *not* usually okay, although marrying someone else right after a divorce is, and neither is "having an affair," at least not for a man.

Getting laid (or talking about getting laid) is an important component of each of the company conventions and a decisive consideration in the selection of a convention site; and the salesmen who succeed in getting laid there soonest are likely to turn out to be the social heroes of the convention, though not necessarily the envy. (That will depend on the quality of whom they find to get laid with.) Getting laid at conventions is usually done in groups of three or four (two decide to go out and try and take along one or two others). Just about everybody in the company gets laid (or seems to), or at least talks as though he does (or did). In fact, it has become virtually *comme il faut* at company conventions for even the very top and very old, impotent men in the company— in fact, *especially* those—to allude slyly and boastfully to their own and each other's sexual misconduct in their welcoming addresses, acknowledgments, introductions, and informal preambles to speeches on graver subjects. Getting laid is a joking matter on all levels of the company, even with people like Green and Horace White. But it's not a matter for Andy Kagle to joke about now.

"Andy, I'm serious," I say.

"So," he says, "am I."

I close the door of my office after Kagle leaves, sealing myself inside and shutting everybody else out, and try to decide what to do about my conversation with Arthur Baron. I cancel my lunch appointment and put my feet up on my desk.

I've got bad feet. I've got a jawbone that's deteriorating and someday soon I'm going to have to have all my teeth pulled. It will hurt. I've got an unhappy wife to support and two unhappy children to take care of. (I've got that other child with irremediable brain damage who is neither happy nor unhappy, and I don't know what will happen to him after we're dead.) I've got eight unhappy people working for me who have problems and unhappy dependents of their own. I've got anxiety; I suppress hysteria. I've got politics on my mind, summer race riots, drugs, violence, and teen-age sex. There are perverts and deviates everywhere who might corrupt or strangle any one of my children. I've got crime in my streets. I've got old age to face. My boy, though only nine, is already worried because he does not know what he wants to be when he grows up. My daughter tells lies. I've got the decline of American civilization and the guilt and ineptitude of the whole government of the United States to carry around on these poor shoulders of mine.

And I find I am being groomed for a better job.

And I find—God help me—that I want it.

My wife is unhappy

My wife is unhappy. She is one of those married women who are very, very bored, and lonely, and I don't know what I can make myself do about it (except get a divorce, and make her unhappier still. I was with a married woman not long ago who told me she felt so lonely at times she turned ice cold and was literally afraid she was freezing to death from inside, and I believe I know what she meant).

My wife is a good person, really, or used to be, and sometimes I'm sorry for her. She drinks now during the day and flirts, or tries to, at parties we go to in the evening, although she really doesn't know how. (She is very bad at flirting—poor thing.) She is not a joyful woman, except on special occasions, and usually when she is at least a little bit high on wine or whiskey. (We don't get along well.) She thinks she has gotten older, heavier, and less attractive than she used to be—and, of course, she is right. She thinks it matters to me, and there she is wrong. I don't think I mind. (If she knew I didn't mind, she'd probably be even more unhappy.) My wife is not bad looking; she's tall, dresses well, and has a good figure, and I'm often proud to have her with me. (She thinks I *never* want her with me.) She thinks I do not love her anymore, and she may be right about that, too.

"You were with Andy Kagle today," she says.

"How can you tell?"

"You're walking with a limp."

There is this wretched habit I have of acquiring the characteristics of other people. I acquire these characteristics indiscriminately, even from people I don't like. If I am with someone who talks loud and fast and assertively, I will begin talking loud and fast right along with him (but by no means always assertively). If I am with someone who drawls lazily and is from the South or West, I will drawl lazily too and begin speaking almost as though I were from the South or West, employing authentic regional idioms as though they were part of my own upbringing, and not of someone else's.

I do not do this voluntarily. It's a weakness, I know, a failure of character or morals, this subtle, sneaky, almost enslaving instinct to be like just about anyone I happen to find myself with. It happens not only in matters of speech, but with physical actions as well, in ways I walk or sit or tilt my head or place my arms or hands. (Often, I am struck with fear that someone I am with will think I am aping him deliberately in order to ridicule and insult him. I try my best to keep this tendency under control.) It operates unconsciously (subconsciously?), whether I am sober or intoxicated (generally, I am a happy, pleasant, humorous drunk), with a determination of its own, in spite of my vigilance and aversion, and usually I do not realize I have slipped into someone else's personality until I am already there. (My wife tells me that at movies now, particularly comedies, I mug and gesticulate right along with the people on the screen, and I cannot say she is wrong.)

If I am lunching or having cocktails after work with Johnny Brown (God's angry man, by nature and coincidence), I will swear and complain a lot and talk and feel tough and strong. If I am with Arthur Baron, I will speak slowly and softly and intelligently and feel gentle and astute and dignified and refined, not only for the time I am with him but for a while afterward; his nature will be my nature until I come up against the next person who has more powerful personality traits than any of my own, or a more formidable business or social position. (When I am with Green, though, I do not feel graceful and arti-

64

culate; I feel clumsy and incompetent—until I am away from him, and then I am apt to begin searching about for glib epigrams to use in my conversations with somebody else.) I often wonder what my own true nature is.

Do I have one?

I always dress well. But no matter what I put on, I always have the disquieting sensation that I am copying somebody; I can always remind myself of somebody else I know who dresses much that same way. I often feel, therefore, that my clothes are not my own. (There are times, in fact, when I open one of my closet doors and am struck with astonishment by the clothes I find hanging inside. They are all mine, of course, but, for a moment, it's as though I had never seen many of them before.) And I sometimes feel that I would not spend so much time and money and energy chasing around after girls and other women if I were not so frequently in the company of other men who do, or talk as though they wanted to. I'm still not sure it's all that much fun (although I *am* sure it's an awful lot of trouble). And if I'm not sure by now, I know I never will be.

If I argue with someone who stammers badly, I am in serious trouble; for I have a slight stammer of my own at times and the conversation soon threatens to disintegrate hopelessly into bursts of meaningless syllables. I am in absolute dread of talking to people who stutter; I have a deathly fear I will want to stutter too, will be lost for life if I ever have to watch the mouth of someone who stutters for more than a sentence or two; when I am with a stutterer, I can, if I let myself, almost feel a delicious, tantalizing quiver take shape and grow in both my lips and strive to break free and go permanently out of control. I am not comfortable in the presence of homosexuals, and I suspect it may be for the same reason (I might be tempted to become like them). I steer clear of people with tics, squints, and facial twitches; these are additional characteristics I *don't* want to acquire. The problem is that I don't know who or what I really am.

If I am with people who are obscene, I am obscene. Who am I? (I'll need three guesses.)

My daughter is not obscene, but her speech is dirty now when she talks to her friends and growing dirty also when she talks to us. (*I* talk dirty too.) She is trying to establish some position with us or provoke some reaction, but my wife and I don't know what or why. She wants to become a part too, I guess, of what she sees is her environment, and she is, I fear, already merging with, dissolving into, her surroundings right before my eyes. She wants to be like other people her age. I cannot stop her; I cannot save her. Something happened to her, too, although I don't know what or when. She is not yet sixteen, and I think she is already lost. Her uniqueness is fading. As a child, she seemed to us to be so different from all other children. She does not seem so different anymore.

Who is she?

It amuses me in a discouraging way to know I borrow adjectives, nouns, verbs, and short phrases from people I am with and frequently find myself trapped inside their smaller vocabularies like a hamster in a cage. Their language becomes my language. My own vocabulary fails me (if it is indeed mine), and I am at a loss to supply even perfectly familiar synonyms. Rather than grope for words of my own, I fasten upon their words and carry their phraseologies away with me for use in subsequent conversations (even though the dialogue I steal may not be first rate).

If I talk to a Negro (*spade,* if I've been talking to a honky who calls a spade a spade), I will, if I am not on guard, begin using not only his vernacular (militant hip or bucolic Uncle Tom), but his pronunciation. I do the same thing with Puerto Rican cabdrivers; if I talk to cabdrivers at all (I try not to; I can't stand the whining malevolence of New York cabdrivers, *except* for the Puerto Ricans), it will be on their level rather than mine. (I don't know what *my* level is, ha, ha.) And the same thing happens when I talk to boys and girls of high school and college age; I bridge the generation gap; I copy them: I employ their argot and display an identification with their tastes and outlooks that I do not always feel. I used to think I was doing it to be charming; now I know I have no choice. (Most of my daughter's friends, particularly her girl friends, like me and look up to me; she doesn't.)

If I'm with Andy Kagle, I will limp.

"You were with Andy Kagle today," my wife says.

We are in the kitchen.

I have indeed been with Andy Kagle; I stop walking with Andy Kagle's limp; and I consider prudently if I have not been talking to my wife in a Spanish accent as well, for the girls Kagle and I were with this time were both Cuban and unattractive. They were prostitutes. Nobody likes to call a prostitute a prostitute anymore (least of all me. They are *hookers, hustlers,* and *call girls*), but that's what they were. Prostitutes. And I have taken the high-minded vow again (even as I was zipping up my pants and getting back into my undershirt, which smelled already under the sleeves from the morning's output of perspiration) that from this day forward, I am simply *not* going to make love anymore to girls I don't like.

We have done better with our whores, Kagle and I, than we have done this afternoon, and we have also done worse. Mine was the better looking of the two (Kagle always wants me to take the better looking of the two), with bleached red hair and black roots. She was not well-educated; but her skin was smooth (no pimples, cysts, or sores), and her clothes were neat. Her nature was gentle, her manner tender. She wanted to save up enough money to open a beauty parlor. She was friendly and obliging (they aren't always), and wanted to please me.

"Do you like to be teased?" she asked me softly.

When Kagle cannot run away from his home and the office by going on a business trip (like the one to Denver he has just got back from), he likes to run away to New York whores in dark hotels or walk-up efficiency apartments with thin walls. He asks me to

67

accompany him. I always refuse. "Oh, come on," he says. And I always go.

I don't enjoy it. (Although I definitely do enjoy my sessions with one of those extraordinary, two-hundred-dollar call girls that are sent my way as a gift every now and then by one of the suppliers I buy from. I tell Kagle about these; all he does is smile. I don't believe he wants a pretty girl in a lovely apartment. I think he wants a whore.) I feel unclean. (I am inevitably repelled by the odor of my undershirt when I put it back on, even though it is my own odor and usually slight. On days when I don't wear an undershirt, the smell is there in my shirt, faint but unmistakable, even if I've used a deodorant. The smell is me—I?—and I guess I can't get away from myself for very long.) I know there is something unholy, something corrupt and definitely passé, about grown men, successful executives like Kagle and me, going cold sober to ordinary whores in our own home town. They aren't pretty or necessary, and they aren't much fun. I don't think Kagle enjoys it, either; we have never gone back to the same girls (although we *have* gone back to the same sleazy hotels).

Kagle always pays and charges it to the company as a legitimate business expense. (One of the things I do enjoy is the idea of fucking the company at the same time.) I pay for the taxi sometimes and buy the bottle of whiskey he likes to bring along. Once I'm there I'm all right (I fit right in); but once I finish, I want to be gone. Generally, I'm ready to leave before he is and depart alone. Kagle hates to go home (even more than I do). If things are going smoothly for him (they don't always, because of his bad leg), I leave him there with his whiskey and his whore. I never really want to go with him at all. He asks. And I do.

I began biting my fingernails pretty much that same way, because someone asked me to. (Lord knows, it wasn't *my* idea. I didn't even know people did such things. And I don't think I was inventive enough to come upon the habit on my own.) I was in the second half of my first year in elementary school, seven years old and already fatherless. (I don't remember much about my father. I did not grieve for him when he died; I acted as though he had not gone, which meant I had to act as though he had not been. I didn't miss him, since I didn't remember him, and I've never thought about him much. Till times like now.) All of my friends in the first grade (I had many friends in the first grade; I have always worked hard to be popular and I have always succeeded) began to bite their fingernails the same week, for no better purpose than to exasperate the teacher (Miss Lamb; in the second grade, it was Mrs. Wolf. I have an uncanny memory for names and similar petty details) and their parents and older sisters. (It originated as a childhood conspiracy.)

"C'mon, bite your nails," they told me.

So I did. I began biting my nails. In a little while, they all stopped. But I didn't. (They grew up and went away, leaving their bad habit with me.) I didn't even try (I know now that I didn't try to stop because I didn't want to and because I understood even then that I would not be able to). And for all these years since, I have been nibbling and gnawing away aggressively, swinishly, and vengefully at my own fingertips, obtaining an enormous satisfaction from these small assaults. (It's not so much a habit, of course, as a compulsion, vicious, uncouth, and frequently painful, but I like it. And I don't think, at this stage, that I would want to live without it, and nobody has been able to tell me why.) And I know now that I will continue chewing away at my fingernails and my surrounding flesh until I die (or until I have all my teeth pulled and am no longer able to. Ha, ha).

Even my handwriting is not my own!

I borrowed it (and never gave it back). I actually copied the handwriting I have now from an older boy who used to work with me in the file room of the automobile casualty insurance company and liked to while away the time between busy periods inventing, practicing, and perfecting a brand-new handwriting. (His own was not good enough.) His name was Tom, or Tommy, depending on who was talking to him or calling for him. He was twenty-one, tall, and very complacent and mature. (He had a good deal to be complacent and mature about, for in addition to creating a new handwriting, he was laying Marie Jencks, the biggest blonde that our casualty company had to offer.) He studied art lackadaisically in the evening and tended to take things easy during the day while he waited for the army to draft him into World War II. Between chores and errands and smokes in the men's room, Tom would sit at the desk in the rear of the file room (out of sight of everyone who went by, for the file room was a cage of cyclone fence that rose from floor to ceiling and jutted right out into the center of the office, where everybody who did pass could look inside at us) and devote himself industriously to his handwriting. And I would sit beside him at that desk in back, tucked out of sight behind a bank of green metal file cabinets containing indexes by name to the accident folders filed by number in the taller banks of larger, greener cabinets standing near the front, to learn and copy and practice his handwriting with him.

It wasn't always easy work. Tom would experiment tirelessly with the arcs and slants and curlicues of a capital *R* or *Y* or *H* or *J*, speaking little, until he had achieved precisely the effect he thought he wanted, and then he would say: "I think that's it now." And if he didn't change his mind in a minute or two with a sober shake of his head, I would slide his sheet of paper with the finished product closer to me and set to work learning and practicing that letter, while he moved ahead with the foundations of design for another member of the alphabet. (Sometimes, with a downcast, disappointed air, he would reverse his judgment about a certain letter after a week or two had elapsed, reject it, and start all over again from scratch.) Some of the letters were simple, but others proved incalculably hard and took an immeasurably long time. We were a pair of dedicated young calligraphers, he and I (I, of course, the apprentice), when we weren't scheming secretly and separately to satisfy the stewing miseries of our respectively emerging lusts; for he, like me (I was to discover one day entirely by coincidence), also had a very hot thing going with one of the women (girls?) in the office (and here, too, he was way ahead of me. He had big, bossy Mrs. Marie Jencks, of all people, who was twenty-eight and married, and he was already getting in regularly down, of all places, in the storeroom. Wow! What a mixed-up maelstrom of people, I felt, when I finally found out about all of us, not realizing then, as I do realize now, that the only thing unusual about any of it was me). By the time old Mrs. Yerger was transferred all the way across the company offices into the file room to get us to do more work or clear us out (even though there was not that much more work to be done. It was Tom, in fact, who taught me that if I just walked around with a blank piece of paper in my hand, I could spend all the time I wanted to doing nothing. I spent a great deal of time doing plenty, or trying to, at a corner of that desk underneath the big Western Union clock, very close to Virginia, that pert and witty older girl of twenty-one, who wore her round breasts loose some days even then, knowing they looked fine that way too if the breasts were good, and liked to arch her back and twist her shoulders slowly with a sleepy sigh, just to roll her breasts from side to side for my pleasure or thrust them toward me), I had Tom's handwriting down pat, and I have been using his handwriting ever since.

I found out about Tom and Marie Jencks only by coincidence one day about five weeks before he left the company to go into the army. (I left the same day he did for a job that I didn't like in a machine shop.) Mrs. Marie Jencks (that was what the brass nameplate on her desk called her) worked in the Personal Injury Department for mild, short Len Lewis, who was head of the Personal Injury Department and who had fallen politely in love, romantically, sexually, idealistically, with my own incorrigible Virginia. (She encouraged him.) I was amazed to find out about all of us, especially amazed about Marie and Tom (more amazed even than I'd been to find my big brother on the floor of that wooden coal shed with Billy Foster's skinny kid sister so many murky years back. Mrs. Marie Jencks was a much bigger

71

catch than Billy Foster's skinny, buck-toothed kid sister). Marie Jencks was one great big *whale* of a catch, and I was in awe.

To me, once I knew about her, she was a fantasy fulfilled (although for somebody else), a luscious enormous, eye-catching, domineering marvel. (And I could not stop staring at her.) She was married. She was tall, blond, and buxom. She was almost twenty-eight. She was striking and attractive (although not pretty. Virginia was prettier). And she was humping lucky, twenty-one-year-old Tom Johnson whenever she wanted to. (What a gorgeous spot for lucky twenty-one-year-old Tom Johnson to be in. It gave little seventeen-year-old Bobby Slocum something good to look forward to.) When Len Lewis was away from his desk, Marie was boss of the whole Personal Injury Department. She was sometimes good-humored, sometimes officious, and I and most of the men and their secretaries who had to deal with her were always a little afraid of her. She was bossy with Tom too; she bossed him down one floor into the moldering storeroom for cabinets of dead records whenever she felt the urge; she bossed him right back upstairs when she was through.

It was because of that storeroom with its two unshaded bulbs dangling overhead from thick black wires like a pair of staring spiders that I found out about Tom and Marie. (I had taken the key; I wanted to meet Virginia; he needed the key to meet Marie.) They did it on the desk. I found that nearly impossible to believe, even though Tom assured me they did it there, and so did Virginia (once I began talking to her about it), and I knew it had to be true. There was no other place but the floor, and that was always dirty. I still couldn't picture it all taking place on the desk. There didn't seem room enough for a woman so tall. (I have since discovered that a *thimble* is room enough when they really want to, and that the planet itself may prove too small when they really don't.)

There was only one key to the door of the storeroom (which made the place ideal for just the sort of thing so many of us, it turned out, had on our minds for so much of the normal business day), and I would not give it to him. I had already made my own plans for another one of the two- or three-minute assignations with Virginia to kiss her and feel her up (before she grew tense and furious all at once with a stark, mysterious terror that always seemed to seize her without warning and for which I was never prepared and could not understand. Her face would blanch, her eyes would darken and dart about anxiously like frightened little mice, and she would tear herself away from me, emitting low, wild, angry gasps and whimpers as she fled in panic and bolted back upstairs. By the time I followed, she would be sitting at her desk beneath the big clock again as though nothing had happened, and she would smile and wink at me salaciously exactly as before. I know now that she was more emotional than I thought and at least a little bit insane. I suppose I loved her then but was too naïve to recognize it. I thought love felt like something else).

"Come on," said Tom. "Gimme the key."

"I can't," I answered.

"I need it."

"So do I."

"I need it now," he said.

"Me too."

"I'm meeting someone there."

"So am I."

"A girl," he explained.

"Me too." (I colored with pride, grinning.)

"Who?" he asked, stepping back to look at me.

"Should I tell you?"

"Why not? I'm your coach, ain't I? Virginia?"

"How do you know?"

"I'm not blind. And I'm not deaf."

"It shows?"

"It shows right out between your legs whenever you stand there and talk to her. You oughta try taking your hand out of your pocket once in a while so we can all get a good look. I'd really like to see that. You oughta carry an accident folder in front of you instead just in case you do have an accident. Pow—

what a property damage case *that* would be. Are you laying her yet?"

"Not yet."

"Do you know how?"

"I'm getting there."

"She can show you how!"

"How do you know?" I asked jealously.

"I can tell. Just do it, that's the best way to learn how. Don't think about it. Just shove it in. You oughta come down now and watch me work it out."

"With who?"

"You'll scream it out all over the place if I tell you."

"No, I won't."

"Gimme the key."

"Tell me who it is."

"Will you keep it quiet?"

"Virginia?" (I felt another pang of jealousy.)

"Marie."

"Jencks?"

"You're screaming."

"Are you laying Marie Jencks?"

"We're laying each other. Don't turn around! She's looking right at us, waiting for you to give me the key, so you better do it—or she'll chop your head off."

"She's married!" I told him with astonishment.

"Can I please have the key?"

I relinquished the key obediently, in deference to his superior achievements; and as soon as he (then she) had gone, I hurried excitedly to the old wooden desk underneath the old, big Western Union clock to postpone my own meeting with Virginia and let her in on what I had just found out. (She was really the best friend I had in the company, and perhaps anywhere else. On days when I was unaccountably sad and lonely or had no money, she would notice and set right about trying to cheer me up or insist on lending me the two or three dollars I needed until payday, even when she had to borrow it from one of the other girls.)

"Why?" she wanted to know, when I asked her

74

to meet me on the staircase instead of in the store-room.

"Can you keep a secret?"

"Sure," she responded brightly. "What do you want to do to me?"

"No, it's about Tom. Would you believe that Tom Johnson and—"

"Of course," she said.

"With—"

"Sure."

"Right *now?*"

"The more often the better, I always say."

"In the *storeroom?*"

"Sometimes they do it in an apartment on Second Avenue. She has a divorced friend who lives there."

"How do *you* know?" I demanded.

"She tells me."

I was flabbergasted. Virginia's cheeks were red with delight and her eyes were twinkling with merri-ment at my expression of amazement.

"How do they do it?" I wanted to know.

"Well, she has this thing of hers, and he has this thing of his, and he takes his—"

"I mean down there! Where do they lie down?"

"On the desk," she told me. "Haven't you ever tried it?"

"I'm going to as soon as they're through."

"Not with me, you aren't. I need a big hotel room. I like to move around a lot."

"You didn't move around so much in that canoe at college," I reminded her.

"I was a dope then," she laughed. "I didn't know I was supposed to. Do *you* want to know a secret?" She motioned me closer. "Come around to here so I can whisper and put my knees against you."

Holding a blank slip of paper, I moved around to her side of the desk and began fussing with folders in a tray there, as though hunting for a particular one. As soon as I drew near her, she swung her knees around against my leg and began rubbing me with them methodically, watching me steadily with a know-ing, kind of mocking smile.

"What's the secret?" I asked.

"Take your hand out of your pocket."

"Fuck you."

"Okay."

"On the desk?"

"Pretend you're working."

"I am. What's the secret?"

Mrs. Yerger was outside the entrance of the file room (Mrs. Yerger was always outside the file room), observing me balefully.

I took my hand out of my pocket, picked up a property damage accident folder, and held it over my hard-on. Virginia saw, of course, and laughed out loud, showing the tiniest tip of shiny tongue between bright red lips and wet white teeth. Her cheeks were touched with red too—they wore them rouged then—and she had dimples. I felt the strongest undertow of affection for her, but it was so inadequate; she was twenty-one, and I was seventeen, and I found myself wishing I were as old as Tom and had a better idea of what to do with her.

"Len Lewis and I," she told me, "meet for drinks and dinner every Thursday night after work. He wants to tell his wife he wants a divorce, but I won't let him. He says that nobody in his whole life ever kissed him the way I do."

I was surprised again, but excited to find this out. I was always fascinated by her sex adventures with other men. (She had a fondness for sheer, silky blouses, and I often had an urge to put my hands on her shoulders when she wore one and delicately caress her. When she wore a sweater, I wanted to put my hands inside and squeeze.)

"Do you sleep with him?" (I was always greedy for details.)

"He's afraid. He's been married all his life and never did anything with anyone else. I feel sorry for him. I don't know what I'll say when I finally get him to ask me to. I like him. But I'm not sure I want to."

I liked Len Lewis too. And I had no doubt that nobody had ever kissed him the way Virginia did, for I had seen him at the office Christmas party with his wife, who was a short, shapeless, soundless woman,

76

as old and meek as he was, and much more wrinkled and gray. For that matter, nobody in *my* whole life had ever kissed *me* the way she did or touched and fondled me the way she could and did over and over again in the storeroom downstairs or on the staircase between floors. I wanted more and more of her; I never got all I wanted. She did not like me to do things to her; she liked to do things to me. We met on the staircase between floors several times each working day, where we would kiss and pet and clutch frantically for the few seconds before she always imagined she heard someone coming and bolted away; or we would meet downstairs in the storeroom for three, four, or five minutes, where she would also pale suddenly and whirl away from me in violent alarm.

I was never angry with her when she ran from me, never felt resentful or cheated; I always felt lucky that I'd had any of her at all. (And I was always sorry to see her so scared. I always wished there were some way I could help.) She told me once (more than once, because I kept bringing it up in order to hear about it again) that in her freshman year at college (she attended Duke University for two years and never went back after her father killed himself one summer) she had been laid in a floating canoe by the backfield star of the varsity football team. I didn't believe her. (I don't think I honestly believed then that *anybody* really got laid, that a boy like me took my thing and put it inside her thing and then went on to do the rest, even though I had seen the drawings and photographs and listened to the dirty jokes and stories.) She kept asking me to get a room. I didn't know how. I asked Tom how to go about renting a hotel room, and he told me, but even after he told me, I still didn't feel I knew how. I had an idea the desk clerk would start beating me up right there in the lobby if I ever tried to register for a hotel room for Virginia and me. And I didn't have the money for something like that. I was only a file clerk. (I didn't even know how to take her to dinner!)

I never really made it with her (I never laid her),

and I'm sorry. After Tom and I left the company together, I never went back, and I never saw or spoke to her again. I tried. I'm sorry. I miss her. I love her. I want her back. I remember her clearly now when I try to remember everything important that ever happened to me. I think of her often as I sit at my desk in my office and have no work for the company I want to do. And I think of her often in the evenings, too, when I sit at home with my wife and my children and the maid and the nurse and have nothing better I want to do there, either, biting my nails addictively like a starving hunchback as I slump in a chair in my living room or study and wish for something novel to occur that will keep me awake until bedtime. I liked the fact that she was short and slightly plump (and wherever my hands fell, there was something full to hold and feel). I remember how clear and smooth and bright her skin was; her dimples deepened when she laughed. She laughed and smiled a lot. I miss that gaiety. Now I *would* know what to do with her. I want another chance. Then I remember who I am; I remember she would still be four years older than I am now, short, overweight, and dumpy, probably, and perhaps something of a talkative bore, which is not the girl I'm yearning for at all. (That person isn't here anymore.) Then I remember she's dead.

(She killed herself, too, just like her father. I tried telephoning her at the office after I got back from overseas. I tried telephoning her again after I'd been married a few years. I was already missing her way back then. She wasn't there. There was somebody new in charge of Property Damage also. I spoke to a crippled man in Personal Injury named Ben Zack.

"Virginia Markowitz?" he said. "Oh, no. She killed herself a year and a half ago. She's not employed here anymore. Didn't you know?")

It was after the war, I think, that the struggle really began.

So that was where the tin lizzie had already carried us to by then, this industrial revolution, to the third largest automobile casualty insurance company in the whole world, with a coarse, tough-talking, married bleached blonde in Personal Injury (PI) and a flirting black-haired girl with thick glasses and very weak eyes in Property Damage (PD), and all of us frying in lechery but poor old Mr. Len Lewis, who was beguiled and fortified by juvenile notions of romance that had no possibility of ever coming true. (By now, he certainly must be dead. He had nothing left coming to him but those kisses from Virginia.) It was a pretty tangled (and funny) (and doleful) situation there in that automobile casualty insurance company, and I didn't begin to learn about most of it until just before Mrs. Yerger came barging into the scene like a hunk of destiny, disguised as new boss of the file room, and scared me out a few weeks later. There were so many startling secrets then that everybody seemed to know but me. Today, I don't think there's a single thing I might find out about anybody in this whole world that would cause me anything more than mild surprise or momentary disappointment. Sudden death, though, still shakes me up, particularly when it strikes somebody who has always been in robust health. (Like my brother.)

Once I did find out about Tom and Marie Jencks, I turned more persistent in my advances to Virginia; it got me nowhere. (I don't think I even knew then what it was I wanted to force her to do.) The funny thing about each of these women (girls?) (women) (girls) was that neither one wanted either of us ever to take the initiative. I had much more freedom with Virginia than Tom enjoyed with Marie Jencks (and got fewer results). I could go to her desk beneath the big clock whenever I chose and talk as dirty as I wanted to, or ask her to meet me on the staircase or in the storeroom; most times she would; sometimes, with her naughty smile, she would be the one to suggest we meet. But she would never let me force her down onto the desk, although she continued to tempt me far enough to try—before she broke away from me and fled. (Why was that? What was there that made her so frightened with me and not frightened at all with the many older boys and men for whom, she

79

claimed, she did put out and always had?) I think
it all would have worked out well with Virginia and
me if we ever had gotten together in an apartment
or hotel room and had plenty of time, worked out
beautifully. (So what?) She would have taught me
to go slow. If I did go slow, she might not have become
frightened; and if she did not grow frightened, she
would have let me do everything to her and showed
me how.

But so what?

It would have passed, sooner or later, just as she
has passed already, just as I am passing now. (Fuck
her, she's dead.) Her case is closed. If she didn't
kill herself, she'd be older than I am now and probably
a pest; she would be stout and wrinkled and suffer
from constipation, gallstones, menopause distur-
bances, and bunioned feet, and I more than likely
would not wish to see her. Everything passes. (That's
what makes it endurable.)

But the memory lives (but not for long. Ha, ha).

Her record may be dead, but it isn't buried; and
I remember also how she used to urge me on after
Marie Jencks once she saw me lusting for that baby
too. I could not stop thinking about Marie that way
after I found out about her and Tom and that desk
in the storeroom. (I used to eat my lunch at that
desk two or three times a week and read the sports
sections of the New York *Daily News* and *Mirror*.)
I wanted her too. I didn't know how to get her.

"Bang her," Virginia would exhort me. "Go get
her."

"How?"

"Goose her."

"You're nuts."

"Grab her by the nipple."

"You're crazy."

All I could decide to do was keep my eye on Tom
and see what he did to get her; and all he did was
nothing. He practiced his handwriting. (He knew
enough to wait and never approach her.) He sat un-

perturbed for days at a time, working on his handwriting with me, and waited tactfully and patiently for her to summon him into her office by buzzer or telephone or by ordering one of the other file clerks (it might be me) to send Tom in.

"Are you busy now?" she would ask.

He would answer: "No."

"Get the key," she would command.

And down to the storeroom they would go (where records and folders of people in accidents were crumbling with age in the file cabinets).

Virginia and I kept track of their comings (ha, ha) and goings. She was truly a stupendous catch for a lucky young man to make (or be made by), although I liked Virginia more (and so, for that matter, did Tom). She seemed twice as large as Virginia, four or eight times as much in pure female bulk, that towering, sarcastic, frequently sympathetic bleached blonde of a twenty-eight-year-old married woman in Personal Injury, who looked solicitously after poor little old Len Lewis (who was suffering seriously from kidney trouble and dangerous related ailments and in all likelihood didn't really want to divorce his poor, old, little wife, to whom he had been married all his life and of whom he was probably still very fond) and did what she could to make his job easier. She was married to a cost accountant with a weak heart (weakened, probably, by her) and she bluntly took control of Tom whenever she wanted to and put him to work banging her down in the storeroom or in her divorced friend's apartment after business hours, in much the same autocratic manner she might use to call him into her office and order him to do some filing.

(Tom never knew when she sent for him the kind of task to which he was going to be put, but he was perfectly willing to take the good with the bad.)

The farthest Tom would ever go toward getting her would be to put himself on display in her office by pretending to hunt for some file. She knew exactly what he was hunting for. Sometimes she would frown, and he would move off immediately, as though in preoccupied continuation of his search for some specific accident folder. Other times she would react as he had hoped, smiling caustically, almost grimacing, and demand:

"Is there something in here you want?"

"Yes."

"Get the key."

And down into the storeroom they would go again.

"I'm not even sure she likes me," Tom confided indifferently to me one afternoon in the file room, focusing much more emotion on the *P*'s and *Q*'s of the handwriting he was practicing than on the statement he was making. "But she sure likes doing it with me."

I could not help wondering if she might not like doing it with me.

So I tried to seduce her. (And failed.) I tried to steal her away from him—not *steal* her *away,* actually, but merely to get, if I could, my own fair share of that musky, estrous, overpowering, inexhaustibly marvelous and voluptuous blond married Viking (who was really just an overgrown, rawboned Scotch-Irish brunette from Buffalo with very large pores). And I got nowhere. Virginia spurred me on energetically with outrageous counsel.

"Go give her a fast bang," she would advise. "She's dying for it right now. A lady can tell. Walk right into her office and get her."

"How?"

"She'll be good for you."

"How?"

"Tell her."

"What?"

"What you want. Come right to the point. That's the best way."

"Oh, sure."

"Grab her by the nipple. Slide your hand up under her dress—"

"She'll kill me."

"No, she won't. Look—Mr. Lewis is out. Go in right now and tell her you've decided you'd like to put it to her."

"She'll lock me up."

"She'll fall in love with you. You'll sweep her off her feet."

"She'll break my head. And put me in jail."

"She won't be able to resist you. You're better looking than Tommy. And more fun, too. You've got nice curly hair."

"She'll tell Len Lewis, or Mrs. Yerger, and have me fired."

"She'll pull her dress up right there, throw open her arms and legs, and sing: 'Oooooooh, come on, baby. Do it to me, like you did to Marie, on Saturday night, Saturd—' "

"Pull up *your* dress and sing," I countered, "if you find me so irresistible. I want to put it to *you*, too."

"Get a hotel room."

"Marie does it on the desk downstairs."

"Marie's got a big round ass."

"So've you."

"I like you, darling," she declared unexpectedly, looking up straight into my eyes. (I was almost swept away by surprise.) "An awful lot. Really, I do. Even though I'm smiling now when I say it—I do mean it."

I was almost too stunned to reply. "What are you talking about?" I whispered fiercely.

"I wish we were older," she continued wistfully in a tone close to some boding lament. "That's what I wish. You know what I wish? I wish you were old enough to knock me around a little."

I was shocked and terrified, almost enraged with her in my confusion and embarrassment. "Why do you talk like that?" I demanded indignantly, afraid that something fateful I did not understand and could not cope with was already taking place. "Why do you say things like that to me now? Right out here in the middle of the office?"

"Because nobody who hears me will believe me," Virginia continued blithely without lowering her voice or altering her expression of beaming innocence. "Not even you. Not a single person around us would take me seriously if I just let my voice get louder and louder steadily until it was almost a shout"—her voice rose clearly and deliberately until it *was* almost a shout and everybody nearby was watching us with amusement—"and suddenly called out, 'I love *you*, Bobby Slocum!' "

(And she had to go and kill herself. Why? She was no longer an employee of the automobile casualty insurance company because she had committed suicide shortly after the war and was no longer employable.)

"You're a riot," I muttered awkwardly with an artificial smile.

"See?" she resumed in her normal voice, as all the people around us bent back to their work. "Nobody believes me. Not even you, do you?"

"What do you want?" I begged of her in bewilderment. "Tell me what to do. Look, Virgin-for-Short, I'm only seventeen years old. And I'm scared. I don't know what's going to happen to me."

"Don't be scared," she answered, and now her voice did go soft with a tender care and affection. "We'll be alone soon in a hotel room, and I'll do things to you that no girl ever did to you before. I promise." (We were never alone in a hotel room. A little while ago in New Orleans, a whore in a night-club made that same promise to me in exactly those words, and then had nothing different to offer when she came to my room.) "Now go get Marie."

"Mrs. Yerger is watching," I noticed.

"She doesn't like me," said Virginia.

"She doesn't like me, either."

"She doesn't like me because I try to have fun with everybody I know. Especially with you."

"I better look busy."

"I'll keep you busy—here." Virginia wrote the number of an accident folder on a sheet of paper. "Find this accident for me," she instructed. "It's a large property damage case with three personal injuries. You can probably get it from Marie Jencks," she added mischievously.

"Yes, Miss Markowitz," I responded heartily enough for Mrs. Yerger to hear me, and started away briskly.

"Oh, and Bobby! Remember—" She beckoned me

back to her desk with an important look. In a low voice, she instructed: "Grab her by the nipple."

So, with Virginia goading me on, I set out to seduce Marie Jencks. I tried in the only way I could think of: by loitering. I loitered on her premises for two or three minutes at a time whenever Len Lewis was away from his desk and I saw her sitting in their office alone. I lurked and hovered in her view perpetually, pretending to search for accident folders, expecting her to look at me one time and perceive suddenly, in a moment of effulgent revelation, that I had dark curly hair and was a better-looking boy than Tom Johnson and much more fun, and that she would then say to me also:

"Are you busy now? Get the key."

I never even came close. The most *I* ever got from her was, "Are you going to spend the rest of your life in here?" or "Why do you keep staring at me all the time like a moonstruck cow?" or, shrewdly (she knew what I was after, all right, the sapient bitch), "Is there anything in here you want?" or, most unkindest cut of all:

"You get out of her now. Send Tom in."

And down to the storeroom Tom would go with her, leaving his handwriting behind in the back of the file room for me to work on alone, and it is his handwriting that I still use. (I wonder who's using Marie.) Tom relied on me to cover for him in case Mrs. Yerger or anyone else came calling for him. And I did.

("Tom."

No answer.

"Tom."

Still no answer.

"Where is that boy, I wonder."

"Downstairs in the storeroom, Mrs. Yerger, laying Marie Jencks on a desk," I could fancy myself replying.)

It was pretty hard, I confess, keeping my thoughts on Tom's handwriting when I knew he was down in the storeroom with her. Usually, my imagination wandered right down there with him (and I was more inclined to make dirty drawings of the two of them instead). That got to be a pretty steamy meeting place, that gloomy, silent, dingy mausoleum for dead and decaying records on the floor below. Occasionally, someone else in the company would really wish to go there in search of an old accident, and barely miss colliding with Tom or me in a new one. It was only one floor down, but descending the two staircases of that one floor to the musty storeroom was like escaping from scrutiny into some dark, cool, not unpleasant underworld, into the safe and soothing privacy of a deep cellar or dusty, wooden coal shed. I enjoyed going there often, even just to eat my sandwiches alone and read the *Mirror* and *Daily News,* or to steal away for a long smoke in the morning or afternoon and meditate over which teams would win the college football games that coming Saturday or what would eventually become of me and my mother and my brother and sister. (My brother is dead already: his heart attacked him one day without warning in the waiting room of his business office, and it was all over for him in a matter of seconds. My mother is dead too. My sister lives far away. We sometimes talk on the telephone.) I imagine ill-humored Mrs. Yerger, who took note of everything, gave that storeroom a very thorough airing once Virginia, Tom, Marie, and I were all gone.

I remember also a rape that nearly took place there one lunchtime when Virginia was trapped with me and two older, bigger boys who also worked in the file room. They would not let her out. She had gone too far, joked and boasted about too much, and now they would not let her go, they said, until she "took care" of the three of us. Virginia grew nervous quickly. We all kept talking and wisecracking compulsively, as though nothing unusual were occurring. One of them had his arms around her shoulders from behind, seeming to hug her playfully, but actually holding her almost helpless and trying to press her to the floor; and the other was soon busy with both hands under her skirt, trying to unsnap her stockings and roll her panties down. I watched, with dread and

86

keen anticipation. All of us were breathing heavily (even I, who was just watching). We wore strained, sick, determined smiles and forced husky laughter out between quick comments in order to sustain for as long as possible the charade that it was all really in fun. It was obviously not in fun. Virginia was terrified after the first few seconds. Her cheeks were chalk white and quivering as she struggled to wrest free. (I never could bear the sight of terror, not in anyone, not in my whole life, not even in people I hate.) Her eyes fell upon mine in wordless panic and appeal. I intervened and let her get away. I was terrified also as I stood up to those two older, bigger boys and insisted they let her go.

"Let her go," I said hesitantly.

"She wants you," one of them said.

"Let her go!" I screamed, with clenched fists.

After Virginia had fled, they shook their heads in unbelieving contempt and told me I was stupid for letting her go just as she was getting ready to put out for the three of us.

Was I stupid?

(I know that by the time we got back upstairs, she was serene and gay again, and not nearly as grateful to me as I took it for granted she would be. And there was no change in her friendliness toward the others. She joked and flirted with them as before, with a show of flattering respect, as though she thought much more of them now. I couldn't understand that. I still can't. I do wonder, though, what would have happened between her and me if I had kept my mouth shut and joined with the others in making her put out for the three of us. Would she have thought more of me too? How could she? But would she? She used to tell me that on her tombstone she wanted an inscription that read:

"Here lies Virginia Markowitz. She was a very good lay, even though she was Jewish."

I bet it isn't there.)

I bet I *was* stupid.

(I know I never got to lay her. And I should have. I think I wanted to. I'd like to lay her now. I wish she hadn't killed herself and was still around for me to call up and make love to, to tell her I care for her and how much she has always meant to me. I'm glad she's not, because I'm not sure I would want her now. I don't know what I want.)

I know I was much more encouraged about my own future because of Virginia, Tom, and Marie Jencks. It was reassuring to learn that so many people *were* getting laid, that the activity was indeed so widespread. It augured well. Tom was twenty-one years old and had a big blond married woman of almost twenty-eight who let him make love to her. I took it for granted that when I was twenty-one, I would have a big blond married woman of twenty-eight who would let me make love to her on a desk also. I thought such women came along automatically.

It never happened, of course.

There was no Marie Jencks for me when I was twenty-one. All I got when I was twenty-one was the right to vote. And by the time I finally did get around to screwing a woman of twenty-eight, it was my wife, and I was thirty-two and already married to her, and that was *not* what I had been daydreaming about at all.

Today when I have anything to do with a woman of twenty-eight, she generally turns out to be not a woman, but a girl, and often just a little girl; she is unmarried and unhappy, or married and lonely. And it isn't the same as it would have been if I had that same girl and were still only seventeen. It is sometimes pleasant, sometimes sad; it is never pleasant for long without turning sad (and uncomfortable, at least for me. Often, they wish to become more devoted to me than I want them to be. I find close relationships suffocating). There is usually something drunken about it (that's my fault, I guess—I like to drink and to get them drinking too), something forlorn and pathological (perhaps in both of us). They like to talk a lot, and they like to listen, to be talked to seriously. (More than anything else, I think, they crave to be spoken to.) I know one or two or three girls near thirty with whom I have become very good friends by now; I don't see any of them too often because our meetings are uneventful (at least for me) and soon turn dull. I meet many young girls I like an awful lot for a while and feel I could love loyally for the rest of my life if I didn't know beforehand that I would grow so bored quickly. That Cuban girl this afternoon was about twenty-six or twenty-eight, and now that I think of her again, she wasn't really so bad. She wasn't really unattractive. She would have been a great girl to have if I were still only a kid of seventeen and knew I could have her whenever I wanted to, and didn't have to pay. She had a small child somewhere being brought up by somebody else. She wanted enough money someday to have her child back and to open her string of beauty parlors.

"Do you like to be teased?" she asked me softly. And when I nodded, she said: "Who doesn't?"

Now that I think of it, she wasn't bad at all.

I don't know what happened to Tom (he could have been killed, for all I know or care); he left me his handwriting, and I still sit at a desk, in my office at the company or in my study at home, and use it. I don't know what finally became of Marie Jencks. I never even found out what happened to me.

Mrs. Yerger, I sense, is still there. (The name is different, but the character is indestructible.) The Mrs. Yergers always survive, unattracted as they are to folly or indiscretion, and so do their grim-faced Mr. Yergers, if there are any (the Mrs. Yergers don't need them), who are indistinguishable from them by everything but gender and dress. The Mrs. Yergers become not only heads of the file room, but mayors, school principals, college deans, majors, judges, government attorneys, colonels, Selective Service board members, American Legion officials, attorney generals, Presidents of the United States of America, and managers of minor departments in companies like mine. Along with Green and Black and Horace White, I have played the part of tyrant myself at times with people in the company who are subordinate to me, and I play it often at home with my wife and my daughter and my son, and even at times with my idiot child, who also doesn't understand what's going on.

("How can you call him that?" my wife will lash out at me with strong emotion. "How can you talk about him that way? He's your own flesh and blood!"

"By definition," I will inform her coldly, "an idiot is any person who lacks the capacity to develop beyond a mental age of three or four, even if he *is* my own flesh and blood.")

I abandon Kagle's limp for the time being and start around in back of her, observing her closely, through the corner of my eye, trying to see how closely she has been observing me (through the corner of *her* eye). She is not wearing her girdle (which is normally a reliable sign that she is in a cordial mood). The round-shouldered colored maid we have now is concealing herself in a far corner of our large kitchen, working noiselessly over a black wooden salad bowl we bought from a different round-shouldered colored woman in Jamaica during a vacation there. She is afraid of me (I think, and I am afraid of her). My wife stands at the stove, stirring red wine into a pan of dark meat that might be chicken livers or chunks of beef. The bottle of wine is more than half empty (or less than half full. Ha, ha). I move behind my wife very carefully toward a glass and some ice cubes (although I am tempted to shout *Olé!* when I think of my Cuban), and I try my best to remember on what terms she and I parted this morning, or went to sleep last night, in order to know if she is still angry with me for something I did or didn't say or do that I am no longer even aware of.

Is she mad or is she glad? I can't remember. And I am unable to tell. So I remain on guard. I bend a bit nearer to her with a cracker and rolled anchovy and perceive suddenly that she is neither mad *nor* glad. It will make not the slightest difference to her whether we parted on good terms or bad, because she has forgotten too.

She has been drinking again, and I can tell, from her downcast look of furtive uncertainty, that *she* also is trying to recall whether we are friends tonight or not. (Am *I* mad or am I glad?) She is waiting for some sign from me. (Am I mad at her for something she said or did wrong or glad with her because she didn't?) I don't know why she is so afraid of me when I am so afraid of her. She is rigid and alert, contrite already (for what? God knows), tense as a bowstring as she stirs her simmering pan and hopes that I'm not angry with *her* for something *she* did or didn't say or do that *she* is unable to remember. It's almost enough to make me laugh.

"You're right," I say, just to get things going for both of us.

"About what?"

"Kagle," I say, and feign Kagle's limp for one step. "We had a few drinks."

"I'm glad they put you in a good mood."

The maid takes it all in spookily with averted eyes. My apprehensions gone, I move to my wife's side and kiss her lightly on the cheek. She turns her face up diffidently, still not completely sure. She smells of wine and expensive perfume.

"Hungry?" she asks.

"I will be. Looks good."

"Let's hope."

The maid glides past us to carry the salad bowl into the dining room.

"How is this one working out?" I ask.

"All right," my wife says. "I had some wine," she adds hastily. "I was using it to cook the chicken livers with. So I thought I'd better try some to make sure it's good."

"Is it good?"

"Good enough." She smiles. "Do you want some?"

"I'll have some bourbon."

"I'll have more wine."

"Kids all right?"

"Yes."

I am off to a fairly good start, I feel, and it may yet turn out that this evening at home will be pleasant. My wife is slightly on the defensive (which will make things easier for both of us). The children (thank heavens) have not come flying at me with grievances and demands. My daughter is in her room, on the telephone. My boy is in his room, watching television. (The set is on loud and I can hear it.) Neither has been much affected by the fact that I am there, that Daddy is home (and I am vaguely hurt by their neglect. A dog would have greeted me with more love). The maid still seems properly subjugated and gives no indication of any incipient Black rebellion. (We pay her well and treat her courteously, and she is probably more at ease in her position with me than I am in my position with her. I am not totally comfortable having maids.) Derek is not nearby, yawping or whimpering or trying to talk, and the nurse (or governess) we have for him now is not hanging around glaring at us as though he were our fault, as though we *wanted* him that way. (Her job, really, is not to nurse or govern, but to keep herself out of sight, and to keep him out of sight as much as possible, even though he is not disagreeable to look at or have around when he is playing quietly with some brightly colored book or infantile doodad.) They are leaving me be. I have my whiskey. Wife has her wine.

"What did you do today?" I ask routinely (before she can ask me).

"Nothing," she replies with a shrug, a confession of failure, a penitent admission that another day has been wasted. "Stayed home. Shopped. Rested. I slept."

"Anybody come over?"

"No."

That is good, if she is telling the truth, for it means that she has been drinking only wine, and probably no more than a little bit at a time, for too much wine makes her sick. I believe she *is* telling the truth, for I don't think my wife has learned how to lie to me yet. (My wife doesn't know how to flirt and doesn't know how to lie to me.) When she does have something she hopes to conceal, she remains silent about it and hopes I will not inquire. (If I ask, she will always tell me. She doesn't like to lie.) I cooperate by not prying when I sense she has a secret she wants to protect. I try to keep away from whatever I think she is trying to hide. I suspect she does the same for me (I suspect she knows a great deal more about me than she discloses). Our conversations, therefore, are largely about nothing, and frequently restrained.

"See you soon," I say, and start away in back of her with my drink. "I want to read the mail."

She nods. I pat her softly on the fanny as I pass. She is pleased, grateful, and presses her ungirdled ass back into my hand with a leer of lewd and tipsy delight.

"Later?" she says. "I hope you're in the mood."

"You know me," I laugh.

I'm sorry to see her this way. (It's not the way she used to be.) I may not love her anymore, but I've known her a long time now, and I do not feel like shouting *Olé*.

I'm sorry my wife drinks now in the afternoon, and perhaps takes a drink or two in the morning as well. I try not to say anything to her about it. That would be humiliating, and I would not want her to fear I was going to start bullying her about that, too. Usually, she will use some offhand way of informing me she's had a little something to drink that afternoon; she met her sister, or the wife of somebody, for lunch or fabric-shopping and had a cocktail or double scotch before coming home, or, as she did just now, she has been cooking with wine. Sometimes she will want to tell me but wait too long and won't, and I will have the feeling then that she is trembling inside herself, wondering if I have noticed and will criticize. (My wife is afraid of me; I don't particularly want her that way, but it makes things easier.) At times I pity her.

She has never been drunk in the daytime (she does get drunk at parties and have a good time—although never at any of our own. My wife is a superior hostess), and neither of the children has ever remarked about her drinking at home during the day, so it may be that she has not let them notice. But I remember that she never used to drink at all; I remember that she never used to flirt. (She never used to swear.) And she is still religious; she goes to church most Sundays and tries to make the rest of us go too. (None of us want to. Once in a while we will, when I decide it's a small enough way of paying her a favor we owe. She isn't quite sure about the minister we have now, and neither am I.)

My wife is also starting to learn how to use dirty words (in much the same self-conscious way other women take up painting at an advanced age or enroll in adult education courses in psychology, art history, or Jean-Paul Sartre). She is not much good at that, either. Her *hell*'s and *damn*'s carry too much emphasis, although her *Oh shit*'s have the ring of authority by now. She is not as convincing as the rest of the men and women in our several social groups in the jaded indifference we affect toward obscenity. My fifteen-year-old daughter is already much better than my wife with dirty words. My daughter uses dirty language with us liberally in order to impress us with her intelligence; often, she uses it directly *at* us (especially at my wife), probing to see how far she will be allowed to go. (She's *not* allowed to go far by me.) And my boy, I can tell, is working up the courage to experiment at home with a dirty word or two. (He isn't sure what the word *fuck* means, although he knows it's dirty. He was under the impression *fuck* was the word for sexual intercourse, until I told him it usually wasn't.)

It is painful for me to recall how my wife was, to know the kind of person she used to be and would have liked to remain, and to see what is happening to her now, as it is painful for me to witness the deterioration of any human being who has ever been dear (or even near) to me, even of chance acquaintances, or total strangers. (A spastic can affect me profoundly, and a person with some other kind of facial or leg paralysis can immobilize me with repugnance. I want to look away. I resent blind people when I see them on the street, grow angry with them for being blind and in danger on the street, and glance about desperately for somebody else to step alongside them before I have to guide them safely

94

across the intersection or around the unexpected side-walk obstruction that throws them abruptly into such pathetic confusion. I will not let myself cope with such human distress; I refuse to accept such reality; I dump it all right down into my unconscious and sit on it as hard as I can. Let it all come out in bad dreams if it has to. I forget them anyway as soon as I wake up.) Martha the typist, that young, plain girl in our office who has bad skin and is going crazy, is a total stranger to me and was already well on her way toward going crazy when she was sent upstairs to us by Personnel (to finish going crazy); I am not responsible; I do not know her; I do not know her mother in Iowa who has married again and will not take her back, or her father (if she still has a father), or anyone else among the many people in this world who should be close to her; yet, if I let it, it could break my heart that she is going crazy. I say nothing to her about how I feel (or could feel). But I always speak kindly to her. My manner is undiscerning. I try not to let her see I care anything at all about what is happening to her (she might turn to me for help, if she knew I knew), and I try not to let myself care. I try not to let her see I know. (She might not know it yet herself.) It would probably be upsetting for her to learn that everyone around her knew she was going crazy.

So I am silent with Martha, and I am silent with my wife, out of the same coarse mixture of sympathy and self-interest, about her drinking and flirting and dirty words, as I was silent also with my mother when she had the first of her brain strokes, and am silent also with everyone else I know in whom I begin to perceive the first signs of irreversible physical decay and approaching infirmity and death. (I write these people off rapidly. They become dead records in my filing system long before they are even gone, at the first indications that they have begun to go.) I say nothing to anybody about anything bad once I see it's already too late for anyone to help. I said nothing to my mother about her brain stroke, even though I was with her when it happened and was the one who finally had to make the telephone call for the doctor. I did not want her to know she was having a brain stroke; and when she did know, I didn't want her to know I knew.

I pretended not to notice when her tongue began rattling suddenly against the roof of her mouth during one of my weekly visits to the apartment in which she lived alone. The same splintered syllable, the same glottal stutter, kept coming out. I masked my surprise and hid my concern. She broke off, that first time, with a puzzled, almost whimsical look, smiled faintly in apology, and tried again to complete what she had started to say. The same thing happened. It happened the next time she tried. And the next. And the time after that, her attempt was not whole-hearted; she seemed to know in advance it was futile, that it was too late. She felt all right otherwise. But she nodded when I suggested we get a doctor; and as I telephoned, the poor old woman sat down and surrendered weakly with a mortified, misty-eyed, bewildered shrug. (She was frightened. And she was ashamed.)

The doctor explained patiently afterward that it was probably not a clot but only a spasm (there was no such things as strokes, he said; there were only hemorrhages, clots, and spasms) in a very small blood vessel in her brain. (Had the affected blood vessel been a larger one, she would have suffered paralysis too on one side and perhaps loss of memory.) But she never spoke again for as long as she lived, although she continued, forgetfully, to try (out of habit, I suppose, rather than from any expectations of success) until the second in her series of spasms (or strokes), and then stopped trying. I would visit her in the nursing home (where she hated to be); I would do all the talking and she would listen and motion for the things she wanted or rise from her chair or bed (until she could no longer stand up, either) and go for them herself. Occasionally, she would jot a request on a scrap of paper. I never mentioned her stroke to her or referred to any of the other growing disabilities that appeared and crept over her remorselessly (arthritis, particularly, and a pervasive physical and mental indolence that blended finally into morbid apathy) as I sat by her bedside during my visits and talked to her about pleasant matters, soon running out of things to say about me, my wife, my children, and my job that I thought might make her feel good. She never knew that Derek had been born with serious brain damage, although she did know he had been born. I always told her he was fine. (I always told her everybody was fine.) We didn't know it either about Derek until he was a few years old, and by then it was too late: we'd already had him; he had already happened. (I wish I were rid of him now, although I don't dare come right out and say so. I suspect all of us in the family feel this way. Except, possibly, my boy, who may reason that if we did get rid of Derek, we could get rid of him, too, and is already concerned that we secretly intend to. My boy watches and absorbs everything having to do with us and Derek, as though waiting to see how we finally dispose of him, which is something, he senses, that sooner or later we will probably have to do.)

My conversation to my mother, like my visits, was of no use to her. I pretended, by not speaking of it, for my sake as well as for hers (for my sake *more* than for hers) that she was not seriously ill and in a nursing home she hated, that she was not crippled and growing older and more crippled daily. I did not want her to know, as she did know (and I knew she knew), as she knew before I did, that she was dying, slowly, in stages, her organs failing and her faculties withering one by one. I brought her food (which, toward the end, when her mind was gone almost entirely and she could barely recollect who I was for more than a minute or two, she would seize with her shriveled fingers and devour ravenously right from the wrapping paper like some famished, caged, wizened, white-haired animal—my mother). I pretended she was perfect and said nothing to her about her condition until she finally died. I was no use to her (except to bring her food), as I am no help now to our typist who is going insane right before my eyes, and am no help either to my wife with her drinking and her flirting and her other rather awkward efforts to be vital and gay. (I have visions these days when I am lying alone in strange beds in hotels or motels, trying to put myself to sleep, of being assailed by filthy hordes of stinging fleas or bedbugs against which I am utterly inept because I am too squeamish to endure them and have no other place to go.) *I don't want my wife ever to find out she drinks too much at parties and sometimes behaves very badly with other people and makes an extremely poor impression when she thinks she is making a very good one!* If she did (if she ever had even an inkling of how clumsy and overbearing she sometimes becomes), the knowledge would crush her (she would be destroyed), and she is already dejected enough.

At home during the day, she drinks only wine; in the evening, before or after dinner, she might drink scotch if I do. Many evenings we will not drink at all. She doesn't really like the taste of whiskey (although she is starting to enjoy the taste of martinis and to welcome that numbing-enlivening effect they mercifully produce so quickly) and doesn't know how to mix cocktails. At parties now, she will drink whatever's handed her as soon as we walk in and try to get a little high as quickly as she can. Then she will stick to that same drink for the rest of the evening. If things have been fairly comfortable between us that day and she is feeling secure, she will have a loud, jolly, friendly good time, with me and everyone else, until she gets drunk (if she does), and sometimes dizzy and sick, and no real harm will be done, although she used to be a quiet, modest girl, somewhat shy and refined, almost demure, always tactful and well-mannered.

If things are not so good, if she is not happy that day with me, my daughter, or herself, she will flirt belligerently. She will usually frighten away the man (or men) she flirts with (they almost never hang around long enough to flirt back) because she doesn't know how; her approach is threatening, her invitation to seduction a challenging attack, and there may be something of a scene if I don't step in quickly enough. It will always be with some man she knows and feels thoroughly safe with (she doesn't really want to flirt

98

at all, I suppose) and usually one who appears to be enjoying himself and bothering no one. (Perhaps he seems smug.) It is saddening for me to watch her; I do not want other people to dislike her.

She will challenge the man openly, sometimes right in the presence of his wife, with a bald and suggestive remark or enticement, sliding her hand heavily up his shoulder blade if he is standing or squeezing the inside of his thigh if he is seated; and then, as though he had already rejected her, turn taunting, vengeful, and contemptuous before he can respond at all. As neatly and promptly as I can, before much damage is done, I will move in to rescue her, to guide her away smoothly with a quip and a smile. I never rebuke her (although I am often furious and ashamed); I humor her, praise her, flatter. I want her to feel pleased with herself. (I don't know why.)

"You're just jealous," she will accuse defiantly, when I have led her away.

"Damned right, I am," I reply with a forced laugh, and sometimes I will put my hands on her intimately to help persuade her I am.

"You'd better be," she'll gloat triumphantly.

We have had better times together, my wife and I, than we are having now; but I do not think we will have them again.

Dinner, my wife says, will be ready soon. My mood is convivial (so many times when I am home with my family, I wish I were somewhere else) and I decide, magnanimously, that tonight (at least) I will do everything I can to make them all happy.

"Hello," I say as my children assemble.

"Hi," says my daughter.

"Hi," says my son.

"What's the matter?" I ask my daughter.

"Nothing," she says.

"Was that a look?"

"No."

"It was a look, wasn't it?"

"I said hello, didn't I?" she retorts, lowering her

voice, maliciously, to a tone of unconcerned innocence. "What do you want me to do?"

(Oh, shit, I meditate pessimistically, my spirits sinking, what the hell is bothering her now?)

"If something's wrong," I persist tolerantly (feeling myself growing incensed), "I wish you'd tell me what it is."

She grits her teeth. "Nothing's wrong."

"Dinner's ready," says my wife.

"I won't like it," says my boy.

"What's bothering her?" I ask my wife loudly, as we move together into the dining room.

"Nothing. I don't know. I never know. Let's sit down. Let's try not to fight tonight. Let's see if we can't get through just one meal without anybody yelling and screaming and getting angry. That shouldn't be too hard, should it?"

"That would suit *me* fine," says my daughter, emphasizing her words to indicate that it might not suit somebody else (me). (She has not looked at me directly yet.)

"It's okay with me," says I.

"I still won't like it," says my boy.

"What does that mean?" I ask.

"I want two hot dogs."

"You can at least taste it," argues my wife.

"What?" asks my daughter.

"You can't keep eating hot dogs all your life."

"If you want them, you'll get them," I promise my son. "Okay?"

"Okay."

"Okay?" I ask my wife. "No fights?"

"All right."

"Amen," I conclude with relief.

"What does that mean?" my boy asks me.

"*Olé*," I answer facetiously.

"What does that mean?"

"Okay. Have you got it?"

"Since when?" intrudes my daughter.

"*Olé*," my boy replies.

"No, it doesn't," says my daughter in her soft, weary monotone without looking up, attempting (I

100

know) to keep the bickering going. *"Olé* doesn't mean okay."

"If you were in a better frame of mind," I josh with her, "I would threaten to wring your neck for that."

"There's nothing wrong with my frame of mind," she replies. "Why don't you threaten to wring my neck anyway?"

"Because you wouldn't realize I was kidding now, and you'd probably think I really wanted to harm you."

"Ha."

"Can't we have a peaceful meal?" pleads my wife. "It shouldn't be so hard to have a peaceful meal together. Should it?"

(I grit *my* teeth.)

"It would be a lot easier," I tell her amiably, "if you didn't keep saying that."

"Forgive me," my wife answers. "Forgive me for breathing."

"Oh, Jesus."

"That's right," says my wife, "swear."

"I didn't mean it that way," I tell her harshly (lying, of course, because that was exactly the way I did mean it). "Honest, I didn't. Look, we all agreed not to argue tonight, didn't we?"

"I know *I* did," says my daughter.

"Then let's not argue. Okay?"

"If you don't shout," says my daughter.

"Olé," says my boy, and we all smile.

(At last we have agreed about something.) Now that we have agreed to relax, we are all very tense. (Now I am sorry I'm there—although I do enjoy my boy. I can think of three girls I like a lot and know a long time—Penny, Jill, and Rosemary—I would rather be with, and the new young one in our Art Department, Jane, who, I bet, I could be having dinner and booze with instead if I had taken the trouble to ask.) None of us at our dining room table seems willing now to risk a remark.

"Should we say grace?" I suggest jokingly in an effort to loosen things up.

"Grace," says my boy, on cue.

101

It's an old family joke that really pleases only my boy; and my daughter's lips droop deliberately with disdain. She holds that scornful expression long enough to make sure I notice. I make believe I don't. I try not to let it rankle me (I know my daughter often finds me childish, and *that* does rankle me. I have a bitter urge to reproach her, to shout at her, to reach out and hit her, to kick her very sharply under the table in the bones of her leg. I have an impulse often to strike back at the members of my family, even the children, when I feel they are insulting me or taking advantage. Sometimes when I see one of them in the process of doing something improper, or making a mistake for which I know I will be justified in blaming them, I do not intercede to help or correct but hold back in joy to watch and wait, as though observing from a distance a wicked scene unfold in some weird dream, actually relishing the opportunity I spy approaching that will enable me to criticize and reprimand them and demand explanations and apologies. It horrifies me; it is something like watching them back fatally toward an open window or the edge of a cliff and offering no warning to save them from injury or death. It is perverse and I try to overcome it. There is this crawling animal flourishing somewhere inside me that I try to keep hidden and that strives to get out, and I don't know what it is or whom it wishes to destroy. I know it is covered with warts. It might be me; it might also be me that it wishes to destroy) and, succeeding in stifling my anger beneath a placid smile, say:

"Pass me the bread, will you, dear?"

My daughter does.

My wife sits opposite me at the head (or foot) of the table, my boy on my left, my daughter on my right. The maid pads back and forth without talking, delivering bowls of food from the kitchen. My wife spoons large portions out into separate plates and passes them. We are silent. We do not feel free any longer to converse without inhibition in front of our colored maids. (I am not even certain of this one's name; they do not stay with us long anymore.)

"The salad is good, Sarah," my wife says.

"I did what you told me."

I am not comfortable having our maids serve us our food at our places (neither are the children), and I won't allow it (even though my wife, I suspect, would still prefer to have it done that way, as it was done in her own family when she was a child, as she still sees it done in good middle-class homes on television and in the movies, and as she imagines it is also done at Buckingham Palace and the White House). I am not comfortable being served by maids *anywhere,* even less so in other people's homes (where I am never certain how much food I am supposed to take, always have difficulty manipulating the serving forks and spoons from a sideways position, and am in continual anxiety that I am going to bump the meat and vegetable platters with my shoulder or elbow and send them spilling to the floor. Of course, that's never happened—yet). I suffer the same discomfort even when they are white (the maids, I mean, not the friends. I don't have any Black friends and probably never will, although I do see more and more pretty Black girls these days that whet my appetite. They're all out of reach for me by now, I guess, unless they're Cuban or Puerto Rican).

"I think it's good," my wife says. "I hope it's good."

"I won't like it," my boy says.

"That's enough," I tell him.

"Okay." He retreats quickly. He cannot stand it when I am displeased with him.

"What is it?" my daughter asks.

"Chicken livers and noodles in that wine sauce you like with beef. I think you'll like it."

"I won't," mumbles my boy.

"Will you at least taste it?"

"I don't like liver."

"It isn't liver. It's chicken."

"It's chicken liver."

"Please taste it."

"I'll taste it," he answers. "And then I'll want my hot dogs."

"Can I have mine?"

My wife and I watch with bated breath as my daughter pokes at the meat solemnly, almost lugubriously, with her fork and touches a small piece to her mouth.

"It's good," she says without enthusiasm and begins eating.

My wife and I are relieved.

(My daughter is somewhat tall and overweight and should be dieting; but my wife, who reminds her endlessly to diet, makes such things as noodles and serves large portions, and my daughter will probably ask for more.)

"It's delicious," I say.

"Can I have my hot dogs?"

"Sarah, put up two frankfurters."

"Can I have the bread back?"

I give my daughter the bread.

"I've got some good news," I begin, and each of them turns to look at me. I am still brimming with excitement (and conceit) over Arthur Baron's conversation with me; and in a sudden, generous welling of affection for them, for all three of them (they *are* my family, and I *am* attached to them), I decide to share my joyful feelings. "Yes, I think I may have some very important news for all of us."

The three of them gaze at me now with such intense curiosity that I find myself forced to break off.

"What?" one of them asks.

"On second thought," I hesitate, "it may not be that important. In fact, now that I think of it, it isn't important at all. It isn't even interesting."

"Then why did you say it?" my daughter wants to know.

"To tantalize you," I kid.

"What in hell does that mean?" my boy asks.

"*Do* you have something?" my wife asks.

"Oh, maybe yes," I tease her jovially, "and maybe no."

"To *tease* us," my daughter exclaims to my boy with mockery and distaste.

(My daughter makes me feel foolish again. And again I have that powerful, momentary, spiteful impulse to injure her, to wound her deeply with a cutting retort, to reach out over the dining room table and smack her hard on the side of the face or neck, to

104

kick her viciously under the table in her ankle or shin. I can do nothing, though, but ignore her and try to maintain my facade of paternal good humor.)

"Then why don't you tell us?" my wife inquires. "Especially if it's good."

"I will," I say. "All I wanted to say," I announce, and my spirit turns manifestly arch and tantalizing again as I pause to butter a piece of bread and take a bite, "is that I think I may have to start playing golf again."

There is a thoughtful, puzzled, almost rebellious silence now as each of them tries to figure out before the others what it is I am waggishly withholding from them and presently intend to disclose.

"Golf?" asks my nine-year-old boy, who is still not certain what kind of game golf is, whether it is a good game or a bad one.

"Yes."

"Why golf?" asks my wife with surprise. (She knows I hate the game.)

"Golf," I repeat.

"You don't even like golf."

"I hate golf. But it may have to be golf."

"Why?"

"I bet he's getting a better job!" my daughter guesses. (In many ways, she is the smartest and most devious of all of us.)

"Are you?" asks my wife.

"Maybe."

"What kind of job?" My wife's reaction is suspicious, almost morose. I know she has assumed secretly for several years that I have been longing for a different job that would take me away from home more often.

"Selling."

"Selling what?" asks my boy.

"Selling selling."

For an instant, my boy is confused, almost stunned by the riddle of my reply. Then he understands it was meant as a joke, and he bursts into laughter. His eyes sparkle, and his face lights up joyously. (Everybody likes my boy.)

"Do you mean it?" probes my wife, studying me. She is still unsure whether to be pleased or not.

"I think so."

"Will you have to travel more than you have to travel now?"

"No. Probably less."

"Will you make more money?" my daughter asks.

"Yes. Maybe a lot more."

"Will we be rich?"

"No."

"Will we ever be rich?"

"No."

"I don't want you to travel more," my boy complains.

"I'm not *going* to travel more," I repeat for him, with a trace of annoyance. "I'm going to travel *less.*" (I begin to regret that I brought it up at all. The questions are coming too swiftly; I can feel my self-satisfaction ebbing away, and an army of irritations mobilizing too rapidly for me to keep track of and control. I am already replying to them with my slight stammer.)

"Are you going to start talking to yourself again?" my boy cannot resist baiting me mischievously.

"I wasn't talking to myself," I declare firmly.

"Yes, you were," my daughter murmurs.

"Like last year?" my boy persists.

"I was not talking to myself," I repeat loudly. "I was practicing a speech."

"You were practicing it to yourself," my boy points out.

"Will they let you make a speech this year?" my daughter asks. "At the company convention?"

"Oh, yes," I respond with a smile.

"A long speech?"

"Oh, yes, indeed. I imagine they might let me make a speech as long as I want to at the company convention this year."

"Will you be working for Andy Kagle?" my wife asks.

The question brings me to a halt.

"A little something like that," I stammer evasively.

(The fun goes out of my family guessing game, and now I *am* sorry that I started it.) I laugh nervously. "It isn't definite yet. And it's all a pretty long way off. Maybe I shouldn't even have mentioned it."

"I'm glad you'll be working for Andy Kagle," my wife asserts. "I don't like Green."

"I didn't say I'd be working for Kagle."

"I don't trust Green."

"Don't you listen?"

"Why are you snapping at me?"

"I don't want you to be a salesman," my daughter exclaims with unexpected emotion, almost in tears. "I don't want you to have to go around to other people's fathers and beg them to buy things from you."

"I'm not going to be a salesman," I protest impatiently. "Look, what's everybody talking about it so much for? I haven't got it yet. And I'm not even sure I'm going to take it."

"You don't have to shout at her," my wife says.

"I'm not shouting."

"Yes, you are," she says. "Don't you hear yourself?"

"I'm sorry I shouted."

"You don't have to snap at everybody, either."

"And I'm sorry I snapped."

My wife is right, this time. Without my realizing it, I have moved from optimistic conceit into a bad temper; and without my being conscious of it, my voice has risen with anger, and I have been shouting at them again. We are all silent at the table now. The children sit with their eyes lowered. They seem too fearful even to fidget. I am guilty. My forehead hurts me (with tension. Another headache is threatening). I am numb with shame. I feel so helpless and uncertain. I wish one of them would say something that would give me a clue, that would point the way I must follow toward an easy apology. (I feel lost.) But no one will speak.

I pounce upon an energetic idea. I whirl upon my son without warning, shoot my index finger out at him, and demand:

"Are you mad or glad?"

"Glad," he cries with laughter and delight, when he recognizes I am joking again and no longer irate.

I spin around toward my daughter and shoot my index finger out at her.

"Are you mad or glad?" I demand with a grin.

"Oh, Daddy," she answers. "Whenever you make one of us unhappy, you always try to get out of it by behaving like a child."

"Oh, shit," I say quietly, stung by her rebuff.

"Must you say that in front of the children?" my wife asks.

"They say it in front of us," I retort. I turn to my daughter. "Say shit."

"Shit," she says.

"Say shit," I say to my son.

He is ready to start crying.

(I want to reach out instinctively to console and reassure him and rumple his soft, sandy hair. I am deeply fond of my boy, although I am not sure anymore how I feel about my daughter.)

"I'm sorry," I tell him quickly. (I have the shameful, shocking apprehension that if I did put my hand out to comfort him, he would cringe reflexively, as though afraid I were going to strike him. I recoil from that thought in pain.) I turn to my daughter. "I'm sorry," I say to her too, earnestly. "You're right, and I'm sorry. I do act like a child." Now it is my eyes that are down. "I think I want another drink," I explain apologetically, as I stand up. "I'm not going to eat anymore. You go on, though. I'll wait in the living room. I'm sorry."

They continue eating after I leave, their voices subdued.

I do such things to them, I know, even when I don't intend to. But I cannot admit this to my wife or children. My wife would not understand. I cannot really say to my wife: "I'm sorry." She would think I was apologizing. My wife and I cannot really talk to each other about the same things anymore; but I sometimes forget this and try. We are no longer close enough for honest conversation (although we *are* close enough for frequent sexual intercourse). She would respond with something as vacuous and frustrating and galling as "You should be," or "You didn't have to snap at everybody," or "You don't have to shout at me that way." As though my snapping or her snapping at me (she can snap too), were any part of the problem. She would say something exactly like that; and I would be brought to a stop again, as though slapped sharply; I would be stunned; I would feel abandoned and isolated again, and I would sink back for safety again inside my dense, dark wave of opaque melancholy; I would feel lonely and I would be brought face to face again with the fact that I have nobody in this world to confide in or reach toward for help; I would miss my mother (and my father?) and my dead big brother, and I would begin daydreaming once again about some new job with a different company that would take me far away from home more often. Someday soon someone may be dropping bombs on us. I will scream:

"The sky is falling! They are dropping bombs! People are on fire! The world is over! It's coming to an end!"

And my wife will reply:

"You don't have to raise your voice to me."

What happened to us? Something did. I was a boy once, and she was a girl, and we were both new. Now we are man and woman, and nothing feels new any longer; everything feels old. I think we liked each other once. I think we used to have fun; at least, it seems that way now, although we were always struggling about one thing or another. I was always struggling to get her clothes off, and she was always struggling to keep them on. I remember things like that. I remember the many times I had to pull my wife's dress up and her panties down because she didn't like to make love outdoors, or even indoors if anyone else was even remotely in the vicinity: in the same house or apartment, in the next room (even at hotels! She would be petrified if she heard someone stirring in the adjoining room), in the *next* apartment, in the *next* house! I remember the way I'd unbutton her blouse almost anywhere to get at her bra and breasts. (Pale blue brassieres still do drive me crazy more than black; she used to wear them.) She was always afraid we'd be caught. I didn't care (although I might have cared if we'd ever been caught). I was always ripping open her slacks or tearing off her bathing suit or tennis shorts and flinging them away somewhere over my back as I went at her as hard and fast as I could every chance I had. I was a pretty hot kid once. I didn't care whether she enjoyed it or not; just as long as *I* got *mine*. I was always trying to jump her. We were with her parents and her younger sister a lot then, and I would grab at her the second they all went out and try to bang her before any of them got back. In the country, during the summer, or at the seashore, I would try to lure her outside the rented house after dark and do it to her on the porch or right down on the ground or sand (although I didn't like the sand in my clothes and hair afterward—and she didn't like the ground, because it hurt her ass and made it black and blue). I was always pulling at her buttons and zippers and clutching and scratching at the snaps and elastic of her underthings. I was absolutely wild for her when she was a girl and I was a boy, absolutely out of my head with volcanic lust. I was all cock and hard-on. I wanted to come, come, come. I would give her no warning, no time to deliberate or converse or prepare or find any excuses for delay, and often she did not understand fully what was happening to her until I had her half undressed and was already swarming all over her, wholly on fire and stone deaf to all her objections and premonitions, and it was too late for her to make me stop. (Sometimes I would sit scheming about her all through family dinner, plotting where and how I would spring at her the moment I had the opportunity and selecting the way in which I would ravish her this time.) No matter where it was I trapped, seized, and finally overcame her (if it was anywhere outside the bolted door of our own bedroom; often it was even *behind* the locked door of our own bedroom), she would recline and heave submissively beneath me with her eyes wide open in gleaming fright, turning her gaze from one side to the

110

other rapidly and distressfully to make certain no one was seeing, listening, or approaching. (I think now that I probably enjoyed her terror and my violence.) I didn't mind that her eyes were open and darting all about and that her strongest emotions were not those of passion or entirely on me, just as long as *I* had her when *I* wanted her and got what *I* wanted; it might, in fact, have added something, that tangy, triumphant sense of frenzied danger, that ability to dominate rather than merely persuade, and I often wish I were driven now by that same hectic mixture of blind ardor, haste, and tension. (It might, in fact, have added a great deal.) Maybe that's what's missing. I lay girls now that are as young as she was then, and much more nimble, profligate, and responsive but it isn't as rich with impulse and excitement and generally not as satisfying afterward. (There is no resistance.) I have more control and maturity now and can manipulate and exploit them coolly and skillfully, but it isn't nearly as much fun anymore as it used to be with her, and I miss her greatly and love us both very deeply when I remember how we used to be then. I have large rooms now with big beds and all the privacy and time I want; the girls have places of their own, or I have Red Parker's apartment in the city and hotel rooms and suites on business trips out of town; but it's all rather tame now, rather predictable and matter-of-fact, even with someone I am with for the very first time (and I often wonder, even while I am in the act of doing it, why I bother. I am no sooner in than I'm thinking about getting out. I no sooner come than I want to go).

"Let's go into the bedroom now," I will say (or they will say).

"All right."

I think it was better the other way with me and my wife when we were both so much younger. "Hurry, hurry," she would urge, beg, moan, pant, demand, murmur, pray, implore frantically as she lay and churned in my grasp, doing everything she could think of to help bring me to an end quickly before we were discovered. And I would work away at her, sometimes grinning when she couldn't see me, and have the time of my life.

That was fun we used to have together. It was fun then (more for me than for her), and it is fun now for both of us to recall and laugh about (when we are laughing). We often reminisce together warmly about some of the crazy times and places I did get her. My wife enjoys looking back even more than I do and has a better memory for separate occasions.

("Remember the time in that boathouse when my father—"

"And your kid sister was doing it all summer—"

"You sound envious."

"She probably got more than I did."

"You had no complaints."

"I did when I found out about her."

"Were you hot for her?"

"Only when I knew about her."

"Are you hot for her now?"

"Don't be crazy. She's a God-damned reactionary bitch now."

"You don't ever say anything to her about—"

"I hardly ever talk to her."

"Remember the time on the lake in that rowboat?"

"Do I!")

I remember the time I once tried to do it to her right on the bottom of a rowboat, far out on a lake. (I remember dead Virginia from my automobile casualty insurance company, and I bet *I* could do it now also in a canoe to a carefree young coed like Virgin-for-Short, but I don't think I would want to anymore, not at my age, not in a canoe.) I did almost everything else to her that day while she wriggled and kissed and fought and hugged and fretted against the bottom of that rowboat, but when it came to the nudeness of it, to the pulling of her things off and my things down, she was terror-stricken by the thought that people might be seeing us from the houses along the shore and, almost weeping miserably, made me stop. So I rowed furiously to a small island a little farther out (I think I must have broken the speed record for rowing that day) and laid her on the ground just inside the woods. She rolled her head from side to side with wide-open eyes flashing in anguish and fear, pleading with me desperately please to stop or please to hurry up and finish before someone came trudging up through the trees and caught us. We were already married then.

It *was* fun, even though we often fought about it bitterly: she would cry, and I would rage if I could not have my way with her in matters of sex and just about everything else. (My feelings were easily hurt.) I used to want to jump her everywhere. We are both glad now that I did. I was always throwing her halters off then or shoving her blouses and sweaters up to go for her breasts and lips like someone starved, suffering the aching, compulsive need and joy in my heart and head and mouth and throat and in the palms of my hands. (What a nutty kid I was, even then.) "Not now," she would say, or "Do you love me?" she would ask. And I would say anything, or nothing, as I pushed and forced myself upon her. It took very little to get me excited then, usually nothing more than the sight of her, or just the thought, when I had been away, that I would be back with her soon. (*Then* I knew what being horny really meant.) When we were alone indoors and knew we had time, I could be different, and so could she; but there were many times when we could not be alone. And the trouble with my wife then was that she did not like to make love *anywhere* outdoors. She did not like to screw in parks, or on beaches, or in bushes, or standing up against walls, doors, or trees (and I did). She did not want to screw in the back of my car (or the front), and I always had to force her. (There was frequently no better place we had for it then; and when there was, I often did not want to wait.) My wife was something of a lady then, and I liked her for that (more than I like her drinking and flirting now, or her raucous tones when she is having a good time at parties and dinners). But I also liked getting laid. There was one whole summer at the lake when she did not want to make love at all because we were sharing the house with her mother and father and sister, and one person or another was always around. That was the summer, I remember, that her sister got knocked up near the end and almost drove her mother and father insane before she would agree to the abortion (it was not that she wanted the baby; she was afraid of surgery), although it could have happened at college the first week she went back. My wife and I were married then, and what was clear (at least to me) was that her kid sister had been making out effortlessly all summer long, while I was having so much trouble, which made me wonder if I had not wasted the better part of that summer trying to get into the wrong sister, my wife. Once I found out about her sister, I wanted to lay her too, even though I didn't like her.

Later, when we had our own place, my wife didn't want to make love until she was certain all of the children were sound asleep and the door to the bedroom was locked and the door to the apartment was double-locked. (God knows who she imagined might sneak in and catch us at it then. Burglars?) There was a long, long period, even when we had our own place, when she did not want to screw any time during the day, even before we had children, and when there was no one else around. (Nowadays, she'll do it with me just about any place, any time, especially if she's had a drink or two.) She needed darkness, even at night; she wanted to be hidden; the lights had to be out, the shades drawn, the doors closed, even the closet doors. She would rather I did not watch her undress and did not gaze at her when she was walking or lying naked; often she came to the bed with her nightgown already on, having removed her clothes privately in the bathroom or closet, even though she knew I would slip it up and off her immediately. Then, though, when conditions were exactly right, once she had made certain she was safe from interruption and concealed from watching eyes, when everything around us was just the way she wanted it, she could be absolutely fine in just about every way and feel proud of herself and me afterward and in between. And she wasn't so bad all those other times when I had to force her and we had to do it fast (she learned rapidly that the more zealously she pitched in to give me what I wanted, the sooner it would be over), although she was never nearly as good at age twenty-eight as my Cuban whore was this afternoon. ("Do you like to be teased?" she purred, and I can hear her purring again. Of course I do. Maybe I never left my wife enough time to tease me then, or even to learn how.)

Nowadays, my wife is much better. Nowadays, my wife is completely different about this whole matter of sex; but so am I. She is almost always amorous nowadays, it seems, and ready to take chances that horrify even me. I can usually tell when she's been thinking about it the instant I walk in, by a bold, questioning, determined look in her eyes and a funny, self-satisfied, slightly twisted smile. I know I am right if she has left her girdle off. (Her girdle is off tonight. I remember when she didn't need a girdle and wouldn't wear one; now she'll seldom go out of the house without a girdle, even though she still doesn't need one.) When she is in the mood, I have only to grip her elbow or nudge her gently toward a couch or bed and I can have her any time I want to and just about anywhere. Or she will come after me. She is always in the mood when she drinks (unless she is sick), and she drinks almost every day now. I have only to pass within arm's reach of her in the kitchen when she is cooking or meet her by accident in one of the hallways and she moves right up against me and is ready to sink down on the spot (she has even had me do it to her on the kitchen floor), in the dark or in brilliant daylight. She lifts her own skirt now, and fumbles impatiently with *my* pants if I am not removing them quickly enough. (I'm not sure I like her this way, although I would have liked it back then, but I'm not so sure about that, either. I'm really not sure I *want* my wife to be as lustful and compliant as one of Kagle's whores or my girl friends, although I know I am dissatisfied with her when she isn't.)

"Do you really have a chance at a better job?" she asks me later, when we are upstairs in our bedroom.

"I think so."

"Much better?"

"And how."

"Will you make more money?"

"And how."

"Oh, boy," she responds.

And she swarms all over me irrepressibly, her arms and legs and mouth opening and entwining, with our bedroom door open and the children probably still awake. And I am the one now who wiggles free and rises from the bed to close and lock the door and extinguish the overhead light.

"You're some girl," I tell her admiringly, after a long, deep embrace during which we are both practically still.

"You did it," she agrees readily, with a boastful laugh, sitting astride me now and rocking back and forth. "You made me this way."

I can't believe it was all my fault.

My daughter's unhappy

Both our children are unhappy, each in his (or her) separate way, and I suppose that is my fault too (although I'm not sure I understand how or why). I no longer think of Derek as one of my children. Or even as mine. I try not to think of him at all; this is becoming easier, even at home when he is nearby with the rest of us, making noise with some red cradle toy or making unintelligible sounds as he endeavors to speak. By now, I don't even like his name. The children don't care for him, either. No one really cares for him, not even the nurses we hire, and they are paid to care for him and to pretend to like him; they are nearly always unmarried women in their late thirties or older; they are very expensive and usually pretend to love him in the beginning; they act adoring and jealously protective of him for just the first few weeks and then turn negligent toward him and impudent and reproachful with the rest of us. We turn nasty with them. They go. They either leave on their own or are fired. My wife and I take turns telling them they must go. I begin to detest all of them almost from the moment we hire them; they don't like me. I hate and fear the one we have now, who is older than I am, superstitious, and forcefully opinionated; she reminds me of Mrs. Yerger. I want to yell dirty things at this nurse now for the debasement Mrs. Yerger made me suffer then. Every older woman I find myself afraid of reminds me of

Mrs. Yerger. Every feeble old woman I see reminds me of my mother. Every young girl who attacks my pride reminds me of my daughter. No one reminds me of my father, which is okay with me, I guess, since I don't remember a father for anyone to remind me of. Except Arthur Baron. I think I may feel a little bit about Arthur Baron the way I might have felt about my father if he had lived a little longer and been nice to me. I hope this one quits soon. I want to be rid of her. If she doesn't quit soon, my wife or I will have to fire her, which never seems to upset any of them as much as it does us, and as much as it would upset me if I were ever fired. This will leave things at home dismal and disorganized for a while. I will go out of town on a business trip until a new one is found. I always like to leave things like that for my wife and her sister to take care of. Her sister is good at things like that. I always like to be out of town when we have to look for a new nurse or move from one house to another. I always like to be somewhere else when anything unpleasant is taking place. We will feel glad to be rid of her when we finally do make her go; but each one has to be replaced; we always have to find another; or we will have to send Derek away early to a home for retarded people and never look at him again. We will erase him, cross him out, file him away—even though we go to visit him three or four times the first year, one or two times the second, and after that perhaps not at all, we will never really look at him again. We will put him out of sight, think of him less and less. He will visit *us,* maybe, in dreams.

"I wonder how he's doing," one of us might think of speculating from time to time, if either of us dared to face the consequences of a reply.

And later:

"Whatever happened to him? You know, that kid we used to have? Derek, I think his name was. The one with something wrong. Are we still in touch with him?"

My wife and I are not able to send him away yet. He is still too little. There is no hope. He is lots of trouble. He has let us down. He needs care constantly, and no one wants to give it to him, not his father, his mother, his sister, or his brother. None of us really even wants to play with him anymore. Although we take turns making believe).

My daughter, who is past fifteen, is a lonely and disgruntled person. (She is much more than disgruntled, I know. She is unhappy; but that's the form her unhappiness tends to take, and that's the nature of the criticism and complaints with which we generally have to contend. I wouldn't mind so much, I think, if she were unhappy and obliging. Like my son. It would make things easier for me. Although it does not seem to make things easier for him.) She is dissatisfied with us and dissatisfied with herself. She is a clever, malicious girl with lots of insight and charm when she isn't morose and rude. She is often mean, often depressed. She resents my wife and me terribly and as much as tells us frequently that she wishes one or both of us were gone or dead. (In fact, she *does* tell us that, in exactly those words.) And it's a lucky thing my wife and I are both sensible enough to remind each other that she really doesn't mean it. (Even though I know she often *does* mean it, and that deep inside her, probably, she often wishes, in melodramatic fantasy, that she were dead also, and that we were at her graveside and sorry.) At least I'm sure she may mean it at the time she says it and perhaps, subconsciously, she harbors that evil wish in regard to us always. Perhaps she really does wish that my wife or I will die soon. It would not be so unnatural for her to do so; it would not be so difficult for me to understand (for didn't I have that same repugnant wish for my mother after she fell sick, and perhaps even earlier, when she began to grow old, once I no longer needed her, and she began to need me? I was impatient for her to die. And told myself she'd be better off). If my daughter is poised, if she is looking smug and wearing her thin-lipped half-smile of calculating villainy when she remarks to my wife or me that she really doesn't think she would mind very much if my wife and/or I fell sick and/or died, I know she does not mean what she is saying; she is speaking for effect; she is merely searching, imma-

119

turely and compulsively, for a painful, punishing clash with us (making sadistic family small talk, so to speak) and slicing out at a sensitive old wound that she knows intuitively will open freely and bleed with pain. (My daughter likes to hurt us. She sometimes professes remorse, but lets us know she doesn't really feel it.) If, however, the statements gush from her in a high shriek or tumble out brokenly in gulping, hysterical sobs, then there is no ignoring the sincerity of her passionate hatred and bottomless misery. She is not, as I said, happy. (In these moments she is pathetic. She would break my heart, if she were somebody else's.)

She has a very pretty face but doesn't believe it. (She has what I believe is called a *low*—or *poor*—*self-image*.) And nothing my wife or I can do will help. I realize now that I have not always given replies to her questions and comments that were appropriate. When she tells me she wishes she were dead, I tell her she will be, sooner or later. When she tells me life is empty and monotonous and that there does not seem to be any point to it, I tell her everybody feels that way now and then, particularly at her age, and that she's probably right. When she told me, in tones of solemn importance, that she hoped to have a lover before she was eighteen and would want to live with him for several years even though she is never going to get married, I nodded approvingly and wisecracked I hoped she'd find one—and was astounded when her face went bloodless with shock and she seemed about to cry. When she asks me if I ever thought of killing myself when I was young, I answer yes. And when she came to me, even that first time, to say she wasn't happy, I told her that I wasn't either and that nobody ought to expect to be. By now, she is able to anticipate many of my sardonic retorts and can mimic my words before I say them. Sometimes this annoys me; other times it amuses me—I don't know *why* there is a difference in my reaction. My error, I think, is that I always speak to her as I would to a grown-up; and all she wants, probably, is for me to talk to her as a child.

I am simply not able to stop myself from saying

things to her I know I shouldn't; sometimes the words escape from me before I can consider them, before I am even aware they have sprung from my mind and are being shaped by my mouth and tongue to fly out between my lips. And I hear my blunt or cutting remarks with a start of astonishment, as though they came from somebody else and were directed harmfully at me as well as at her, as though they had their source in some dark and frightening area of my soul with which I am not in communication. It is that same weird, perverse, glowering part of me that shelters my recurring impulse to kick Kagle's lame leg very hard, and to kick my daughter's leg under the table or strike her (I am never really tempted to hit my wife or my boy, and I never have. I don't think I have. I have never hit my daughter either. Or kicked her), and it nourishes refreshingly that thrilling desire of mine to say very cruel things to people I like who are in trouble and confide in me and request my sympathy or help. I do rejoice momentarily in the misfortunes of friends. I cannot condone their weakness; I cannot forgive them for being in need; I experience undeniable gladness that I enjoy suppressing. I like finding out I'm better off than somebody else. There are things going on inside me I cannot control and do not admire.

My daughter doesn't laugh much anymore (she enjoys my boy a great deal, but picks on him often with bad intent) and has few interests or pleasures. (The same seems true of the boys and girls who remain her friends. They like music but not much, not as much as they seem to wish they could. None are cheerful. All are glum and creepy, usually. They cast a pall. I hope they outgrow it. I don't know how to talk to them.) She sits alone in her room for long periods of time doing absolutely nothing but thinking (I sit alone in my study for long periods of time doing absolutely the same thing); and what she likes to think about most is herself; what interests her most is herself; what she broods about most is herself; what she likes to talk about most is herself. She is not much different from me, I suppose. I think, though, that I was happier than she is when I was young, and that all the boys and girls I grew up with and went to elementary school with and high school with were also much happier than she and her friends. I like to think that. But I really didn't know these other boys and girls as well as I know her. And perhaps they were not so happy as I think they were. And perhaps I was not. I didn't have as much to do with them when we were out of school and not in the street; I did not know them in the home and did not know them when they were alone. And I'm not so confident anymore that my own recollections of my childhood are as infallible as I have always believed them to be. I also think I may have been *more* unhappy than my daughter when I was young, and felt even more entrapped than she does in my own sense of pathless isolation. There are long gaps in my past that remain obscure and give no clue. There are cryptic rumblings inside them but no flashes of recall. They are pitch black and remain that way, and all the things I was and all the changes and things that happened to me then will be lost to me forever unless I find them. No one else will. Where are they? Where are those scattered, ripped pieces of that fragmented little boy and bewildered young man who turned out to be me? There are times now when it seems to me that I may not have been any place at all for long periods of time. What ever happened to all those truly important parts of my past that no longer exist in my memory and have been ignored or forgotten by everyone else? No one will ever recall them. It is too late to gather me all up and put me together again. My life, therefore, is not entirely credible. I have trouble believing it. I can believe that it was me (*I*. I know) with Virginia in the storeroom of the automobile casualty insurance company and me with my wife making love on our honeymoon and me who is bored, melancholy, and reflective in my office at the company now, or in my study at home; but I can't *really* believe it was *really* me (*I*. Even though I know it's true) who sang those silly military songs exuberantly so long ago as we marched slovenly along in formation in uniform, sorted accident reports in an insurance office, filed folders, shot crap and played cards for pennies, nickles, and dimes, had satisfactory erotic dreams and was thankful for them, masturbated, and was thankful that I could, read the comic strips and sports pages of the New York *Daily News* and the New York *Mirror,* which, alas, is now defunct —soon there won't be anything left—said good-bye to my mother five mornings each week if I reminded myself to say anything at all to her when I left, carried a brown paper bag containing an apple and two baloney, egg, or canned salmon sandwiches with me into Manhattan for lunch, had tantrums as a child in frenzied and incoherent arguments at home with my mother or sister and wept inconsolably over matters I could not understand or explain, was a hardy and impetuous patrol leader in the beaver patrol of the Boy Scouts of America for many years and worked to earn merit badges, masturbated some more, even as a Boy Scout, and rode back and forth to my automobile casualty insurance company each working day on a very stuffy subway car crowded with tired, hostile, grimy adults who glared, sighed, snored, and sweated. That was somebody else, not me—I insist on that; it exists in my memory but that's all; like a children's story; it is way outside the concrete experience of the person I am now and was then; it never happened—I do insist on that—not to me; I *know* I did not spend so much of myself doing only *that;* so there must have been a second person who grew up alongside me (or *inside* me) and filled in for me on occasions to experience things of which I did not wish to become a part. And there was even a third person of whom I am aware only dimly and about whom I know almost nothing, only that he is there. And I am aware of still one more person whom I am not even aware of; and this one watches everything shrewdly, even me, from some secure hideout in my mind in which he remains invisible and anonymous, and makes stern, censorious judgments, about everything, even me. He hardly ever sleeps. I am lacking in sequence for everything but my succession of jobs, love affairs, and fornications; and these are not important; none matters more than any

123

of the others; except that they do give me some sense of a connected past.

Who cares if I get Kagle's job or not? Or if I do get into young Jane in the Art Department's pants before Christmas or that I was never able to graduate myself into laying older-girl Virginia on the desk in the storeroom of the automobile casualty insurance company or in a bed in a hotel, although I did squeeze her good tits many times and feel the smooth inside of her thighs?

I care. I want the money. I want the prestige. I want the acclaim, and congratulations. And Kagle will care. And Green will care, and Johnny Brown will care so much he might punch me in the jaw as soon as he learns about it, and I know already I will have to begin making plans beforehand for coping with him tactfully or getting rid of him altogether, even though he's good. But will it matter, will it make a difference? No. Do I want it? Yes. (*Should* I want it? Nah. But I do, I do, dammit. I do.)

And there's no mistaking, either, the fact that my daughter does honestly covet the greater freedom enjoyed by girls and boys she knows who *have* lost a father or a mother through accident or illness, or whose parents are divorced or separated. (Even though they don't really seem to be enjoying it; they just seem to have more freedom.)

"Who the hell would take care of you if we *were* divorced, or if we were killed in a plane or automobile accident?" I try to explain to her tolerantly one evening during one of those "frank" (and generally abusive) discussions she persists in inaugurating regularly, usually when she observes that I have settled myself alone in my study to do some work or read a magazine. "You couldn't live alone. You know that. Who would feed you and clean up after you, help you pick your clothes out and remind you to brush your teeth and help you keep your weight down? You'd have to live with someone, you know. So it might as well be us. You know, you get some pretty God-damned *good* things from us, too."

"I wish," says my wife, "that you wouldn't swear so much when you talk to the children. And that you didn't always have to yell. Can't you see you're only scaring her?"

"Can't you make her keep out of it?" says my daughter to me, sullenly, about my wife.

"And *I* wish," I reply to my wife—

"She's always butting in."

—in a growl that rises menacingly.

But I don't know what I wish (except that I damn well wish I were somewhere else), so I grind my jaws shut without completing my sentence. (My voice does have a tendency to get loud whenever I am irritated, frustrated, or attacked. And I will stammer ferociously if I attempt to speak a long sentence with strong emotion.)

I wish I knew what to wish.

I wish my daughter would stop complaining and feeling so sorry for herself all the time and start trying to make the best of things. She doesn't think much of us. She is nervous, spiteful, embittered, and vindictive. She is approaching sweet sixteen, smokes, and hates us both intensely—at least part of the time (if not nearly all of the time). I don't know what we have done, or failed to do, to account for it all: I don't know what she blames us for; but she blames us for something. (I grow pretty damned spiteful and embittered myself at my inability to please her, at our failure to make her happy. And I often strike back at her in clever, malign ways. I enjoy striking back at her. Revenge is sweet, even against her. And she is not yet sixteen. I sometimes find myself wishing that she would run away from home, just to make things easier for me.) I know my daughter hates us because she makes a point of telling us so. She may hate us singly or she may hate us both together: she is versatile, my darling little girl, at least in this one respect, extremely gifted; without straining herself unduly, she can hate all three of us simultaneously, my son included, or she can begin hating him separately without apparent reason and be oblivious to us; or she can hate Derek, his nurse, our house, our community. She can, of course, hate herself. With uncommon resourcefulness, she can even *stop* hating us for a little while, just to throw us off stride into an unguarded state of well-being that leaves us wide open for her next piercing assault. She is perverse, and proud of it. My daughter can't (or won't) learn chemistry, grammar, or plane geometry easily; but she did learn how to smoke cigarettes at an early age (even inhale, she boasts. Marijuana, too, she intimates, without being asked) and to say *motherfucker* so effortlessly as to appear to have been saying it unselfconsciously to us at home all her life; and she did learn how to hate us and say cruel things that hurt my feelings and reduce my wife to plaintive tears. It took my wife and me ten or fifteen years of full-time marriage and hard and constant practice to learn how to hate each other with good, wholesome vigor and elation (when we do hate each other. We do not hate each other all the time), but my precocious daughter has learned how to do it already. It may be a talent she has, a genuine aptitude (if it is, it's the only talent she has. I am often quite furious with her, but I won't give her the satisfaction of showing it. I am often cruelly sarcastic with her in return). She hates my wife much more, and much more often, than she hates me, which is ironic and unfair, because my wife loves and cares for her without limit or restraint and would lay down her life for her. (And I would not.) But I get my share too. (She has enough hatred to go around.)

It doesn't really bother me so much anymore that my daughter hates me (I won't let it); by now, I expect it, I am inured to it, and I am willing to bow to her assertion that there is good reason for her hatred, although I don't know what that good reason is (except that I have grown inured to it, which is reason enough, I suppose).

Usually, she will come uninvited to my study to interrupt me when I'm working or reading a newsmagazine (or pretending to work or read) to tell me (in a tense, thin, childlike voice that she endeavors valorously to hold steady and self-assured) that she has arrived at the conclusion (never *come to,* but always *arrived*) that she doesn't have any real feelings for my wife or me any longer, thinks ___ of her mother and of me too and finds it impossible to respect us, in fact, by now really dislikes us both very much; and that, terrible as she knows it must sound, and even though she will admit that she probably ought to be ashamed of herself—but isn't—for feeling the way she does, she is certain that she really wouldn't be sorry if Mommy (my wife) were killed in an automobile accident, like Alice Harmon's mother—Alice Harmon, in fact, can't make herself feel sorry about her mother at all—or if I were to get sick and die of a brain tumor, like Betsy Anderson's father; that she wouldn't actually take any pleasure in it, she wants me to know, and isn't actually wishing for that to happen, she wants me to understand, and might even regret it a little if it did, as she would regret it if it happened to anyone she knew, but she just doesn't think it would be the biggest tragedy in *her* life if I did get a stroke or a brain tumor, provided I died quickly and didn't need someone to take care of me for a long time, like some of those people who have brain tumors or strokes and go on living like vegetables, and is not saying all this just to start an argument with me or make me feel bad, but is only saying so because that just happens to be the way she feels, and she knows I want to know the way she really feels—don't I?—because I am her father and she is my daughter. And then, if I have let her progress that far (sometimes I cut her off gruffly as soon as she begins and kick her out right then), she might volunteer the information (again), with that same affected air of casual, unmotivated reflection (still struggling to keep her small voice from wavering and her trembling fingers from picking at things) that if my wife and I ever do get divorced, as she knows we have considered doing, and feels we *should* consider doing, since we are not so happy together anyway and are not very much alike, she doesn't think she would want to have to live with either one of us but would prefer to be sent away to boarding school, like Christine Murray, who is very happy now that she doesn't have to live with either one of her parents anymore, or even maybe to school in Switzerland, where she knows she will be content. In fact, she has arrived at the conclusion

127

by now that she would be much better off living away from us, anyway, even if we don't get a divorce, and that we would probably be much happier without her too, since she can tell we don't really want her there. Wouldn't we?

Sometimes (with spiteful goals of my own) I will hear her through with the silence of a stone, letting her go on this way for as long as she is able, saying absolutely nothing and gazing at her all the while with a heavy expression that yields no flicker of emotion, forcing her to go on and on with increasing dismay and befuddlement (although I look at her, she must wonder if I am listening to her, if I hear her) as the smug, malevolent composure with which she entered crumbles away into terrified misgivings and she is left, at last, standing mute and foolishly before me, shivering and exhausted, bereft of all her former confidence and determination. (I can outfox her every time.) And then (when she has run out of all things to say and I know I have outfoxed her) if I maintain my silence and continue to stare at her oppressively with my dull, heavy, unresponsive look, she might stammer lamely, in a final, desperate attempt at bravado that fails:

"I'm only trying to be frank with you."

And then, with victory palpably before me, I might decide to speak; I might decide to move in skillfully for my own attack, simulating an air of smug composure that seeks mockingly to impersonate her own.

"No," I will say enigmatically.

(And this will confuse her.)

"No what?" she must ask.

"No, you're not."

"Not what?" she is forced to inquire, timid and suspicious now. "What do you mean?"

"You're not trying to be frank. You're trying to be anything but frank, so please don't use that as an excuse for your bad nature."

"What do you mean?"

"Aren't you?"

"I don't know. What do you mean?"

"Don't you know what I mean?" I inquire with cool, invigorating vengeance. She shakes her head.

"What I mean is that you aren't trying to be frank and that you *are* trying to say the most shocking and outrageous things you can think of in order to hurt my feelings and make me angry at you."

"Why would I do that?"

"Angry enough to yell and begin punishing you."

"Why would I do that?"

"Because that's the way you are."

"Why would I want you to punish me?"

"Because that *is* the way you are. Don't you see? And that's the way you want me to feel. Don't you see that? Don't you think I can see it?"

"What do you mean?"

"That's what I mean."

"It's a matter of supreme indifference to me," she rejoins loftily, "how you feel."

"Then why bother," I mimic just as loftily, "to tell me at all?"

"What do you mean?"

"I mean that if how I feel is really a matter of such supreme indifference to you, why bother to ever talk to me at all?"

"What should I do?"

"Unless you want something."

"And you wonder why I bite my nails and can't sleep well and why I eat too much."

"Don't blame your eating too much on me."

"What about the rest?"

"I eat too much also."

"You don't think very much of me," she alleges. "Do you?"

"Not right now. How much do you think of yourself?"

"I was only trying to be honest."

"Bull."

"You want me to be honest, don't you?"

"No."

"You don't?"

"Of course not. Why should I?"

An unexpected answer like that always outfoxes her, strikes her speechless for a few moments, makes her stammer and regret even further that she came barging into my study so rashly in the first place to start up with me. If she tries to continue the contest, her voice will drop to a diffident murmur that is almost too faint to be heard (I will pretend not to hear any of it and make her repeat each remark); or she will explode suddenly in a snarling, unintelligible, dramatic outburst and storm away in total defeat, banging some furniture or slamming a door. (I can outfox her easily every time.) But she never seems to learn (or she *has* learned and is drawn self-destructively to repeat these same cheerless defeats), so we go through innumerable repetitions of these same annoying, time-wasting, belittling (she makes fun of me because I'm getting fat. And getting bald. And I strike back by being faster, keener, and better informed in my repartee) "frank" and "honest" disputes with each other (I manage to win them all, although I sometimes feel wounded afterward) over money, smoking, sex, marijuana, late hours, dirty words, schoolwork, drugs, Blacks, freedom (hers), yelling, bullying, and insults to my wife.

"What will you do," she will ask baitingly, "if I come home with a Black boyfriend?"

This is a peculiarly ingenious stroke of hers that requires lightning dexterity to counter and with which she does succeed in confounding and vanquishing my wife. There is no way out, and I am tempted to award her accolades: if I tell her I'd object, I'm a racist; if I tell her I wouldn't, I have no regard for her. My wife succumbs by taking her seriously. I survive by skirting the trap.

"I would *still* ask you to clean up your room," I reply nimbly. "And to stop reading my mail and showing my bank statements to your friends."

Of course I'm a racist! And so is she. Who the devil isn't?

"That's not answering the question," she is intelligent enough to sulk. "And you know it."

"Bring one home and see," I challenge her with a snicker, because I know she is not ready to try *that* one on us yet.

She wants me to promise her now that she'll have her own car. She is willing to promise she'll give up smoking cigarettes in return. I used to order her not to smoke because of the risk of cancer, until I grew so weary of bickering with her over that subject that I stopped caring whether she smoked or not, despite the risk of cancer. (I did my best for a while as a responsible parent. And it did no good.) So now she smokes regularly (she says), over a pack a day (she says), but I don't believe her, for she could be lying about that too. (She lies about everything. She lies to her teachers too.) But she is not allowed to smoke in the house, which makes it easier for my wife and me to pretend that she doesn't smoke at all. And perhaps she doesn't. (Really, who cares? I don't. And I don't like to have to feel forced to pretend to. If she didn't tell us, I wouldn't have to.)

"I do smoke," she insists. "I even inhale. I guess it's a regular habit with me by now. I don't think I could stop smoking cigarettes now even if I wanted to."

"It's your life," I answer placidly.

"Over a pack a day, sometimes two. I know you wouldn't want me to be a sneak about anything like that, would you?"

"Yes."

"What?"

"I do."

"You would?"

"Of course."

"A sneak?"

"Yes."

"What do you mean?" Her eyes cloud with uncertainty and her mouth begins to quiver. I have just outfoxed her again.

"I do want you to be a sneak." I continue breezily, and zero in for the kill. "About smoking, and all those dirty, really very vulgar words and phrases you're so fond of using so openly."

"You use them."

"I'm an adult. And a man."

"Mommy uses them."

"Not the same ones you do."

"Mommy's a prude."

"You're a child."

"I'm sixteen."

"You're fifteen and a half."

"I'm nearer to sixteen."

"So?"

"Can't you say anything more than that?"

"Like what?"

"You always like to give short answers when we argue. You think it's a good trick."

"It is."

"You're so sarcastic."

"Be a sneak," I tell her sarcastically. "I'm not being sarcastic now. It will make things easier for all of us. I give you that advice as a pal, as a really devoted father to a young daughter. Sneak outside on the porch or into the garage when you want to smoke or burn that crappy incense or do something else you don't want us to know about. And close the door of your room when you're on the telephone so we won't have to listen to you complain about us to all of your friends or see those crappy sex novels you read instead of the books you're supposed to be reading for school. You can get away with much more that way. By being a good sneak. Just don't let me find out about it. Because if I do find out, I'm going to have to do something about it. I'm going to have to disapprove and get angry and punish you, and other things like that, and that will make you unhappy and me unhappy."

"Why will it make *you* unhappy?" she wants to know.

"Because you're my daughter. And I really don't enjoy seeing you unhappy."

"Really?"

"Yes."

"Ha."

"And because I don't like to waste so much time fighting with you and yelling at you when I have other things I'd rather be doing."

"Like what?"

"Anything."

"What?"

"Working. Reading a magazine."

"Why must you say that? Why must you be this way?"

132

(I don't know.) "What way?"

"You know."

"I don't." (I do.)

"Why can't you ever pay me a compliment without taking it back?"

"What compliment?"

"You always have to have the last word, don't you?"

"No."

"See?"

"I'm not going to say another word."

"Now you're trying to turn the whole thing into a big joke, aren't you?" she says reprovingly. "You always have to try to turn everything into a big joke, don't you?"

(I'm contrite. I feel a little bit shamed. But I try not to let it show.)

"Let me work now," I tell her quietly.

"I want to talk."

"Please. I was working when you came in."

"You were reading a magazine."

"That's part of my work. And I have to prepare a program for the next company convention and work on two speeches."

"Where is it? The convention."

"Puerto Rico again."

"Can I help with the speeches?"

"No, I don't think so. Not yet."

"Is it more important than me?"

"It's something I want to get done tonight."

"I want to talk now."

"Not now."

"Why?"

"No."

"Why not?"

"No."

"You never want to talk to me."

"Please get out now."

(I know by now that I don't have too much in common with children, not even with my own, and that I dislike getting involved in long conversations with them. I really don't enjoy children for more than a couple of minutes at a time. It is difficult for me to keep interested in what they say and difficult for me to think of things to say that might interest them. So I no longer try.) Sometimes, when my daughter is in buoyant spirits (for some reason) and feeling exceptionally strong and sure of herself, she will sweep into my study audaciously without any pretext or apology and, as though she and I were commonly on the most familiar terms, settle herself imperiously on my couch as though for a lengthy, top-level consultation, and begin complaining to me about my wife, grossly miscalculating my response, assuming mistakenly, I guess, that because my wife and I fight so much, I will welcome her allegiance. (I don't allow her to speak disrespectfully about my wife; she ought to know that by now.) It used to be that when my daughter was small, and it sounded so beguiling and precocious, I would encourage her to find fault with my wife (my wife would delight in this also, because my daughter really was so bright and entertaining), which may be one reason she reverts to it so frequently now. But I don't like it now; and I will defend my wife (even when my daughter's complaints and unflattering comments are accurate and justified). Or I will cut her off curtly almost as soon as she begins, and kick her out with a stern admonition. My daughter's impression about me is correct: there are times when I simply don't want to talk to her. (She is generally so contentious and depressing. My boy is always easier to take—everybody says that. He is more straightforward and generous and much more likable; unlike my daughter, and me, he never rejoices in the misfortunes of other people; instead, he grows grave and worried in the presence of anything woeful, watching always to ascertain if any in the ungovernable whirl of events around him pose any danger to his own existence.) There are times now when I'm plain fed up with her, when I have had all I am able to take, when I just don't want to hear my daughter tell me one more time that I'm no good as a father and my wife is no good as a mother, that the home is no good as a home and the family no good as a family, and that Derek (our idiot child, of course) and all the rest of us are spoiling her life, even though it all might be true.

So what? What if it all *is* true? (My mother wasn't much better; and my father was much worse, ha, ha. He was hardly around at all after he died. Ha, ha.) Maybe it *is* my fault that she does so poorly at school and lacks confidence in herself and bites her fingernails and doesn't sleep well, and even my fault that she eats too much and is heavy and is having a boring and excruciating time of it. But, so what? (I've got my excuses ready too.) What good does it do anyone to know that? Even if I agree (and I often do agree, just to frustrate and befuddle her), it doesn't change anything, it doesn't make anything easier for her. So why must she dwell on it? It has grown so boring by now—it never leads anywhere—just plain boring to the point of maddening irritation (which is obviously all she hopes to achieve with me now, all she feels now that she *can* obtain from life, to goad me ruthlessly into these states of furious and intolerable resentment in which I stammer, spit, bellow, and launch myself into blustering denunciations that cannot be concluded with dignified grammatical coherence, and which are enough to bring that detestable, unmistakable glint of baleful satisfaction into her cunning eyes).

(What does she want from me?)

"You know," she might begin with deceptive tranquillity, "I really don't think I have anything in common with Mommy anymore. And I don't think you have, either. I don't know why you still stay married to her. I know you're incompatible."

(*She* doesn't even know what incompatible means.)

If I do (to her enormous surprise and chagrin) cut her off right then and kick her out of my study, it is not improbable that she will go straight to my wife (pals with her, all at once) and begin complaining to *her* about *me!* (And she, of course, is the one who never wants to be a sneak!) And then my wife, who is manipulated all too easily by my daughter, will come barging back into my study unsuspectingly to take up the cudgels for her, emboldened in her

135

adventure by her sense of mercy. My daughter, smiling surreptitiously, will lurk in the background, anticipating with gleaming relish the fight that she hopes will now break out between my wife and me. (My boy, on the other hand, is appalled when any two of us quarrel and always looks unnerved and nauseated.) It is my daughter's brazen look of gloating expectation, I think, more than anything else, that inevitably fills me with rage, and with a vicious need to retaliate.

"She says," my wife says, "that you kicked her out of your study just now. She says she came in here to talk to you and you wouldn't listen to her. She says you never want to listen to her. You made her get out before she could even say anything."

I hold my breath for a second or two and pretend to meditate.

"Did she?" I ask.

"Yes."

"Uh-huh."

"Didn't you?"

"He did."

"Uh-huh."

"Did he?"

"Why would I say so?"

"Uh-huh."

"Well?"

"Well?"

"Yes."

"What?"

"You just heard her, didn't you? You kicked her out."

"Is that right?" I ask my daughter tonelessly, staring at her with a look of frigid scorn.

"Didn't you?"

"And did she chance to tell you," I say to my wife, "what it was she wanted to talk to me about?"

"That isn't fair!" my daughter blurts out in alarm. Her startled gaze shoots to the doorway as though she wishes she could run out.

"No."

"Oh."

"What?"

"I kind of thought she might have been careless

136

enough to leave that out. That she wouldn't mind very much, for example, if you got sick and died. She didn't tell you that?"

"That's not true!" my daughter cries.

"Or that she really doesn't think she would care very much if you or I got killed in an automobile or plane crash, like Alice whatever-the-hell-her-last-name-is Harmon's mother, or passed away from a stroke or a brain tumor."

"I didn't say that!"

"You could."

"I didn't."

"You have."

"That isn't what I wanted to talk about!"

"I know. What she does want to talk to me about is that she doesn't think you and I have anything in common and wonders why I continue to stick it out with you instead of getting a divorce. Is that it?"

"I only began that way."

"No? Then let's continue. What was it, then, that you did want to talk to me about?"

"Oh, never mind," my daughter mumbles in moping embarrassment and lowers her eyes.

"No, please," I persist. "I want to. I want to give you that chance to talk to me you always say I never do."

"Why can't you leave her alone now?" my wife demands.

"She's trying to tear us apart, my dear. Don't you see?"

"Why can't we all be nice to each other?" my wife wonders aloud imploringly out of the innate goodness of her heart.

"Must I listen to a sentence like that?"

"What's wrong with it?" my wife retorts sharply. "What's wrong with wishing we would all try to get along once in a while instead of picking on each other all the time?"

"We don't 'pick' on each other all the time," my daughter interjects condescendingly in a tone of sulky contempt (trying to insinuate herself back onto my side in opposition to my wife). I am familiar with this tactic of hers. She flicks her gaze to my face tentatively to see if I am going to let her succeed.

I ignore the overture.

(That's what my wife's innate goodness of heart gets her.)

"I'm tired," I remark deliberately with an exaggerated sigh.

"That's because you drink too much before—"

"I'm tired," I interrupt resolutely, letting my voice get louder in order to drown out my wife's, "of listening to you tell me I drink too much before I come home, and listening to her tell me over and over again how bad you and I are and how much she hates me. I've got better ways to spend my time. Let her hate me. Hate me if you want to, and if you think it solves your problems for you. You've got my permission. I don't care if she hates me. But I do mind, God dammit, if she comes in here to tell me about it every God-damned time I sit down in here and try to do some work."

"He was reading a magazine."

"That's my work."

"She doesn't hate you!" my wife declares.

"What do I care?" I answer. "It's a matter of supreme indifference to me whether she hates me or not."

"And you're supposed to be so intelligent!" my wife exclaims.

"What does *that* mean?"

"She wants you to pay some attention to her once in a while. Can't you see that? And you're supposed to be so intelligent."

"Will you stop that?"

"You think you're always so smart, don't you?"

"Stop."

"All right. But if you'd only take the trouble to look at her once in a while, and listen to her, you'd see she doesn't hate you. She loves you. You never even show you know."

"Okay."

"You make her feel like a nuisance."

"Okay, I said."

"She doesn't hate you."

138

"Okay!"

"Okay."

I turn to stare at my daughter searchingly, my face still hard and scornful and belligerent (my defenses are up until I can make certain hers are down). She is standing perfectly still, as though meekly awaiting a verdict. I am awaiting some sign from her. She looks humble and penitent. She is alone. Her downcast eyes are grave and moist, and her ashen lips are pinched together sadly and are twitching, as though, despite all the forces of will she has amassed to hold her poor self together, she is going to collapse into shambles before us and begin crying helplessly, without pride. She is tense. My feelings soften with a sensation of irremediable loss (of something precious gone forever, of someone dear destroyed) as I study her pale, drooping, vulnerable face. I am tense too. I am unable to speak (maybe I do love her), and for a second I am struck with the notion that my wife is right, that perhaps my daughter doesn't hate me and does love me, and perhaps does need to have me know it (and needs to know also, perhaps, that maybe I think well of her). And I begin to feel that maybe *I do care very much whether she hates me or not!* (I don't want her to!) She *must* matter to me, I think, for I am nearly overcome with grief and pity by her look of tearful misery (and I want to cry myself), and I want to put my arms out to her shoulders to hold her gently and console her and confess and apologize (even though I have a vivid premonition suddenly that this is all a typical trick, and she will pull away from me in a taunting, jubilant affront as soon as I do reach out to comfort her, leaving me standing there ridiculously with my empty hands outstretched in the air, abashed and infuriated). I decide to risk it anyway—she is so pathetic and forlorn: I know I can survive the rebuff if it comes. Smiling tenderly, stepping toward her repentently, I reach my hands out to take her in my arms, apologize, and hug her gently.

She pulls away from me with a vicious sneer.

And I find myself standing there stupidly with my empty hands in the air, feeling hurt and foolish.

And my wife picks exactly that moment to cry:

"I'm the one she hates! Not you! I'm the one she can't stand!"

And I turn around to gape at her incredulously. (I had forgotten she was even there.)

"Don't you ever hear her?" my wife continues stridently, and runs toward my daughter as though she intends to smack her. My daughter flinches, but holds her ground steadily, glaring insultingly up into my wife's eyes with stubborn defiance, daring her, with a small, cold smile, to do more. "What have I ever done to you?" my wife shouts at her. "What have I ever done to her that she should hate me so much? Look at her! Don't you see the way she's looking at me right now?"

"Christ, yes!" I shout back at my wife. "What the hell do you think I was talking about? Why the hell do you think I kick her out?"

"And you—you're no better!" my wife accuses me. "You don't care either, do you?"

"Oh, Jesus!" I wail.

"Nobody in this house gives a damn about me," my wife laments. "Nobody ever loved me. Not in my whole life. Not even my own mother. Am I so horrible? What did I ever do to you or anyone else that you should all hate me so much? What makes me so horrible that you should all feel you can treat me this way? Tell me."

"Oh, shit!" I groan disgustedly.

"Don't talk to me that way."

"Must I really spend the rest of my life in rotten conversation like this?"

"What's so rotten about me?"

"Nothing."

"What do I do that's so horrible?"

And I find myself wondering once again just what in the mystifying hell an able, well-read, fairly intelligent, sensitive, personable, successful minor organization executive like myself, sound in health (if not in tooth), provocative in wit, still virile and still attractive to many susceptible ladies my own age and much younger, is doing engaged seriously in such a low, directionless argument with two such people (children) as *them*, my shallow, melancholy, slightly inebriated, self-pitying wife (I often try to figure out what it was I ever saw in her so long ago that made me think I loved her and wanted to spend the rest of my life with her, except her good and willing ass, which is still not so bad and now even more willing. All in all, in fact, in the long run, I think I enjoy fucking my wife more than I do any of the others, although most of the ones I have gone with a second time or more have been pretty good, too, and full of very surprising surprises, for a while. Jane in the Art Department will be a headache—I sense that already; she is gullible and unsophisticated and she likes to talk; her skin will be so clear and smooth it will almost hum to my touch, but she is still too young and pleasant, or simple-minded, to make much sense to me now. Some girls laugh a bit too loudly at just about everything amusing I say and drive me batty, between erections, once I recognize they laugh so readily and talk too much. That will be young, sweet, pleasant Jane. I know her already. But I also know I will grab for it lecherously at the next company party or sooner; and that I don't think I will want her to keep on working there with me after I do: she is a present I intend to give myself for Christmas this year, or earlier, and I am already in the process of wrapping her up) and my depressing, self-centered, self-pitying daughter, when I would much rather be concentrating on something else, on those two speeches I want to begin outlining (I like to get started on important things well in advance, on a long convention speech in case I am moved up into Kagle's job by then and am nominally in charge of the whole affair, and on my customary, unexciting, three-minute speech about the plans and activities of my department in case I am not moved up into Kagle's job and am still working for Green, who probably won't let me give it this time, either. I hate Green and will never forgive him or forget him for what he did to me at the convention by not letting me speak. I really don't want Andy Kagle's job—I never did want to do that kind of work or have power over so many people—but I will be heartbroken now if they don't give it to me: I will feel betrayed and disgraced, and I will want to slink away alone into someplace dark and weep and never come out. I am too weak to refuse it, and too vain to be indifferent to the honor. I don't even really need the extra money) and on the list of changes I will want to recommend when I am promoted into Kagle's job. (I will want to show Arthur Baron and Horace White that I am ready. There are people in nearly all our offices I will want to be rid of. I wish I could be rid of Green now, although I don't know who could replace him.)

"Tell me," my wife repeats shrilly. "What do I do?"

"You give me," I answer, "a pain in the ass. *Both* of you!" I add emphatically, with a long, warning look at my daughter to let her know unmistakably that I am including her also this time in my ire, and to deprive her of that pasty, crafty glee she customarily evinces whenever I turn abusive to my wife.

"Don't yell at me," my wife snaps.

"I wasn't yelling," I explain. "I was speaking emphatically."

"I can yell too, you know."

"You are."

"And don't say things like that to me, not in front of the children. Ever again. I don't care how you talk to me when we're alone."

"Like what?"

"What you said."

"Then stop being one."

"You're so clever."

"I know."

"It's no wonder they use such filthy language, when they listen to you. It's no wonder they talk to me the way they do."

"Oh, stop."

"I'm not going to let you talk to me with such disrespect," my wife goes on vehemently. "Not anymore. Not even when we're alone. I'm not going to put up with it. Do you hear me?"

"Fuck off now," I tell her quietly. "Both of you."

My wife is stung. Tears spurt into her eyes. (I

142

am sorry immediately. I feel small and shameful already for having said that.)

"I could kill you for that," she tells me softly.

"Then kill me," I taunt.

"I wish there was someplace I could go."

"I'll find one."

"I wish I had money of my own."

"I'll give it to you."

"That's some way," my daughter observes softly in a petulant tone, "for a father to talk to a fifteen-year-old child."

"Go—" I begin (and pause to conceal a smile, for her reproof is humorous and ingratiating, and I am tempted to laugh and congratulate her) "—away to boarding school."

"I wish I could."

"You can."

"You stop me."

"Not anymore. And that's some way," I exclaim, "for a fifteen-year-old child to talk to her father."

"I didn't—"

"Yes, you—"

"I only started—"

"—and you know it. I get—you know something, kid? I bet you'll never guess in a million years what I get from all these frank and honest discussions of yours that you insist on having with me."

"Headaches."

"You guessed!" I declare, hoping that I will be able to make her laugh. "I get piercing headaches," I continue (pompously, after I fail, for I feel myself inflating grandly, and crossly, with a delicious thrill of outrage. I am nearly ecstatic with grievance, and I forge ahead vigorously in joyous pursuit of revenge). "Yes, I get piercing headaches from all those brain tumors and cerebral hemorrhages you keep giving me. And stabbing chest pains from all the heart attacks you keep telling me you wouldn't feel so unhappy about if I got. *I* would feel unhappy if I got one! In fact, I'm starting to feel pretty damned miserable from having to listen to both of *you* tell me all the time how miserable *you* feel." My wife and daughter are silent now and cowering submissively (and a flood

143

of self-righteous gratification begins to permeate and sweeten my throbbing sense of injury. I feel so sorry for myself it is almost unbearably delicious. I also feel mighty: I feel potent and articulate, and part of me wishes that Green or someone else I yearn to impress, like Jane, or Horace White, or perhaps some terribly rich and famous beauty with marvelous tits and glossy hair, were in a position to witness me so fluent and dominating). "I'm sick," I remark misleadingly in a falling voice, just to puzzle them further a moment. "Yes, by now I am sick and tired of having both of you people come barging in here, into *my* study, whenever you feel like it, just to tell me what a lousy husband and father you think I am."

"You were reading a magazine," my wife remarks.

"You too?" I jeer.

"We're going."

"This *is* my study," I remind her caustically (and desperately) in a surly, rising voice, as she turns to leave. "Isn't it? And now that I think of it, just what the hell are both of you doing in here right now—in *my* study—when I've got so many important things I want to get done?"

"Which is more important?" my wife makes the mistake of asking. "Your own wife and daughter, or those other important things?"

"Please get out," I answer. "That's the kind of question I never want to be asked again the rest of my life."

"All right. We'll go."

"So go."

"Come on."

"No, stay!" I blurt out suddenly at both of them.

"We're going."

"You stay!" I demand.

"Aren't we?"

(All at once, it is of obsessive importance to me—more important to me now than anything else in the whole world—that *they* stay, and that *I* be the one who is driven out. Out of *my* study. My eyes fill with tears; I don't know why; they are tears not of anger but of injured pride. It's a tantrum, and I am obliged to give myself up to it unresistingly.)

"I'll go!" I cry, as both of them stare at me in bafflement. I stride toward the door with tears of martyred grief. "And stop sneaking these extra chairs in," I add, with what sounds like a sniffle.

"What?"

"You know what I mean. And all of you always take all my pencils and never bring them back."

"What are you talking about?"

"Whenever you redecorate. This God-damned house. You dump chairs in here. As though I won't notice."

My wife is bewildered. And I am pleased. (I am enjoying my fit exquisitely. I am still a little boy. I am a deserted little boy I know who will never grow older and never change, who goes away and then comes back. He is badly bruised and very lonely. He is thin. He makes me sad whenever I remember him. He is still alive, yet out of my control. This is as much as he ever became. He never goes far and always comes back. I can't help him. Between us now there is a cavernous void. He is always nearby.) And when I whirl away again exultantly to storm out, leaving my silent wife and daughter standing there, in *my* study, at such a grave moral disadvantage, I see my son watching in the doorway. And I stamp on him before I can stop.

"Ow!" he wails.

"Oh!" I gasp.

He has been waiting there stealthily, taking everything in.

"It's okay!" he assures me breathlessly.

Clutching his foot, hopping lamely on the other, he shrinks away from me against the doorjamb, as though I had stepped on him on purpose, and intend to step on him again.

"Did I hurt you?" I demand.

"It's *okay.*"

"But did I hurt you? I'm sorry."

"It's *okay!* I mean it. It doesn't hurt!"

"I didn't mean to step on you. Then why are you rubbing your ankle?"

145

"Because you hurt me a little bit. Before. But it's okay now. I mean it. Really, it's okay." (He is supplicating anxiously for me to believe he is okay, pleading with me to stop pulverizing him beneath the crushing weight of my overwhelming solicitude. "Leave me alone—please!" is what I realize he is actually screaming at me fiercely, and it slashes me to the heart to acknowledge that. I take a small step back.) "See?" he asks timorously, and demonstrates.

He puts his foot to the floor and tests it gingerly, proving to me he is able to stand without holding on. I see a minute bruise on the surface of his skin, a negligible, white scrape left by the edge of my shoe, a tiny laceration of the dermatological tissue covering the ankle, no injury of any seriousness. (He is probably the only person in the world for whom I would do almost anything I could to shield from all torment and harm. Yet I fail continually; I can't seem to help him, I do seem to harm him. Things happen to him over which I have no power and of which I am often not even aware until the process has been completed and the damage to him done. In my dreams sometimes he is in mortal danger, and I cannot move quickly enough to save him. My thighs weigh tons. My feet are anchored. He perishes, but the tragedy, in my dreams, is always mine. In real life, he is suffering already from secret tortures he is reluctant to divulge, and from so many others he is unable to comprehend and describe. He is afraid of war and crime. Anyone in uniform intimidates him. He is afraid of stealing: he is afraid to steal anything and afraid of having things stolen from him.) He seems out of breath and waxen with fright as he stands below me now watching me stand there watching him (the delicate oval pods beneath his eyes are a pathological blue), and he is trembling in such violent consternation as he waits for me to do something that it seems he must certainly shake himself into broken little pieces if I don't reach out instantly to hold him together. (I don't reach out. I have that sinking, intuitive feeling again that if I do put my hand out toward him, he will think I am going to hit him and fall back from me in dread. I don't know why he feels so often that I am going

146

to hit him when I never do; I never have; I don't know why both he and my daughter believe I used to beat them a great deal when they were smaller, when I don't believe I ever struck either one of them at all. My boy can hurt me in so many ways he doesn't suspect and against which I have no strength to defend myself. Or maybe he does suspect. And does do it with motive. When I think of him, I think of me.) And I know why he is quaking now, squirming awkwardly and plucking nervously and obliviously at the small bulge of penis inside his pants as though he is tingling to urinate. I know I must have seemed enormous to him as I spun wrathfully to storm away and stamped down blindly upon him. I must have seemed inhuman, gigantic, like that monstrous, dark hairy, splayfooted tyrant (that flying cock elsewhere is not the only fur-bearing blot) on that ugly father-card in the Rorschach test.

"Then what are you looking so unhappy about?" I want to know timidly. "If it doesn't hurt."

"Your yelling."

"I'm not yelling."

"You *were* yelling. Before."

"I'm not yelling now. I wasn't even yelling at *you*," I argue with comic fervor, trying to appease him. I want to make *him* smile too. (I can't stand to see him upset, particularly when I am the cause. I smother furious impulses against him when he fails to be as fully content with life and me as I would like him to be.) "Was I?"

"No," he replies without hesitation, twisting in one place again (as though he would like to wrest his feet free from the floor and fly away) and patting his knees spasmodically with fluttering palms. "But you're *going* to yell at me," he guesses cagily, with a gleam of insight in his eyes. "Aren't you?"

"No, no, no, no," I assure him. "I'm not going to yell at you."

"You will. I know you will."

"I won't. Why should I yell at you?"

"You see? I told you."

"I'm not."

"You're yelling already."

"I'm not yelling!"

"Ain't he yelling?"

"I don't think he knows *what* he's doing."

"That's good," I compliment my wife acidly. "That will cool things down."

"You know you're impossible?" she answers. "Whenever you get this way."

"I'm possible."

"He's possible," my daughter intones ruefully.

"Are you going to yell at me now?" my boy asks.

"I'm not going to yell at you at all," I tell him. "I was speaking loudly only to be *emphatic*," I explain to him almost in a whisper, forcing myself to smile and imposing on my words a scrupulous and conciliatory calm. I squat to my heels directly in front of him, bringing my face almost to a level with his own, and look instructively into his eyes. He lets me take his hands. Tissues inside his hands, I feel, are beating and lurching like little fishes. (Everybody in my family trembles at home but me, even though I don't want them to. I brood and sulk and moan a good deal and wish I were someplace else. I tremble elsewhere. At the office. In my sleep. Alone at airports waiting for planes. In unfamiliar hotel rooms in cities I don't like, unless I drink myself sodden and have some girl or woman I can stand who is able to spend most of the night with me. I don't like being alone at night and always leave a small light on when I have to be. Being dead tired doesn't help; in fact, exhaustion is worse, for I don't sleep any sounder and my defenses are low and laggard. Repulsive thoughts swarm over them and invade my mind like streams of lice or other small, beetle-brown, biting insects or animals, and I am slow to choke them off and force them back down where they came from. There is this animal, I sometimes imagine, that creeps up on paws in the night when my eyes are closed and eats at my face—but that's another childish story. My dreams are demoralizing. I won't reveal them. I have castration fears. I have castration dreams. I had a dream once of my mother with black mussels growing on her legs, and now I know what it meant.) "Please don't be afraid of me," I urge him tenderly, almost begging. "I'm not going to do anything to hurt you or scare you. Now or ever."

"It's okay," he says, trying to comfort me.

"You can trust me. I'm not yelling at you now, am I? I'm speaking softly. Ain't I?"

He nods mistrustfully (and I want to raise my voice and begin yelling at him again to make him believe I never yell at him at all. But I don't. I don't want to scare him again. I don't ever really want to frighten any of them and am always sorry and disgusted with myself afterward when I do. Almost always. But only *after* I succeed in bullying them; if I try to bully them and fail, I am distraught. And frightened. I am sorry now that I have just intimidated them all; and in speaking to my boy, I am trying to apologize to my wife and daughter as well. I want them to see I am sorry; but I don't want to say so. I want to be forgiven).

"Why do you look that way?" I ask him, in a troubled, slightly nagging voice (pleading with him to relax and feel free and safe and happy with me). "Why do you look so worried?"

"It's okay."

"You can trust me," I promise.

"It's just the way I look."

"And I wasn't yelling at you before, either," I continue uncontrollably. "Sometimes when a person raises his voice and speaks loudly, it isn't because he's yelling at you or even angry, but only because he wants you to believe what he's saying. He does it for . . . *emphasis*. He wants to be . . . *emphatic*. That's what the word *emphatic* means." I pause in annoyance as I see my boy catch my daughter's eyes for an instant and then roll his gaze upward with a dramatic look of tedium (as both my children are apt to do ostentatiously when one of us is lecturing them at length for doing something we deem hazardous, or inundating them with unnecessary directions or repetitious questions. I would rather have him bored with me now and making fun than panic-stricken. So I continue peaceably, persuasively, instead of reprimanding him tartly, although my dignity *was* offended for a second). "Now that's what I was doing when I raised my voice a bit before," I continue. "I was being . . . *emphatic*. I wanted you to believe that I wasn't going to yell at you and that I wasn't angry with you. And it was exactly the same when I was speaking with them," I lie. "I wasn't yelling at them, either."

"I know," he says. "I know it now."

"And I'm not yelling at you now, am I?"

"No."

"So I was right, wasn't I?"

"Yes. It's okay."

"Good. I'm glad you understand. And that's why . . ." I conclude wryly, with a smile—and somehow I know he guesses the joke I'm about to make and that he is going to interrupt and make it for me. I pause, to give him time.

". . . you yelled at me!" he says.

"Right!" I guffaw.

(Our minds are very much alike, his and mine, in our humor and our forebodings.)

"Do *I*," he ventures ahead boldly on his wave of success, with a sidelong glance at my wife that glitters with impish intent, "give you a pain in the ass, too?"

"Oh, my!" I exclaim. (My first impulse is to guffaw again; my next is to protect him from any sanctimonious reproof that might come from my wife for his using the word *ass*. Quickly, clowning, laughing, mugging with grossly burlesqued alarm, before my wife can react at all, I cry:) "Now, *she's* going to yell at you!"

"She's not!"

"No?"

"Are you?"

But my wife is glad (not mad) and laughs merrily with relief (because she sees I am glad now, too, and not mad at her or my daughter anymore).

"No, but you're a devil and a rascal," she upbraids him affectionately. "Because *you knew* I wouldn't yell at you this time if you said that word."

"What word?" asks my boy, with a feigned look of innocence. "Ass?"

"Don't say it again!"

"Ass?"

150

"You're *not* going to make *me* say it!"

"What? Ass?" asks my daughter, joining in friskily.

"I give up." My wife throws her arms out mirth-fully in exasperation. "What am I going to do with them?"

"Say ass," I advise.

"Ass!" my wife blares obligingly, extending her face out toward both of them like an elephant's trunk. They roar with gulping laughter. "Ass! Ass, ass, ass, ass, ass!"

All of them are laughing hysterically now.

My daughter is unable to keep her balance in the sweeping exhilaration she experiences at finding herself released so unexpectedly, without penalty, from the excoriating conflict she had devised and in which she had so swiftly found herself the tortured victim. She falls against my boy joyously; they hug each other with immense delight and go staggering wildly all about my study, bumping into us and each other and into the superfluous chairs my wife keeps sneaking in when she has no better place to put them. My boy is pleased with himself beyond measure, beside himself with glee and ecstasy at having used his dirty word with impetuous imagination and gotten away with it and at having transported us all to a spirit of warmth and generous good feeling from the savage rancor with which we had been smashing each other. We are close now, intimate, respectful, and informal. The children bump and hug each other and continue to laugh hilariously. I watch them with affection (feeling complacent and benign). I am glad they are mine.

"They're really such good kids," my wife murmurs pensively in my ear, so that only I will hear.

I nod in agreement, feeling wistful and pleased (with myself, too, and with her). I slip my arm around her waist and draw her to my side. She moves willingly, her body limber, and fits herself against me compliantly. I get an erection. (I would lay her now if we were alone. We would lay each other.) I slide my hand down over her ass and follow the curve in at the bottom toward her box. She stretches away.

"Later," she cautions guardedly.

"No, now," I demand, teasingly.

"You're crazy."

"I might not have it later."

"You will. You'd better," she laughs. "I'll see that you do."

I laugh too.

And that is the needful service performed for us so regularly and artlessly by this angelic little boy of mine ("He isn't real," my daughter has complained about him enviously. "He's never mean. He never gets mad."), who is no better off than the rest of us (who may be considerably worse off, in fact, because he is only nine and has already been frightened of just about *everything*, heights and kidnapping, sharks, crabs, drunks, adults who stare, sheriffs, unkempt handymen, wars, Italians, and me. He isn't afraid of monsters or ghosts so much, because monsters and ghosts are silly. He is afraid of human beings. He veers away from cripples. He welcomes the phenomenon of cops, because he has the dim hope they will safeguard him from all the rest, even from me), to draw us together again by reminding us who we are and what we know of each other, to stop the three of us just in time and make us step back—by evoking and recalling to us the great need and capacity for affection each of us has hidden away very deep inside, like a yawning wound, affection for him, and perhaps for each other—from mangling each other willfully, brutally, and irreparably, with much malice and happiness aforethought, if we have not maimed each other permanently already. I believe he pulls us together as a family and keeps us together. (I often think of leaving and always have. My daughter can't wait to get away, or says she can't.) I think we will fall apart as a family when he grows up and moves away. (I love him so much I just know he is going to die.)

"You like him more than me," my daughter has said.

"No," I answer, lying, because I do not always wish to outfox her, and because she sometimes seems so barren of hope that I find myself grieving silently alongside her, as though at an open coffin or grave in which her future is lying dead already. (She is not yet sweet sixteen, but it sometimes seems to both of us that she has already missed all boats. When?) "But you must admit, darling, that in many ways, he is much more likable."

"I know."

They are not so funny to us while they are taking place, these corrosive family arguments that my daughter provokes so malignantly, and they do not always end in bedroom trysts for me and my wife and gales of gleeful laughter for the children. They are excruciating, especially for her. I wish she would write book reports instead, or do complicated jigsaw puzzles with one thousand pieces when she finds herself with lots of time and no exciting way to spend it. (I wish she would fall in love or something.)

But she can't stop.

(It's her compulsion.)

She must continue to agitate, like some dark and moody burrowing creature with a drive to undermine and destroy. I (we) do not know what it is she wants that she feels we can give her (she wants to be beautiful, willowy, brilliant, famous, rich, and talented—and who can blame her? We would like her to be all that too. Perhaps she knows it. But we don't insist), and she does not tell us. She does not know. Sometimes she confides in us without belligerence or guile. She confesses. She stands before us listlessly, her head bowed in disgrace, and, in words that force their way out from her soul and flow from her lips in a low, pining, abject monotone, she says:

"I have nothing to do."

It breaks my wife's heart when my daughter has nothing to do.

I will not let it break mine.

My daughter bites her fingernails, and I suppose that is my fault too. (At least it's something to do. My boy has poor posture, and so do I.) She began biting

153

her nails around the age of five. My boy used to suck his thumb in his sleep and raised a swollen white lump (it was the color of fungus or peeling, dead skin) on the joint of his finger that handicapped him at play and stigmatized him in the daytime by reminding him of its cause. We couldn't make him stop. We put casings of evil-odored bandages on his thumb at bedtime, but he sucked at it anyway. We even tried the vile-tasting liquid we had used without avail years before to discourage my daughter from biting her fingernails. That didn't work, either, so she still bites them. I don't know how he finally stopped: I don't know how he ever made himself stop doing things in his sleep. (Often, I can stop unpleasant dreams from developing by bounding wide awake alertly at their first portentous overtures as though in response to some well-recognized primal alarm—like a good censor or movie director I can yell "Cut!" at the first specter of something askew in my dream scripts and make them start all over again in another direction. The words I actually speak to myself are "Oh, no! None of that again"—and keeping guard vigilantly over my slumbering intelligence until my dreams rewrite themselves into scenes and themes that are more to my taste. Then I can relax securely, fall back into sleep, and give them free rein. I can stop these unwelcome dreams from proceeding only if they start as I am sifting down into sleep and am still in touch with myself. Often, I cannot; and I lie in darkness like a limbless baby while they run their ruthless course through me rampantly as though I were a helpless and disembodied mind, or this tiny, armless, legless baby still imprisoned motionlessly in a cradle or womb. I can't bear them. I forget them. They leave traces. I have them often. I have them whenever I want them.)

(I know so many things I'm afraid to find out.)

She is a poor sleeper, my daughter, and, except for short-lived, unfounded spells of euphoric gaiety and plan-making (which flare so suddenly and extravagantly as to seem almost feverish), prefers to cling to the tragic view she takes of her own possibilities. She is easily alarmed and often jittery. She is

154

probably a virgin. (If she weren't, she would tell me. When she isn't, she will—I visualize that approaching occasion reluctantly more and more frequently—and I look ahead grimly to the day or evening she marches into my study to mock me with *that*. What am I supposed to say? I will laugh it off, of course, minimize its importance, so as not to send her into promiscuity and perversion on one side or frigidity and abstinence on the other. What a dilemma.

"Well, I'm sure other girls your age do it too, my dear," I can hear myself saying with suave insouciance, flicking the white ash off a cigar I do not smoke. "I imagine you're not the first. Don't they?"

What will I really feel?) She lacks confidence in herself and, like my boy (and me), is wary of strangers and ill at ease with people to whom she has just been introduced. (I, on the other hand, am a good sleeper at times—although I like to pretend I'm not—especially when I am sleeping at home with my wife, although I usually wait until I can no longer keep awake before I go to sleep. Ha, ha. When I sleep away from home with my wife, I will have a nightmare the first or second night, usually the same one: a strange man is entering illegally through the door, which I have locked, and drawing near, a burglar, rapist, kidnapper, or assassin; he seems to be Black but changes; I think he is carrying a knife; I try to scream but can make no sound. I have this same bad dream at home often, even though I carefully lock all my doors before going to sleep. I have had it dozens and dozens of times. I have always had it. I must make some sound, though, while I am having the dream and trying in vain to scream, for my wife awakens with the noise of my struggles and rouses me by calling my name and tells me, as though I didn't know, that I was having a nightmare. Sometimes, even when I am trapped deep in my agony and whatever menaces me is moving right up to my bedside, some different section of me is tuned in omnisciently to the nature of the experience, knows and reassures me it is all just a very bad dream and watches from outside it tranquilly and smugly and waits expectantly, with enjoyment, for my wife to be disturbed by my noises and motions and to call to me by my name and shake me awake by the shoulder to tell me I was having a nightmare. I think people have more than one brain. I like the idea of scaring my wife with my nightmares. Sometimes, when *she* is having a nightmare, I revenge myself on her by *not* waking her up and allowing it to torture her for as long as it wants to, while I watch her from outside, idly and smugly, leaning on my elbow. I have piss dreams too, but they are funny. I think they are. When I am sleeping away from home without my wife, I am often worried I will have this same bad dream, or a different one just as horrifying. Who will wake me? Will I survive it if no one does? I don't have this dream when I'm alone. Will I be embarrassed and apologetic with whoever wakes me in the next room or same bed? There are many nights now when I am grabbed wildly by insomnia the instant my head touches the pillow and am then tumbled about violently all night long. My body—particularly my legs, shoulders, and elbows—is heavy and unmanageable; I have no place to put them; my soul is fragile; my mind is tissue thin and easily pierced by emotions and images. I can do nothing at all. My head fills and races with disconnected thoughts. By now, I can identify this tumultuous insomnia in the first second or two; I no longer try to overcome it. It is useless. I give in to it with a sinking feeling. I lie and wait resignedly, submitting, keeping my eyes closed because that's easier, and depend on morning to come and rescue me or for sleep to steal upon me unawares after several hours and snatch me away from those buffeting cataracts of fantasy, fury, reminiscence, and speculation—all of it inconsequential—that race through my head in such torrential splashes. Poor me. I'm not sure I'm such a good sleeper after all, although I can generally doze off easily after lunch and sexual intercourse. I am surprised when I awake in the morning after a seizure of insomnia to realize I have been asleep; I am often aghast upon awakening from a sound, dreamless sleep to realize how far away from life I have been, and how defenseless I was while I was there. It is almost as though I truly am afraid of the dark. Like my daughter. And my boy.

Like I used to be as a child. And later. I might be unable to return. I don't like to lose touch with consciousness entirely. Dreams, even very bad, weird dreams, are my only contact with reality when I sleep; I want them; I even welcome headaches at night; I am out of existence. Where am I, then, when I am not? Filed away? I worry about things like that lately and did when I was small. All the things I worry about now I worried about more when I was small. I worry about the need for surgery someday for just that reason; the cutting, hammering, sawing, and stitching are all obnoxious enough; but the thought of anesthesia that benumbs the mind totally is even more repelling. Where will I be in that bottomless, measureless time between the moment they lower the cone over my nose and mouth and instruct me to breathe deeply, as they did when I was a kid and had my tonsils out, and again when I was married already and had two impacted wisdom teeth pulled, and the moment the first thought stirs in my brain again and I, like Jesus from the cave or Lazarus from the grave, am miraculously resurrected? I think an authentic miracle takes place in the universe every time I come awake again after going to sleep. What is happening to me when I am not conscious of myself? Where do I go? Where have I been? Who watches over me when I am gone to make sure I do get back? If I die under anesthesia, I will certainly be the last one to find out I have departed. I try my wife's tranquilizers when I feel it might be impossible for me to sleep and think they might help. I don't want sleeping pills; they bring to mind visions and aromas of old-fashioned funeral parlors, dentists' offices, and wax fruit. Years back when my daughter was small, she would materialize in our bedroom in the black hours of night, or in the doorway of the living room if one or the other of us was up late, all at once she would just *be* there; and make faint, odd, rustling noises that were barely audible—we would *feel* them somehow rather than hear them—until she forced us to look up and take notice of her. She could not speak; her mouth seemed numb; she could only reply with a grunting and drowsy incoherence to the sharp ques-

157

tions we fired at her and she did not remember when we questioned her again in the morning about it after we had made her return to her own room. Or claimed she didn't. We tried gropingly to relate these episodes to her tonsillectomy; but they had started earlier, and there had been no complication over the operation, at the hospital or at home, before or afterward. Just disillusionment. She had expected something different. It soon stopped. And we soon stopped thinking about it, since she seemed to have gotten over it. When my boy's tonsils were taken out, he didn't want to stay in his room, either. There were no complications, they told us. But for a little while afterward, he would sneak into our room in the dead of night and curl up to sleep on the carpet at the foot of our bed. He did not want to be alone. If he came in too soon, when we were still awake, we would make him go back to his own room and tell him he could leave a lamp on; sometimes we would yell; but he would always return, or try to, no matter how many times we yelled, stealing back into our room over and over again as quietly and slyly as he could, like some yearning creature newly born, and curl up on the floor against the foot of the bed. We would find him there when we awoke, lying on his side like a well-formed fetus, sucking his thumb. It was a chilling, heart-sickening experience for us to clamber out of sleep each day and receive as our first blow of the new morning the shocking sensation that there was another living being in the room with us. When we closed the lock of our bedroom door to keep him away, he would sleep curled up on the floor just outside. If one of us had to leave our bedroom for something in the middle of the night, we would strike his body unexpectedly as it lay there when we opened the door and almost scream with fright. If we got out of bed in the darkness, we were afraid we might step on him. We could have let him come into bed with us, of course; we wanted to. But a doctor told us no. We didn't like to see him that way. We did not want to shut him out. I'm sorry now we did. I think the doctor was wrong. I don't know what else we should have done.) She is very touchy and defensive and will interpret even the mildest suggestions about herself as ferocious personal attacks. She is prone to disparaging herself unfairly, and she takes issue with us intensely when we defend or praise her. She will occasionally start to cry, as though *we* were doing the belittling. She has a definite gift for placing me in predicaments like that. She is not as tall and stout as she thinks she is, her skin is not as oily as she fears it is, and her face is much, much prettier than she is willing to believe. She is actually quite attractive. But she doesn't believe her eyes; and she cannot believe our assurances.

She envies all other girls she knows for one quality or another (this one's figure, that one's hair, the next one's money, the next one's brains or talents) and does not know who it is she should want to emulate. (Now that she is tall for her age, she feels mammoth and clumsy. When she was shorter than most of her friends, she was convinced that only very tall girls were ever considered beautiful. When she was slender, she felt flat and sexless. Now that she is overweight a bit and has large developing breasts, she feels ungainly and believes that boys only fall in love with girls who are slim and have straight bellies.) This might be funny, if it were not so real for her. She cannot decide, for example, whether she wants her breasts (tits) to be larger or smaller. (This might be funny too, if she did not brood over the matter mournfully for long, silent stretches during which she is very much withdrawn. Sometimes she sits with us and is worlds away.

"A penny for your thoughts," I used to say.

Now I get no answer to this gambit, just a look of disdain.)

She feels she is not much good for anything; and she isn't. But who cares? Who cares if she does not have any special aptitudes, talents, beauty, or social skills? *She* cares. (And perhaps *I* care. And my wife. And perhaps we have let her know we care. If we said to her that we did not care about things like that, she would say to us that we did not care about her at all. She knows all the tricks. How can I tell my daughter she is the most marvelous, beauti-

159

ful teen-age girl in the whole world when we both know she isn't? What answer can I give when she asks me how she compares to other girls who outshine her in one way or another?) She cares a great deal. (And so, perhaps, do I.)

"Are you very disappointed in me?" she asks periodically.

"No, of course not," I answer. "Why should I be?"

She knows many people and is lonely, and almost never seems to have a good time. (This is infuriating to us, her obdurate refusal to be happy and have fun, although we try not to look at it in just that light. But I know I have been so enraged with her at times for having nothing to do that I have wanted to seize her fiercely by the shoulders, my darling little girl, and shake her, pummel her frenziedly on the face and shoulders with the sides of both my fists, and scream:

"Be happy—God dammit! You selfish little bitch! Can't you see our lives depend on it?"

I have never done that, of course, or even mentioned the impulse to my wife, who would be repelled by the brutal ugliness of the urge and regard it as abnormal and depraved—even though I know she experiences this same brutal and abnormal impulse herself. And about my wife's own endless nigglings with my daughter, I have commented:

"I hope you understand that it's really your own happiness you're thinking about, and not hers."

"That isn't true." My wife was adamant in objection. "Don't you think I *want* her to be happy? I'm thinking of her!"

"Balls," I replied, or wanted to.

Because I know it was my wife who sent her into a paroxysm of weeping by suggesting to her, apropos of nothing else we were talking about, that she have a sweet sixteen party; for it has been an unmentioned secret that she never knows enough boys and girls she likes at any one time, or who like her, to compose a decent celebration for her, and that this is one of the poignant sources of her unhappiness.) She thinks of herself as unpopular. She makes friends easily and

160

discards them callously. She is still shy with boys. (She has already had, I think, at least one bad sex experience of some kind and is looking forward apprehensively to having some more.) She is not comfortable with boys in the house when I am there. Was my wife as innocent in her proposal as she seemed, or did she make the suggestion with sly, and perhaps unconscious, cruelty? I don't know. Probably she was innocent, for my wife tends to look back with nostalgia on what she remembers as the enjoyable occasions of her own girlhood. My wife reveled like a princess in the sweet sixteen party her own mother made for her, or thinks she did. (Perhaps it was the last time in her life she was allowed to feel important.) My wife is one of these warm-hearted, sentimental human beings who are drawn to see some good in everyone (when I let her) and to project the rosiest colorations onto past experiences, with the result that her recollections are often inaccurate. She likes to think she loved her mother, but she knows she hated her. Her girlhood was tortured, not happy. She hates her younger sister and always has. (At least I didn't begin hating *my* mother until she became a burden to me. I still have sad, yearning dreams about my mother in which I am young and she is going away. And there are tears drying in the corners of my eyes when I open them.)

My daughter doesn't really like her friends very much (she shuffles them in and out of her good graces arbitrarily), and neither do I, with the exception of one classmate half a year older who is slim and pretty and secretive and who, I am just about convinced, is flirting with me, leading me on. (I encourage her.) She is not, my daughter tells me, a virgin anymore. She has a knowing, searching air about her that sets her apart from the others. She keeps her look on me when I am near, and I keep mine on hers. I'm not sure which one of us started it. I think it was me. (Perhaps we recognize something, the same thing, in each other, and *she* thinks that I am flirting with her, which may be true, but if I am, I am only kidding. I *hope* I'm only kidding.) Sixteen would be *too* young, even for me. (Or would it? *Someone* is going to be laying that provocative, pretty, hot-pantsed little girl soon, if someone isn't doing it already, and why shouldn't it be me, instead of some callow, arrogant wise guy of eighteen or twenty-one, who would not relish her as much as I would, regale and intoxicate her with the spell of flattery and small attentions I could weave, or savor the piquant degeneracy of it nearly as much as I would be certain to. Although I'm not so sure I would want to tell anyone about *this* one.) No, sixteen *is* too young (young enough to be my daughter, ha, ha), and I turn irritable whenever my daughter comes out of her room to chat with us wearing only a nightgown or a robe that she doesn't always keep fully closed on top or bottom. (I don't know where to look.) I either walk right out without explanation (seething with anger but saying nothing) or command her in a brusque, irascible voice to put a robe on or put her legs together, or keep the robe she does have on closed around the neck and down below her knees if she wants to stay. She is always astounded by my outburst; her eyes open wide. (She does not seem to understand why I am behaving that way. I cannot explain to her; I can't even explain it to my wife. I find it hard to believe my daughter is really that naïve. But what other interpretation is there?) Afterwards, I am displeased with myself for reacting so violently. (But there is little I can say to apologize. Where am I supposed to look when my tall and budding buxom daughter comes in to talk to me wearing almost nothing, sprawls down negligently with her legs apart, her robe open? How am I supposed to feel? Nobody ever told me.) They are all morbidly alike, the girls and boys in this somber social circle of adolescents of which my daughter is a part (none are happy), much more so than the girls and boys and men and women I work with in the company (although, to them, *we* might seem all alike). None are well-adjusted. (*I* am well-adjusted, which is not exactly the best recommendation for adjustment, is it?) They manifest defiance, displeasure, lassitude, and indifference. They generally have nothing they want to do. There is nothing they want to be when they grow up; they have no idols. (Neither have I. There is now no one else I would rather be than me—even though I don't really like me and am not even sure who it is I am.) They are not comfortable with adults (me); they pose and attitudinize when they are with us; they strive to be as reticent and solitary as moles. They do not want us to hear what they say when they talk to each other. I used to believe they were always feigning; now I believe they really are as cynical and disheartened as they think they are pretending to be. They don't want to be doctors when they grow up, or aviators, or heavyweight champions of the world. They don't really want to be lawyers. None of them wants to be President of the United States, Chief of Staff, Chairman of the Board of E. I. du Pont de Nemours & Co., or me. (Why should they? There are enough other people to do that kind of work. Me, for instance. I will do it because by now I have nothing else I *can* do.) They have good reason to be so pessimistic, I feel; the pity is they found it out so soon.

Some of the girls and some of the boys always do seem to be having an easier time of it than the others, but this only lasts a little while for any of them, and even my daughter will surface buoyantly every now and then and whiz along vivaciously until something happens (sometimes that something is so elusive that it cannot even be identified; it is almost as though she suddenly runs out of her supply of joy the way a car runs out of gas) that breaks her morale and dissolves her confidence, and she sinks back sluggishly and safely into her accustomed mire of regret. Some of the boys she goes with swagger and boast a good deal more than the others, but the worldly self-assurance they affect is transparently unreal. If not, if they really were as tough and egotistical and domineering and amoral as they wish to appear, I would find them obnoxious and insufferable, for I have seen my daughter with these boys in crowded cars, and I did not like what I saw, or imagined. (But what difference does that make?)

What difference does it make, really, what she is or isn't doing already with those boys I could so easily dislike, and even perhaps with girls (just about all

163

of the young girls I do it with these days brag now about having done it, at least once, with other girls too), in those crowded cars she drives in to pizza joints with loud music (I don't really like most of their music, although I sometimes pretend to just to please my daughter) or to parties with the same loud music in other people's darkened houses—as long as they don't drive recklessly and get killed or maimed in an automobile accident?

(What difference does it make anymore who is screwing whom?) It is already too late for anything else. It is too late, I think, for me to stop her or change her, and I would not know anymore how to try. Something happened to both my children that I cannot explain and cannot undo. I can't be good to them, it seems, even when I want to.

"Listen," I say to both of them anxiously, practically pleading with them to allow me to help them. "What do you want to be when you grow up? Tell me. What do you want to do?"

"I don't ever want to get married," my daughter mumbles moodily, "or ever have children."

"Work in a filling station," my boy answers.

"Well, that's a bit better." I approve, nodding with a look of praise. Why not? Own his own business? It makes some sense. Profitable franchise: Exxon, Texaco, Sunoco, Shell, Gulf? Sure. It's something. A start. Okay. "Why?"

"I like the smell of gasoline."

Christ!

"Jack, you've got kids," I appeal to Green at the office, almost in desperation. "That are older than mine. You've got a boy in college, haven't you? What does he want to be when he gets out?"

"A suicide."

"I'm not joking."

"You think I am? I've got a daughter in college too. She has abortions. Between suicide attempts. She lays bums. They don't want to continue. There've been three attempts between them. That I know about. One by slashing, two by drugs. It sounds like Paul Revere, doesn't it? They're both on drugs. My new

164

wife is crazy too. So is her mother. So is mine. It's not my business anymore."

"I'm sorry. I didn't know."

"Go do some work. It's not your business either."

He has written his children off, filed them away, closed them out like dead records that are not his business anymore. But I still have my children, and I wish to engulf them in devotion and safeguard them against every slight. (I want them to believe I love them.)

"Listen," I exclaim to them frantically, "you don't have to do what everybody else does. You can be whatever you want to be. I'll help. You don't have to join the Cub Scouts or play baseball or go to Sunday school or even to college. What do you want to do?"

"Join the Cub Scouts and play baseball," says my boy.

"Go into my room and play my records now," says my daughter.

Good God—has it happened to them already? They don't care. Or they don't know. When did it happen? Where? Where was I when the decisions were made that determined he would want to join the Cub Scouts and play baseball now, and all she would want to do is go into her room to talk on the telephone and play her phonograph records? Is it really too late?

It is too late, I feel, for me to save her, or even to help her, and I really don't think I would know what to do anymore to try (except to sit apathetically and watch her go her unhappy way). It would do no more good for me to try to change her now than it has done in the past, when she was more credulous and suggestible and more eager to please. I have tried; I have taunted, reasoned, thundered, whined, disciplined, flattered, and cajoled, to no avail and perhaps much harm, until I confessed to myself one day that it was not merely hypocritical of me, but futile, and therefore foolish. Then I stopped. (Now I go through perfunctory routines. I acknowledged to myself also that I was not really as exercised as I maintained by her shortcomings and mistakes and by the frameworks for future disasters that I watched her constructing. All that seemed calamitous to me

165

was her disobedience, and her unwillingness to believe me. All that endangers me now is her resistance and disrespect.) What was the purpose in continuing to try to influence her (other than to be able to say someday—now—that I tried)? I know I have no power over her now. (If I knew she were about to become a heroin addict and then a common prostitute, I wouldn't know what to do to avert it. I would rail and curse *my* fate; but none of that would help. So I wouldn't try at all.) She doesn't know yet that I have no power over her; so I bluff, and for the time being (redundancy coming) we have a *modus vivendi*. (All I have left is the power to cripple her.) Where was the morality, duty, and good sense in trying to turn her into a kind of person I do not like and one that she was probably never able to become anyway? I know where it will end (and I do not like it. I do not like knowing it. But what can I do? Nothing. I know that much too). She is already what she is, already well on her way to being what she is destined to become, good and/or bad, and I don't think there is any longer a single thing I or anyone else can do at present to help her or change her. She is going to become a lonely, nervous, contemporary, female human being. (She is too smart to be dumb.) She is much smarter than my wife, which means for one thing (unlike my wife, so far) that she will sleep with other women's husbands (and that she will not be overly impressed, for long, with her own). I can't stop that. I cannot fight and nullify a whole culture, an environment, an epoch, a past (especially when it's my own past and environment as well as hers, and I myself am such a large part of hers), and I have made my own adjustment to them all so contemptibly. Why should I expect her (or even want her) to be different from other girls and women I know and like? (Except that they are not happy.) (But who is?) If she isn't really smoking a pack of cigarettes a day outside the house this year, she will smoke a pack of cigarettes a day outside the house next year. And if she isn't screwing for one or more of the boys she knows now, she'll be screwing

166

for them later, and doing other commonplace sex stunts with them as well.

"That's some thing to say about your own daughter," my wife remarks, with a grimace of revulsion.

"Even if it's true?"

"Yes."

(And yet that is precisely the thing we *both* would say about her if she were not our own daughter, for my wife and I have engaged in this same derogatory speculation about most of my daughter's friends and about other people's daughters her own age and younger.)

It is not a matter of morals anymore, or even of decision; it is only a matter of time. (And my wife, who has a romantic loyalty to the way things *ought* to be, ignores her own past. She prefers to forget that even *we* were doing it all to each other before we were married.)

And what's the use of making believe it isn't? I know where my daughter is heading from the girls I know who have already been there. She will not go to church like my wife. (She goes now every third or fourth Sunday only to placate my wife and place her under an emotional debt for which she will later obtain exorbitant payment. She makes fun of the service while she is there and trades laughing, side-long glances with my boy, who already finds the whole extraordinary ritual somewhat silly.) She will drink whiskey for a while instead; then stop; then start in again after she's been married several years and drink whiskey regularly from then on, like my wife. She will have two children or three and be divorced (unlike my wife), and she will marry a second time if she and the children are still young when the first marriage breaks up. She will smoke marijuana (who doesn't? Even Ivy League fraternity boys on the executive level at the company smoke it now, and so do I when it's proffered at any of the parties I attend in town without my wife), if she isn't doing so already; if she doesn't smoke pot and hash at least once in high school, she will smoke it when I send her away to college and everyone interesting she meets there is already smoking it. She will get laid. (There is just no other way to deal with that fact; and the best one can wish for her in this area is that she enjoy it wholesomely from the start. Although I find it hard to wish it. And I hope she never decides to confide in me about *that*.) She will go wild for a while (and think she is free), have all-night revels and bull sessions, complain about her teachers and curriculum requirements, have no interest in any of her academic subjects but get passing grades in all with very little work, if she doesn't drop out altogether because of sheer dejection and torpor (which she will eulogize into something mystic and exalted, like superior intelligence). She will experiment with pep pills (ups), barbiturates (downs), mescaline, and LSD, if LSD remains in vogue; she will have group sex (at least once), homosexual sex (at least once, and at least once more with a male present as a spectator and participant), be friendly with fags, poets, snobs, nihilists, and megalomaniacs, dress like other girls, have abortions (at least one, or lie and say she did. Just about every young girl I meet these days has had at least one abortion, or claims she did, and feels compelled to boast about it to me), and sleep, for a while, with Negroes, even though she will probably enjoy none of it, and might really not want to do *any* of it. (She is a strong-minded girl who is far too weak to withstand a popular trend.) If it isn't one type of self-destruction and self-degradation she cultivates for a while, it is certain to be another; and she will emerge, if she is lucky, from this period of wanton profligacy and determined self-expression after two-and-one-half to four-and-two-thirds years feeling tense, worthless, spent, and remorseful, having searched everywhere and found nothing, with no ego at all, and pine for just one good, stable, interesting man to marry (like myself) and live happily ever after with. She will wish she had children. (She won't find that one man she wants, of course, because we're not that good.) I hope she stays away from addictive drugs so that she will be able to come out of it when she decides she wants to. I hope she doesn't get pregnant and have to have that abortion. I hope she doesn't insist on telling me about any of it. (I hope she never falls so deeply into some kind of trouble that I have to find out. I hope she doesn't get killed in a car crash.)

I know this bumpy terrain too well, and I know she is already bouncing and tumbling through it downhill, with a will and momentum that cannot be stayed and which is not really entirely of her own choosing (no matter what she elects to believe). The die is cast (*iacta alea est*), although I don't know when her dice were rolled or who did the throwing. (I know I didn't.) I know I must have done some horribly damaging things to her when she was little, but I can't remember what those things were or when I did them. (I swear I did not want to. There have been times I wanted to hurt, I'll admit, but never seriously, I swear, and not permanently.) My daughter is already plunging downhill into her own tangled future, careening bruisingly from one obstruction right into another, and I can no more halt her descent than I could catch a boulder in an avalanche. (*I* would be destroyed also if I tried. She is on her way, she is no longer mine.) She is skidding and falling ahead resolutely out of control, into times of arid, incomprehensible turmoil that contain no enticement and offer nothing alluring, except having something else to do and getting free of us. ("Think positive, please," I have urged her tartly. "What do you want to be? What do you want to do?" If I were presented with those same questions, I would not have a good answer anymore either. A suicide? Why not? What's better? A filling station? No. But, what's the hurry? If I did not have girls to play around with and such serious problems at home to contend with, I think, sweet, bleeding Jesus, I would go out of my mind from this fucking job of mine.)

And I tend to feel that she and I have come by now to a point of tacit agreement, our *modus vivendi*, to the mutual understanding that each of us has already written the other off, that neither of us really belongs to the other any longer, and that we are both merely keeping up appearances, going through perfunctory routines (as I wrote my mother off a long time before I buried her, and, as I now believe, she did the same with me. She saw through me, I think, dim and old and speechless as she was, and indulged and babied me correctly by letting me indulge and baby her as she wasted away in that nursing home during those final months of awkward visits in which I did nothing more useful than bring her highly seasoned things to eat and sit by her bedside for almost an hour gazing stealthily at my watch and babbling blithe, patent nonsense in which she showed little interest. That was all the solace I could produce for each of us in those final moments we were to spend with each other in all eternity. What a chance I had, we had, to say something. Nothing came out. I'll bet, now, that these inconvenient, unproductive visits were no more pleasant for her than they were for me. I made them because she was my mother; she endured them, I think, because I was her son. She was always perceptive and would see into me), biding our time, my daughter and I, as we go through the formalities of pretending to be still related. She lives here, follows loose procedures, and has dinner with us; I talk to her, buy her things, and will continue to profess to be interested in her until she is old enough to go away to college or move away somewhere else, as she never ceases stressing she wishes to do.

"Someday soon," she says, "maybe this summer when school is over, I think I would like to live in a place of my own. An apartment or studio. In the city. Either by myself or with just one friend. And then in the fall, I think I would like to go away to boarding school. I don't really like any of my friends here."

"I will help you," I reply noncommittally (and know instantaneously that it is the wrong thing for me to say. I had not intended this time to be unkind. But the words themselves carry a sting of rejection that makes me smart with compunction). "Seriously. I will help you find a decent, safe place, and I'll give you the money you need to pay for it and live there."

"I meant it."

"So do I."

"You're making a joke out of it."

"You'll need my help. You'll need me to sign the lease. You're too young."

"I want to live my own life."

"Who's stopping you?" I retort. (And now I know we *are* contending with each other in another one of those abrasive battles of wits.) "It seems to me you can, now that I've offered to pay the bills and said I'd let you go."

I can outfox my daughter easily just about every time.

(Even when I don't want to. I can't keep my mouth shut.) I don't know what else to do when we spar like that and she tries to show me she is as good as I am. (She isn't. Should I let her win?) She hurts me, and I hurt her; she strikes me, and I strike back. She likes to browbeat my wife and me into spending excessive sums of money on her for things that have not much value to her once she owns them (it is one method she has found of exercising power over us); I permit her to succeed, without resistance, comment, or complaint (it's a method *I* have found of outfoxing her. And it is easier for me in the long run to let these really rather negligible amounts of money go than to keep quarreling with her over them in a series of emotional discussions that might not be concluded otherwise. I win victories over her, I have found, by giving in to just about everything nettlesome she proposes). She thinks I am immature. It *galls* me to hear her say so (even when she says it with approval, when I *am* succeeding in making her laugh, it irks me to hear her tell me that I never fully grew up and that I am, in her opinion, still as playful and childish as a little boy. My boy is frequently distressed and offended when I try to make him and my daughter laugh in public, by singing, walking funny, or making unexpected, loud wisecracks in elevators, drugstores, or supermarkets), and I have taken to wondering (wishing) bitterly now and then after the most disruptive of these sessions with her, as I sit stewing resentfully in discontent and suffering so much sympathy for myself, why she does not oblige me by running far away from home like so many other unhappy girls her age (I guess I might be sorry if

171

she did. I wouldn't miss her, I think, since we don't actually have that much to do with each other anymore, but I would have to go through such elaborate efforts to find her and so many clumsy conversations with other people about her having run away) and make things easier for me by leaving me in peace. And it is my wife, of all people, who brings me to a halt on these occasions, who makes me stop and reflect when I am feeling most murderous and sour, when I am out of my mind with wrath and aboil with a blazing yen for revenge, my wife who utters the words that shed some light, and even hope, and make me remember what I ought never allow myself to forget. She calls me stupid; she tells me I am rotten, self-centered, insane; that I am "no good" (and I regret again that I ever confided to my wife the words I think my mother tried to say to me in the nursing home the last time she spoke). It is my wife, maudlin, discouraged, repetitious, often inane, who, abused by my daughter and oppressive to her in return, berates me with grief and compassion and makes the surprising observation that puts my daughter back into vivid focus suddenly. In tears, crying quietly (I have no patience anymore with women who cry, and my wife knows it and tries not to), it is my wife who remonstrates with me, defending her:

"She's just a little girl."

My daughter is just a little girl, and I try to outfox her in argument. (I just can't help it.) I talk to her as I would to a grown-up, to Kagle, Green, Jane, or my wife, cleverly, cogently, glibly, bitingly. I react to her unpleasant moods as I would to some insulting adult my own age or older. I try to embarrass and defeat her in debate: I want to top her always when we trade taunts and wisecracks, and I usually succeed. (If I can't be funnier, I can always get angrier and grasp my victory that way.) I am ashamed; she makes me forget she is only a child. It is very important to me that I beat her in all our contests. When we discuss or dispute anything, I must be the one to deliver the most intelligent opinions. (I compete with

172

her.) If my daughter criticizes me or complains about me or makes a disparaging joke (even a very humorous and lighthearted one), I can be as affronted, hurt, and unnerved as though some stinging jibe had been inflicted upon me by Green. (I will hide my feelings from both of them, although I suspect Green sees into my skull and knows everything that takes place there. I may even want to cry.) I will sulk (and it is almost as though my daughter is the adult and I am the child). Our roles are reversed; and it is somewhat eerie. (I depend on her. I wanted security from her; I do not get it. Instead, she troubles me with her problems. She takes my time. I do get some of this security from my little boy—so far. "Who do you like?" I can fire at him almost any time with a grin. "I love you, Daddy," he will cry with joy, and hurl himself forward to embrace me with an ardor that jars us both. But he is afraid of spiders and bees—so am I—and of crumbling ankle bones, and I sense much trouble ahead for both of us. I have never felt only sadness at the death of a friend or relative or the departure to a faraway place of someone I like, or even perhaps love. Always there has been simultaneously a marked undercurrent of relief, a release, a secret, unabashed sigh of "Well, at least that's over with now, isn't it?" I wonder how I would feel about the death of a child.) She still has power to wound me; I have power to wound her (so maybe we have not really written each other off entirely yet. Maybe that's why we want to, we are dangerous to each other. My wife can't hurt me. My daughter can). I don't want to hurt her. I do not want her to hurt me. I want her to like me. (I want Green to like me, and everyone else I meet in the whole world to like me, except the people I've already met, handled, found inconsequential, and forgot about.) I want her to obey and admire me (and will hit back brutally at her when she is rude or disparaging). I can't bear defiance from any member of my family (or from waiters or other public servants who are supposed to be subordinate, although I often keep silent with these others and nurse my injuries covertly). I want respect from my daughter and continual kindness. I don't get it.

"She doesn't dislike you," my wife will say to me, when I go to her sometimes for help and advice. "She adores you. Can't you tell?"

"She never says she does."

"Neither do you."

"I don't adore me."

"You know what I mean. Why are you joking now if you really care?"

"She's always angry," I complain. "Even when she isn't really angry, she comes in and pretends she's angry and then she gets angry. She does that with you too."

"That's why she's so sensitive when you're angry with her or pay no attention to her or when you're even too busy to talk to her when she comes into your study to talk to you."

"She never really has anything she wants to talk to me about."

"She doesn't know what to say."

"To me?"

"She doesn't know what else to talk about that will interest you."

"Then why does she try?"

"She wants to impress you."

"She doesn't have to."

"Then why does she try? Your mind is always someplace else. You always act as though we're intruding and you wish you were someplace else. With me, too."

"Stop it, for now, will you? We aren't talking about you. Or I will wish I were someplace else."

"I'm sorry. I didn't mean to say that now."

"Yes, you did. Or you wouldn't have said it."

"Do you want to pick on me?"

"All she does is tell you she can't stand me, and all she does is come into my study to tell me she can't stand you and start a fight with me about one thing or another."

"She doesn't know what else to say to you."

"What am I supposed to do?"

"She's shy."

"With me?"

"That's why she goes into your study so often to interrupt you. She wants you to pay some attention to her and tell her she's pretty."

"She isn't so pretty when she says some of those things she does."

"Don't you think she's pretty anyway?"

"Do you?"

"She could be. I think she could be very pretty if she'd lose some weight and take better care of her face and her hair."

"Why do you serve such fattening meals and keep cake and candy and ice cream in the house?"

"I know. I don't know why. I forget."

"None of us want it but you. And her."

"I won't do it anymore."

"I don't know what to say to her."

"She doesn't know what to say to you."

"I don't know how to talk to her when she tells me she thinks she's fat and ugly or asks me to tell her honestly, if she wasn't my daughter, would I think she was pretty. Would I like her? She's not fat and she isn't ugly, and she knows it. What am I supposed to say?"

"She doesn't know what else to say to you. She's afraid to say anything else. I don't know what to say to you either. I have trouble talking to her too."

"What are you talking about?"

"None of us know what to say to you. You're always so irritable. You always get so mad."

"Oh, come on."

"It's true. You make us feel so stupid. You try to."

"I'm not that bad."

"Maybe if you came home earlier or didn't sleep in the city so often."

"What has that got to do with anything we're talking about? I work late."

"Or came home less often. Sometimes we all get along better when you aren't here."

"Maybe I shouldn't come home at all."

"I didn't mean that."

"Are you suggesting a divorce?"

"No. You know that. Why are you bringing that up so quickly?"

"What are you complaining about?"

"I'm not. I'm sorry I said that. I don't know. I don't know why. I didn't mean to say that."

"Yes, you did. Or you wouldn't have said that, either. People say what they mean."

"So do you. She thinks you hate her."

"I don't. Sometimes I do. When she gets me mad."

"She says you never look at her."

"What the hell does *that* mean?"

"That you never look right at her, even when you're talking to her. She says you always look off to the side somewhere. She notices things like that. She thinks you despise her so much you can't even bring yourself to look at her."

"She's nuts. That's not true."

"Do you look at her?"

"Sure, I do. I don't know. I think I do. Why shouldn't I?"

"She thinks you don't love her."

"It isn't true."

"Do you love her?"

"Of course I do. Do you?"

"You know I do."

"You're always criticizing her. More than I do."

"She's afraid."

"Of what?"

"You."

"Shit."

"We never know what kind of mood you're in."

"That's some way we live."

"We never know what it's safe to say around you."

"*I'm* afraid."

"Of what?"

"What do you think of that? Of you. Of all of you. You've got me walking on eggs, you're all so God-damned touchy and afraid. Do you think I *want* you all afraid of me? I never know what I can say either around here without hurting somebody's feelings. It's worse than being with Green or Arthur Baron or Horace White. It inhibits me, in my own house. No wonder I yell a lot. Do I really yell so much?"

176

"All the time now."

"I don't always mean to."

"You're always so irritable."

"I'm irritable all the time now. I'm always tired."

"Maybe you're working too hard."

"I don't work hard. I worry a lot."

"Maybe you should try to get an easier job."

"Don't you ever listen to me?"

"One where you wouldn't have to work so hard."

"I said I don't work hard."

"Well, maybe you should try to get another job."

"I am trying to get another job."

"Will it be harder or easier?"

"Easier, I think. More responsibility, but much less pressure. More money. More worry. I don't know."

"Will you be able to make speeches?"

"What are you talking about?"

"You know what I mean. Speeches."

"Yeah. All I want."

"I hate Jack Green," she says.

"Why?" I retort suspiciously.

"He's a lousy bastard," she declares passionately. "I'll never forgive him for what he did to you."

"What?" I ask, feeling my face burn suddenly and a tense, protective anger begin to rise.

"Not letting you make that speech at the convention last year, like everyone else. I bet he's jealous of you, that's why. I'm surprised Arthur Baron let him do that to you."

"It wasn't that important."

"I know how hard you worked on it. I know how small it must have made you feel."

"Are you doing this deliberately?"

"But how did it make you feel?"

"I don't feel any bigger being reminded of it now."

"See?" she says. "You're too sensitive to things like that. Maybe you shouldn't take this new job if you have to work too hard and worry more."

"Maybe I won't. To hell with the money and the prestige and the success."

"I don't think you ought to travel more."

"I don't think you can keep your mind on one

177

subject for more than one minute at a time, can you?"

"That's just the kind of remark you would make to me. That's just the kind of remark you would make to her, too."

"I made it to you. Let's not fight now. I didn't come in here for that this time. You and I can fight later."

"I'm not trying to fight."

"Then stop needling me like an oh-so-innocent bitch. Or that I'm too dumb to know what you're doing. That speech is none of your business. Why bring it up all the God-damned time if it really makes you so angry? You do it just to remind me."

"And I'm not angry at what you said just now about my mind. I know you think I'm the dumbest person who ever lived. And I'm not trying to pick on you now. But did you hear how you sounded just now? That's just the kind of thing you would say to her. That's just the way you would sound to her. Try to remember when you talk to her that she's only fifteen and a half years old."

My wife is right.

I do not talk to my daughter as I should to a child, or would if she were somebody else's. I'm not nice to her. If my little boy misbehaves, I respond to him dotingly as a careless, mischievous, or overtired little boy who needs a kiss and a hug and the mildest of reprimands; it is a normal, predictable, endearing mistake, and I correct him tolerantly in an almost deferential way. If my teen-age daughter does something wrong, it is something *wrong*: it is an insulting, intentional, inexcusable attack against me that requires swift and severe retribution. (I do not treat them the same.) I wonder why. Is it because she's a daughter? Or a first child, for whom my aspirations were too high, and in whom I am now therefore disappointed? Or is it that she is already in her teens, growing up and away from me, slipping free from my authority, already preparing to live without me, to challenge frontally my wisdom, morality, and ability, and threatening to dislodge me, if she can, from my shaky stronghold of dictatorial self-esteem? Will I have to endure and survive these same assaults and rejections from my little boy when he grows up too? I hope not, for I would derive no satisfaction (I think) in vanquishing him. (Thank God my third child is an idiot: I really don't mean that. What I do mean is that thank goodness I will at least be spared a rebellion from him. I know how I will feel when Derek dies, or when he is finally sent away: relieved, liberated, and I will release a long-compressed breath and say, perhaps even aloud to someone whom I may feel I can trust:

"Well, at last that's over with too now, isn't he?")

I try to remember when this rivalry between my daughter and me first began. I can't. It sometimes seems that we have always been this way with each other, that we have never gotten along any better or differently. I would like to make my daughter less miserable if I can, to help her to be happier and much more pleased with herself. I don't know how. (I like to trap my daughter in carelessness and lies in order to make her admit she's sorry.)

"She wants to know you love her," my wife says. "She doesn't think you do."

"Well, I do. She knows it."

"How?"

"I think I do."

"By your actions? You never tell her."

"That isn't so."

"When?"

"She's my daughter. I can't say 'I love you' to my own daughter."

"Why not?"

"It sounds like incest."

"Only to you. She thinks you're disappointed in her."

"*You* are. You certainly let her know you are."

"Only because I know she can be better. She could be a good dancer or actress or piano player now if only she'd stuck to things when she was younger. She had so much talent. She could still study dancing or acting."

"So don't deny it. Don't accuse me of that, too."

"I know what happened to me. I wish I'd stuck to something. Like my mother wanted me to. I wish

179

my father had kept out of it and let my mother make me practice more. I might be something today."

"You could be the king of France."

"I'm your wife. You never say 'I love you' to me either."

"You're my wife, I don't have to."

"That isn't funny now."

"Are we talking about you again?"

"I'm not talking about that now. I don't know what to talk about. I don't know what to do with myself. I don't know how to kill time. What am I supposed to do with time if I don't know how to kill it?"

"Have another drink."

"All right. Will you get it?"

"Sure. I don't know what to do about my daughter."

"Me neither," my wife intones in a distant, hollow voice. "She breaks my heart," she adds fretfully. "She can be such a *bitch* when she wants to hurt me."

"I know."

"You too. A bastard. You can be such a bastard. You could at least try to be friendly with her when she wants to talk to you. Even if it hurts."

"I do. And it does hurt."

"That's why she does it. It's the only way she knows how to make you notice her."

"What about you?"

"Maybe me too. I don't even have that way anymore. I don't think you even care anymore whether I'm nasty or not. I think you just don't care."

(Maybe she is right.)

My wife can wring my conscience for a little while (if I decide to let her), but she does not have the power to hurt me anymore (which is why I think I feel secure with her, why I even might have decided it would be good for me to marry her). She wishes she did. She would like to know she means more to me than she thinks she does, would like to believe I need her. (I don't. I don't think I do. I don't let her know I do.) She wants me to tell her I love her, although she has stopped asking me to (I bring her a box of chocolates every Saint Valentine's Day now, and she is pleased to receive it, although we both

180

know it is only a box of chocolates. Still, it *is* a box of chocolates, and everybody in the family enjoys eating chocolates but me), just as she has too much pride (or good sense) to delve into the subject of my sleeping away from home so often or hint that I might be sleeping with other girls (as she does surmise about other married men we know. If *that* ever hopped out into the open between us, like that little mouse I was afraid of in our apartment in the city so long ago, *she* would have to do something about it, *she* would have to act—and I know she does not want to. I know that she, like me, prefers to keep us together until time, or life, runs out). I know I don't want my daughter to grow up to become the kind of girl I run around with now (none of whom can hurt me either. I pick them for that, reject them, in fact, in advance, before I even take up with them), but I don't know what kind of girl I *do* want her to become. (She will never become the king of France either.) She will never dance on the stage of the Radio City Music Hall. She will be some boy's girl friend for a short while, then some other boy's, and then an unhappy wife and mother who will get along no better with her children than I get along with mine, and I don't know what else she *can* become or anything I can do to help her toward something *better*—except nothing. (There are really so few things that *can* happen to people in this lifetime of ours, so few alternatives, so little any of us *can* become, although neither my wife nor daughter realizes that yet.)

"You never like to talk to me, do you?" my daughter says to me softly and earnestly, speaking this time not merely for effect.

"Yes, I do," I reply, avoiding her eyes guiltily. (She is vulnerable in her candor. I do not want to hurt her.)

"You don't even like to look at me."

"I'm looking at you now."

"Only because I just said so. You were looking over my shoulder, like you always do, until I just said so."

"I was watching a fly. I thought I saw one. When I do look at you, you want to know why I'm staring

181

at you. You do the same thing with Mommy. *You* yell."

"If I come in here to talk to you, you always look annoyed because I'm interrupting you, even when you're not doing anything but reading a magazine or writing on a pad."

"Sometimes you keep saying good night to me for an hour or two and keep coming back in with something else you want to take up with me. Five or six times. I keep thinking you've gone to bed and I can concentrate and you keep coming back in and interrupting me. Sometimes I think you do it for spite, just to keep interrupting me."

"I keep thinking of other things to say."

"I'm not always that way."

"I'm the only one who ever comes in here."

"Am I always that way?"

"Everybody else is afraid to."

"Except the maid," I say, trying a mild joke.

"I'm not counting her."

"I do come in here to work, or to get away from all of you for a little while and relax. I don't know why everyone around here is so afraid of me when I never do anything to anybody or even threaten to. Just because I like to be alone every now and then. I know *I* certainly don't get the impression that people around here are afraid to come in here and interrupt me when they want to, or do or say anything else to me, for that matter. Everybody always is."

"You spend nearly all your time at home in here. We have to come in here when we want to talk to you."

"I have a lot of work to do. I make a lot of money. Even though it may not seem like much to you. My work is hard."

"You keep saying it's easy."

"Sometimes it's hard. You know I do a lot of work in here. Sometimes when I just seem to be scribbling things on a pad or reading I'm actually thinking or doing work that I'll need in the morning the next day. It isn't always easy to do it at the office."

"If you ever do say you want to speak to me, it's

only to criticize me or warn me or yell at me for something you think I did."

"That's not true."

"It is."

"Is it?"

"You never come into my room."

"Is *that* true?"

"When do you?"

"You told us not to come in. You don't want me to. You keep the door closed all the time and you ask me to please get out if I do knock and come in."

"That's because you never come in."

"That doesn't make sense, does it?"

"Yes, it does. Mommy would know what I mean. You never want to come in."

"I thought you didn't like Mommy."

"Sometimes I do. She knows what I mean. All you ever do when you come into my room is tell me to open a window and pick my clothes up off the floor."

"Somebody has to."

"Mommy does."

"But they're still always on the floor."

"Sooner or later they get picked up. Don't they? I don't think that's so important. I don't think that's the most important thing you have to talk to me about. Is it?"

"I'll try never to say that to you again. What is important?"

"I've got posters on my wall and some funny lampshades that I painted myself and some funny collages that I made out of magazine advertisements. And I'm reading a book by D. H. Lawrence that I'm really enjoying very much. I think it's the best book I ever read."

"I'm interested in all that," I tell her. "I'd like to see your posters and your funny lampshades and collages. What's the book by D. H. Lawrence?"

"You don't like D. H. Lawrence."

"My own taste isn't too good. I'd like to see what you've done with your room."

"Now?"

183

"If you'd let me."

She shakes her head. "You don't want to. You'd only pretend to look around for a second and then tell me to pick my clothes up off the floor."

"Are they on the floor?"

"You see? You're only interested in joking. You're not really interested in anything I do. You're only interested in yourself. You're not interested in me."

"You're not interested in me," I retaliate gently. "When I do start to ask you questions about yourself, you think I'm snooping into your affairs or trying to trap you in a lie or something."

"You usually are."

"Not always. You do tell lies. You do have things you try to hide."

"You won't let me hide them. You want to know everything. Mommy too."

"Sometimes they're things we should know."

"Sometimes they've got nothing to do with you."

"How can I tell until I find out what they are?"

"You could take my word."

"I can't. You know that."

"That's very flattering."

"You do lie a lot."

"You don't enjoy talking with me. You never want to discuss things with me or tell me anything. Unless it's to make me do my homework. Mommy spends more time talking to me than you do."

"Then why don't you like her more?"

"I don't like what she says."

"You aren't being fair. If I do try to tell you something about the company or my work, you usually sneer and make snotty wisecracks. You don't think the work I do is important."

"You don't think it's important, either. You just do it to make money."

"I think making money for you and the rest of the family is important. And doing my work well enough to maintain my self-respect is important, even though the work itself isn't. You know, it's not always so pleasant for me to have the work I do at the company ridiculed by you and your brother. Even though you're joking, and I'm not always sure you are. I spend so much of my life at it."

(*Why* must I win this argument? And why must I use this whining plea for pity to do it? Why must I show off for her and myself and exult in my fine logic and more expert command of language and details—in a battle of wits with a fifteen-year-old child, my own? I could just as easily say, "You're right. I'm sorry. Please forgive me." Even though *I'm* right and not really sorry. I could say so anyway. But I can't. And I *am* winning, for her look of resolution is failing, her hesitations are growing, and now it is her gaze that is shiftily avoiding mine. I relax complacently, with a momentary tingle of scorn for my inferior adversary, my teen-age daughter. I am a shit. But at least I am a successful one.)

My daughter replies apologetically. "I'm interested in your work," she tries to defend herself. "Sometimes I ask you questions."

"I always answer them."

"With a wisecrack."

"I know you're going to sneer."

"If you didn't wisecrack, maybe I wouldn't sneer."

"I promise never to wisecrack again," I wisecrack.

"*That's* a wisecrack," she says. (She is bright, and I am pleased with her alertness.)

"So is that," I retort (before I can restrain myself, for I suppose I have to show her that I am at least as good).

My daughter doesn't return my smile. "See? You're grinning already," she charges in a low, accusing tone. "You're turning it into a joke. Even now, when we're supposed to be serious."

I turn my eyes from her face and look past her shoulder uneasily at the bookcase on the wall. "I'm sorry. I was only trying to make you feel better. I was trying to make you laugh."

"I don't think there's anything funny."

"No, I'm not. I'm sorry if you thought so."

"You like to turn everything into a joke."

"I don't. Now don't get rude. Or I'll have to."

185

"You start making fun of me. You never want to talk seriously to any of us."

"That isn't true. That's the third time you've made me deny it."

"You always try to laugh and joke your way out whenever something serious comes up."

"That's the fourth."

"Or you get angry and bossy and begin yelling, like you're starting to do now."

"I'm sorry," I say, and pause to lower my voice. "It's my personality, I guess. And my nerves. I'm not really proud of it. What you have to try to remember, honey, and nobody seems to, is that I've got feelings too, that I get headaches, that I can't always control my own moods even though I seem to be the one in charge. I'm not always happy either. Please go on talking to me."

"Why should I?"

"Don't you want to?"

"You don't enjoy talking to me."

"Yes, I do."

"Now?"

"Yes. Tell me what you want to. That's how I'll know. Please. Otherwise I always have to guess."

"Was Derek born the way he is?"

"Yes. Of course. We think so."

"Or was it caused by something one of us did?"

"He was born that way."

"Why?"

"Nobody knows. We all think he was. That's part of the problem. Nobody knows what happened to him."

"Maybe that's what I'll be when I go to college. An anthropologist."

"Geneticist."

"Did you have to say that now?"

"You want to learn, don't you?"

"Not always."

"I thought you'd like to know the difference when you make a mistake."

"Not now. You knew what I meant. You didn't have to stop me just to show you're smarter. Did you?"

"You're very smart. You're very bright and very clever. Maybe you should be a lawyer. That's a compliment. I don't pay you compliments often."

"I'll say."

"You like to force people into a corner. I'm the same way."

"I think I try to be like you."

"I was happier."

"Was your family disappointed in you?"

"I can't remember. Is yours?"

"I don't know."

"I think my mother was. But later on, not when I was a child. When I was older and moved away."

"You never kiss me," my daughter says. "Or hug me. Or kid with me. Like other fathers."

She has black, large shadows under her eyes, which are swollen, gummy, and red suddenly, and she looks more wretched than any other human being I have ever stared at before. (I want to wrench my gaze away.)

"You stopped wanting me to kiss you," I explained softly with tenderness, feeling enormous pity for her (and for myself. Whenever I feel sorry for someone, I find that I also feel sorry for myself). "I used to. I used to want to hug you and kiss you. Then you began to pull away from me or draw your face back with a funny expression and make a disgusted sound. And laugh. As a joke at first, I thought. But then it became a habit, and you pulled away from me every time and made that same face and disgusted sound every time I tried to kiss you."

"So now you've stopped trying."

"It wasn't pleasant for me to be insulted that way."

"Were you hurt?" There is that glitter of too much eagerness in her expression. "Did it make you unhappy?"

"Yes." We are talking in monotones. (I don't remember when it really did begin to hurt me deeply each time she pulled away from my demonstrations of affection with signs of mock revulsion; and I also don't remember when it stopped bothering me at all.) "I was very unhappy. My feelings were hurt."

"You never said so."

"I wouldn't give you the satisfaction."

"I was little then."

"It was still very painful."

"I was just a little girl then. Wouldn't you give up just a little bit of your pride to satisfy me, if that's what I wanted?"

"No. I didn't."

"Would you do it now?"

"I'm not."

"You won't?"

"No. I don't think so. I don't think I'll ever let you get any satisfaction out of me that way."

"You must be very disappointed in me?"

"Why?"

"I'll bet you are. You and Mommy both."

"Why should we be?"

"I know *she* is. I'm not good at anything."

"Like what? Neither am I."

"I've got a greasy scalp and skin. And pimples. I'm not pretty."

"Yes, you are."

"I'm too tall and fat."

"For what?"

"I'm not even sure I want to be. I don't know what I'd do even if I was good at anything."

"Like what?"

"Like art. I can't paint or sculpt. I'm not very smart. I'm not good at music. I don't study ballet."

"I don't study ballet either."

"It's not funny!"

"I'm not trying to be." (I *was* trying to be.) "We're not good at those things either."

"I'm not even rich."

"That's my fault, not yours."

"At least that would be something. I could be proud of that. Are we ever going to be? I mean really rich, like Jean's father, or Grace."

"No. Unless you do it."

"I can't do anything. Should I be ashamed?"

"Of what?"

"Because we're poor."

"We aren't poor."

"Of you."

"At least you're frank."

"Should I be?"

"What would you expect me to say?"

"The truth."

"Of me? I hope not. Being ashamed is something you either are or aren't, not something you do because you should or shouldn't. I do well enough. Jean is ashamed of her father because he's mean and stupid, and thinks I'm better. Isn't she? So is Grace. I think Grace likes me a lot more than she does her father."

"I'm never going to be anything."

"Everybody is something."

"You know what I mean."

"Like what?"

"Famous."

"Few of us are."

"I don't blame you. I don't blame you for being disappointed in me."

"We're not. Do you think we'd be disappointed in you just because you aren't good at anything?"

"Then you never even expected anything of me, did you?" she accuses, with a sudden surge of emotion that catches me by surprise.

"Now you're not being fair!" I insist.

"It's not funny."

"Honey, I—"

But she is gone, disappearing intransigently with a look of mournful loathing as I put my arms out to comfort her (and I am left again by myself in my study with my empty hands outstretched in the air, reaching out toward nothing that is there).

There is something I have done to her (or am doing to her now) for which she refuses to forgive me, and I don't know what that something is (or even if it is to her I am doing it. I know she acts angry and hurt when I am drunk or even a little high. She does not like it either when I flirt with her friends). I try to remember when it began, this mordant, stultifying sorrow into which she sneaks away to bury herself so often. I know it was nothing that happened this year, for she was not much different last year, and it was nothing that happened last year for she was not much different then than the year before.

(She is not much different at fifteen from what she was at twelve and not much different at twelve from what she was at nine.) Almost as far back as I can recall, in fact, she has always been pretty much the same person she is now, only smaller. And yet, there must have been a break somewhere, an end and a starting point, a critical interval in her development of some breadth and duration that I cannot remember or did not notice (just as there must certainly have been a similar start of metamorphosis somewhere back in my own past that I took no notice of then and cannot remember now), for she was an infant once (indeed she was, I do remember that), a playful, chubby, gleeful, curious, active, giggling, responsive baby, easily pleased, quickly interested, and happily diverted. (Whatever happened to it, that baby she was? Where did it go? Where is it now? And how did it get there? Such beings, such things, just don't happen one day and stop happening the next. Do they? What happened to the lovely little me that once was? I remember certain things about him well and know he used to be.) What happened to her early childhood, that unmarked waste between the infant we had then and the daughter we have now and have kept reasonably good track of? (Where is it? Where was it? When—I can remember intact everything in *her* history, and I don't know—did it take place? I know this much: there was a cheerful baby girl in a high chair in my house once who ate and drank with a hearty appetite and laughed a lot with spontaneous zest; she isn't here now; and there is no trace of her anywhere. And I am sure of this much: there was a little boy who surprised his big brother with a girl in a coal shed once and had a lump of coal thrown at him, and opened a door once on his father and mother embracing in bed, or thinks he did; the mother and father are dead, and the little boy is missing; I don't know where he came from; I don't know where I went; I don't know all that's happened to me since. I miss him. I'd love to know where he's been.) Where in her lifetime (and in mine too, of course) was that legendary happy childhood I used to hear so much about (those carefree days of joy and sunshine, ha, ha, that birthright) that she is entitled as a human being to be enjoying even right now (along with all those other moldering, moody, incapacitated kids her own age who are her friends) and should be at liberty to look back upon fearlessly later with intense and enriching gratification (like my wife, whose childhood was really like some kind of suffocating ashland until *I* swept into the picture and carried her away from unhappiness into her present life of uninterruptable bliss. Ha, ha) when life turns old, threadbare (teeth come out, toes abrade, arches begin to ache and spinal columns too, and shoes no longer fit), dry, and sour? Where is that pleasurable childhood everybody keeps thinking everybody else has? I know I didn't have one (although I might have thought I did and could have thought I knew why I didn't in case I thought I didn't). If I was unhappy, I could always tell myself it was because my father was dead. If my daughter is unhappy, she might feel it's because *her* father is alive!

(Freud or not, I have never been able to figure out how I really did feel about my mother, whether I liked her or not, or even felt either way about her at all. I think I felt nothing. I had the same feeling, or absence of feeling most of the time, toward the other members of my family and my best friend, with whom I am not on very friendly terms anymore. We grew tired of each other, and I am relieved. He needed money; I couldn't give it generously more than once. I have never been sure I ever really cared for anyone in this whole world but myself and my little boy. But I still do have these grief-filled dreams about my mother. There's a part of me I can't find that is connected to her still as though by an invisible live wire transmitting throbs. It refuses to die with her, and will continue to live inside me, probably, for as long as I survive. In my final coma, I suppose, even if I live to be a million, my self-control will lapse and I will die moaning: "Ma. Momma. Momma." Which is pretty much the way I began. I feel lucky sometimes that I don't remember my father, that he died without making an impression upon me, or I might be having dreams about him, too. In case I ain't having them already. He might have fucked up my life even more just by being around if he had lived, just the way I seem to be fucking up everyone else's around me. Even though I don't want to. I swear to Christ I never consciously wanted to. Maybe I am having bad dreams about him anyway and just don't know it. Soon after I die, nobody will ever think about him again. And soon after my children die, nobody will ever think of me.)

I had no happy childhood, if I recall correctly, and neither did my wife (who prefers to recollect *in*correctly, when I let her), and my boy, at nine, though he laughs a lot and is intent on making many good jokes, is running into stormy weather already, even though I do everything I can to try to make things easier for him. (With my daughter, I've stopped trying. There does not seem to be any way left to propitiate her, except to allow her to continue forcing us to buy expensive things for her and yield her those minute, transitory victories of ego that evaporate in an instant and dump her right back down where she was, in that same vacant, unlighted predicament of not knowing what to do next, no different than before. It was easier for me to spend the eight or eighty dollars on her than to argue with her why I shouldn't.) I forage through experience to try to discover when my daughter was different from now, and I must go very far back indeed to find her radiant in a high chair (she was a gorgeous, lovable child, and I feel a wistful pang of love and regret when I remember) at a birthday party in her honor, when she was either two or three years old. (What a difference there is between a baby and the person it becomes.) She is our only child. Relatives from both sides of the family are present. My wife and I are younger. My mother is alive. Many people have assembled. The apartment bustles. Our attention is dispersed. We are absorbed in each other, and my little girl is forgotten until she suddenly strikes the tableboard of the high chair sharply with the plastic pink party spoon clutched in her dimpled fist and calls out clearly and gloriously:

"Good girl, grandma!"

It takes a moment for all of us to comprehend. And when we do, all simultaneously it seems, we roar with laughter and begin applauding and congratulating this little girl and ourselves exuberantly (and my daughter, seeing this response of raucous gaiety she has stimulated, bounces and rocks with glee so vigorously in her high chair that we fear she will fall out or topple over), for my mother (her hair was not all white yet, her face not all disiccated and creased) had merely lifted a glass to her lips and drained it of some strawberry punch. But my daughter was watching her. And when my daughter, who was herself being trained then by my wife and me to drink from a glass and faithfully rewarded with handclaps of delight and cries of "Good girl!" whenever she succeeded, saw my mother drink from a glass, she banged her own hands down with delight and approval and called out:

"Good girl, grandma!"

(Not long afterward, my mother could not drink from a glass unless someone held it to her lips.)

It was a small thing, an incident of tiny surprise, but it filled the room with rolling waves of tremendous pleasure and warmth. (All of us there were happier people then and closer to each other than we have ever been since.) All of us rejoiced and united in merry praise of my daughter and made the sunniest predictions, and my daughter was so exhilarated by the sheer volume and intensity of such good feeling and elation that she sang out "Good girl, grandma!" two or three more times (no longer spontaneously, but with discerning calculation) and bounced and rocked on her throne of a high chair, giggling her hearty laugh, luxuriating in her triumph and in the looks and words of adoration directed toward her. (She knew. I was proud of her then, I remember. So pleased with what she had said. So devoted and protective.) All of us marveled breathlessly at her cheerful wit and beauty (she was our miracle) and foresaw sparkling attainments. And even my mother, who tended to be cynical toward everything superstitious, was convinced, she declared, that my daughter had been born under an exceedingly lucky star and would enjoy a brilliant, happy, unblemished future. My daughter really was a darling child, and everybody loved her then, even me.

That was just about the last time I saw my daughter so happy. That was just about the last time I saw my mother happy. It was shortly afterward that I made my decision not to invite my mother to live with us, which meant she would have to live the rest of her life alone. Words were not necessary. The omission itself was an indelible statement. (She never asked, never made me say so. She made it easy for me. She was very kind to me about that.) Although I would have dinner with her every other week, at her apartment or ours, and on appropriate family holidays. (I would even drive her home. None of us wanted her, not my wife, not my daughter, not my sister, not me.) Not much after that, she suffered the first in a series of crippling brain spasms that robbed her at the outset of her ability to speak and at the end of her ability to think or remember. (As my mother faded away, speechless, in one direction, Derek emerged, speechless, from the other.) And there you have *my* tragic chronicle of the continuity of human experience, of this great chain of being, and the sad legacy of pain and repudiation that one generation of Slocums gets and gives to another, at least in my day. (I got little. I gave back less.) I have this unfading picture in my mind (this candid snapshot, ha, ha), and it can never be altered (as I have a similar distinct picture of my hand on Virginia's full, loosely bound breast for the first time or the amazingly silken feel of the tissuey things between her legs the first time she let me touch her there), of this festive, family birthday celebration in honor of my little girl at which my old mother and my infant daughter are joyful together for perhaps the very last time. And there I am between them, sturdy, youthful, prospering, virile (fossilized and immobilized between them as though between bookends, without knowing how I got there, without knowing how I will ever get out), saddled already with the grinding responsibility of

194

making them, and others, happy, when it has been all I can do from my beginning to hold my own head up straight enough to look existence squarely in the eye without making guileful wisecracks about it or sobbing out loud for help. Who put me here? How will I ever get out? Will I ever be somebody lucky? What decided to sort me into precisely this slot? (What the fuck makes anyone think *I* am in control, that I can be any different from what I am? I can't even control my reveries. Virginia's tit is as meaningful to me now as my mother's whole life and death. Both of them are dead. The rest of us are on the way. I can almost hear my wife, or my second wife, if I ever have one, or somebody else, saying:

"Won't you wheel Mr. Slocum out of the shade into the sunlight now? I think he looks a little cold."

A vacuum cleaner that works well is more important to me than the atom bomb, and it makes not the slightest difference to anyone I know that the earth revolves around the sun instead of vice versa, or the moon around the earth, although the measured ebb and flow of the tides may be of some interest to mariners and clam diggers, but who cares about them? Green is more important to me than God. So, for that matter, is Kagle and the man who handles my dry cleaning, and a transistor radio that is playing too loud is a larger catastrophe to me than the next Mexican earthquake. "Someday"—it must have crossed my mother's mind at least once, after my denial and rejection of her, since she was only human—"this will happen to you." Although she was too generous to me ever to say so. But I know it must have crossed her mind.)

"When I was a baby," my daughter asks, "did you ever play with me?"

"Sure," I reply. "What do you think?" A warning shudder of some kind shoots through me at her question, turning my skin icy.

"Did you ever pick me up and toss me into the air," she inquires, "or give me piggyback rides, or tell me stories before I went to bed, or carry me around in your arms and talk baby talk to me and say very funny things?"

"All the time," I answer. "Of course, I did." Her

195

look of doubt shocks me. "What kind of monster do you think I am?"

"You don't do anything like that now."

"You're a big girl now. I always yell out hello when I come home, don't I? You don't even answer."

"Did I have parties when I was little? Birthday parties?"

"You sure did. Very beautiful parties. Mommy went to a lot of trouble to make them very good ones."

"I don't remember them."

"Yes, you do. You mention them."

"I mean when I was very little. And all our relatives came and made a big fuss over me and gave me expensive presents?"

"Yes. I used to play with you a lot. I used to go right in to see you every day as soon as I came home from work. You were the first person I wanted to see. I always played with you."

"Mommy told me you did. But I didn't believe her."

"What kind of person do you think I am?"

"You're never the same. You always change. Sometimes you laugh at something I do. Sometimes you get angry and annoyed when I do exactly the same thing and want me to go away. I don't like it when you drink. I never know what to expect."

"You're like that too."

"You're a father."

"It isn't easy."

"You don't know how to be a father."

"I try to be. I always tried my best. I try now. I used to play with you every night as soon as I came home from work," I rush on earnestly, the words pouring from me in a torrent of virtuous reminiscence as I seize the chance to explain to her once and for all and exonerate myself forever from whatever blame and neglect she charges me with. "I even played baseball with you with a plastic bat and ball when you were a little girl and didn't know it was a boy's game, and taught you how to swim. I'm the one who taught you. I asked you to put your face down in the water and float and promised that nothing bad would happen to you if you trusted me and did. You believed me then and weren't afraid. And that's how I taught you. Every day as soon as I came home from work, you were just a little baby then and we lived in the city, I would take my hat off, I wore a hat then, one of those funny fedoras with brims that people still wear, and put my head down near you and let you grab my hair. You used to love to do that. Maybe because I had a lot more hair then, ha, ha. You were just a tiny little girl then and couldn't even stand or walk. I would kiss Mommy on the cheek when I walked in and go right in to see you every day as soon as I came home. I would bend my head down and you would grab my hair with both your little hands and pull, and you would laugh and bounce and scream and kick your legs with such wild excitement that we were always afraid you were going to bounce right off the bed or kick your way right out of the crib. Ha, ha. You would giggle like crazy. And Mommy would watch and laugh too. We used to do that every day as soon as I got home from work. And later when you were older," I go on rabidly in obsessive recollection, "after you had your tonsils out and came back from the hospital, I used to have to tell you a story every night before you went to sleep, or you wouldn't go to sleep. You insisted. It was *your right,* ha, ha, to have a story from me. Every night, and it usually had to be the same story. You didn't like new ones. First it was *Cinderella* and then it was *Peter Pan* too after you saw *Peter Pan* on television. I used to have to act *Peter Pan* out for you. You would make me. I bet I nearly broke my legs every night jumping from the couch to the floor when I pretended to fly for you. Ha, ha. Then there was *Peter and the Wolf,* and *Siegfried*—I once read you the whole story of *Siegfried,* and you were so soft-hearted then that you even began to cry in sympathy for that dumb blockhead Siegfried, so I never read it to you again—and that one about the rabbit and the tar baby, and for a while I tried telling you *The Little Boy Who Cried Wolf,* but you didn't like that one at all because the little boy got eaten up at the end, I think, so we went back to *Peter*

197

Pan and *Cinderella.* And in *Cinderella,* whenever I came to the part where the prince asks Cinderella to marry him, you would interrupt and answer: 'Sure, prince! Don't you remember? Mommy does. 'Sure, prince!' you would cry, ha, ha, and we would both laugh. And Mommy would stand in the doorway and listen, and she would laugh too. When I was out of town, I would try to get to a telephone in the evening before you went to sleep and tell you the story long distance. And I had to tell you the stories in exactly the same way every time. You would make me, ha, ha. If I changed a line or ever tried to leave something out just to speed things up, you would correct me right away very severely and make me do it exactly the way you wanted me to. Oh, you were so strict and determined. Like a stern little princess. Ha, ha. You knew all the stories by heart, and you didn't want me to change a word. Every night. Ha, ha. Don't you remember?"

But she doesn't believe me.

And I don't care.

My little boy is having difficulties

My little boy is having a difficult time of it in school this year, in gym, in math, and in classes stressing public speaking. And just about everywhere else, it seems. (At home with me. With my wife. My daughter. My boy seems to be having a difficult time of it in school every year now when the new term starts, but each year seems to grow worse. He is, I'm afraid, starting to "let me down.")

He hates gym and public speaking. He used to like gym. (He never liked public speaking.) Now he dreads gym, with its incessant regimen of exercises that he cannot perform well: chinning, push-ups, rope climbing, and tumbling. He abhors rope climbing, chinning, and push-ups and is stricken almost speechless (you can almost see that bulbous, leaden lump jamming his throat) by this reluctance even to talk about them (as though merely to mention his hatred of these ridiculous gymnastic demonstrations would be to violate some clandestine taboo surrounding them and to be sentenced to perform them awkwardly and feebly, with everyone watching, still one more time). My boy hates Forgione, the squat, barrel-chested, simian gym teacher with forests of black, wiry hair curling out all over him everywhere, even through the weave of his white T-shirt, except on his head, who can break me in two with his bare hands if he ever decided he wanted to, and who tries to be helpful and encouraging to my frightened little

199

boy in his blunt, domineering, primitive way and only succeeds in frightening him further.

"He doesn't have a good competitive spirit," Forgione asserts to me complainingly. "He lacks a true will to win."

"I don't have one either, Mr. Forgione," I reply to him tamely, in an effort to get on his good side. "Maybe he gets it from me."

"That can't be true, Mr. Slocum," Forgione says. "Everybody's got a competitive spirit."

"Then why doesn't he?"

"That's what I mean," says Forgione.

My boy can turn frozen and look mucous green with trepidation some mornings when he knows he will have to go to gym later that day, or deliver some kind of oral report in one of his classes, and he will disclose to us that he doesn't feel well and thinks he might want to vomit. His chest feels empty, he says, and sometimes his arms and legs feel drained of all substance as well (if I understand correctly what he is trying to say. He feels he might fall if he tries to stand, simply sag and fold inward and sink to the floor like someone deflated and without skeleton). He does not like to have to make oral reports in class.

("It is good training for him," the school says. I know from my own small experience at addressing groups that it is no training at all.)

Sometimes, he has hinted, he will not do as well as he is able to on written reports in order to escape being called upon to read what he has written aloud from the front of the classroom as an example to others of what is superior. (He lacks the true will to win.) He never likes to be called upon in class unless he is positive he has the right answer. (He almost never, his teachers tell us, raises his hand to volunteer a reply.) He is a gifted, hard-working student; he is inhibited; he is a quick, intuitive learner. He is afraid to be wrong. He always seems to know much more about everything than he is disposed to reveal. (He thinks a lot. I can't always make him out.) He fathoms privately, his clear face grave and remote. He worries. (Or seems to. Sometimes when I ask him what he looks so worried about, he glances up at me with a flicker of astonishment and replies that he isn't worrying. I don't know if he is lying to me or not. I worry a lot that he may be worrying.)

It is impossible for us to tell anymore whether he likes school or not (he used to like school. Or seemed to) although he generally manages to adapt to the different people and procedures of each new school year and then begins enjoying himself immensely. It takes a while; and he girds himself for the effort. He is distant with people he doesn't like; he grows close swiftly with schoolmates he does. (He is guileful enough by instinct, it seems, to get on friendly and respectful terms with tough guys and bullies.) He makes many friends. (He has started to keep things from me, and I don't like it. I ask questions. I try to pry details loose from him. He tries to hold on to them. I don't want him to. I want him to confide in me.)

Once he does make friends in school and sees himself adapting capably to whatever new systems of authority and social codes prevail, everything tends (or has tended till now. Knock wood. Ha, ha) sooner or later to turn out fine: he does well; he survives; and he celebrates the miracle of his survival with boisterous, optimistic horseplay and industry unless something, even *one* thing of some meaning to him, goes wrong for him drastically (this year so far it is gym and Forgione, with those push-ups, tumbling, and chinning, and that vertical rope climbing to the high ceiling of the gymnasium with its theoretical danger of growing scared and dizzy and falling, or freezing in panic halfway up, or down, although nobody I've ever heard of has. Some kids his age, he tells me, can already go almost halfway up without using their feet. Like monkeys. He, like me, never will be able to—he can't get more than a single hoist above the resting knot at the bottom of the thick, bristling rope—but I won't ever want to climb ropes again, and he does. And public speaking. This year, the school has decided to emphasize public speaking in the early grades. Why? They don't explain. Are they related, public speaking and physical agility?

I am reminded of those mysterious, musty dreams of danger I have—I think everybody must have them—in which I am unable to move any muscles and unable to speak or scream or even to utter that single word I want to, *Help,* unable to make any noises at all except the ones that force themselves upward through my throat to wake my wife and then fill me with a delicious sense of gladness when I understand that she is calling my name and shaking my shoulder to awaken me. I guess I must really hate her at times. Often I will pretend to be asleep for a few moments after I realize I am not and continue my unintelligible moaning just so that she will have to continue trying to awaken me. I like the concern in her voice. My wife feels responsible for my bad dreams; I am pleased she does, make no effort to exonerate her, and feel she really is to blame when I have one. I use them to punish her. I keep digressing to me. I keep digressing from me. I wish my wife had bigger tits. I wish my wife had smaller tits. I think I really do love my little boy, though, the way a father should. At least I feel I do), and then he is apt to come very close to falling completely to pieces, to crumpling like a frail, inanimate bundle of little boy's clothes or spilling out emotionally all over the room like a sack of broken chips of some kind—potato, poker, wooden—into a frenzy of melancholy anguish that is at once both petrifying and shattering (to us as well as to him. My wife and I go numb with terror at even the vaguest possibility of something wrong with either of our children. Thanks to Derek. My wife does not want my little boy to grow up to be a fag and worries sneakily that he will. I know she does, because I worry often about that same thing, but not as often as she does. I don't want my boy to be a fag. I have no reason yet to think he will. But I just don't want him to).

My little boy is only nine years old and not yet able to deal like an adult with certain kinds of opposition and frustrations (and we do not know yet what all those kinds are; it seems to us he often does not even want to try; warding things off becomes for him so futile and exhausting an endeavor as to be, at

202

times, possibly just not worthwhile; he would almost sooner give up, stop struggling; it would be so much easier and more sensible, his regretful manner of tired resignation often implies, to simply stop striving, yield, and let the very worst of all those things he foresees overtake, violate, and destroy him, to succumb and once and for all be done. He used to be afraid of weird things rising from beneath his bed. Better to let them all rise up, he may feel now, than continue waiting constantly for it all to happen to him anyway no matter what precautions are taken, since sooner or later, inevitably, it must, and never feeling safe enough for long to cease listening for mortal disaster's relentless approach. It comes on footsteps that are almost audible. I think he may feel this way about himself, because I feel this same way about both of us).

(I know how it feels to have to feel this way.)

(It doesn't feel good.)

I know how it feels to have to begin speculating ominously weeks before each summer ends and the new school year begins about the innumerable ordeals massing ahead of him. (I know how it feels to be notified of an office meeting scheduled to take place and have no idea what it's going to be about. I know that I am already troubled grimly and sadly about whether or not I will be allowed to make even my three-minute speech at the company convention in Puerto Rico this year, let alone about what will become of me if I do have Kagle's job by then and have to take charge of the whole event. Will I be good? As good as I know my three-minute speech last year would have been if Green had let me give it? I think I hate that bastard Green too, but I'd rather not admit that to my wife. Why would I want to admit to anyone that I hate and fear the man I work for, yet continue to work for him? Why do I let myself agonize over what even at best would have been no more than an amusing three-minute speech? The sky is falling, tumbling down on all our heads, and I sit shedding tears over an unhealing scratch on a very tender vanity. At least my boy's problems are real. They occupy space. They dangle from the ceiling of a gymnasium

203

and glower at him from the dark and evil face of a physical education teacher.) To his young and practical mind it seems so pointless to have to go through one school year making complicated adjustments to people, young, old, good, neutral, and bad, only to have the relationships all terminated when spring ends and summer comes (for him, and for me now too, the year begins in September and closes out in June. Summer marks time. Summer is for taking inventory, adding bank balances, and fucking around in); and then have to go through the same harrowing process in the fall of adapting to new relationships that he knows from the start will be dissolved as well the following spring (as methodically and insensibly as the changes in seasons themselves, and for no more beneficial purpose. The seasons do not change because we want them to), leaving him isolated once more outside some sheltering context (the home, obviously, has not been substantial enough) inside which he can orient himself securely with some conviction that it is going to last awhile and maintain meanings and directions that will not blur and alter suddenly without explanation. (Where is a frame of reference now for any of us that extends even the distance to the horizon, only eighteen miles away?) My boy puzzles over things like that.

("How far is the horizon?"

"Eighteen miles at sea level," I answer rapidly. "Or only fourteen. I forget which."

"Why sea level?"

"I don't know. Maybe if you're up higher you can see farther.")

He puzzles over things like that well in advance (although not in these words, which are mine. He is only nine and lacks my vocabulary. Where was I when I was nine? Isolated among friends in elementary school too, where it was mandatory that I see a dentist twice a year to have my teeth fixed and have my head examined once or twice a year by a nurse right in the classroom, along with all the other kids, whites, Blacks, Jews, Italians, for nits, without any of us ever being told what nits were, although intonations signaled they were bad. That was a test

I always passed. I don't know how I would have survived if I had ever failed. Once a girl peed in her seat in the classroom during a geography test and everyone knew it. I don't know how she survived. I don't think I could have ever survived if I had ever peed in my seat in the classroom during a geography test).

When my boy puzzles over things in advance, he tends to puzzle over things that perplex or torment him. (He almost never sees anything good in store for him. He has wishes; he never sees them coming true, even though he knows I promise and give him just about everything he asks for and everything else I think he wants and should have. When he does chance to think about something pleasant that is likely to happen to him, his reveries turn negative: he begins grieving it won't. He loses it before he even has it. He is like our salesmen, and me, wired by experience to expect, and long for, the worst—just to have it over with.) They pollute his summers for him. (The early part of each summer is marred for him by the need to acclimate himself to the surroundings of whatever beach or country house we have decided to rent that year. He won't go away to camp, and neither will my daughter ever go again, although they don't enjoy being with us. We never know what to do with Derek. It is always so embarrassing to hide him; and equally embarrassing to disclose him. The latter part of the summer is ruined for him by the approaching fall. Sometimes, to my chagrin as well as his, the cares of early summer and late summer overlap, so that if one set subsides for a while, the other is present already, gnawing at his peace of mind. Sometimes he pisses me off, and I begin to worry about everything too, including the feelings of enmity toward him that start fermenting inside me. I'm afraid I am beginning to dislike him.)

I know (and am annoyed) that weeks before the end of summer he begins fretting despondently about all the trials he knows are lying in wait for him: the schoolwork, the accomplishments expected of him in gym (he welcomes running and dodging games, at which he is swift, nimble, and foxy), the new teachers, the old teachers, the principal, the assistant principal, the shop teacher, and the science teacher (he has always been leery of shop teachers and sicence teachers. Perhaps because they are men), the music teacher (will this one also require him to stand up in turn and sing solo a few notes in order to determine into which section of the chorus to classify him for those times when they have to perform at the weekly school assemblies?), the student monitors from grades higher than his own (boys bigger and stronger than himself with license to order him about, and older, taller girls with badges and arm bands of authority and with embryonic breasts starting to swell forward toward him mysteriously and threateningly. I remember how it was when I was small), and the boys and girls familiar to him from the preceding school year who will not be in his class again. He laments the loss of children he knows, boys *and* girls, even those he does *not* like, who move away into different communities or are transferred by their parents into private schools (more and more of us seem to be transferring our children into private schools, which are expensive and not much good, and then transferring them out again into other private schools that are not much better. We don't like the heads of these private schools. More and more things seem to be slipping into a state of dissolution, and soon there will be nothing left. No more newspapers, magazines, or department stores. No more movie houses. Just discount stores and drugs. More and more of us, I think—not just me—really don't care *what* happens to our children, as long as it doesn't happen to them too soon) or the one or two who drowned or got hit by cars during the summer (the incidence of accidents suffered each year by children we know corresponds with portentous accuracy to the incidence of accidents suffered by adults I know in the company. Martha in our department is going crazy), and those others who, as a consequence of inexorable and unfathomable processes in operation in offices downstairs (adults toiling assiduously with records of living children that are dead already on sheets and cards in folders and cabinets) have been separated from him (like our tonsils and our baby teeth) and scattered about into different classrooms. He hates changing from teachers who have been kind to him.

("What are you worrying about?" I will ask him when I can no longer endure in silence the thought that he might be worrying alone.

"I'm not worrying," he will reply.

I wish I could be more of a help to him. I wish he would let me try.)

"What are you worrying about?" I will ask again.

"I'm not worrying," he answers, looking up at me an instant with a glimmer of surprise.

"What makes you look so glum?"

"I was thinking."

"What were you thinking about," I persist with a smile, "that makes you look so worried?"

"I don't know. I forgot already."

"You looked so glum."

"I don't know what that means."

"Sad."

"I'm not sad."

"Tired?"

"Maybe I'm sleepy."

"Do you stay up late?"

"Sometimes I don't fall asleep right away."

I sometimes wonder if he really worries as much as I think he does. I sometimes think he worries more. He is a cautious little thing (or seems to be. I know I worry for him and expect the worst to happen to him also. So does my wife. I used to worry about my daughter too when she was little, but now she is past fifteen, and the worst hasn't happened. What is the worst? I'm not sure). Maybe the worst *has* happened and went unrecognized, because my boy, now that I look back, has never had an easy time of things (and my daughter is having a lousy time of it now, unless she is acting too. Wouldn't it be funny if both were acting more unhappy than they are merely to spite and upset us? Ha, ha. I wouldn't find it funny at all. Even as an infant in a playpen he always seemed to be siphoning everything around him in through large, mysterious, intelligent eyes and judging everything he absorbed tentatively before making up his mind and allowing himself to react—even when he reacted spontaneously, as when grinning or giggling suddenly, there always seemed to be a premeditated delay, an infinitesimal lag, but a lag nonetheless, during which a decision had been arrived at. Even an offer of money, or an ice cream pop, would bring a moment's weighty consideration before acceptance. I lose patience with him often. I shout and shame him sometimes—then deny I shouted and try to persuade him I was only being *emphatic*. It's no way to build confidence. I try to be generous and companionable to make up for it.

"Say yes or no," I demand of him in explanation. "What difference would it make if you are wrong? What would you lose by making a mistake?"

He is confused.

He is afraid of making mistakes.

So he makes them with me by vacillating).

I know he must wonder now why his life has been arranged to be so unceasingly difficult (why I shout at him so frequently, or seem to, why I undoubtedly *will* do raise my voice) or if there ever *will* come a time of tranquillity and bliss for him in which no new implacable demons are waiting in ambush for him, stirring in time as the moment of contact draws near, making ready for him, practically in view. (I know I wonder all of that for him. When will he be able to relax and take things easy, so I can relax and take things easy too?)

"Tell me, what do you want to do?" I ask him so many times out of disconsolate, moody concern. "What do you want to be?"

"I would like to learn how to drive a car someday."

"Everybody does that."

"If I can. Do you think I will?"

He likes the smell of gasoline and is afraid of fire, height, and speed (but not of airplanes, if he is in one).

How weary (I feel) he must be already of challenges and adversity, like a spent and weatherbeaten old man (homunculus), or a resigned, moribund, white-haired old woman embracing her own demise with relief. Often, when something of a particularly eroding nature seems to be preying on his mind, a shadow of gaunt consternation will fall across his fragile, fine features, a stricken look of transfixing amazement, as though he is troubled deeply by the fact that he is troubled at all.

He hardly seems altogether at ease anywhere but at home, although he has always laughed a great deal when with people he knows. He makes jokes. He has wit and a talent for giddy and imaginative tricks. They are mainly verbal, always harmless, usually successful by one light or another. He seeks safety and invisibility in humor. (I do too. I find it in sex, which is always humorous too.) And he labors industriously to surround himself inside a womblike atmosphere of compassion and good spirit and survive there eternally (like the me I really think I am, I think, swaddled cunningly inside my cocoon, hiding secretly in a foxhole no one knows is there), dissembling, peeping out guardedly nearly all the time (one part of me anyway) to reassure himself (myself) that our outer shell of protection is still there and intact (and we are there and intact too), recoiling hastily (searching in horror for some unobstructed avenue of escape, I am sure, and searching in horror in vain) when we spy or think we spy any omen of any hazard of puncture, deflation, and disintegration. (He is upset by basketball, which he does not understand.) His impulse always is to be endearing; he wants no enemies, dislikes disagreements, and does not enjoy competition. He feels least in jeopardy when everyone around him is happy and sated with contentment (he feigns complete indifference to Derek when we let him and tries to pretend he is able to ignore him); he feels most in jeopardy in proximity to somebody sullen or someone manifesting anger, especially me. (He is as much afraid of me at times, I believe, as he is of any sullen stranger glaring to himself in a cafeteria, or even as he is of Forgione, or Forgione's assistant, with their demands for rope climbing, chinning, tumbling, push-ups, and basketball games that my little boy finds impossible to do well and baffling

209

to understand.) He is the only member of my household who hesitates to come into my study to interrupt me. (He is even too diffident to come inside to say good night to me at bedtime, though I keep asking him to do so and keep assuring him that I will not mind.

"Good night," he will call out to me from the hallway, keeping himself so deeply withdrawn that I will be unable to see him when I turn my head and look up, and recede skittishly into his own room unless I call right back:

"Good night. Come in here a minute. Will you?")

Unless I make him. Once I do make him step inside my study to talk to me, we have little to say to each other. He brings a barrier with him. Or I have one of my own. But I do want to talk to him. We have nothing to talk about. I have to search for questions. He is unresponsive. He makes me interrogate him; he gives one-word replies. I think he knows I am not really interested in answers to the questions I ask him—he seems cross and stubborn with me for even trying.

He is wary of strange men with mean, sinister faces and of wild-eyed men and women in the street who talk out loud explosively to themselves. (He keeps an eye out for them always. Many of them use such filthy language.) He is unnerved by erratic behavior of any kind (even mine when I'm drunk or kidding around in certain ways in public or with his friends. He prefers me to remain dignified when other people are around). If I do lose my temper with my wife or my daughter, or if one or the other of them begins shouting at me, my boy is apt to continue fretting over our abrupt motions and cruel threats and accusations long after the argument has ended and the rest of us are back on favorable terms. My wife and I make endeavors now not to quarrel in front of the children, mainly because of the bad effect our fights have on him (and the salubrious effect they generally have on my daughter. They cheer her up. My daughter will come sniffing up avidly whenever she scents the elements of a marital quarrel brewing and will often gratuitously, and shrewdly, supply the remark needed to make it erupt, although she will sometimes blanch and shrink out of sight in dismay if the outbursts she had hurried up so enthusiastically to observe, and so hopefully to participate in, turn more vicious and hurtful than she could have envisioned. There were times, in large, noisy, crowded cafeterias or restaurants near sports arenas, circuses, or shopping centers, or in hotel lobbies or railroad stations or other cavernous, ceilinged areas in which we found ourselves surrounded by strangers, when he would feel that someone there was glaring at him with hot fury and cold dislike, planning something hurtful. He told me this; and sometimes he would describe and single out the person, always without daring to turn his own face around to look again. When I moved my own eyes swiftly to gaze at the man he was indicating, I was unable to be positive he was wrong. But I always told him he was imagining it. I did this to reassure him). He has a patient habit of mulling things over privately for long periods of time, roving through his mind in search of keys to secret riddles, and I am often unable to determine positively if he is indeed bogged down in something clutching and constraining or if he is merely relaxing and I am only imagining that he is in difficulty. (I make him enigmatic. I do not want my boy to be troubled by things he is unwilling to discuss with me, even if I am prominent among the things that are troubling him. I do not like him to keep things from me. I would like to know he confides in me. I would like to be certain he is eager to answer all my questions fully, even though his answers might be lacking in excitement and amount to little of interest to either of us. How can I know something he is thinking about is boring until I know what it is? I would like him to want to tell me everything he thinks of even before it occurs to me to ask. He is, after all, really my only son, and I think he should understand how much I need him.)

He is a good-looking son, kind and inquisitive, and everyone likes him (or seems to. You never can tell with people. Although he can. I know I do). He has fine, sandy hair, a sense of humor impish and intelligent, and pale, slight shoulders and arms.

He is not strong. He is slim. His health is good. (We are pleased with him. My daughter is pleased with him now too, although she used to be envious and nasty, and we all enjoy talking about him to others.) It is like pulling teeth from him sometimes to get him to complain. (We tend to think of him as happy and to diagnose his occasional episodes of disobedience, resistance, or distress as symptoms of fatigue or sore throat and fever or as normal lapses into tolerable, childish misconduct.) He is a good little boy and always has been. He is, as my wife or I reflect aloud with pride on occasions, almost too good to be true (and he isn't! Something's wrong, and I think I have always known it, although I have never been brave enough to say so or even to face the thought without diverging from it in haste. All my wife worries about is that he not grow up to be a homosexual, although there is not a single reason to suspect he will. I worry about that only a little.

"He's being good just to spite me!" my daughter will allege impulsively in his presence during some of those playful or tempestuous disputes one or the other is always instigating, sometimes in humor, sometimes with virulence. "Nobody is that *good* all the time."

"Lesbo," he retorts winningly.

And we are all compelled to chuckle in affectionate appreciation, although my wife is not certain such language is appropriate in front of us or healthy or proper for either one of our children to use, or even know).

But something *is* wrong, I think, although I have always kept my chilling doubts to myself (as though by not taking notice of anything unpleasant that might be emerging, it will go away. There are people who believe they cure their own cancers that way. My wife. Something bad is going to happen to him. I know that now. I know it will. And something bad is going to happen to me too, because it does happen to him. Perhaps it is happening to him already. I think it is. It started far back) with the foolish, unarticulated prayer that (primarily for *my* benefit, rather than his) it would heal itself adequately by

212

and by and spare me the anguish and difficulty of having to deal with it, or at least that it would remain dormant and undetected by anyone else until I have lived out my allotted three score years and ten in joy, prosperity, and fullest contentment (ha, ha. And am dead, of natural causes) and can no longer be harmed by whatever tragedy it is that pains and cripples him severely (I can't stand pain) or strikes him down fatally. I am skeptical about my chances, for I have noticed that people tend to grow up pretty much the way they began; and hidden somewhere inside every bluff or quiet man and woman I know, I think, is the fully formed, but uncompleted, little boy or girl that once was and will always remain as it always has been, suspended lonesomely inside its own past, waiting hopefully, vainly, to resume, longing insatiably for company, pining desolately for that time to come when it will be safe and sane and possible to burst outside exuberantly, stretch its arms, fill its lungs with invigorating air, without fear at last, and call:

"Hey! Here I am. Couldn't you find me? Can't we be together now?"

And hiding inside of me somewhere, I know (I feel him inside me. I feel it beyond all doubt), is a timid little boy just like my son who wants to be his best friend and wishes he could come outside and play.

On the positive side, he seems to be outgrowing his fear of bees, spiders, caterpillars, crabs, and jellyfish, he tells me, and I want very much to believe him.

"I am," he repeats, insistently. "The last time I saw a bee I didn't even want to move away."

"But were you afraid?" I question him closely. "Did the bee come near you?"

"I was with someone," he admits.

He is marvelous at math and good at science, but no longer cares to excel in either (to the chagrin of his teachers, who express disappointment with him. He is puzzled by their disapproval). Mixed in with all his confusion, I'm sure, is an unresolved

Oedipal conflict of staggering dimensions and attendant horrifying castration fears (mine, of course), but he is still too young, ha, ha, to be bothered by any of *that* stuff now.

He thinks (I think) that he is much smaller than he actually is. I think he thinks he is funny looking and disappointing and that we want to abandon him, take him somewhere far, and leave him there. For what reason we should want to do this he doesn't know; he doesn't say. (Maybe he believes we want to abandon him because we think he's too small. He isn't small. He is average, and only seems small in comparison to boys his age who are taller. He is a little small, and it's no use telling him he isn't.)

It used to be that when we brought him someplace he had never been before, or even to certain places he had been, to somebody's home, or to a public place that was deserted or one that was noisy and crowded (dark or bright didn't matter. He didn't like crowds; he didn't like emptiness. Or the taking him there. Or taking him anywhere. When we went, he was not convinced we were going where we told him we were going until we got there and not sure when we were there that we intended to bring him back), he would maneuver craftily to keep his shoulder or hand against my wife or me, persevere at remaining in physical touch with one or the other of us, at least until he had scrutinized his surroundings and us to his satisfaction and concluded that the time had not yet come (that it was not yet the occasion of his doom. Sentence had already been passed. Only the moment of execution remained in doubt). He wants to hold on tight to what he knows he has (even though he is far from pleased by what he knows he has). He does not want to lose us. He does not want to be alone, not even at home, and usually leaves the door to his room open. He doesn't spend much time inside it. (He is disturbed when he comes upon doors to other rooms in the house that are closed. The door to my daughter's room is always closed, almost as a flamboyant gesture of spite. Ours may be open or closed. And evenings and mornings when my wife and I make love, or one of us thinks there's a possibility we might, it is closed. We don't feel we want anybody to watch. Group sex will never be for us.) He does not want to be with people he doesn't trust; and he does not trust people he has not known long. He does not always trust us. (So who else does he have?) He would take hold of our hands and be unwilling to let go. We were often embarrassed. We made him let go.

"Let go," we would coax. "Let go of my hand. Please let go now."

The blood would drain from his cheeks and lips (which would turn blue. His lips would take on a bluish tinge when he was very tense). He would tremble, swallow, and gag; especially if, after forcing him to let go, we then also forced him to go off somewhere alone to play or told him to sit in one place while we moved out of sight to another. He always hung back an instant with a sickened, pleading look whenever we told him to go off someplace and play. So we stopped. (He would not want anyone to see his painful apprehension, even while baring it to us. We have stopped making him come with us to places he does not want to go. He has the choice of remaining home without us. My daughter is usually too busy now to devote much attention to him.) He is always saddened and disconcerted when one of our Black maids or white nurses leaves (even though he might not like her. He usually does not like them and wants no more to do with them than he has to). He feels we may be planning to get rid of him the same way.

"Do you want to get rid of Derek?" he has asked.

"No," I have lied.

"Do you want to get rid of me?"

"No. Why should we want to do that?"

"Do you want to get rid of anyone?"

"No."

"People who work for you?"

"No. Just one. Why should we want to get rid of you? You're too good."

"Suppose I wasn't?"

"You'd still be too good."

"Sometimes," he confesses ruefully, with a soft (perhaps tricky) smile, "I dream at night that I'm all alone someplace and I don't know where to go. And I cry. When I wake up, my eyes are wet. Sometimes," he continues humbly, now that he has decided to tell, "I'm not even asleep when I have this dream."

His look is sad when he finishes, and he waits in silence for my answer with a searching, sagacious air.

(I do not know anymore whether he tells me things like this because they are true, or because he observes how strongly they affect me. Mistrust and acrimony are starting to cloud my emotions toward him. More and more frequently, I am incited to react toward him contentiously and competitively, the way I do toward my daughter. I try not to.

"Are you angry?" he will ask.

"No," I will lie.)

Or, as he asked of us one day when we dressed him in a shirt, knitted tie, and jacket to take him to what we told him was the circus (it *was* to the circus, although he did not seem to believe it, and he looked so lovable, wholesome, and neat in the pink tattersall shirt I had bought for him in the Boys' Shop at Brooks Brothers and miniature blue blazer we had also bought him from Brooks Brothers, with his shiny, silken hair—which was his own and not from Brooks Brothers, ha, ha—clean, wet, parted, and combed.

"Am I clean enough?" he asked, turning from the full-length mirror after he had been scrubbed and dried and dressed.

"Clean as a whistle," I assured him.

"Shiny clean," added my wife):

"Are you going to put me in a taxi and leave me there?"

"No, of course not!" I retort with anger, appalled. "Now why in the world would we want to do that?"

He responds with a self-effacing shrug. "I don't know."

But he does seem to know.

216

"Are you playing games with me?" I demand. "Or do you really mean that? Do you really think we would leave you in a cab? What would the cabdriver say?"

"Can I ask you?" he requests meekly.

"What?"

"What I want to."

"I won't get angry."

"You're angry now."

"I won't get angrier."

"Go ahead," my wife says.

"If you do want to get rid of me, how will you do it?"

"With hugs and kisses," I answer in exasperation. "You're ruining the whole day. This is a hell of a conversation to be having with a handsome boy who's all dressed up in a tattersall shirt, tie, and blazer. And we're taking you to lunch at a fine restaurant too."

"I don't want to go."

"Yes, you do."

"You'll enjoy it."

"I don't even want to go to the circus."

"Yes, you do."

"You'll enjoy it."

I don't like the subway. (I have had scared terrifying fantasies centered around him in which he does get lost, or has been misplaced, on a subway, but never thoughts or dreams in which I leave him someplace deliberately, or even want to. The door closes between us before we can both get on or off together, separating us. Or we are walking together and I turn my head away for an instant, and when I turn it back, he is gone. Or I forget about him: he slips my mind: and I remember only afterward, when he is no longer present and has disappeared without trace from my dream, that he is supposed to be with me. I am unable to guess where he has gone. There is only void. I feel lonely then, and it is not possible to be certain which one of us has been lost. I feel lost too.)

He withdraws from bad smells (he thinks, perhaps, of rot, poison gas, or suffocation. He does not want to fly to the moon, ever, and neither do I) and is alarmed by unexpected loud noises (or creeping, mystifying, stealthy ones. So am I, and so, for that matter, are antelopes. He tends to believe that he is the only one who reacts to such things, and that he is the only one who ever feels in danger). He cannot understand why wars, muggings, bees, math, spiders, basketball, rope climbing, nausea, ferocious, menacing men (real and deduced), and public speaking all have to be there for him to contend with, lying in wait for him visibly, stinking, inevitable, unmovable, and unappeasable (and, frankly, neither do I, although there does not seem to be much that I or anyone else can do about it. It is the custom); why he is expected to work harder at math and learn much more and attach more importance to it just because he is good at it, and why his classroom teachers (most of them female), who used to be so delighted with him because of his precocious insight into numbers, are now disappointed with him because he has lost interest in math for math's sake and why they let him know they are displeased (they feel he has rejected them. He has let them down); or why he must try harder, strive to excel, determine to be better than all other boys in pushball, kickball, throwball, shoveball, dodgeball, baseball, volleyball. (It all does seem indeed like an awful lot of balls for a young little man like him to have to carry around, doesn't it?) He particularly hates basketball. He does not know what he is supposed to do (and will not let me explain to him. He will ask a specific question and accept only the answer to that question and no more. He cuts me off curtly if I try to go on. He rebuffs me). He is never sure when to shoot and when to pass, and he is too self-conscious and ashamed to confess his predicament and ask. He has never made a basket; he is afraid to try; he never shoots unless people on his team all yell at him: "Shoot! Shoot!" Then he shoots and misses. He is never able to keep straight in his mind when he is supposed to block and obstruct and when he is supposed to catch, pass, cooperate, and shoot. He relies on his instincts, and his instincts are not reliable. In the bewildering disintegration of his judgment, he tends to lose track of which of the other kids are on his team and which are on the other as the thumping action swarms and slithers around him (like the grasping, unfurling long legs of a large spider, I would imagine. He has never told me this). He passes the ball away to opponents and commits other errors just as conspicuous, and he is pushed and yelled at as a result (and often does not know why. He does not learn from these mistakes because he does not understand what they are. The danger that he may repeat them hobbles his thinking and increases the chances that he will). Forgione shakes his head in disgust. My boy takes it all in. (I imagine all of this too and melt with pity for him.) My boy would like to make baskets and be able to pass and dribble flawlessly. (He doesn't want to shoot because he knows he will miss.) He is afraid to play basketball and wishes he didn't have to.

By now, he does not want to go to school at all on days he has gym. (Or public speaking. Or knows he must make an oral report or read a written one.) He has gym three days a week; he worries about gym three of the other four days. (Saturdays he takes off. One-day school holidays afford no surcease. Unless they fall on a day he has gym. Then he is ecstatic.) By now, he is afraid of Forgione, and feels despised, and of the assistant gym teacher (whose name he doesn't know; nor does anyone, he seems to indicate, and he does not describe him, so I have no idea how old or large he is), which must be another ghastly danger for him to have to stave off. (How would *you* like to be a tame, somewhat shy and unaggressive little boy of nine, somewhat shorter and thinner than average, and find yourself put three times a week, every Monday, Wednesday, and Friday, as regularly and inexorably as the sun sets and the sky darkens and the globe turns black and dead and spooky with no warm promise that anyone anywhere ever will awaken again, into the somber, iron custody of someone named Forgione, older, broader, and much larger than yourself, a dreadful, powerful, broadshouldered man who is hairy, hard-muscled, and barrel-chested and wears immaculate tight white or navy-blue T-shirts that seem as firm and unpitying as the figure of flesh and bone they encase like a mold, whose ferocious, dark eyes you never had courage enough to meet and whose assistant's name you did not ask or were not able to remember, and who did not seem to like you or approve of you? He could do whatever he wanted to you. He could do whatever he wanted to me.)

"He doesn't try to win," Forgione asserts to me in reproach about my boy after I can no longer, in good conscience, postpone going to the school to remonstrate with him privately on behalf of my boy.

(My wife has been nagging me to speak to Forgione or to complain about Forgione to the principal, which I hesitate to do because that would be sneaky and perhaps unnecessary and perhaps even produce disastrous repercussions.

"It's *your* child, isn't it?"

It *is* my child, and I suppose I really can't, in good conscience, have him suffering such nauseating sorrow three mornings a week, as systematically as clockwork, can I, although there may prove to be nothing I can do about alleviating the situation without making a raucous pest of myself, and I am not like that. There must be something I can do. I have a shaming feeling there is something other fathers would do.)

"I'm sure he does his best."

"He doesn't want to beat the next fellow."

"That's his nature, I guess," I murmur apologetically.

"That's not his nature, Mr. Slocum," Forgione persists sententiously. "He wasn't born that way."

"That's his nature now."

"He doesn't have that true competitive spirit. He doesn't try his best to win. He lacks a will to win."

"You aren't going to give him one by picking on him, Mr. Forgione," I venture timidly, in as harmless a tone as I can manage.

"I don't pick on him, Mr. Slocum," he protests earnestly. "I try to help."

"He's afraid of you, Mr. Forgione. He used to enjoy coming to gym and have fun playing games.

When he was little, he always liked to play. Now he doesn't. Now he doesn't want to come here at all."

"He has to come here. Unless he has a medical excuse."

"I'll have to get him one."

"You're not blaming that on me?" he protests defensively.

"I'm not trying to blame it on anyone." The advantage, I feel, is now mine, and I continue with more confidence. "I'm trying to find some way of making the situation here easier for him."

"How is he at home?"

"Fine. When he doesn't have to worry about coming here."

"It's no good to make things too easy for him."

"I don't want to make things too easy."

"He has to learn to cope."

"With what? Rope climbing?"

"He has to do that here. He'll have to do it other places."

"Where?"

"In high school. In the army, maybe. He has to do lots of things he doesn't want to if he wants to get ahead."

"I don't want to argue with you."

"*I* don't."

"I want to try to help him try to work things out."

"I help him," Forgione maintains. "I try to encourage him, Mr. Slocum. I try to give him a will to win. He don't have one. When he's ahead in one of the relay races, do you know what he does? He starts laughing. He does that. And then slows down and waits for the other guys to catch up. Can you imagine? The other kids on his team don't like that. That's no way to run a race, Mr. Slocum. Would you say that's a way to run a race?"

"No." I shake my head and try to bury a smile. (Good for you, kid, I want to cheer out loud. But it's not so good for him.) "I guess not."

I have to chuckle softly (and Forgione grins and chuckles softly also, shaking his trim, swarthy head complacently in the mistaken belief that I am chuckling because I share his incredulity), for I can visualize my boy clearly far out in front in one of his relay races, laughing that deep, reverberating, unrestrained laugh that sometimes erupts from him, staggering with merriment as he toils to keep going and motioning liberally for the other kids in the race to catch up so they can all laugh together and run alongside each other as they continue their game (after all, it is only a game). I am gratified, I am thrilled, by this picture of my boy but I know I must not reveal this to Forgione (or display any mockery or superiority), for Forgione does have him totally at his mercy three times a week and can get back at me effectively by inflicting all sorts of threats and punishments on him (while I am safely encapsulated in my very good job in my office at the company, smothering in accumulating hours, aging and suffocating in stultifying boredom or quivering intolerably with my repressed hysteria, or otherwise ambitiously preoccupied in something idle or sensual. Who can possibly imagine all the vicious crimes and atrocious accidents that might befall my boy or my wife or my daughter or Derek while I am biting my nails at my desk or peeing in a urinal here or ducking encounters with Green or feeling Betty's, Laura's, or Mildred's tit in Red Parker's apartment or flirting with Jane in the narrow corridor outside the Art Department? I can. I can imagine them all, and then fabricate new ones without end. Disasters troop across my mind unbidden and unheralded like independent members of a ghoulish caravan from hell or from some other sick and painful place. I seek skeletons in decaying winding sheets as I study company reports, and they aren't grinning. I smell strange dust. I shudder and am disgusted. I am often contemptuous of myself for imagining the catastrophes I do. They are not worthy of me, and I will often catch myself at it with a scornful rebuke and make myself get busy on something immediately to evade the sinking feeling in my chest and the network of tremors I experience coming alive inside me like a wicker basket of escaping lizards. Or a gale of colorless moths beating their wings. Or I telephone home in order to make sure that everyone is all right, as far as whoever answers the telephone there knows. The most I can generally find out, though, is that there has been no news of anything bad. Even if I undertook daily the fantastic effort of calling each member of my family in turn at the different places they are, I would have no binding assurance that some tragedy had not struck the first one I called by the time I had finished talking to the last one. Of course, I could use three or four telephones and get them all on at the same time. At least that way I could be sure—until I hung up. At least a policeman or ambulance attendant does not pick up the telephone when I call home, and I am thankful for that. In these situations, it's a case of no news being good news, I always say. Until the bad news comes. Ha, ha. I'll bet I haven't said that once. Until just now. Ha, ha again). And I therefore dare not risk offending Forgione, or cause him to dislike me, for my little boy's sake (if not, eventually, for my own. What troubles him troubles me). So I am meek, humble, respectful.

"Does he have to race?" I inquire. I am deferential and disarming with Forgione. I control my urge to be sarcastic: I do feel superior to him, and afraid; I know I am better than he is, and that I am weaker. "Isn't there something else they can do? Or him?"

"Life is hard, Mr. Slocum," Forgione philosophizes (and I would like to tell him to take his philosophizing and shove it up his ass). "He has to learn now that he has to be better than the next fellow. That's one of the lessons we try to teach him today to prepare him for tomorrow."

"I feel sorry for the next fellow."

"Ha, ha."

"Who is the next fellow? Poor bastard."

"Ha, ha."

"Maybe he's the next fellow."

"That's why we train him now. You wouldn't want that to happen to him, would you? You wouldn't want him to be the next fellow that everyone's better than, would you?"

"No. He's this fellow to me. He's the one I care about. That's why I came to the school to speak to you."

"Maybe I am riding him a little too hard. But that's only for his own good. It's better to be too hard than too easy. Sometimes."

"Mr. Forgione, you have children, don't you?" I argue back in a reasoning, slightly more determined manner (inasmuch as he has not yet smitten me dead with the short-handled hammer of his fist and has retreated to a position of vindicating himself). "You know I can't just look the other way and allow a child of mine to come here if he's going to be so upset by things or because he thinks you pick on him. Would you do that?"

"I don't pick on him, Mr. Slocum," Forgione objects quickly, swallowing uncomfortably, his neck bobbing with emotion. "Did he tell you that?"

"No. But I think he feels that way."

"I try to help him. I don't pick on him. It's his friends. It's all his friends that pick on him. They get angry and begin to yell at him when he slows down and starts laughing and doesn't try to win. Or when he passes the basketball deliberately—he does it deliberately, Mr. Slocum, I swear he does. Like a joke. He throws it away—to some kid on the other team just to give him a chance to make some points or to surprise the kids on his own team. For a joke. That's some joke, isn't it? He throws the ball away when someone charges at him. He gets scared. It's his friends that get angry and start to yell at him—not me. I just try to get him to do things right so they won't. That's when they really get sore and turn on him, and then he starts moping and looks like he's gonna cry and says he feels sick or has a sore throat and wants to see the nurse and go home. He acts like a baby. He turns green. I don't like to say this, Mr. Slocum, but sometimes he acts like a baby."

(I could kill Forgione for that; I could kill him right there on the spot because what he says is true and I didn't want anyone to notice.) "He *is* only a kid, you know." I fake an indulgent laugh.

"He's nine years old."

"How old is that?"

"That's time to start learning some responsibility and discipline."

"I don't want to argue with you."

"I don't. I tell you this, Mr. Slocum. He's got to learn to start facing things."

"He's trying. He's trying very hard."

"Then they don't want him on their team. They complain to me that they don't want him on their team if he's not going to try. It's no secret. They do it right in front of him. Now they complain to me that they don't want him on their basketball team because he isn't any good. That isn't such a funny joke to kids who are playing their hearts out to win. What am *I* supposed to do? Whose side should *I* take? Can't *you* do something?"

"That's why I came here. To try."

"Can't *you* talk to him, Mr. Slocum? And try to explain to him why he should try to do things straight and right. It would be better for him, not me."

It would indeed. With no great effort I can picture my little boy looking scared and green with Forgione, for I have seen him often enough looking that same way with me when we are in some unfamiliar place and he thinks I'm going to leave him there or that I am going to try to make him dive from a diving board. How can I explain to Forgione that I like my little boy pretty much the way he is (do I? I'm not sure), that it's all right with me if he's not competitive, aggressive, or outstanding, although there are times, I must admit to myself, when I wish he were more so, when I am displeased with him because he isn't, and would probably be more proud of him if he were. And I guess he must know that too.

He does not know yet that I have come to Forgione to try to obtain special favors for him, and I do not want him to find out. I think he might be too mortified, feel too nakedly degraded, ever to be able to face Forgione again. And I know that I will be peeved with him when I leave for having made it necessary for me to come (and for spoiling my morning and most of my peace of mind the evening before after I made my decision to go to Forgione once and for all and was already regretting it), and that I would like to kick all those other snarling, snapping little

kids in the ass and smash their smelly, snotty, bellicose little heads together for ganging against him.
(And making it necessary for me to do something.
Oh, shit—I sometimes think I could be so happy alone,
but I know I would not be.)

"Can't you leave him out for a little while, if he
asks you to?"

"Is that what he wants?"

"Yes, I think so. Although I don't think he will
ask you. And I will talk to him. But don't say anything."

"If that's what he wants, sure. I don't pick on him,
Mr. Slocum."

"Maybe he'll get a little of his confidence back.
Just for a few days."

"I try to help."

"Tell him he looks a little tired or something."

"Have him come to me with an excuse. Let him
limp a little or bring a note from you saying he
feels sick. So the other kids don't find out and make
fun of him."

"It wouldn't be a lie. On days when he has gym,
he does feel sick and feels like throwing up. He doesn't
eat breakfast. He comes to school without eating
anything."

"I didn't know that. Does he say anything about
me?"

"Only a little. Nothing bad. That he's scared and
can't do things. He didn't ask me to come here."

"I'm only trying to help him when I get on him
to try to make him do better and try harder. I'm
just trying to get him to realize his maximum potential
so he'll do the best he can and be much better off.
You ought to tell him I said that."

"I don't even want him to know I came here. Let
him do push-ups or something for a few days and
see what happens when we take the pressure off.
Okay?"

"He's no good at push-ups, either. Or at chinning,
sit-ups, rope climbing, or tumbling. In fact, I don't
think I could give your boy a good rating at anything,
Mr. Slocum. But running. He's pretty fast. But he
doesn't always try. He kids around."

(I have to suppress another smile.) "Maybe that's hereditary," I say. "I was never much good at anything either."

"Oh, no, Mr. Slocum," Mr. Forgione corrects me with a laugh. "Anybody can be good at anything physical if he works steadily to develop himself."

"I hope so," I concede diplomatically. "I know I used to spend a lot of time in gyms," I lie. "But I never seemed to improve very much."

"You've got a good build. I can see that from here. Your boy could be a fine athlete, Mr. Slocum, if he'd only apply himself harder. He can run like a weasel and has quick reflexes. You should see the way he flinches when he thinks I'm gonna yell at him. Or one of the kids."

"He may be afraid to ask you. Even if I give him the note."

"I know what to do."

"He might be too embarrassed. And you won't tell him I spoke to you. I wouldn't want him to know."

"Sure. No."

"And you're not going to get even, are you? Take it out on him because I came here to ask?"

"No, of course not," Forgione exclaimed indignantly. "Why would I want to do that?" (Because you're human, I think.) "What kind of a man do you think I am?"

"Cro-Magnon," I reply crisply.

(But that, of course, I say to myself. Outside myself, I laugh softly in a pretense of congeniality. I wonder if the time will ever come when I will begin, without recognizing I am doing it and without detecting the change, saying out loud the things I now say privately to myself or verbalize in contemplation and if I will therefore become psychotic or one of those men—more often than not they are women—who talk out loud to themselves on sidewalks and buses. If that happens, I will blend my inner world with my outer world and be disoriented in both. I will be pathetic. I have trouble enough deciding which is which now and which one is the true one. I worry gravely about all lapses of self-control. I think it may already be happening, that I do talk to myself out loud—my children tease me and say I did talk to myself out loud while rehearsing the speech I wasn't allowed to give at last year's convention—sometimes when I'm drunk or very deeply immersed in work or introspection. Sometimes I catch myself almost mouthing words that I intend to write down when I get to my desk at the office or in my study at home, or that I plan to say to whoever it is I am on my way to meet. At least, I think I always catch myself in time. I can't be sure. There may be times already when I don't. I know I occasionally do gesticulate with hands and head when preparing myself for conversations, but that is almost in the nature of a rehearsal of which I am aware. I am so afraid that I will start talking to myself someday that I feel I already do. People will make fun of me. Or look the other way and pretend I'm not. I suffer chest pains frequently because I'm so afraid of suffering chest pains someday and dying of a heart attack. My brother died of a heart attack while waiting for something in the waiting room of his office, and my father died of something else while I was still just a little boy, and my mother, as I can't forget, was struck down in her old age by a number, some of them too subtle and minute in individual effect to be counted, of cerebral vascular accidents, as they are euphemistically called—they did not seem like "accidents"—that set her tongue clattering inside her mouth when she tried to talk and turned the rest of her, eventually, to bloodless pulp. God, how I grew to detest the sight of her! And wanted to cry, in love, sympathy, and self-pity, and would not let myself do anything like that. I kept control. I was strong. I can be strong and unemotional when it comes to someone else. I think I may worry as much about talking out loud to myself as I worry about stuttering. I think some of my dreams may be homosexual. I think I'm afraid I might start stuttering incurably when I even think that thought of being homosexual. I don't know why I feel that way about those dreams. And I also feel that some of my other dreams may be heterosexual, and I do know why. I am chasing and pumping away with girls in those dreams and almost

228

get there, almost get all the way in, but never do. I never even come. They always break off unfinished. Is it my mother? Nude and cooperative? And know also that much of my waking life is composed of defenses against behavior I am not aware of and would find difficult to justify. Why do I feel like crying so often and why do I refuse to let myself do so . . . ever? There are times, afterward, when I wish I did and regret I didn't. I often used to feel like crying after quarreling with my daughter. I am no longer proud that I can remain unmoved. I hope desperately that my little boy never finds out I'm a fag if that is what I really am, although I think I might derive some nasty gratification if my wife began to harass herself about that possibility. I hope I never lose control of myself in anything. I never have, not even with a girl. I wish I wanted to. I'm glad I don't. I hope I never have a stroke that makes me stutter or renders me paralyzed or speechless. I hope I never have a heart attack. I hope I'm never senile and pee in my pants and want to molest children. I wonder what kind of person would come out if I ever did erase all my inhibitions at once, what kind of being is bottled up inside me now. Would I like him? I think not. There's more than one of me, probably. There's more than just an id; I know that; I could live with my id if I ever looked upon it whole, sort of snuggle up and get cozy with it, exchange smutty stories. Deep down inside, I might really be great. Deep down inside, I think not. I hope I never live to see the real me come out. He might say and do things that would embarrass me and plunge him into serious trouble, and I hope I am dead and buried by the time he does. Ha, ha.)

"Ha, ha, Forgione," is what I do say, to indicate to Forgione that my question was not intended to be taken seriously. "I do. I really do, Mr. Forgione."

"What?"

"Appreciate it. I'm glad you understand."

"That's okay, Mr. Slocum. I'd do that to help any kid."

"Thank you, Mr. Forgione. I feel much better now."

I put my hand out eagerly in order to shake his, and find that I feel much worse when I depart from him.

I went there braced for battle, prepared to take on all comers, if necessary. I have won my point too easily, and go away feeling I have lost. I am depressed. *Good God!* I catch myself wondering as I commute into the city by train to my office again. *What in the world have I done to my poor little boy now?* I find myself furious with my wife for having prodded me to go there. Suppose Forgione is intent upon revenge? I don't want to have to go looking around for a private school to transfer my little boy to, not now; yet Forgione can make me. I am in his power, and he is not in mine. Last year it was a saturnine battle-ax of an arts and crafts teacher (*his* Mrs. Yerger, and mine too again, for that time. For every season there is a Mrs. Yerger, it seems—there always has been—and a Forgione too) that came very close to making me move him out of his public school (he pleaded with me to let him stay) into an expensive private one that might have turned out to be just as evil. This year it is sturdy, umber Forgione, with his damned gym and muscular physique. (We moved to Connecticut to get away from Negroes. Now I've got this stocky Italian weight-lifter to worry about.) Does Forgione, as I now feel absolutely certain, resent my having come to the school to complain to him (did I make a very bad impression on Forgione?) and criticize and interfere with his work in relation to my child? Will he strike back at me, with immense personal satisfaction, by browbeating and disgracing my boy even more than he already has? Tune in the next day to find out. And I do tune in shakily all the next day to find out, with a telephone call home at lunchtime (to ask, ostensibly, if there is any important mail, but really to make certain he is still alive, that no word of his death has come from school) and with another telephone call home late in the afternoon.

"Guess what?" my boy exclaims cheerfully, answering the phone (to my vast relief and amazement).

For Forgione, bless his noble heart, turns out fine. (I am more tense about gym than my boy at breakfast that morning. My coffee is flavored with the bitter taste of bile. Forgione is an executioner, masked in dire, enigmatic intentions, and I ponder all day long in my office over what kinds of criminal atrocities are being committed against my boy behind the brick walls, closed doors, and blind windows of that penitential institution of a school. I am more tense than my boy because I can objectify anxieties he does not even know he suffers from yet. I have an imagination that is infinitely more sophisticated and convoluted. He does not know yet about Leopold and Loeb, and I do. He does not know about cunning, older, polymorphous perverts, driven and deranged, who brutalize and murder children for no good reason. I have the same scorching foresights he has of strange, fierce, scowling men abducting, harming, dismembering him, and there are days—or used to be when we lived in the city, and still are, even now that we have retreated into the suburbs—when I will glare accusingly and belligerently, bluffing, of course, at every strange man I see in his vicinity—handymen, delivery men, construction men, insurance men, even clergymen—as potential kidnappers, sadists, ruffians, degenerates, or mad murderers who torture and mutilate their disbelieving victims before and after killing them, even though I know *that's* impossible. I picture it anyway. And now Forgione's face is swimming among them, heartless, symbolic, carnal, alien. I am crazy: no wonder my boy tends to be fearful. For a long time in the city I was too fearful to allow him to walk to school alone, even though the school building was only a few blocks away and other kids his own age were already doing it; at the same time, I kept urging him to get up the courage to try it, pointing out to him that he was big enough and intelligent enough and would have to do it someday, and assuring him that nothing would happen to him if he waited always for the light to turn green and looked in all directions before stepping from the curb and crossing each street. I was afraid he'd get lost. I am afraid of traffic accidents. I also feared drunkards, junkies, unhappy laborers, explosions, bigger, bullying school-boys, and truants from high school come to prey on the smaller children in elementary school, most of them Black, Puerto Rican, or Italian, who would take his ice cream money, tear his clothes, bloody his face, or pull his ears off; I was even afraid of falling cornices, and so, I think, was he. I would telephone the house two or three times a day from my office to ask if any important mail had come or my dry cleaning, but really to make sure that everyone there was still alive, as far as anyone who was there could tell—if no one answered the phone when somebody should have, I would think of calling the police, the apartment building superintendent, or one of the neighbors—to verify that he had made it back home safely from school for lunch—which meant, by deduction, that he had made it *to* school safely after breakfast—and that he had found his way back home successfully again after school—which meant, once more, that he had made it back safely *to* school after lunch, that day.

"Do you want to talk to him?" my wife would ask.

"Only if he has anything he wants to say to me."

"He doesn't. Do you have anything you want to say to Daddy?"

"No."

"Do you want to ask him anything?"

"No."

"He doesn't. You sound disappointed."

I would *be* disappointed. I'd feel he should *want* to talk to me, even though he had nothing specific to ask or tell. Hadn't I worried about *him?*

I would brood about that too: his ingratitude. After all, I was investing so much of my feelings in *him,* wasn't I?

Every trip from home for him then was, for me, another venture into unknown perils that were inching close. I would feel about him the way I believe I used to feel about my wife and daughter, the way some passive part of me still feels every time I walk up the ramp into an airplane on an ordinary business trip: I'm not sure I will ever come down. Wouldn't it be ridiculous for me to die on an ordinary business trip? Every day that he and I and the rest of us remain alive is another miracle. Isn't it wonderful that we can still be here and have not yet been knocked off by some accident or crime? I think that. I don't trust cars. God knows who may be driving the ones close enough to collide with us. I don't trust my wife when she is driving, especially now that I know she drinks during the day, and I don't like my daughter at night in a car driven by some kid who might be drunk also or loony with drugs. I don't really worry as much as I used to about my wife and daughter, possibly because they have both survived early childhood and seem old enough now to take care of themselves, or possibly because I no longer care for them as much as I used to, as much as I know I do care about my boy and myself. I do have morbid outlooks about myself; I don't like closed doors, sick friends, bad news. And my boy is still young and vulnerable enough, we feel, and he does too, to be very much in need of our love and our protection. And I know I do care for him, and I worry nervously about what jeopardy I have placed him in with Forgione, who— God bless him again—turns out to be just fine indeed.) Forgione, in fact, proves a surprisingly good-hearted man, and he is more generous and discreet with my boy than I would have thought him capable.

"I don't have to do anything in gym anymore," my boy continues with elation. "I don't even have to play. Until I want to."

And from that day on, my boy is a swaggering princeling. (But it does not, of course, last.) He treasures his respite in the beginning (he thinks he's smart); he basks in leisure, luxuriates in school and at home. Along with boys with plaster casts on hands and arms and legs and those with heart damage or other seriously crippling deformities, he is allowed to remain out of the games and races and to pass the time in the gymnasium watching and strutting, although he is required to report there and remain for the entire period. (There is one boy in the school his own age who is totally blind, and he is excused from gym. The school keeps him as an experiment.)

233

My boy spends his time in gym strolling **around** the outskirts of activities, he tells me, feeling superior. (He is pulling a fast one, he feels, and wants others to observe that.) He feels he ought to be envied. (He isn't. He is only a temporary novelty.) In a short while, though, and all at once, a transformation occurs, a draining of confidence, and he flickers in sallow indecision. He perceives that he does not want to be different (perhaps he is startled by the threat that what he thinks he is faking will prove to be real and that he is facing the risk of being excluded permanently, like those other boys his own age who do have heart murmurs of pathological origin and are not allowed to play, and all those others we always see wheeling and hobbling about who are disabled and deformed).

He wants to be the same as healthy ones, part of a normal group (before he is left behind and finds he can no longer catch up), even though he does not esteem the group and does not enjoy what the group is doing. He does not enjoy being classified with those who are weak and crippled (and cannot even band together into a group of their own, because they are handicapped in separate ways) and exiled and ostracized. So he stops faking fatigue, a limp, and a sore throat and goes to Forgione to report he thinks he feels okay again.

And back he plunges voluntarily into games and races (and into chinning, rope climbing, and tumbling, as well, which he still hates but consents to endure, for he cannot declare himself fit for games and races but not for gymnastics). And now he roars like a lion and fights like a tiger; he runs like a weasel and says "hubba, hubba, hubba" dutifully like an eager beaver.

("Mr. Forgione says nice things about me now," he discloses to us smugly one day.

"I scored four points today," he tells us another. "I was the second best on my team.")

And he learns it is easy enough for him to be good enough in sports if he has that true will to win (and even, perhaps, in gymnastics, if he applies himself), just as it is very easy for him to be good enough in math (even without applying himself). He is not the best at anything, but he is good enough (and lots of fun), and the ones who are the best enjoy him and want him on their teams now. (They are tougher, bigger kids, and he is one of them now.) He keeps cumulative (clandestine) records (in his mind) of his own and all other kids' triumphs and failures in pushball, punchball, kickball, throwball, shoveball, upball, assball, and baseball (he is back now with all his balls, ha, ha) and is aware always of how he stands in comparison with others. (He is like our sales staff at the company.) In relay races and in basketball, he will connive to place himself opposite some fat boy on the other team whom he knows he can beat. (He feels guilty about that fat boy, and sorry for him. But someone is going to beat the fat boy anyway, so it might as well be him.) It is not so much that he wishes to look good but that he wants to avoid looking bad. It doesn't really bother me anymore that my boy does not want to be best.

"Maybe I do," he hints enigmatically.

"Then why don't you try?"

"Maybe I know I can't," he replies, with a trace of a mysterious smile (and it is impossible for me to know, as I study him, whether he means what he implies or is merely practicing slyly some cryptic and discerning and unpleasant game he has devised to confound me. Is he clever enough for that?).

At least we do know he is smug: on days when he does do as well as he hopes to in gym, when no one makes fun of him or criticizes, or when nothing at all happens to him there (or in public speaking), he comes home confident, jubilant, and composed, swaggering almost conceitedly with an exalted view of himself, so it all isn't all bad. On days, though, when something bad happens, he turns cranky and anguished and declares he hates things and people, so it isn't all good either. He sits motionless, then rises abruptly to move about in rage and shame that he only expresses in dribs, yearning (we see) to cry, but restraining himself unhappily. It is pitiful to watch him (my wife and I want to cry too), and infuriating (I want to yell at him in displeasure, perhaps beat him, for reacting so disconsolately). He doesn't want to talk about unpleasant events beyond a certain point. And he continues to try as hard as he can at chinning, push-ups, and rope climbing. He improves, but slowly (and he probably is already gazing ahead in discouragement to high school and more chinning, push-ups, and rope climbing and to swimming nude with others in the chlorinated pool. He probably will not want to swim nude. I know I didn't. If he is like so many of the rest of us, he will think that his cock is small and in danger of vanishing. I will have to tell him, if he lets me, to stare at it in the mirror if he wants to see it look as large as it appears to other people. I will not go into the phenomenon of foreshortening, unless he asks me. He does not like having his hair cut, even when we leave it long, and is afraid of having his teeth pulled or his gums injected with Novocain. If he had to have his tonsils taken out now, he would probably refuse to cooperate and would have to be lugged to the hospital by force. We clipped them from him at the right time. He doesn't like injections of any kind, except those in the side of his ass when he really does have a red throat and is too disoriented by fever to remember he's afraid). And Forgione is pleased with his "hubba, hubba, hubba," for my boy, under Forgione's tutelage, tries hard now, competes vigorously, and has developed (or at least displays for Forgione, Forgione's assistant, and others in the gymnasium) that good competitive spirit.

"You didn't tell me," my boy murmurs to me accusingly, "that you went to see him."

"How did you find out?"

"I did."

"Who told you?"

"I did. You told me. Just now. By answering me. I guessed. You did. Didn't you?"

"You ought to be a lawyer too."

"I figured it out."

"You wanted me to do something, didn't you? I know you did."

"You didn't tell me," he answers peevishly. "So I'd know."

"What else did you think I could do?"

He shrugs.

"You aren't being fair to me now. If you don't tell me what else you think I could do."

"I don't know."

"You're glad I did. Aren't you now?"

And soon, almost imperceptibly, because things have worked out so well for him, he moves back to worrying again about going to school on days when he has gym (and public speaking), worrying that he might perform poorly and his team might not win because of him. Because he has shown a good competitive spirit and a true will to win, he is now afraid of losing. He does not want the blame. He is afraid of making errors in baseball, mistakes in basketball, stumbling or dropping the beanbag in relay races, and getting part way up the rope and being unable to come down, ever, without falling. And soon, at breakfast on days he has gym, he is depressed and pasty again and complaining of nausea and red throats. He has bellyaches and doesn't want to eat, and I am right back where I started from. (I get nauseated when I see him this way, and I don't eat either.)

"Do you want me to speak to Forgione again?"

"No, I'll manage."

"I will if you want me to."

"I don't."

"Or to someone else. I can go to the principal."

"No, don't. I'll manage."

"Big shot," I respond with a laugh, trying to buoy him up. "You don't even know what *manage* means."

"No. But I will, anyway."

"Okay."

And he does. So far.

(While I watch.)

(And wait.)

He is waiting too.

(For what? He doesn't know. I don't have to ask.)

The pity of it is that (instead of waiting) he could probably be having a good time if he would only stop waiting and were allowed to develop and do things his own way. But he has never been allowed to (I wasn't allowed to either, and nobody else I can think of was); he is not being allowed to; and he will never be allowed to, not by me, by my wife, by himself, or by others. (I wonder what we would all grow up to be if we were never ordered about by anybody else. Apes, probably. Instead of babies.) The "others" are all virtually superfluous by now, even Forgione: there is enough right here at the family hearth to shackle, twist, and subdue him (and render him and all the rest of us all the more susceptible to haphazard, unfriendly "others" like Forgione and Horace White, with whom I really have little contact, and whom I know I would be afraid of even if I did not have to be. He's got the whammy on me. We were put into that relationship from the beginning, before we even met. And he is a simpleton. Horace White is a simpleton; yet, I was prepared to kneel before him even before I knew he existed. What has happened to my boy and me to make us so subservient?). Only my daughter has never attempted to improve, damage, educate, or train him (just to dominate and manipulate him) once she succeeded in tearing her way through that draining, turbulent period of stunned and bitter wrath that raged through her like a flame at his having been brought into her home and family at all (even though she had been taught and promised for months that a brand-new baby brother or sister for her, and a baby for us also, would be coming into the house soon and wasn't she happy and lucky? The irony is that she would have felt equally deprived if we had permitted her to remain an only child. She did not want Derek either and blames herself for his affliction—at times —because she cursed him silently before he was delivered and wished him harm). She used to try to injure my boy when he was an infant in his crib or lying prone or supine, unable yet to walk or squirm away to safety, on our bed or on our blanket on the floor or sitting in his stroller or his high chair or his playpen. (She tried to push him over and he did not know what was happening.) When he was learning to walk she would knock him down if we were not alert enough to stop her. She would try to put her fingers in his eyes. Now she's stopped. They get along well now, affectionately (unless she is with friends and does not want him around), and almost never have any serious disagreements. (He gives in readily.) My daughter does not like me to shout at him: she cannot bear it when I lose my temper with him and begin shouting, and she will often scurry away in flight with her head down or whirl upon me hysterically and harangue me (and then scurry away before I can reply and defend myself. That's another tactic of hers, and I am often caught unawares and find myself shouting abuse or explanations into empty space after she has sped away. That makes me angrier). Sometimes when I do lose my temper with him (usually without realizing I have done so until afterward) and begin to bark demeaning, threatening remarks (I have called him "sissy" more than once merely by warning him contemptuously not to act like one, although I never intend to do just that while I am doing it and will detest myself afterward for having done so and seek some face-saving way of apologizing to him. Usually by letting him see I am no longer angry with him and offering to buy him something expensive I think he wants), shouting, probably (without knowing I am doing so and denying that I am if charged), with my lips deranged, probably, and my teeth bared and my whole red or bloodless face glaring at him, probably, my daughter will fling herself between us heedlessly to shield him from me, holding her ground there to defend him against me and actually start to cry.

"What are you doing to him?" she will demand, with tears forming and spilling from the corners of her eyes. "Why can't you leave him alone?"

She does not yield so readily to emotion when my fight is with her. When my fight is with her, she tries (with fortitude, perversity, with face-saving spite) *not* to let me make her cry (not to give me the satisfaction of seeing I can affect her even remotely. I am a matter of "supreme indifference" to her), as though that is what I want to do. (It often is.) I always desist as soon as I see I can, curbing my own spiteful intentions and drawing back from her mercifully.

(Nothing is suppressed in our family.)

(In our family, everything is suppressed.)

On the other hand, my daughter can be cruel to my boy when she is with her friends and feels no need to show him off, shutting him out rudely, discouraging especially those slouching, mumbling teen-age boys from kidding with him or tossing a ball or paying any attention to him at all. She does not want him around when she is with her friends. (She does not like to share.) She will separate them and chase him away, snapping:

"Don't bother with him. Don't let him bother you. Go back to your room."

He does not know what is happening to him when this does. He does not know what is happening to him now. He wants to be like other boys he thinks, mistakenly, we want him to be like. He thinks he is not now the person anyone wants him to be. We don't want him to be like everybody else. We want him to be like we want him to be (but we haven't spelled that out yet even to ourselves. So how could *he* know?). We want him to be different, and superior. (But we also want him to be not much different. Frankly, I don't know what I want him to be—except no trouble. He does not know yet what he's supposed to want to be when he grows up, except that he now knows he is not supposed to want to work in a filling station. And I can't guide him. A doctor? He has no idols. A lawyer? I wouldn't want that. I have no models to give him. James Pierpont Morgan II? August Belmont, Jr. III? Clara Bow? At least I had people like Joe DiMaggio, Babe Ruth, Joe Louis, and Cordell Hull I could want to be when I grew up, although I'm glad now that I didn't grow up to be any of them. But I still don't know yet what I want to be when I do grow up. Or even what I *should* want to be. I'd like to be rich. I know this much: I don't want to be President of the United States. They have bad reputations, and ruin neighborhoods.) So he struggles manfully (childishly), doggedly, dazedly to change himself into everybody else his age. He wishes to be able to conform successfully without effort or thought. He wants to wear, at nine years old, what other boys of nine or ten are wearing (even though he might not like what they are wearing) and experience the same enthusiasms and frustrations. (He really doesn't care about baseball anymore, I feel, and also feel he doesn't know that yet. One time when I was very young and had doubts, probably, that I would ever grow larger or older—there must have been a time, I think I recall, when I was unable to believe I would ever be any different from the lonely, isolated little boy I was then—I wanted to be a jockey in a cerise and white cap and ride race horses, even though I had never been on a horse and was too frightened even to step near the ponderous, spiritless ones that delivered ice or milk or laundry or dropped dead in the street, like people—I never could feel friendly with my brother's wife after he died and never see her now, am not clear in my mind anymore just where in New Jersey or Long Island she and her two children, my niece and my nephew, live—and soon attracted dense, buzzing clouds of green and blue pot-bellied flies. As a jockey in a red and white cap astride a huge, speeding, lunging thoroughbred, I think I felt I could trick everyone into believing I was a tiny man instead of a little boy. I'm glad I never became a jockey. I would be too heavy now and would not win many races.) And this is unfortunate in many ways (not for me, but for him) because there is so much about him entirely his own that is profoundly endearing (there is also much about him that he would be better off without, and maybe he will be able to shed that all someday, although I doubt by now that he will be able to shed any of it. By now I feel we remain pretty much the same. We grow scar tissue instead, or corns and callouses in our soul that cover, and we forget, when we can, what's there. Until occasions remind us); and what there is about him that is good, I'm afraid, we all (not my daughter, but me, my wife, Forgione, the world, and even those dusty, ghostly rocks and craters familiar to us on the moon now, connoting dark times and transparent specters) collaborate to destroy. (Even Derek exerts a haunting effect upon him, and tall buildings. If we were stones instead of people we would have an effect upon him, perhaps that same one. Everything does. Perhaps we are stones to him. I do not know how he thinks of us. I know I do not always think of my children as children. I know I remember my father now and other dim adult males from my early childhood, and even my big brother then when he was alive and I was small, as figures of voiceless stone capable of swift, unobservable journeys from one locale to another and communicating always obscure intimations of awful, indefinable things about to occur.) He has a lively, imaginative taste for the comic, some courage, and a warm heart; and even the colored maid we have now, who pads about on tiptoe in my presence and is rarely valiant enough to talk in anything louder than a faltering mumble, will grin at something unpredictably funny he has said or done and blurt out impulsively:

"That boy. Oh, that boy of yours. He is really something."

We think so too (we are somewhat vain and braggarty about those precocious intuitions and idiosyncracies of his in which we can take proprietary delight) and (like rigid, high-powered machines not really in charge of ourselves) operate automatically to change him—to harden him, soften him, smarten him, desensitize him—lying to him and to ourselves (as I lied, and knew I was lying, when I filed my mother away into that repulsive nursing home that I described to her and others with false energy as being beautiful, new, and comfortable as a modern hotel) that it is for his own good. (And not for ours.)

"Be good," we fire at him. "Don't be afraid. You can do it. Try. Try harder. You can be anything you want to be. Don't do that. You're getting me angry."

(Maybe it is for his own good.)

(And maybe it isn't.)

And even the nurse we have for Derek now, who is considerate to none of us (and especially dislikes my daughter, who is defiant and impolite to her and never truckles at all), not even to Derek anymore,

I suspect, singles my boy out periodically for loud flattery that embarrasses him and clumsy, possessive hugs that make him miserable as he sees her scowling reproachfully at the rest of us in taunting contrast, even though she does not approve of the way he acts toward Derek either.

"It's no wonder he doesn't want to play with him," she has censured the rest of us in his presence, "when he sees how the rest of you treat him. None of you want to play with him."

My boy does not like Derek's nurse or the harsh spotlight of her praise. (I think he senses he is being used by her to get at us.) He is actually afraid of her, as he is afraid of most of his teachers and the school nurse, and wishes, without evincing any of his dislike (he is always afraid to show antagonism to anyone), to avoid all possibilities for conversation with her and to escape her pinches, touches, and embraces. (He finds her obnoxious.)

"Get rid of her," I decide on cranky impulse and snap at my wife.

She sighs. "I don't want to have to start again."

"She isn't even good to him. She doesn't keep him clean."

"Where should I go?"

"Get someone young this time, can't you?"

"Where?"

"I wish we could get someone who would really like him. You can't. I know. They don't want to have to take care of him either."

"Maybe I should do it. Maybe I should devote my whole life to taking care of him."

"Holy you."

"What do you mean?"

"Become a nun."

"Maybe I should."

"Not if you think about it that way. You don't mean it. You'd probably be worse to him than any of them."

"Fuck you."

"I like the way you swear now," I joke. "You say 'Fuck you' much better than you used to."

"Practice. You taught me."

"I'm proud."

"Only with you. You make it very easy to say 'Fuck you' to you."

"You do it better too."

"Any complaints?"

"Not at this moment."

"Well fuck you again."

She rolls away from me. We are nearly naked. I continue laughing.

"I'm trying to," I tell her, coaxing her back. "I'm trying to get you to."

"Maybe we should start thinking about sending him away someplace."

"Maybe we should stop talking about him now."

"I want to."

"No."

"Where he'll be much better off."

"No, I said."

"We'll have to, sooner or later. Think about it, I mean. You never want to think about it."

"I don't want to talk about it."

"We'll have the money now. Won't we?"

"You don't understand, do you?"

"I'm asking."

"If I decide to take the job. I've got money enough for that anyway. It isn't money."

"Maybe you should decide to take it."

"I don't want to talk about it now."

"I'm talking about the job."

"I don't want to talk about that, either. No, you're not. You're not talking about the job. You lie a lot about yourself."

"We have to talk about it sometime. We're going to have to decide. Stop a minute, will you? You can't keep ducking away forever."

"I can till I die."

"Don't joke about it."

"And leave you with him?"

"Don't joke about that, either."

"And her. And him too. Won't *you* be busy."

"None of that's funny."

"Don't you want me to die?"

"You know I can't stand talking about things like that."

"He's still too small. I don't want to talk about him now. When the kids might hear."

"Should I lock the door?"

"You're just as bad," I remind her. "If I say yes, you say no. When I say send him away, you say we can't."

"It's for his own good."

"No, it's not."

"Maybe we should send them all away," she observes hopelessly.

"What do you mean by that?"

"I don't know what I mean," she retracts. "The kids are embarrassed by him. Ashamed. Maybe we should send them both away and keep him."

"How would it help to send them away?"

"I didn't mean it. You know that. I'm just feeling bad. They don't like to have their friends come to the house and have to see him. Neither do we."

"Talk about yourself. I'm more comfortable about him than you are."

"No, you're not. You just pretend. You put on an act. He makes everyone uncomfortable. He makes everyone who comes here put on an act."

"Fire the old cunt."

"How would that help?"

"It would help us. She's rude to everyone."

"Don't use that word. You know I don't like it."

"That's why I use it. You ought to get used to it by now. I am. In fact, I'm starting to get very used to it right now."

"It's easy for you."

"Sure."

"I know you. You'll probably be out of town the day I tell this one she has to go and the day the new one comes."

"You bet."

"You can laugh about it. You don't even want to interview them."

"I don't know what to ask."

"And then you're disappointed. You're never satisfied with the one I get."

"I'm just glad you can get anybody at all."

"Until you get used to them. Until you can't stand them and then want me to fire them."

"Get a young one, can't you? Can't you get a psychology major or something?"

"We need someone full time. She has to do everything for him. He can't do anything. You never like to face anything unpleasant."

"Do you?"

"Don't you ever feel guilty doing this while we're talking about the children, or even Derek?"

"No. Why?"

"Even the day my grandmother died you wanted to make me do it."

"I wanted to make you do it the day your father died too."

"Don't say that. You know how I felt."

"What does one thing have to do with another?"

"I do. I don't feel right about it."

"Why should I?"

"It doesn't seem right."

"Do you want me to stop? I will if you want me to."

"It seems all wrong now. It seems dirty again. I don't know. I don't feel right."

"Don't you like feeling dirty?"

"No. You do."

"You feel fine."

"Am I coarse? Am I ever common?"

"Now I do. Yeah, I guess I do feel guilty. You did that. You do that a lot. We don't do it that often when we're talking about the kids or something serious."

"I feel dirty."

"Then I will stop. It's no fun for me. Do you want me to?"

"Lying here talking about sending him away."

"You were doing that. I wasn't. Is that what's making you feel dirty? Or me?"

"Do you love me?"

"I'm trying to. My hardest. Feel how hard I'm trying to love you."

"Don't do that."

"This?"

"You know what I mean."

"This?"

"Fuck you again."

"Lock the door."

"You lock the door, since you're feeling so peppy."

"Fire the old cunt."

"Christ, you're vulgar," she says, and means it.

"You're profane," I answer. "Suppose your new minister could hear you now. I bet he'd like to see you now. Aren't you glad I'm vulgar?"

"No feelings."

"Feelings," I maintain. "Plenty of feelings. Feel my feelings."

"No, I'm not glad."

"What do you want?"

"I don't know. I'm ready."

"I'll lock the door."

"I'll start looking around."

"I think he's getting much better, isn't he?"

"No."

"Don't you?"

"He isn't. You always say that."

"If I don't, you do."

"I know," she admits.

"I think he listens more. He understands now. He keeps himself cleaner."

She shakes her head firmly. "I don't think she's doing him any good at all."

"Don't you see it?"

"No. He's not supposed to get better. He's never going to. That's what they say."

"Then let's fire that fucking old cunt. None of us like her. She doesn't like us. She reminds me of old Mrs. Yerger, falling into decay."

"Who's Mrs. Yerger?"

"A woman I used to work for. When I was a kid."

"Did you ever do it to her?"

"Christ, no. She was worse than my mother."

"I'm ready, I said. Why do you keep doing that?"

"I like it. You're supposed to like it too. All bosom and no breasts."

"Like me?"

"Unlike you."

"I've got small breasts. You keep telling me."

"They're big enough. I like them small."

"You've tried any other kind?"

"Never."

"Did you lock the door?"

"Yeah. How come *you're* so worried?"

"*Locked* it?"

"Open up."

I close my eyes sometimes when I'm making love to my wife and try to think of somebody better than Mrs. Yerger or Derek's old hag of a nurse to spice things up. I try to think of pink and fecund Virginia and can't: she is all silk and exotic fragrance when we begin, but my imagination lets me down and she withers rapidly in my mind into what she would be today if she hadn't gassed herself in her prime (although I doubt *she* thought of it as her prime, ha, ha), a short, dumpy pain-in-the-ass (like just about all the rest. I wish these women's-lib people would hurry up and liberate themselves and make themselves better companions for sexists like me. And for each other) of an offensively chattering woman ten years older than my wife, nearly (Oh, God dammit, why can't some things other than stone remain always as they used to be?), and much less attractive physically, with large pores, a shrill, grating, demanding voice, low-cut dresses with tops of wrinkling boobs, and too much giggling and red makeup. I am much better off with my wife, I know; so I open my eyes and look at her (and that delays my coming until I am ready. I wish I did have some sensational young sexpot in the city I could use in my erotic reveries at home. But I don't: just about all the girls I do succeed in getting and keeping are sad in one way or another and faintly insipid. So I tend to utilize my own wife in my sex fantasies, even while I'm right there fucking her. That's the kind of faithful husband I am. Sometimes when I'm in bed with another girl in the city or out of town and find I'm already sorry I started, I close my eyes and pretend I'm fucking my wife. Such fidelity. My wife should be honored to learn she rises in my thoughts on such occasions when we are apart, but I don't think I'll tell her. She might not like it as much as I do).

I know my boy doesn't like it when our bedroom door is locked (and used to say so before he began to intuit secret sex inside. I think my daughter said to him once:

"They fuck in there.").

Or when Derek's nurse reaches out to snare him in gnarled fingers on bloated hands and crush him against her musty, collapsing bodice (neither would I. Like Mrs. Yerger's, there is massive, slovenly, thrusting front with no suggestion of anything else in back but stale and folding space), and more than once, in debased supplication, he has wretchedly admonished my wife:

"It's your fault. Why do you let her do it to me? I wish she'd stop touching and pushing and squeezing me like that. I don't even like her. Can't you make her leave me alone?"

"Please try to leave him alone," my wife has said to the nurse countless times politely and awkwardly. It has done no good. "It upsets him. He doesn't like anyone to pay too much attention to him. Don't do things for him. He'd rather do them himself. And try not to touch and hug him so much if you can. He's funny. He doesn't like to be touched and kissed. He really doesn't like it from anyone."

"He doesn't mind it from me," the warted witch cackles back. "I have a way with children. He likes me. I can tell. He likes the way I cuddle him and he likes the way I smell. I always keep myself very clean because I know how children feel about smells."

He doesn't like to be hugged or kissed or touched by anyone, in or out of our family, although he has the mannerism of bumping slightly against me with his shoulder when he is feeling close to me or leaning a moment against my wife (except my daughter, with whom he likes to roughhouse and wrestle, and who enjoys tussling with him when she has time. When he was younger, two, three, four, or five, he used to get hard-ons regularly with my wife when she was bathing, powdering, or dressing him, point to them

249

and comment and inquire about them to both of us with pleased and open curiosity. They even tickled and felt good, he let us know. And we would reply to him intelligently and frankly because we did not want to inhibit him. It was okay with us if he had hard-ons; if anything, we were proud to see them. Today he no longer waves them gloriously in front of my wife or me and doesn't talk about them to us. I can't remember if I had hard-ons at nine. I think I can remember having sneaky, scary, tinglings in my tiny cock much earlier as I sat or hovered near my mother in her bedroom and watched her dressing or removing her street clothes to drape herself into one of her housecoats that always hung shapeless and looked faded. I remember her pink or colorless corsets with those dangling garter snaps and bone or celluloid stays that were always going in or out, although I don't remember knowing what a corset was for. I know I remember sitting mute and devious in her bedroom *just* to watch. Why else would I want to, if not out of sexual longing? I also remember having dreams later about exactly the same thing: my mother is in her corset and slip and I am prowling about her bedroom pretending to be occupied with something else. My boy gives money away to other kids. I know I shouldn't care), but he has a special aversion to Derek's nurse (to *all* Derek's nurses, and so do I. And to all of our maids. When he comes into the kitchen for something to eat, he would like to be able to get it himself, and so would I. None of the nurses are young; and all seem to have a peculiar and individual ugliness about them, a lantern jaw, missing tooth, scarred eyebrow, or infected lip. Even when they don't, they do), for he senses some potential destiny for him, some crippling danger, in the fact that she is called a nurse and that she has come to dwell with us only because Derek has a damaged brain, that she came to us from somebody else who had a damaged brain, and that, when she asks for a day off and never returns or when my wife fires her, she will move from here to somebody else with a damaged brain. (He never imagined, I bet, and neither did I, that there are so many people with

250

damaged brains.) She is a veiled harbinger, a jinx, a spinning pointer, a bearer of fatal tidings (he confuses cause and effect, I think, blaming her presence in our home for Derek's condition, instead of Derek's condition for her presence in our home), and he does not want to be singled out by her as next. Yet, he does not want to be forgotten.

"When you were in Puerto Rico," he says, "three years ago, were you very sad?"

His question was unexpected. "That was two years ago," I correct.

"Three."

"I think you're right."

"Two years ago your convention was in Florida."

"You are right. No, I wasn't sad. Were you?"

"I thought you weren't coming back,"

"Is that why? I did come back, didn't I? You didn't say anything about it."

"I was too sad. I was angry at you also."

"How come?"

"I don't know."

"At what?"

Shrugging, he says he doesn't know.

"Are you angry at me still?"

"I get angry every time you have to go away."

"Are you angry at me now?"

"Do you have to go away again?"

"Will you have to be angry?"

"Will you have to go?"

"Yes."

"I guess I won't. Maybe I won't."

"I miss you when I'm there."

"Do you have a good time?" he asks.

I pause a moment to reflect. "I do," I answer frankly. "All in all. I work very hard. At the beginning. And worry a lot. But then I relax and have a good time."

"You don't telephone from conventions."

"It's hard."

"That's why I'm not sure you're coming back. You get very mean to everyone here before you go to a convention."

"No, I don't."

"Yes, you do. You don't listen when we talk to you and you yell a lot."

"No, I don't."

"You do."

"Is that true?"

"Yes. And you lock yourself in your room or the basement and talk to yourself."

"I don't *talk* to myself," I answer with annoyance, and then smile. "I rehearse. I practice a speech and a slide show I know I have to give at the convention."

"That's talking to yourself. Isn't it?"

"I want to make sure I can do it right and that I won't forget any of it when I have to give it."

"I get scared when I have to speak in front of the class."

"So do I. I know you do."

"Does rope climbing scare you?"

"Yes. And I'm never going to climb another one, now that I don't have to."

"Do you like it?"

"Rope climbing?"

"Making speeches?"

"I think so. I like to be asked, anyway. I get nervous too. But I enjoy it. Especially afterward."

"I'm always afraid that I'll forget what I'm supposed to say. Or that I'll get sick and have to vomit while I'm doing it. Do you know why I'm afraid to swim? I think if I ever started to drown, I'd be ashamed to call the lifeguard."

"You'd call him."

"Or that somebody in the class or the teacher won't like me. It. What I say."

"That's why I work so hard and practice so much. And why I get a little angry if one of you interrupts me. To make sure I remember it."

"Do you always remember?"

"Not at the convention. I've never been able to give one. My boss always stops me."

"Green," he guesses with certainty.

"Yes."

"I don't like Green, either," he confides, lowering his eyes. "Because you're afraid of him."

"I'm not afraid of him."

"You don't like him."

"I like him okay."

"You have to work for him."

"That's part of the trouble. When people have to work for other people, they don't always get along well with the people they have to take orders from. But it doesn't mean I don't like him. Or that I'm afraid of him."

"Do you?"

"No. But I like him more than a lot of the others."

"Why do you have to work in a place where you don't like so many people?"

"Because I like it. I have to."

"Do you know what I'm afraid of?" he asks, looking up at me with interest.

"Lots of things."

"Do you know what else I'm afraid of?"

"Lots more things."

"I'm serious."

"What?"

"That you won't come back."

"I'm surprised. I never thought you thought about that."

"I do."

"All the time? Or only at conventions?"

"All the time. But mostly at conventions. Because you're away so long."

"Sometimes I call. When I get there."

"And other times when you're away long. I don't mind so much if it's just for a day. I start to feel you won't come back."

"I always have. I'm here now, ain't I? I'm going to have to die sometime."

"I don't want you to."

"I'll try not to."

"Sometimes I do."

"Do what?" I am more shocked than offended.

"Want you to."

"To die?"

"I'm not sure. When I'm angry. Or have dreams."

"You're never angry."

"I get angry a lot when you go away," he pushes

253

on intently. "No. I don't want you to die. Ever. I don't want to die either. Are you angry?"

"No. Are you?"

"No. I don't think I would be afraid so much if I were with you and Mommy instead of here. I don't want to be left alone."

"You wouldn't be alone. You'd be with Mommy. A person can't be afraid all the time of all the bad things that might happen to him."

"I can," he snickers mournfully.

I smile back at him in response. "No, you can't. Not even you. I'll bet I can name a lot of things you're afraid of that you don't even have time to be afraid of all the time."

"Don't," he exclaims, with mock alarm.

"I won't," I promise sympathetically. "Something comes along that takes our mind away. Should we talk about things that make you laugh instead? Have some fun? Kid around?"

"All right," he answers, with a momentary smile.

"You begin."

"Can a person's blood turn to water?"

"Huh?"

"That's what somebody told me."

"That's what makes you laugh?"

"No. I keep worrying about it."

"When did he tell you?"

"A few months ago."

"Why didn't you ask me sooner?"

"I wanted to think about it. He said he read it in the paper."

"I don't think so."

"That's what one of the kids at school told me. That a person's blood can turn to water and he dies."

"He was probably talking about leukemia."

"What's that?" he inquires sharply.

"I knew it was a mistake to tell you," I reply, with a regretful click of the tongue. "Even as I was saying it. It's a disease of the blood. Something happens to the white corpuscles."

"Does it turn to water?"

"No. I don't think so. Not water. Something like it happens, though."

"Do people die from it?"

"Sometimes."

"Do kids like me get it?"

"I don't think so," I lie.

"It was a kid he said he read about. He said it was a kid who died from it."

"Maybe they do then. I think that once in a while—"

"Don't tell me about it," he interrupts, putting both hands up in another comical gesture of awestruck horror that is both histrionic and real.

"I already have."

"Don't tell me any more."

"You always do that," I criticize him kindly. "You ask me all the questions you can think of about something terrible and then when I finish answering them you tell me, 'don't tell me about it.' "

"Are you angry?"

"Do I look it? No, of course not."

"Sometimes I can't tell."

"Sure, you can. You keep telling me I yell all the time. No, I'm not angry. I want you to talk to me about the things you're thinking about, especially the things you can't figure out."

"Do you? I will."

"I do. Ask me anything."

"Do you fuck Mommy," he asks. "You said I could," he pleads hastily, as he sees me gape at him in surprise.

"Yes, you can," I answer. "Sometimes."

"Why?"

"It feels good, that's why. It's kind of fun. Do you know what it means?"

He shakes his head unsurely. "Is it all right for me to ask you?"

"It's all right to ask if I do. I think it would be better to ask someone else what it is. It would also be a little better if you used a different word."

"I don't know a different word. Screw?"

"That's almost the same. You can use the word you want. It's a little funny, though, to use it with me. Use it. I suppose it's good enough."

"Are you angry with me?"

"No. Why do you keep asking me that? Don't you know when I'm angry or not?"

"Not all the time."

"I thought I yelled so much."

"Not all the time. Sometimes you don't talk at all. Or you talk to yourself."

"I don't talk to myself."

"You bite your nails and don't even listen to any of us."

"Do I? What makes you think I'm angry when I'm like that?"

"We're all afraid."

"That doesn't mean I am. Sometimes I'm just feeling unhappy. Or concentrating. I can be unhappy too, can't I?"

"Would Mommy be angry if I asked her?"

"What?"

"If you fuck her."

"Only because of that word. Maybe not. Don't do it in front of anyone."

"I better not."

"You already asked me. I already told you. If you ask her too, it wouldn't be to find out, would it? It would just be to see if she gets angry."

"Was it all right? To ask you?"

"You already asked me that three times. I'm not angry. Do you want me to be angry?"

"I thought you'd be. I bet other kids' fathers would be."

"Maybe I ought to be. I'm better than other kids' fathers. Is that why you keep asking me? Are you trying to make me angry?"

He shakes his head positively. "No. I don't like it when you're angry. I can tell. You're starting to get angry now, aren't you?"

"I don't like it, either. And I'm not."

"Emphasis?" he remembers.

"Emphasis," I confirm.

"I don't like Derek," he remarks without pause. He wears a troubled, injured look.

"You're not supposed to say that," I instruct him mildly. "You're not supposed to feel that way, either."

256

"Do you?"

"You're not supposed to ask that."

"You just told me I could ask you anything. That's another thing I always think about."

"Yes. You can. It was okay for you to say what you did and ask me. And it was also okay for me to answer you the way I did. It was all right for both of us. Can you understand that? I hope that's not too confusing for you. I'm not trying to duck out on the question."

"Am I supposed to say it or not? I don't know."

"I don't know," I admit resignedly. "I'm not sure I like Derek, either, the situation I mean, the way he is, maybe even him too. I'm not sure. But we often have to live with things we don't like. Like my job. Me too. I don't know what to do about him yet. And nobody can help me."

"He makes me uncomfortable."

"He makes me uncomfortable."

"I'm ashamed to bring friends here. I think they'll make jokes about me."

"So are we. But we try not to be. We shouldn't be. And you should try not to be too. It's not our fault, it really isn't, so we pretend we aren't. Ashamed. What else?"

"Money."

"What about it?"

"You want me to tell you what's on my mind, don't you?"

"Yours too?"

"Do we have any?"

"What do you want?"

"That's not why."

"What is?"

"You buy me everything."

"So far."

"Have we got too much?"

"For what? We're not millionaires."

"Have we got enough?"

"For what?"

"You make it hard," he charges. "You're kidding now. And I'm not."

"To give away?" I kid some more, taunting.

"You give money away," he rejoins in defense.

"To cancer and things like that. Not to other people. Not to kids. I don't shovel it out to kids I hardly even know like it's too hot for me to hold on to."

"Leukemia?" he asks.

"I knew you'd ask that. Do you want me to?"

He shrugs almost indifferently. "I would like it, I think. But don't take it away from cancer."

"I knew you'd start worrying about leukemia the second I told you. I'm sorry I told you."

"I'm not worrying about it. I don't even know what it is yet."

"Don't you ever worry about things you don't know about?"

"Like what?"

"Why should I tell you if you don't know about them?"

"Now I'll worry about them. Now I'll worry about things to worry about," he adds, with another gloomy laugh.

"That's what a lot of people do worry about."

"You don't like me to give money away," he observes. "It makes you angry, doesn't it?"

"Is that why you do it?"

"I'm not gonna tell."

"You're not gonna do it."

"Yeah?"

"I'll kick your ass," I warn him jocularly.

I am happy we are talking together so freely. (I relish those moments when he seems to enjoy being with me.)

He used to give money away (probably still does, or will start giving money away again when the warm weather comes and he finds himself outside the house a lot with other kids), pennies, nickels, and dimes (money that *we* gave him for himself, or that he took from us, although I don't believe he has started stealing coins from us yet or lighting matches. That will come with masturbation. That's the way it came with me. I stole coins from everyone in my family and set fire secretly to everything I could find in the medicine cabinet that I discovered would burn with a flame. I squeezed blackheads from my face and fiddled with

258

cigarette lighters with enormous fires. And jerked off. We didn't want him to. I used to try to explicate for him with professional authority why it was improper for him to give presents that we gave to him away to somebody else, and that the money we gave to him was a present. It was talking to the wall. He would hear me out dutifully every time; but he would not grasp what I meant. His face was vacant, patient, and condescending. I did not know what I meant either, or why I even tried to make him stop. And continued to try. It was only pennies, nickels, and dimes, and yet I moved in on him with the same zealous dedication with which I used to attack the blackheads around my nose and squeeze from my skin tiny yellow filaments that could have been pus. I think I felt him ungrateful). I think he still does give money away, for I have noticed that he and his friends, like my daughter, who is not normally generous, and some of her closest friends, tend to give money and other things back and forth to each other without keeping record or demanding return. I *hope* he does (even though I've told him he shouldn't), for I would like him to be unselfish. So why did I harangue him? I would like him to grow up to be one of these young people I see so many of today who seem to want to be very good to each other. They even lend cars. We never lent cars. I wish *I* were one of them; I wish I had a second chance to be young and could be part of them. I wish I could be sure they are as happy and satisfied as I think they are. (My daughter isn't happy, and neither is my son, and maybe she will be, and so will my son. Maybe they still have a chance.) Every once in a while my gaze falls on a young boy and a young girl (she doesn't even have to be pretty) walking or sitting in public with their arms around each other trustingly and intimately and I can almost fall down in pain with piercing envy and lust. No, not lust. Envy. Longing. Every once in a while I do find myself with a young girl something like that; but I think she thinks I'm "square," even though she may like me (and sleep with me) for a while. And *I* think she's right:

I *am* square. I am even gauche. I even feel gauche when I'm making my pitch for some girl with my customary flip, suggestive (and predictable) (and trite) repartee, and I think less of myself for being that way even while I am that way and see myself succeeding. I don't enjoy adultery, really. I'm not even sure I enjoy getting laid. Sometimes it's okay. Other times it's only coming. Is there supposed to be more? There used to be. There used to be much more heat. My wife and I used to upbraid him fiercely each time we learned, through crafty and persistent interrogation, that he had given money away again. Sometimes it would not even be to a kid he liked much or knew particularly well, but to one he had just met that summer who simply happened to be with him on the boardwalk or street and seemed to want it more. Sometimes that was the only reason he gave us for doing it. He gives cookies away too, and candy, and lets other children play with his toys, even when new. For some reason, it still galls me (my wife reacts similarly—a mood of jealousy and rejection is what I feel) when we see him permit some other kid to play with some new present we have just given him. (We feel it is still ours, rather than his.)

I used to try to observe him closely to detect if there were patterns, to see if there were any categories of personality or experience into which the different kids he gave his pennies and nickels and dimes to—I'm not sure if he ever gave away as much as a dime—could be made to fit. I didn't find any. He knew we studied him and discussed him. I told him he was imagining it. Sometimes he *was* imagining it when I said so; other times he was not. I still watch him. (If my boy ever does get the feeling he was spied upon, mulled over, and talked about when he was young, he would not be entirely wrong. It will not be entirely a delusion.) I feel so foolish and so ashamed for the way I acted (and perhaps will act again). No more than a penny, nickel, or dime was ever involved. But what furors we raised, my adult wife and I; how outraged and scandalized we were that this five- or six-

or seven-year-old child of ours had given away a penny, nickel, or dime he had gotten from us or somebody else and did not want for himself. We didn't yell at him. We did worse; we patronized, belittled. We were never really angry with him, never deliberately very mean. But we pretended to be (which must have baffled him even more), and we would raise our voices (not yelling, but for *emphasis*), and cock our eyes at him in ridicule, amusement, and disbelief. We would cackle and smirk and make jovial, wry wisecracks as we closed in and down upon him in heartless, patronizing argument (while my daughter, who was covetous of the greater consideration she felt he received, would regard us reproachfully from a corner in which she had chosen to hide, too young and still too reserved herself then to object vituperatively the way she frequently does now) that he must not, ought not, simply should not give his money away.

"Why?"

(Why not, indeed? Who knows? We didn't. Although we took it for granted we did.) We were unfailingly good-natured and convivial as we took pains to convey to him (it was our responsibility as parents to do so, we made plain), repeatedly, that we loved him as much as ever anyway and were not punishing him by criticizing him and were not really mad; but we did rebuke him diligently in cordial, tolerant tones (ganging up on him, two of us at a time) as we tried to educate him, and we did try, emphatically, tenaciously, maniacally, to elucidate patiently for him why what he was doing was not wise or correct.

And the problem was that we could not explain. (We had no explanation that made sense even to us. It is difficult to be persuasive when the only answer to his *Why?* is a lame and dogmatic *Because*. We were worse to him, I feel now, than Forgione has ever been, more cruel and demoralizing than any teacher. I am overwhelmed with remorse. And yet, I know instinctively that I will do it again if he does it again and I catch him, or at least I will feel the urge to. I hope I restrain myself. I know I feel that what he does is wrong. I don't know why it is wrong.

261

I don't know why I feel it is.) I know we were unable to present to him a single truthful and convincing reason why he ought not to give his pennies, nickels, and dimes away to other children if he wanted to. We actually put him on notice that, not to punish him, but only to teach him a lesson, we were going to punish him by teaching him a lesson. We would withhold money for stipulated periods of time: we would not give him any the next time he wanted some; or instead of money for ice cream, soda, or candy, we would give him the ice cream, soda, candy itself, because we did not feel he could be trusted with money; or tell him, so magisterially, that he would have the money to buy his own now if he had not gone and given it away as we warned him not to.

("See? We told you.")

It crossed my mind whimsically to demand also that he always eat it all up himself right before our eyes (rather than run the risk he might give someone a bite from his Popsicle or candy bar), but I never went quite that far. (I am all heart, ha, ha.)

He was so uncomfortable through all these discussions and inquisitions (he didn't know what to do or where or how to look; no matter how much we joshed and chuckled to put him at ease, he was never at ease. His doubtful smile was always forced and wavering as he strained to joke back cordially with us and asked questions and gave answers to ours in a profound and abortive effort to understand just what in the world it was we had grown so determined to teach him, and why) I suppose he really wanted to give up and cry: when I look back now and recall his delicate, furrowed expression, his lowered, obliging voice, it seems evident (now) that he had come awfully close to tears, but he would not (because we did not want him to) let them flow: he masked it well (but I know him better now): he flashed his doubtful smile often at us instead, from one to the other of us, as we harangued and excoriated him affably and he groped undecidedly, with knitted brow, to catch on to and hold what we felt we had explained so fluently.

"Suppose you want the penny later, or tomorrow?" I would point out by way of benevolent illustration.

"Then I'll get another one," he would answer.

"Where?"

"Here."

"From who?"

"From you."

"I won't give you one."

He squinted. "How come?" he asked in puzzlement.

"Because I won't," I said, with a conclusive gloat.

"How come?"

I shrugged.

"Then I'll get it from Mommy."

"Will you?"

"I won't give you one either."

"How come?" He draws back a bit and gazes at my wife.

"You just gave one away before, didn't you? That's how little you thought of it."

He sees us watching him in silence, waiting for his next attempt.

"From the boy I gave it to," he says. "I'll get it from him."

"He won't have it."

"He won't give it to you."

"He'll spend it by then. That's why he wanted it."

"Do you think everyone's so generous?"

"Or he won't give it to you. Not everyone is as generous as you are."

"Or as rich."

"Or as well off. We're not rich."

"So you see? Do you?"

"We won't give it to you."

"You won't have one tomorrow."

My boy is befuddled and gapes at us searchingly, still straining to smile and endeavoring to make some sense of the situation, twisting in confusion (and plucking rapidly, distractedly, at his penis) as he waits for a hint, seeks hopefully to detect some beam of light that will illuminate it as some kind of well-intentioned practical joke.

("Don't pull at your penis," I am tempted to reprimand him, but I don't.)

"Do you have to go to the bathroom?" my wife
does inquire peremptorily. He shakes his head with
surprise, wondering why she has asked.

He cannot figure out what has just happened to
him. A tremor of uncertainty shivers through him as
he turns, looking frozen, from one to the other of us
and finds himself deserted by both.

"How come?" he asks plaintively, and now a note
of misery and total resignation perforates his voice.
(He is ready to capitulate if he has to.)

"To," I summarize with lofty and deliberate relish,
"teach you a lesson."

What a prick I was.

What a selfish, small, obtuse, and insensitive prick.
I am glum with shame and repentance now when
I remember those smug and tyrannical persecutions
of my little boy (and will be sickened with shame
and repentance afterward when I inflict them on him
again. How can I stop myself?). For my own part
(I plead guilty, your honor, but with an explanation,
sir), I honestly believe I was motivated mainly by
a protective and furious desire to safeguard him against
being taken advantage of by other children (even
by my daughter. I never could stand to see him taken
advantage of. It was as though I myself were undergoing the helpless humiliation of being tricked, turned
into a sucker. My own pride and ego would drip
with wounded recognition. That's when I have been
most enraged by him, when I wanted to smash and
annihilate him, at those times when I felt, in a flaring
outbreak of nearly unbridled bitterness, that he was
allowing himself to be victimized and bullied by other
children. So *I* bullied and victimized him, instead). I
have loved and grieved for him almost from the day
he was born, from the time I first noticed his lonesome,
ingrained predilection for staring pensively out from
his crib or playpen (my daughter was not that way,
and neither was Derek, who seemed placid and normal at the beginning). And I loved him also for his
naïve candor and absence of hostility, pitied him

(and gave him black marks sullenly) for his tender impulses and for his many nameless and immobilizing forebodings; he seemed lost and distant and passive to me in a way it seemed I had once been myself and still feel I am at times when my guard lets down and all my strength ebbs away; I have always wanted him immune to abuse and defeat. So I abused and defeated him instead with my unctuous homilies, my meddlesome intrusions on his behalf, with my nagging, endless admonitions and discourses. I never could bear to see him unhappy (and would find it difficult to pardon him whenever he was); so I made him unhappier still (purging myself of some of my own distress in the act of doing so), but always feeling smirched immediately afterwards. (I can never sustain satisfaction from humbling him, as I usually can do when I humble my daughter, and always do when I win fights with my wife. With my wife by now, I think it no longer matters very much either way to either one of us whether I make her happy or unhappy; the difference is not so great nor the effect lasting; by now, I think we have learned how to get through the rest of our lives with each other and are both already more than halfway there. Who would ever have believed long, long ago that I would live as long as I have? But my boy is still only just beginning.) What a blind, petty, domineering, and sanctimonious prick I truly was. He simply could not see, and we simply could not show him. And even while all of these disputes were going on (it was usually during the summer in the country or at the beach, where I rent a house and all of us go almost every year and none of us ever have a good time. None of us but Derek. Who is able to take what simple pleasures he enjoys anywhere, even at home. Like Martha going crazy slowly in our office, hearing voices that bring a glow of pleasuré to her face and playing games on country outings somewhere else as she gazes over the carriage of her typewriter at the blank green wall just a foot or two in front of her. I wonder how she will finally go under, how she will elect to do it, and whose responsibility this Martha our typist really is,

Green, who hired her, or Personnel's, who screened and recommended her. She is not mine. At least in the summer, I can stay alone in the city more when the family is away and am free to have as much fun as I can find), my wife and I were charmed extremely by his peculiar generosity (if that's what it was) and beguiling good nature (we would smile at each other in fond and complacent self-approval and comment about him in fascination:

"He's really something, isn't he?"

"And how. So lovable.").

We were enchanted by his novel unselfishness; we talked about him with gusto to other people, feeling fortunate and superior because he was ours and we were able to do so. We fished for envious praise from other parents, soliciting, collecting, devouring, and waxing fat and glib on good comments about him in corpulent self-esteem. (What a vain and vainglorious, hypocritical, and egotistical prick.) And even then (indisputably now), if we had been asked to pick between a child who liberally gave away his pennies, nickels, and dimes that he did not want or need for himself and one who would always hoard them only for his own use, we would have chosen exactly what we had. We *liked* what we had.

(So why did I try to change him?)

Why did we proscribe and threaten and interrogate? (Why did we feel so affronted?) Why did we not chortle and prattle complacently to him also (as we did in conceit to our friends) because he gave those pennies, nickels, and dimes away, instead of only criticizing and reprimanding him and extracting reluctant confessions and recalcitrant vows? (If I were him—*he*, I know—I think I would hate me now. Why can't I leave him alone? Why can't I leave *it* alone, even now?)

And, of course, most contemptible of all, we did give him his penny, his nickel, or his dime the very next time he asked for it (he was invariably right about that, too, and we were invariably wrong), and his dollar or his dollar and a half for the movies, although we generally could not refrain from giving him something of a sermon with it. (Waste Not, Want Not. He could anticipate our catechism with unsettling accuracy and frequently would recite the words right along with us, especially if our daughter was present, for she could join in with him. I begin to perceive what a stereotype I am only when I realize how often my daughter and my boy can predict and mimic my remarks with such verbatim precision. Have I really become so calculable a bore to them without my knowing it? I smart secretly when they succeed in aping me and do not forgive them easily. I forget, rather than forgive. I do not like them to ridicule me.) And we *knew* we would give him the money he wanted the next time he asked, even as we were declaring to him that we would not. So why did we confound and torture him (put him through the wringer) and make him stand there and take it? Why did we make him feel, perhaps (and perhaps intentionally), like something bizarre, different, like some kind of freak?

(For a penny and a nickel or a dime.)

To teach him, we told ourselves, a lesson.

(What was that lesson?)

(We never found it. We didn't even look.)

"Have you learned your lesson?" I would catechize him further the next time he came to me for money.

"Yes."

"What is your lesson?" I would make him recite.

"I shouldn't give money away."

"Will you give it away?"

"No."

"Promise?"

"I want gum, Daddy."

"Do you promise?"

"I promise."

"What do you promise?"

"I won't give it away."

"What will you do with it?"

"Spend it."

"On who?"

"On gum."

"On what?"

"On me. I want gum, Daddy. Don't you understand? I just want some gum now."

"If I give you more than one penny, what will you do?"

"Buy more gum."

"And if I give you no pennies, what will you do?"

"Buy no gum."

"But you had pennies yesterday, didn't you? If you didn't give them away you wouldn't have to ask me for any today, would you?"

"Suppose I spent them yesterday? I'd have to ask you for some today anyway, wouldn't I?"

"I suppose you would. But do you understand now why you shouldn't give money away?"

"Yes."

"Do you?"

"Yes."

"Why? Why is it wrong for you to give money away?"

"Because," he begins—and his eyes gleam suddenly in anticipation and he finds it is impossible to resist giving the impish reply that comes to his mind—"because," he repeats, with a reckless, mischievous laugh and decides to plunge ahead with his joke, "it makes you and Mommy angry."

What a nice kid.

I am so pleased. And I have to laugh along with him to let him know the risk was a good one and that I am not going to make him pay for it.

We have brisk, Socratic dialogues, he and I, on just about everything (the lines fly crisply in rhythmic questions and answers), and we both enjoy them. (With my daughter, I have arguments and demoralizing discussions that tend to become overladen with personal imputations and denials, even when she starts out discussing, objectively and dispassionately, life and its meaning or her friends or mine. She has many comments to make about the people my wife and I know, as though they were any of her business.) I am Socrates, he is the pupil. (Or so it seems, until I review some of our conversations when I am alone, and then it often seems that *he* is Socrates. I know I love him. He loves me. He is nice. I am not.

"You're nice, Daddy," he exclaims to me frequently. He hugs me a lot.

"You know, Daddy, you're really nice sometimes," even my daughter remarks to me every now and then.

So maybe I'm not really always as bad as I think I am. I enjoy being praised, by anyone, even by members of my family. It makes me feel important; I grow expansive. Nobody is good always. Everybody is good sometime.) And there is no predicting in what directions our words will fly, for there is no telling in advance what closely guarded observations of his might suddenly spring to his tongue and flash out almost involuntarily, or what preoccupations, deliberately, after tense, inner centuries of concentrated brooding and speculation, he might choose without preliminaries to bring out into the open. (And once he does decide, there will be no deterring him.

"Did you have to fuck Mommy to get me?" he has asked.

"That's not why," I told him.

"Why what?"

"Why we did it or why we got you."

"It's how, though, isn't it?" He doesn't seem to like the idea.)

He won't take chances he doesn't have to. (Neither will I. Except with girls, and even then I tend to play it very safe.) He has never, to my knowledge, been in a fist fight. (I wouldn't get in one now either unless it was clearly a matter of life or death. The apple has not fallen far from the tree.) He has no taste for bullying or beating children smaller or weaker. He tries as best he can to avoid associating with anyone he's afraid of, even at the cost of giving up activities he enjoys or forfeiting the companionship of other children he likes. He does not know what to do when an older or tougher or even smaller kid shoves him or shouts at him or when a roving band takes away his bicycle or his baseball bat (as did happen to him in the park in the city on successive days that first time I was away at the company convention in Puerto Rico; maybe that's why he still does not like me to go away anywhere in an airplane, although I would not have been there with him in the afternoon anyway to protect him and his bicycle and his baseball bat from that gang of Puerto Rican kids one day and Negro kids the next, so maybe it is not. Other parents, mothers, were there, and they couldn't. Everything is so much more confusing than it ought to be). On the other hand, he is capable of acts of great courage and emotional strength that leave my wife and me flabbergasted. (We compliment ourselves on these, too.) He will sit still and docile if a doctor or dentist tells him he is about to hurt him and submit without flinching (though white as a sheet, or sallow, and with the tips of his fingers trembling) to whatever he has been told has to be done to him. *I* will flinch for him. *I* feel dizzy and am compelled to look away in terror and nausea when his slim arm is bared by a doctor working speedily to inoculate him or take blood. I see on his face in a doctor's or dentist's office that same sickly pallor I recognize now from mornings when he has to face Forgione later in the gymnasium or give an oral report in one of his classes (the whole impression I have of his person when he looks this way is one of phlegm. His total substance is phlegm. But he is certainly not *phlegmatic*. Ha, ha). He says nothing in objection as he submits, but I know that *he* is nauseated too: his gut is constricted, his limbs are tubes, and he fears he may yell for help and embarrass us all (and I am so shaken to see him this way that *I* can scream in agony for him. I could not bear it when he had his tonsils out and I saw the tiny, crescent crust of dried blood looped out the bottom of his right or left nostril. I'm not certain which. My mind is no longer clear on such details, but that doesn't matter. There was a ringing in my head when they wheeled him back into the room, and my wife had to spring to me quickly to grip me by the arm and lead me to a chair, or I think I might have fallen). I hope he does not have to have a tooth pulled until he is old enough and hardy enough to bear it without my support, bear it much more courageously than I would be able to bear having one of his teeth pulled out now. I am so glad he no longer seems as frightened of me as he used to be, not even of my yelling or my acidulous sarcasm when I am feeling unhappy or suffering from a headache. (I remember some of the things I used to taunt and bully him about, like giving money away or being afraid to try to dive or sail or ski or ice skate, and I am saddened by shame, for a minute or two; I find it remarkable that he has been able to forgive me and forget, if indeed he has forgiven me, for maybe *he* remembers too. I think he remembers everything. He may even remember which nostril of his it was that bore that staining crust of blood when he was transported back to us inside the hospital room, but I don't want to ask him because I don't want to remind him of that deep and shattering trauma I suffered when he had his tonsils and adenoids pulled and clipped out and from which I am not sure either one of us will ever recover fully. He suffered too and did not want to stay in his own room when we brought him home from the hospital with his throat that hurt so much he could not speak or smile without pain. When he forgot and cracked a joke in a slow, croaking voice and began to smile he was stunned by the sharp reminder of pain. We made him return to his own room. It was a pretty room with decals on the wall and a hi-diddle-diddle mobile hanging from the ceiling in the center. In the hospital, he was thirsty when he woke up, but we could not give him water until all the ether fumes had evaporated. He would vomit, they told us. So we didn't. His eyelids were blue.)

I thank God that he no longer seems to include me among the clouded swarms of demonic, treacherous, sneaky, heartless, creeping, climbing, crawling, brutal, blood-spilling, overtowering crooks, kidnappers, ghosts, and murderers that infiltrate his dreams (and mine) and of whom, just about all his small life, I understand now, he has been in such profound and enervating dread. (He sensed these malign phantoms and villains rather than saw them, he said when we brought him home from the hospital with his cut throat, but he could hear them also at the same time. Lying awake listening for noises, he would hear the same creaks and footfalls we all do; but he would imagine human beings coming to get

271

him, scaling stone by stone the outside wall of our apartment building, boring downward from the roof toward his bedroom, descending from an opening in the sky to the sill of his fragile glass window. Their faces were hooded or shaped in shadows they carried with them like shawls.

"Why didn't you call us?" I asked. "Why didn't you tell us, instead of trying to come into our room? We thought you were just lonely. Why didn't you call me instead of just lying there and being scared? I would have sat with you. Or Mommy."

"You would have told me I was imagining it."

"You were imagining it."

"I hear animals too. That's why I didn't call you.")

There was that one unreal period when he began to believe that I was not really me!

(Who else I could be he was not able to say.)

He began to suspect that I was no longer really me but someone vicious masquerading as me who had penetrated his household disguised as me in order to trick him and take him away from me. (Was he goading me? He was too small.) It was not possible to disprove him; every denial, every reference to reason and fact was part of the deception. Of course I would say everything I did say if he was right. I only proved him right. I could not prove I was me.

"Why should I want to?" I asked. "Why should anybody want to?"

"I don't know."

"Why should I tell you I'm me if I'm not?"

"To trick me."

"Why would I want to do that?"

"To take me away."

"To where?"

"Mommy too. To get me."

"Why would we do that when we've already got you here with us now anyway, haven't we?"

"I don't know."

"Do you think we already did get you and took you away and brought you here?"

"I don't know."

"I guess we did do all that anyway, didn't we?"

"I don't know."

Now, at least, he does know I am me and feels a bit more secure about that. (Or else understands that it makes no difference, for, if I am not me, he has to adjust nonetheless to whoever else I am. He is in my clutches now, in either event, and must remain—no one will rescue him—until he grows old enough, if he survives, to go away. When my own tonsils were taken out I awoke in pain at night in a darkened hospital ward with no parents there and no nurses. Everything was dark. There was only darkness in that very strange place. I could make out forms. Nothing moved. And thirst. God—what thirst. I was racked with thirst. I felt I would die if nobody gave me water, and nobody did. Nothing was there, except the eerie outlines of other beds that might have been empty. Nobody came until morning. The night was endless. I knew it would never end.

"Give him water," a doctor with a brown and gray mustache barked crossly at the nurses in the morning. "Give him water."

That's the last I remember. They had forgotten.)

I think he believes me now, more readily than he used to, I think he feels a little bit more at home with us, I think he trusts me more. (At least he knows now that I am me, although neither one of us is all that positive who that me we know I am is.) I think he does trust me more now, for he is not as submissive and dependent as he always used to be and has confidence enough sometimes (in me? Or in himself?) to say no to me, to refuse to do or say something he is asked to, although he is still extremely cautious about tempting anyone's wrath. He will not always give me answers about himself to questions I ask. He has never shown anger to me or my wife and hardly ever to my daughter. Is it possible he has never felt it? No. What does he do with the anger he feels? Ventilates it in dreams. And I'll bet he has been saving a lot of it up too, the way other kids accumulate comic books or bubble-gum cards. I'll bet he must hate me at times. (I think I would hate him.) I know he baits me on occasion, but usually as a lark, when we are feeling good toward each other.

"I am going to give you something," he says to a kid in my presence, with a sidelong glance in my direction, "and you don't have to give me anything back. Okay?"

(I suppress an outraged and admiring snort. I cannot believe that this impertinent little rogue of mine will really do what I sense he's going to.)

"What?" The other little boy is not sure he has understood.

"I am going to give you something," my boy repeats slowly, making certain I am attentive, "and you don't have to give me anything back. Okay? Something you want."

"What is it?"

"All right?"

Dubiously, the other boy nods.

"It's something you want."

And, to the other boy's astonishment, my boy pushes upon him the nickel he has just wheedled from me to buy more gum.

I am incredulous.

"Now, Daddy," he starts right in the instant we are alone, with his clenched hands on his hips and his head cocked to one side indignantly, in perfect imitation of me, then shakes a finger at me, again in extravagant mimicry, and launches into talk too rapid for me to interrupt. "I want you to behave and listen to me so you don't do or say anything to embarrass me here because you don't understand and I am the boss and I don't want you to and I will punish you if you do and punish you if you don't do what I want you to so you better not or I will smack you too and no television for a week because I say so do you hear and is that clear? You're laughing!" he explodes with a grin. "I can see you're laughing, Daddy, and I don't want you to pretend you're not and make believe you're angry at what I did and then forget you're making believe and really get angry. You do that sometimes you know, Daddy. Don't you?"

"Are you finished?" I ask, with my hands still

on my hips. "That's a mighty long speech for a little piss-ass like you who sometimes hardly talks at all."

"Are you mad?" he inquires uneasily.

"No, I'm glad. But do you think just because you made me laugh I'm going to let you get away with what you did?"

"It was mine."

"It was mine before I gave it to you."

"It was mine after you gave it to me. Don't embarrass me in public."

"Are you imitating me again? Don't think you can get away with that forever."

"We're in public, aren't we? I don't want you to do anything that will make people stop and listen."

"I'm not doing anything at all but listening to you."

"You're standing."

"So are you."

"With your hands on your hips, just like an actor on television. Let's walk. Let's walk, I said."

"Now *you're* like an actor on television, shaking your finger at me."

"You're embarrassing me," he charges.

"No, I'm not."

"But you're going to," he predicts, "aren't you?"

"Why should I embarrass you?"

"Are you going to yell at me?"

"Am I yelling at you?"

"Are you going to be mad?"

"Am I mad?"

"You *are* embarrassing me," he accuses triumphantly. "You're being sarcastic."

"Big shot!" I tell him sarcastically. "You don't even know what embarrass means."

"Yes, I do. And I know what sarcastic means. It means when you're doing something I don't want you to do."

"I'm not doing anything you don't want me to do. I'm not doing anything at all but standing here, so how can I be embarrassing you?"

"You're asking me questions, aren't you? Why do you keep asking me questions?"

"Why don't you answer them?"

"I'm going to tell Mommy," he threatens. "I'm going to tell Mommy you drank whiskey."

"She won't believe you. She'll know it's a lie."

"How come?"

"Your nose will grow."

"How come?"

"A person's nose grows when he tells a lie."

"Then *your* nose is growing," he counters. "Because *that's* a lie."

"Then why would my nose be growing if it's a lie?"

"I'm going to sock you one, Daddy," he squeals in frustration, as he feels himself outsmarted.

"Why are you twisting around so much? Stand still."

"I think I'm nervous," he guesses.

"Do you have to pee? Then why are you picking at your pecker?"

"I don't like that."

(He stops picking at his pecker. I'm sorry I said it.)

"She'll smell my breath," I resume, to change *that* subject. "She won't smell whiskey, and that's how she'll know you're lying."

"I'm going to kick you," he says. "I think I'm going to kick you in the shins."

"Why?" I ask in surprise.

"Because," he says. "Because whenever I kick you in the shins or sock you one you begin wrestling with me and we laugh a lot, so I think I'll do it to make you laugh a lot."

"I'll kick your ass."

"I'm going to tell Mommy you said a dirty word to me."

"So what? I say dirty words to her."

"She doesn't like it. She'll fight with you."

"We don't fight."

"You fight a lot. She'll smack you."

"She doesn't smack me."

"She cries."

"No, she doesn't."

"Sometimes she does."

276

"You talk too much. And notice too much. Sometimes you get them all mixed up."

"I wish I knew somebody who could beat you up," he tells me, kidding.

"Why?"

"I'm going to call a cop."

"Why?"

"To smack you."

"He's not allowed to."

"You smack me."

"I'm allowed to. And I don't smack you."

"You used to."

"I did not. In your whole life I bet I never smacked you once."

"Once you did. When I was little. I remember."

"If I did, I'm sorry. But I don't think I did. I don't smack you now. Do I?"

"You're going to. Aren't you?"

"For what?"

"You know."

"I'm not."

"You promise?"

"I promise."

"You promise you won't smack me?"

"I promise."

"You really promise you won't smack me?"

"I promise. I won't smack you. Don't you believe me?"

"I believe you," he says.

And *wham*—he kicks me in the shin!

I leap a mile into the air, howling with surprise, and I know I must look funny as hell to him as I go hopping around in outrage, stroking and fanning my stinging leg. He does not laugh immediately: he frowns instead, wondering, I guess, if he has perhaps gone too far and is now in trouble, until he sees and hears me guffaw and understands that I am neither hurt nor displeased. Then his own face opens radiantly in a sunburst of relief and he begins laughing in exultation. I exaggerate all my own comic motions in order to keep him laughing and then to trap him with a sneak attack. He is doubled over in quaking merriment, clutching his belly and gulping and sighing helplessly, and all at once I am upon him: I hurl myself at him while he is bent over laughing, and we fall to the ground wrestling. It is not much of a match. At the beginning, I tickle his ribs to keep him giggling and gasping for air and render him defenseless. We grapple awhile until I grow winded, and then I turn limp to allow him to pin me. I am out of breath, and the match is his if he wants it. But he isn't satisfied. He grows cocky and careless: he wishes to savor his victory; and instead of pinning me, he elects to experiment in torturing me with some useless armlocks and toeholds. My breath is back, I decide to teach him a lesson (another lesson. The subject of this lesson, I suppose, is that one should strike while the iron is hot. The truly disgusting thing about all these platitudinous lessons for getting ahead is that sooner or later they all turn out to be true). So, while my boy is fiddling tranquilly with my fingers, my toes, and my foot, not certain really what to do with any of them, I bunch my muscles treacherously, fill my lungs for the effort, and, in one brief and explosive heave, flip him up and over and around down into the sand. He whoops in fearful, thrilled excitement at my new determination, and he kicks and twists and elbows wildly with joy, a lithe, laughing, healthy little animal trying energetically to fight and wiggle free as I swarm down upon him. (Now I cannot let him win; if I do, he'll know it's only because I did let him, and then he'll know that he has lost.) It is no contest at all now that I have my wind back and am going about it in earnest. I employ my greater bulk (much of it solid flab, ha, ha) to force him down into place. It is relatively easy for me to grasp both his wrists in one of my hands, to immobilize his legs beneath the pressing weight of my own and end his kicking. In just a few more seconds it is over; and he gives up. I have him nailed to the ground in a regulation pin. We stare at each other smiling, our faces inches apart.

"I win," he jokes.

"Then let me up," I joke back.

"Only if you surrender," he says.

"I surrender," I reply.

"Then I'll let you up," he says.

I let him go and we rise slowly, breathing hard and feeling close to each other.

"You know, Daddy," he starts right in with pious gravity, trying to divert me, assuming an owlish and censorious expression as austerely as a judge, "I really did win, because you threw sand in my eyes and tickled me and that's not allowed."

"I did not," I retort fliply.

"Did you tickle me? You liar."

"That's allowed. You can tickle."

"You don't laugh."

"You don't know how to tickle."

"That's why it's not fair."

"It is fair. And furthermore," I continue, "I didn't throw sand."

"I can say you did."

"And did you know, by the way, that it's a lovely day today because the sun is shining and the bay is calm and blue, and there are nine or seven planets—"

"Nine."

"—of which Mercury is the closest to the sun and . . ."

"Pluto."

". . . Pluto is the farthest?"

"Did you hear about the homosexual astronauts?" he asks.

"Yes. They went to Uranus. And if, as they say, there are seven days in each week and fifty-two weeks in each year, how come there are three hundred and sixty-five days in the year instead of three hundred and sixty-four?"

He pauses to calculate. "How come?" he queries. "I never thought about that."

"I don't know. I never thought about it either."

"Is that what you want to talk about now?" he asks disconsolately.

"No. But if you want to stall, I'll stall along with you. You're not fooling me."

"I'm going to tell Mommy," he threatens again. "I'm going to tell Mommy you threw sand in my eyes."

"*I'm* going to tell her," I rejoin.

"Are you?" His manner turns solemn.

"What?"

"Going to tell her?"

"What?"

"You know."

"What?"

"What I did."

"Did you do something?" I inquire with airy candor.

"You know."

"I can't remember."

"What I gave away."

"Did you give something away?"

"Daddy, you know I gave a nickel away."

"When? You give a lot of nickels away."

"Just before. When you were right here."

"Why?"

"You won't know."

"Tell me why. How do you know?"

"You'll get angry and start yelling or begin to tease me or make fun of me."

"I won't. I promise."

"I wanted to," he states simply.

"That's no answer."

"I knew you'd say that."

"I knew you'd say that."

"I said you wouldn't understand."

"He didn't ask you for it," I argue. "He couldn't believe his eyes when you gave it to him. I don't think you even know him that long. I'll bet you don't even like him that much. Do you?"

"You're getting angry," he sulks. "I knew you would."

"I'm not."

"You're starting to yell, aren't you?"

"I'm just raising my voice."

"You see?"

"You're faking," I charge, and give him a tickling poke in the ribs. "And I know you're faking, so stop faking and trying to pretend you can fool me. Answer."

He grins sheepishly, exposed and pleased. "I don't

280

know. I don't know if I like him or not. I only met him yesterday."

"See? I'm smart. Then why? You know what I mean. Why did you give your money to him?"

"You'll think I'm crazy."

"Maybe you are."

"Then I won't tell you."

"I know you aren't."

"Do I have to?"

"Yes. No. You want to. I can see you do. So you have to. Come on."

"I wanted to give him something," he explains very softly. "And that was all I had."

"Why did you want to give him something?"

"I don't know."

He tells me this so plainly, truthfully, innocently as to make it seem the most plausible and obvious reason imaginable. And I do understand. His frankness is touching, and I feel like reaching out to embrace him right there on the spot and rewarding him with dollar bills. I want to kiss him (but I think he will be embarrassed if I do, because we are out in public). I want to tousle his hair lightly. (I do.) Tenderly, I say to him:

"That's still no answer."

"How come?" he inquires with interest.

"It doesn't tell why."

"It's why."

"It doesn't tell why you wanted to give him something. Why did you want to give him something?"

"I think I know. You sure keep after me, don't you?"

"Why did you want to give him something?"

"Do I have to tell?"

"No. Not if you don't want to."

"I was happy," he states with a shrug, squinting uncomfortably in the sunlight, looking a little pained and self-conscious.

"Yeah?"

"And whenever I feel happy," he continues, "I like to give something away. Is that all right?"

"Sure." (I feel again that I want to kiss him.)

"It's okay?" He can hardly trust his good fortune.

"And I'm glad you were happy. Why were you happy?"

"Now it gets a little crazy."

"Go ahead. You're not crazy."

"Because I knew I was going to give it away." He pauses a moment to giggle nervously. "To tease you," he admits. "Then when I knew I was happy about that, I wanted to give the nickel away because I was happy about wanting to give the nickel away. Is it okay?"

"You're making me laugh."

"You're not mad?"

"Can't you see that you're making me laugh? How can I be mad?"

"Then I'll tell you something else," he squeals with ebullient gaiety. "Sometimes I feel like laughing for no reason at all. Then I feel like laughing just because I know I feel like laughing. You're smiling!" he cries suddenly, pointing a finger at my face, and begins shrieking with laughter. "Why are you smiling?"

"Because you're funny!" I shout back at him. "It's funny, that's why. You're funny, that's why."

"Are you gonna tell Mommy I gave money away?"

"Are you? You can't tell her either if I don't. Otherwise I'll get in trouble."

"You can tell her," he decides.

"Then you can tell her too."

"Was it all right?"

"Sure," I comfort him. "It was all right. In fact, it was better than all right. It was very nice. And I'm glad you talked to me. You don't always talk to me." I rest the palm of my hand lightly on the back of his head as we start walking again and head toward the boardwalk. My hand feels unnatural there, as though I am stretching a small elbow and arm muscle into an unaccustomed position. I move my hand to his shoulder; I feel a strain there too. (I am not used to holding my boy, I realize. I am not used to holding my daughter either.) "But suppose—" I want to prepare him and shield him against everything injurious in the world, and I cannot stop myself.

He pulls away from me with an impatient lurch

of his shoulders, frowning. "Daddy, I knew you were going to say that!"

"And I knew you were going to say that," I laugh in reply, but my heartiness is false. "What else am I going to say?"

"I want it for myself later or tomorrow? Then I'll get it back from him. But suppose—"

"Yeah?"

"—he doesn't have it or won't give it to you?"

"He won't."

"Then I'll get another nickel. From who?"

"I won't give it to you."

"From you. I won't give it to you."

"I won't. I warn you."

"You will," he replies to me directly, ending his imitation of us. "You always say that. You always say you won't. And then you always do. So why do you say that? Won't you?"

"Yes," I concede in a long syllable of total surrender, succumbing pleasurably to his childlike charm and intelligence. "I'll give it to you. I'll even give it to you now before you want it."

So what, his sage and ironic expression seems to say to me, am I making such a bogus fuss about? "I knew you would," he summarizes in triumph. He walks beside me with a lighter, more contented step.

"I always will, I want you to know. Do you?" I watch him nod; I see his brow tightening a bit with recollection and perplexity. "We're pretty good pals now, ain't we?" I ask. "You and me?"

"I used to be afraid of you."

"I hope you're not, now."

"Not as much."

"You don't have to be. I won't ever hurt you. And I'll always give you everything you need. Don't you know that? I just yell a lot."

After a moment more of deep reflection, he allows himself to bump against me softly with his shoulder as I often see him do with other boys I know he likes. (It is the friendliest answer he could have given me.) I bump him back the same way in response. He smiles to himself.

"Daddy, I love you!" he exclaims with excitement,

and throws his face against my hip to kiss me and hug me. "I hope you never die."

(I hope so too.) I crook my arm around his shoulders and hug him in return. Very swiftly, before he can be embarrassed by it and stop me, I kiss the top of his head, brush my lips against his silken, light-brown hair. (I steal a kiss.) I love him too and hope that *he* never dies.

I have the recurring fear that he will die before I do. I cannot let that happen. He is too dear to me. I know him now, and I know he is a much more valuable person to me than the Secretary of the Treasury and the Secretary of Defense, the Majority Leader and the Minority Whip. He is more important to me than the President of the United States of America. (I think more of my boy's life than I do of his.) I Pledge my Allegiance to *him*. (I never mention this heresy to anyone, of course.) I will never permit them to harm him.

But what *would* I do to protect him? I think I know what I would do. Nothing.

"Don't worry," I have promised him in earnest. "I will never let anything bad happen to you."

He is afraid of the government, the army, the Pentagon, the police. (And so am I.)

"I won't ever let them hurt you or take you away."

And what is there, really, that I *can* do? Except nothing.

So I do nothing.

I can connive (that gives me time), as I connive now in my job at the company (connive to survive, keep alive till five), but that's about all. And time may soon run out.

Who *am* I? I think I'm beginning to find out. I am a stick: I am a broken waterlogged branch floating with my own crowd in this one nation of ours, indivisible (unfortunately), under God, with liberty and justice for all who are speedy enough to seize them first and hog them away from the rest. Some melting pot. If all of us in this vast, fabulous land of ours could come together and take time to exchange a few words with our neighbors and fellow countrymen, those words would be *Bastard! Wop! Nigger! Whitey! Kike! Spic!* I don't like people who run things. I don't like Horace White, who is hard to take seriously (and yet I must).

"If you ever write a book," he has said to me, and meant it, because such things are important to him, "I would like you to put my name in it."

Horace White is a pale, insipid man of many small distinctions. He likes to see his name in the newspapers. He is an honorary deputy something or other of the City of New York (even though his legal residence is in Connecticut) and has an undistinguished bronze shield proclaiming that distinction affixed to the bumper of his automobile. The letters on the license plate of his automobile form his complete monogram (HOW); the numerals advance each year to give his age. (We think he lies about his age.) No one has ever been able to describe specifically what he does here in the company, except to be who he is, to have money, own stock, and be related in two collateral ways to one or more of the founders and directors. And I must toady to him. And I do.

If I were poor, I believe I might want to overthrow the government by force. I'm very glad, however, that everyone poor *isn't* trying to overthrow the government, because I'm not poor. I don't know why every Negro maid doesn't steal from her white employer (but I'm glad our Negro maid doesn't, or at least has not let us find out she does). If I were Black *and* poor, I don't think I'd have any reason for obeying any law other than the risk of being caught. As it is, though, I'm glad colored people do obey the law (most of them, anyway), because I am afraid of Negroes and have moved away from them. I am afraid of cops. But I'm glad there are cops and wish there were more.

(I don't like cops.)

(Except when they're around to protect me.)

I do not talk about any of this even to my wife, who, as she grows more lonely, old, and disappointed, is turning, like her sister, into a sour conservative who is opposed to happiness. (She is going to vote reactionary this year. I won't talk politics with her. I don't care how she votes.) I keep my own counsel and drift speechlessly with my crowd. I float.

I float like algae in a colony of green scum, while my wife and I grow old, my daughter grows older and more dissatisfied with herself and with me (I see other girls her age who seem perfectly fine. Some are prettier. Others act more sure of themselves. At least they are doing some of the things she says she'd like to do, including getting laid, but never even tries. And get better grades. What do I care what grades she gets? I do. And I have to pretend I care very much, otherwise she will feel I am not interested in her at all), and my little boy grows up tortured and puzzled, uncertain who, beside himself, he is supposed to be (or who, if he thinks like I do, himself even is. Go find him. Go find me. Lost somewhere deep inside his small self already is the smaller boy he used to be, the original article. Or is there? If that is not so, if there is no vanished and irretrievable little me and him so starkly different from what each of us since has been forced to become, if there is no wandering, desolate lost little being I yearn for and started from so far back in my history who took a sudden, inevitable lurch into some inaccessible black recess at a moment when I must have been staring the other way, for I am unable to pinpoint the moment, and left me disoriented all by myself to continue willy-nilly on my own—then how the fuck did I ever get here? Somebody pushed me. Somebody must have set me off in this direction, and clusters of other hands must have touched themselves to the controls at various times, for I would not have picked this way for the world. He has never been found. Lost: one child, age unknown, goes by the name of me. And I can't keep looking back for sight of him to ask him hopefully where did you go and what did you mean. He would be too young still even to know what I was talking about—he was just a kid when he left me, he is younger than my own child—let alone succor me with the wise,

286

experienced knowledge I need from him. What will I talk about to so many of those lined, ruddy faces with bloodshot, puffy eyes if Green does permit me to make my three-minute speech in Puerto Rico this year? I'll need jokes, quick jokes—ha, ha, ha—a few at the beginning and a very good one at the end, ha, ha, and all in only three minutes. We might just as well float like algae in colonies of green scum for as long as the tides will continue to carry us, and when they no longer support us, then what?) or which of the many dangers he pictures are real and which are merely hideous and fantastic daydreams. (Drowning is real. Being plucked from bed by a hook from an opening in the sky while lying helplessly asleep is not.) They are more than merely daydreams; they flood his consciousness at night in the darkness when we think he is asleep. Leaving a night light on makes no difference. It is impossible for us ever to know with certainty whether he is asleep or awake. If we peek in on him to check, he will often pretend to be asleep in order to avoid having us criticize him for being awake. I feel, without any real cause for believing so, that he always hears my wife and me make love or at least knows when we have done so. My daughter, at least, makes sure we hear her when she is up. She runs water or plays records or barges in on us without knocking to settle something once and for all. Not him. He is stealthy. I used to want to rumple my daughter's hair too, pat her head affectionately or touch or kiss her cheek or throw a hugging arm around her shoulders, but she began to shrink away from me as she grew up, kidding at first, I thought, and I would always pretend to be hurt. And then those times came when I began to comprehend that she was no longer kidding, and I no longer had to pretend I was really hurt. I really was hurt—and now I pretend I am not. Something took place, I felt, that made me awful to her, incited her disapproval and inspired her to overlook no opportunity to show it. There were times I felt she was after me in revenge. I don't know what it was I did or didn't do, and I still don't know what to do about it or even if there's anything I ought to try. Soon she'll be away at college.

I feel awkward when I have to touch her. She recoils from me, as though the tiniest physical contact with me would disgust her, or flinches, as though I were going to inflict pain. I never hit her! The most I have ever done, the most I ever do now, is shove her roughly in the shoulder when I have to. The most my wife ever does is start to slap her face when they're fighting, but makes her motion slowly enough to enable my daughter to block or avoid the blow; my daughter can inflame my wife to such anger almost at will and then reduce her to hysterical, muddled weeping. I am always stricken with bewilderment for a moment by my daughter's unexpected flashes of alarm. I am always contrite and flooded with such immense guilt and shame because my daughter thinks instinctively that I intend to hit her—or reacts as though she does. Is she waiting tensely, has she been waiting tensely all these years, for some tremendous blow from us? Does she honestly believe, when I flick my hand out to brush a loose eyelash from her cheek or a crumb of food, that I intend to hit her in the face? Or is she, as I frequently surmise now (perhaps irrationally), merely pretending, consciously and diabolically simulating such terror because she understands how keenly it shocks and saddens me? She is cunning enough for all of that, I think. It runs in the family: she gets it from me: don't I sometimes let my wife suffer through her strangling, moaning nightmares now by making no effort to rouse her from them? And glory in my advantageous position as I watch and listen? Don't I often exaggerate the agony of my own horrible dreams and feign to be more deeply entrapped in them than I am in order to make her labor longer, harder, and more compassionately to wake me from them? I do not understand my daughter any longer and I cannot cope with her successfully or make it possible for her to cope with me. So I try not to try. I wait, and hope for things to run their course. I do not understand my son, either. He is too young to be so magnanimous. He gave cookies away also. That was also the summer he tried to give cookies away to another kid and almost got a punch in the nose in return.

"Here, you can have a cookie," he said to the little boy who had dropped in to the summer house we had rented to play with him while we were all still having breakfast.

The boy gulped it down in a twinkling. Then the boy gazed hungrily at the remaining round chocolate cookie, which my boy was rolling about contemplatively on the tablecloth as he dawdled over his glass of milk. With a flicker of surprised recognition, my boy took note of the hungering stare.

"You can have this one too," he offers. "Here."

The boy stiffens as though offended and pulls back with a look of hostility. Suddenly, to my own amazement, he is enraged and befuddled and shakes his head in vigorous resentment.

"What do you mean?" he demands.

"Why? Don't you want it?" My boy pushes it part way across the table to him.

"You had it in your mouth."

"No, I didn't."

"It fell on the floor."

"No." My boy is taken aback and sounds defensive and apologetic. (He looks like he's lying.)

"It's dirty," the other boy accuses.

"It isn't. I'm not lying. You don't have to take it."

"Why don't you want it?"

"Because you want it. Don't you? I had some."

The other boy is furious, too flustered anymore to trust himself to speak, and his face turns fiery as he sits there in hatred and continues shaking his head adamantly. My boy whitens. The fists of the other boy are clenched and raised, and he is ready to fight; but I am there, sitting forbiddingly (ready to fight too, I feel. If he tries to hit my boy, I believe I will take his arm and break it). He sputters in tongue-tied, gagging wrath, shoves the second cookie roughly back across the table so it falls over the edge, and gallops out of our house, his mouth writhing and his downcast eyes almost spilling over with steaming tears of bellicose frustration. He feels, somehow, that he has been made a fool of. My little boy is blank with consternation; his face is like a crossword puzzle; he cannot understand what he has just done, simply by offering cookies, to cost him a friend and make for himself a young, new enemy who wishes to injure him. He looks about wanly in pleading confusion and tries to smile.

"You can't give things away, not so generously," I explain for him, with a weak, sympathizing smile.

"Why?" he asks.

I shrug. "I don't know. People get suspicious."

"I don't like bugs," he complains. "I don't like it here. Do we have to spend the whole summer?"

"We do. I don't like it here either."

"You go to the city."

"I have to. I'm glad we didn't send you away to camp. I'm glad you're here when I come out."

"I'm not."

That was also the summer in which my boy was having a difficult time of it (my boy has always been having a difficult time of it, it seems, and my wife and I are finding it more and more fatiguing) in the play group in which we enrolled him to insure that he would have fun and much to do with other kids during the day. At the beginning, he was very happy there and eager to go. He was astonished and overjoyed to find himself among so many other boys his own age whom he considered his friends. Boisterously and proudly, he would point them out to us when he came upon them on the boardwalk at night or at the beach or in different parts of town.

"That's my friend," he would announce with elation. "That's my friend. I know him. I know him from play group. That's my friend also." Sometimes he would wave and they would rush to greet each other or they would bump shoulders wordlessly in recognition as they passed. "That's my friend also from play group," he would continue every time. "That's my friend too. He's older."

He took so much pleasure in having them, as though he had never before conceived it possible that he could be on sociable terms with so many people. He was radiant when any came to the house looking for him; he would entice them inside to show them off.

("This is my friend," he would say. "These are my friends."

My daughter was that way too when she was little, still is with boys, but much more subtle and blasé in the manner in which she takes pains to let us see or find out about a boy she wants us to think is interested in her. I wonder what in the world my wife and I ever did to our children to make them believe we thought they would never be able to make friends. I'm not sure anymore that we did anything, that all of it is our fault.) It was almost as though he could not contain quietly all the intense happiness he was experiencing.

It did not last. It ended early for him. Things soon began happening at that play group to disquiet him, and before long he was as reluctant to go there as he is now to go to gym and Forgione. He welcomed the foot races and the guessing games and play-skits indoors on rainy days; but there was rope climbing there too (but only for the older boys, we were able to find out) and a trampoline in view that he was leery of (so was I. And so was my wife. I don't know what my boy thought because I did not want to generate any apprehension in him by asking, but I know what I thought: I was afraid he might go bouncing up all the way to the surface of the moon, bump his head, and come bouncing back down to that trampoline on the back of his neck with his spine broken and both his legs and arms paralyzed—I just did not want him to have to try it), and far in advance he was tormented by the deep-water swimming test he was told all the boys in his age group would have to pass before the summer was over and be given lessons to pass. (He didn't even want the lessons. There were also constant rumors of jellyfish in the water, and sea lice and horseshoe crabs.) There were rumors of boxing bouts and wrestling matches; he spied a pair of boxing gloves on a hook in a shed and believed he would have to fight (although there never was any boxing or wrestling. There never was *anything* dangerous there for the children. It was a good day camp, I guess, as far as good day camps go, but I

291

soon found myself detesting it because my boy began having difficulties there). New games were introduced quickly that my boy did not understand and other children from previous years there did, and no one, not the counselors or any of his friends in the play group, took sufficient time to explain or was tolerant and considerate of his blunders when he made them. He was too shy to ask any question more than once, even when the reply he received was incomprehensible or incomplete; he was doing things wrong consistently. The counselors were busy flirting with each other. (That old stewing concupiscence was germinating hotly there too. The girls wore knitted T-shirts; many wore no bras, and even the tiny-titted ones looked good. It's so much sweeter when you're young, so much hotter, so much more fun. I wish I had that frenetic heat back now instead of this sluggish, processed lust I put myself through and frequently have to make a laborious effort to enjoy.) I hardly blamed them, although I blamed them like hell at the time when their negligence affected my own boy. (I remember my own scalding, urgent drives and fits for two summers in the woods as a camp counselor near a camp with girl counselors just across the lake. There were many activities the two camps did together. I really didn't give a fuck about the welfare or development of any of the kids, so long as they didn't drown, get scarlet fever or polio, or kill each other with ropes or rocks. All I had my entire soul concentrated on for most of those summers was reaching some bold and naughty juicy slut of an experienced girl from town or the other camp who would meet me on the ground in the woods and make me come fast. So I wouldn't have to do it myself. Oh, how I always wanted to come. I used to enjoy doing it to myself in those days as much as I enjoyed it any other way.) He felt himself sinking steadily into disgrace. He was less and less able to figure out what to do. He faked limps at play group in order to be excused from activities he was not utterly positive he understood and began complaining at home at breakfast of nausea and sore throats. (It was like it is at school now. There was no beginning, it seems, and there might be no end.)

One morning he retched and seemed to throw up the very little he had eaten because he did not want to go. We took his temperature, and he had no fever. We made him go. (It was wrong of us to make him go. I know that now, and everybody we talk to about it says it was wrong. But nobody has been able to tell me what would have been right.)

I wandered by there secretly later that day to observe him, and I was jubilant at what I saw. It was a relay race, and he was ten yards ahead, my joyous little boy (I was so proud to spy him), carrying a heavy medicine ball in his arms that he had to deliver to the next runner on his team. He was laughing; his giggles rang out clearly over everything; he was laughing so hard as he ran that he was faltering in his stride, and his knees wobbled and buckled; he was reeling with greater and greater outpourings of laughter and soon staggering and almost falling, doubled over with his deep, choking blasts of irrepressible merriment, as he leaped and stumbled and lumbered and galloped through the sand, slowing down steadily, intentionally, it appeared, for he was motioning heartily to the fat, wheezing, unhappy little boy he was racing against on the other team to hurry and catch up, so they could laugh together and run the rest of the way side by side, as though he had something funny he wished to reveal to him before they got there.

My boy was still laughing (his face and teeth and mouth were all gleaming) when he handed the medicine ball off to the next boy on his team, who, instead of running, flung it back at his feet, and a whole surly gang of enraged people, it seemed, including some of those tall, sun-tanned counselors in white T-shirts, descended upon him like ferocious animals and began screaming and swearing at him. (A few were soon screaming at each other and shoving. My heart stopped and I was frozen to the spot. I could not believe it.) It was a mob scene. My boy was aghast. He did not know how he had sinned. He did not know what to do. As he stood there dumbfounded, twisting grotesquely in bewilderment, a bigger, broad-shouldered boy with black hair and a furious face charged up to him out of the swirl of others like a bull gone berserk and rammed him viciously- in the chest with the hardened heels of both hands. My boy fell back a few steps (his knees were buckling again), turned white as a sheet (Oh, God, I thought—he's going to vomit, or faint. Or cry. And make me ashamed), and waited limply. He did nothing else. He stood there. He did not speak or protest, or cast his eyes about. He did not even lift his arms to protect himself or hit back as the other boys made ready to run at him again; but he did not look as though he intended to flee or beg for help. (I shuddered and thought that *I* might puke.) The other boy rushed forward again and slammed my boy in the chest with his open hands, then stood daringly with his fist poised high in an open challenge to my boy to begin fighting back. Again my boy staggered backward a few steps from the force, recovered his balance, and just waited. He would not fight back; he would not defend himself; but he would not run away, and he would not ask anyone for aid or pity. That much seemed clear; there was defiance in his stillness. For a fleeting instant, I was enthralled by the dignity and courage I sensed he was showing just by holding his ground and waiting for the next battering charge. He would not move to save himself. (I do not move to save myself.) For a second, I could actually make myself feel proud. But that wasn't enough. I wanted him to have more guts. (I wish *I* had more guts.) I heard myself rooting for him to strike back.

"Move, you dope!" I pleaded to myself. "Why don't you *move*, you dope!"

And then, with a numbing, devastating shock that made my head feel faint, I saw that his eyes were red and swollen and brimming with tears and that his lips were bloodless as ashes and quivering. And then I understood why he did not move: he could not move. He was paralyzed. He was devoid of all power and ability to act or think. He could not even panic. He did not move because he could not move. He did not speak because he could not speak. He did not hit back because he could not hit back. He did not cry out or cast his gaze about for help because he couldn't: the thought was not there. He had no voice. Here was that bad dream of mine coming to life. Here was onrushing death and degradation bearing down upon him once more in the senseless, stupid action of a little, slightly sturdier boy (looming suddenly in this situation as large as a giant) whom my boy recently tried to give two chocolate cookies to (it was the same one. Or maybe it wasn't) and he could not move (neither could I) to avert it or mouth the words necessary to call attention to it and release himself from that lifelong, terrifying nightmare of mine. (I am there, and someone can get me—I am dead already because I cannot free my feet or yell for help—I am speechless too—although I feel I want to.) He was affixed. He was frozen to his spot too (as I was frozen to mine). He was fossilized, flat, brittle, and destructible. He was already dead if anyone wanted to kill him. One of the play group counselors (in slow motion, it looked to me) intervened just then to save him (two counselors, actually, the second a chunky blond girl with big breasts. Breasts seem to be growing bigger and bouncier on young girls these days. They seem to be growing them bigger on older girls too and middle-aged women. In summer, the beaches hang with them. I like breasts, until I begin to see so much of so many of them. I used to like them more) and get things going again, and I realized I'd been holding my breath just about all the time and that all my muscles were tensed for violence (and arrested by the urge to use them). I realized that if that other little boy, whom I already hated, had charged at my little boy one more time, I might have lost control and stormed into that children's play area like someone roaring and insane and smitten him dead right then and there. (Or else, in a reaction away from that impulse, I would have murdered my boy.) If I found that I was able to move myself at all. (I will never know if I was petrified too.)

I left when they were all playing again.

I was very good to my boy the rest of that day. (I was so good to him, and sensitive, that I did not even tell him or my wife what I had seen. He had been afraid to fight.)

The next day, as I more or less foresaw, he did not want to go to play group again. He didn't say so; he merely said he didn't feel well but would probably be all right if we told him he had to go. He looked wretched and pasty, and my heart went out to him silently because I knew (I thought I knew) what he felt. He went. We told him he did have to go and took him. Leaving with us for play group that morning (our daughter was away at camp that summer, where she was having a difficult time of it too, if we could believe her), he looked as miserable and ill in spirit as he did on that bleak and drizzling, unnatural dawn we rode with him to the hospital to have his tonsils—and his adenoids—taken out (I keep forgetting those adenoids. I don't even know what adenoids are, except that they are there and dangling, somewhere up inside the nose. Maybe nobody knows what adenoids really are. I once felt pretty witty telling a young girl from Ann Arbor that adenoids were undescended testicles), and, numb with gloom ourselves that dark and heavy morning, strove to make casual conversation with him in the taxicab that I wished would speed faster and *be* there at the hospital already before one of the three of us passed out or passed away from the sheer strain of the approaching event, like that jolly and innocently empty conversation I always used to try to make with my mother in the nursing home during those tedious and sickening visits with her that soon served no purpose at all. I could just as easily have sent my small food parcels into the room by mail or with one of the nurses and departed immediately (and spared myself the gruesome ordeal of watching her fumble with fragments of fish and meat and candy and cake with her deformed and trembling fingers and dabbing the greasy, crumbling pieces into her lips. She did not want me to feed her). But I was her son: I was her dutiful son (ha, ha, and willing to suffer penitentially with her part of every weekend at first, then every other weekend, then every third or fourth weekend, until she began to fail rapidly, when, for some hypocritical reason, to absolve myself, it turned into every weekend again for five or ten or fifteen minutes), but not an especially grateful one. Neither one of us was grateful to the other. I was not grateful to her for having been my mother (it had become by then an unjust imposition. Why could she not have gone away unnoticed, as my father had done, inconveniencing me not at all?); and she was not grateful to me for my visits or the news and things to eat I brought her. What little conversation we had was forced. Angered silence would have been better. She missed her mother.

"Ma," she moaned deliriously again and again from her drugged and agitated stupor near the end, her glazed, reddened eyes showing unfocused fright and welling with tears, and that was almost all she had to say, except for what I think she had to say to me at the end.

I like her more now than I did when she was alive.

My mother was almost eighty when she died, and her memory had gone almost entirely, but she died crying for her mother, and I suppose that I shall die crying for mine (if the Lord, in his infinite mercy, allows me to live long enough. Ha, ha). So much of misfortune seems a matter of timing. We were late coming for him that day, and we saw him, half a block from the play area, standing alone on the sidewalk in his bare feet and bawling loudly, helplessly, because he thought we were never going to come for him at all. (I was incensed when I saw him. We were simply late. Nothing else had happened.) Other people, children and grown-ups, looked at my boy curiously as they walked past and saw him standing there crying: none of them offered to help, none of them questioned him. (Good God—even *I* will help a small child who seems to be in trouble, if no one else does.) He did nothing when he saw us, except shriek more piercingly, quail more frantically, in a tortured plea for us to rescue him from whatever odd spell was holding him to that spot in terror. (I was so deeply incensed with him for a moment that I was actually tempted to stop with a sneer and delay going to him.) He was convulsed with grief by the idea that we had abandoned him, just because we were a little bit late, that we had left him there purposely because we were dissatisfied and disgusted with him, and that he was never going to see us again or have anyone to take care of him.

I was infuriated. He knew the way home. It wasn't far. The walk was uncomplicated. Many mornings we would let him lead us from the house to the boardwalk to the play group just to show him he could get there alone safely and then let him lead us back afterward to demonstrate to himself and us that he also knew how to return. The village was small, there were hardly any cars, it was impossible to get lost—if he did, he could always follow the boardwalk or ask somebody for directions. He knew that too. (We were always pressing him to ask people for directions when he was unsure, but he was afraid of strangers, even children his own age, and reluctant to talk to them. When he did, he mumbled inaudibly with lowered eyes, and whoever he asked always requested him sharply to repeat what he had just said.

"Do you know how to get there?" my wife and I would ask. "You know how. Are you sure you won't get lost? Which way do you turn from here? Do you see you can't get lost? Even if you turned here instead of there or a block later you would still wind up on the boardwalk or the main avenue. You can just follow the people or ask somebody if you do get lost. Will you get lost?")

Yet he had gone only far enough to be almost out of sight of the play group area, where the few remaining counselors were languidly cleaning things up, and could go no farther. Even when he recognized us and saw us coming he did not move, as though even to budge one hair's-width from that agonizing place he occupied would be to risk fainting away over some invisible precipice and swoon out of existence. He remained stationary on the pavement in that single spot on his tiny bare feet as though every bone in his ankles had already been crushed (I noticed then, I think, for the first time, how his feet pronate, how his arches are almost flat, and how large and sharp and close to the ground his ankle bones are) and even to continue standing there was excruciating

298

and unendurable. He couldn't move and he couldn't stay where he was. (He did not rush to us.) He howled. We were salvation, God, his only hope for life, but we had to go all the way to him in order to save him, while his gaping, glistening eyes fastened on us frantically. He would not (could not) take even one step toward us to assist in his own rescue and abbreviate his torment. (It was pitiful, pathetic, heartrending; and I fought back violent surges of anger and impatience and the feeling I might lose control and start berating him right then and there. I wanted to hit him. I felt he deserved it and felt I would have done so if he were older and bigger.) My wife quickened her pace and moved out ahead of me and I plucked at her elbow to hold her back.

"Don't run!" I hissed at her. "You'll scare him."

But it was me he waited for, my presence and protection he needed, and he did not begin walking again until he had felt my hand and was able to grip it solidly. (I had the impression then, as I have now, that if we had turned away from him and gone back, or if, for some unavoidable reason, we had not come for him that day at all, he would have remained stranded unalterably on that same spot at which by invisible forces he had been brought to a stop, a tiny mark on the surface of the world no greater than the dimensions of his own naked footprints, until he had perished or collapsed from exposure, hunger, thirst, fear, or fatigue, or until some unnaturally concerned and curious lady or man had gone searching for a policeman to notify him that there was a small boy standing in one place on the sidewalk who had been crying there all day and night and was in danger of dying from starvation, fright, or loneliness. I had the feeling then, and I sometimes have it now, that he would have failed to survive without my wife and me, will not be able ever to exist without the two of us to sustain him, and he may have that feeling too. What will he do when we die? What will Derek do?)

"If you were swimming," he asked me recently, "and thought you were going to drown, would you yell for the lifeguard and let everybody on the beach

299

see them save you? Or would you let yourself drown?"

I don't know which I'd do. I do know, though, that I no longer go swimming in water over my head.

I would be embarrassed to yell for the lifeguard.

I would be embarrassed to call for a doctor at night if I was having a heart attack but wasn't sure.

"You don't have to be afraid," I told him.

He clung to my hand and walked beside me gingerly with his head down, making each step he took on his bare feet a delicate, probing test. His chest panted, his ribs and breastbone heaving as though they might splinter and stab through his fine translucent skin.

"I don't feel well," he said. His tears dried slowly, staining. "I felt sick."

"We'll take your temperature. Do you feel sick?"

"I was afraid you were never coming for me."

"If you really feel sick when we get back to the house we'll call a doctor and have him fix you up, so you've got nothing to worry about."

"I didn't feel well this morning either."

"I don't know what you're so scared about. You couldn't get lost coming back to the house even if you tried."

"I knew you'd think I was making it up."

He didn't go back to play group the following morning. He didn't want to and we didn't make him. (He adored us for allowing him to stay at home.) He never went back.

"Don't you want to go back there at all?" I asked at breakfast on Sunday.

"He doesn't."

We let it drop.

But after that he had little to do. He had no other kids to play with, no more friends. He spent much of each day on the beach with us, sifting sand. And saying nearly nothing. He wanted to remain indoors a great deal. He read picture books and built lots of models of cars, planes, and aircraft carriers that he took no pride in completing and no joy in preserving. He had no interest in anything. He reread comic books and stared torpidly and sporadically at the television set. He offered to help my wife with the house-

300

work. (This made her nervous.) His attention span was nil; he could not concentrate for long on any of the jigsaw puzzles we bought him. He seemed forgetful. He glued himself to us and went with us almost everywhere, holding on. He did not want to go into town but did not want to be left behind.

("Must you both go?" he would ask despondently.)

He did not want to be left alone and tried to remain with one or both of us always, except at bedtime, when he had to go off into his own room in a different part of the house (and even then he would awake very early each morning—sometimes he awoke in the middle of the night—and ease into the doorway of our bedroom just to assure himself that we were still there and breathing. He remained there persistently, making enough soft noises to disturb one or the other of us.

"What is it?" my wife or I would demand in an exasperated groan. "What do you want?"

"Breakfast," he would lie, if it was already light.

It was spooky. I sometimes had the feeling he never slept at all but merely pretended to and lay awake in his bed watching the window and counting the minutes until he could bear his solitude no longer and felt it was safer to come in to us). He exuded always an air of abject apology, even as he loitered about the kitchen and handed my wife things to help her with the cooking and dishwashing. (My wife had a fear that he would begin wearing her aprons and then other articles of her clothing. What would we do if he turned into a transvestite? And so did I. I pretended to be eager to teach him how to play chess, in order to distract him from my wife and help the time pass, and he pretended to be eager to learn. But neither one of us was really interested, and we soon stopped, even though we could not think of much else for him to do.) It was useless and cruel to urge him to go out and play. There was no one he could play with. He did not want to be with, talk to, be seen by, or even look at any of the boys and girls from the play group, not even any of those he used to hail with glee and point out proudly as his friends. Whenever he walked with us someplace and any came into view, nodding, waving, grinning, or calling hello to him by name, he stiffened and turned his gaze away in angry resolution, offering no response. And soon, no more of them did. They were no longer his friends. It was eerie. It was as though he had never met any of them. He continued to stiffen anyway, tensely and wrathfully, each time we walked and he saw any of them, as though expecting something he loathed to happen. Nothing did. I was angry too and wanted often to slam him on the arm with my fist and shove him toward them roughly with a command to begin playing with them again and have fun.

It was an agony for all of us.

It was the worst summer I ever spent. None of us knew what to do. My wife and I were all he had, and we were not so sure we liked him anymore, although, we never said exactly that. Derek was still a baby in a crib. We didn't know about him yet. And my daughter was away at camp that year for the first time, where she was having a lonely and miserable time of it too, if we could believe her, because all the other girls had been there before and fell easily into cliques, while she was left a friendless outsider. Or so she maintained to us in her letters. We didn't believe her. She wanted to come home: in every letter, she wrote that she wanted to come home; sometimes she wrote *only* to tell us she wanted to come home. We didn't believe her. Some children don't write home enough; ours wrote *too much,* three or four, five times a week, and our spirits sank every time we saw another letter from her. We did not know whether to believe her or not. We thought she was telling us such things solely to make us unhappy. Even at so early an age she was crafty enough to feign crisis and despair just to afflict us with indecision and guilt. She knew how to hurt. From what we were able to learn from other parents with children at the same camp, she seemed to be having no worse a time of it than normal. I wondered why she wrote so often if she had nothing else to say. I did not want to go see her on visiting day. I didn't miss her—I didn't have a chance to, with those damn letters. What for? It meant a long drive on a hot day, a reunion filled with accusations and dejection, another wasted weekend. When we got there, though, she seemed all right and genuinely glad we had come. She behaved as though she had missed us, which was a thing that had not occurred to me and which she had not once, I am sure, put into her letters. Under an elm tree, where no one else could hear us, I asked her point-blank if she wanted me to take her back with us. I even offered to invent some face-saving explanation: my mother was seriously ill, which was true. She said no and seemed to have many smiling friends and sang the camp songs lustily along with the rest of them. She lost the color war. Later, she was to charge that I had bullied her into saying no, and I imagined I saw tears in her eyes and felt a lump in her throat as we drove off for the rest of the summer and she stood at the roadside staring after us with a somber, unmoving face, refusing stolidly to wave good-bye. And those same urgent, whimpering, peremptory letters insisting we bring her home began again and continued in a ceaseless stream. Why, we wondered, although we never lamented it to each other in precisely these words, couldn't she leave us alone, why could she not have the decency to leave us in peace now that we had gone to so much trouble and considerable expense to get her out of our way for eight weeks? She wrote letters to our boy marked PERSONAL in which she pleaded with him—and lavishly promised him things, including to be kinder and more generous with him in the future forever—to do everything he could to get us to let her come home because she was so miserable away from us, at a time when he himself was so downtrodden with sorrow over his own suffering that he could scarcely muster the courage to speak to us about anything at all. Most of his talk with us was monosyllabic replies to questions, mumbled in undertones. One would think she enjoyed being with us, had been satisfied in our company in the past, which was not true. All our summers have been bad. And most of our Sundays. And still are. How I dread those three- and four-day weekends. I wish my wife and I played tennis or enjoyed going on boats for sailing or fishing. But I don't; I don't even enjoy people who do. I don't enjoy anything anymore. I didn't know how to explain to my boy just what the hell was going on with my daughter each time he received another letter from her declaring she was miserable and begging him to beg us to allow her to come home.

"Why won't you let her?" he would inquire with extreme reserve.

"I'm not stopping her."

I didn't *know* what was going on.

"Do you want to come?" I told her by telephone. "Pack up and come. I'll drive up for you now."

"No."

I did know that she was persecuting me. She could indeed have been homesick and unhappy; but she was also using that unhappiness with cool detachment and calculation to upset and oppress us all—as she persecutes me deliberately that same way still, I feel—and that was how we passed the time.

Somehow the time passed; it must have passed very slowly for him. (He liked playing baseball then—and enjoyed being good at it. He loved catching flies and getting hits and scooting around the bases. Now he had nobody to play with.) Somehow, the time always passes (doesn't it, with no help from us and in spite of anything that is going on, as it passes for me now at the company, as it passed ultimately for my much younger daughter then away at camp, and passes now uneventfully for my wife at home with the help of a sneaky and avenging slurp from the wine bottle every half hour or so during the morning and afternoon and an energetic bang in the box from me at night one or two times a week or so if I come home and feel up to it, and as it passed for my poor old mother when she was bedridden with arthritis and painful, cramping limbs and joints and stricken speechless by her brain spasms and just about all she had left to her, for that last, little while, was a consciousness that understood dismally how little she had left. All she had left was me. Yet, she held on, clawed fingers and all, even in those final comas, she held on stubbornly and willfully for dear life, ha, ha, but her kidneys failed her treacherously, it was a stealthy, unsuspected betrayal from underneath, and in the end, ha, ha, she died, crying for her mother, moaning "Ma! Ma! Ma!" in a drone that was clear and loud although the doctor said she felt no pain and did not know what was happening. How did *he* know? Then I could bury her. At last I could bury her, although she had died about sixteen months before. I had a mother once who died sixteen months before she was buried. At least as far as I was concerned. My sister lives far away with diabetes and other family problems of her own and didn't come to the funeral. I didn't want her to and told her it wasn't necessary. I would handle and pay for everything. We aren't close. I wasn't close to my mother. I was mad at her.

"Hey, look, Ma," I could have argued with her with good reason any time during those sixteen months. "You're dead already, don't you know? You died one day exactly two, four, six, eight, ten, twelve months ago right in front of my eyes, and now you're just hanging around. I didn't know it at the time but I felt it, and I turned away from you with a lump in my throat and sobbed, or wanted to, and grieved for you secretly, for over a week because something inside me knew that you were dead and gone. You were dead but not gone. I lost my mother a while ago and keep remembering and losing her again. But you're not her. You're just hanging around. Now you're just hanging around, ruining my weekends and costing me money, splotching my moods and splattering my future. You've been hanging around ever since. You're depressing everybody. What do you want me to do? What are you hanging around for?"

Oh, boy. Oh, boy, oh, boy, oh, boy. I never could say that, even to myself, while she was alive. But that was the way I think I felt. I can say it now. That was the longest I had to wait for anyone's funeral, and she waited with me almost as long. God willing, I will have to wait even longer for my own. Soon, I know, I will have to start. I know how I will begin. I'll have bladder and prostate trouble—that's if I'm lucky, and don't have a coronary occlusion or stroke first. Perhaps some hernia or hemorrhoid operation will be thrown in gratuitously also just to divert me from my bladder and prostate troubles while I'm hanging around waiting for my burial services to be allowed by law to begin. But I know I'll probably want to hang around as long as I can too, pain, pity, self-revulsion and all, clinging with weakening fingers to vaporous mirages above the bedsheets and muttering "Ma! Ma! Ma! Ma!" to the end, instead of "ha, ha, ha." Perhaps only then, when there is room left in the brain for just one memory, and throat and mouth left for just one word, will Green, White, Black, Brown, Kagle, Arthur Baron, wife's sister, three-minute speeches in Puerto Rico, and a drunken, blowsy, young whore I didn't even want in Detroit last week ridiculing me obstreperously, at a party, as she rejected advances I did not even make, perhaps only then will galling events and presences like these be expunged from my teeming inventory of trivial slights and defeats I've never been able to absorb and detoxify and will be filed away with me into oblivion and dead records once and for all. That's the way I will put an end to the world. I will not want to go. They will have to drag me down writhing and moaning, I like to think now, while I fight with mind, eyes, ears to remain, but I know I will probably be undermined also by a liver or two kidneys while I'm concentrating all my forces on top, and I will lose the battle without even knowing I have gone. I will give up the ghost without sensing I am doing so. Morphine will help befog me. I don't ever want to go. I hope I outlive everyone, even my children, my wife, and the Rocky Mountains. I don't think I will. There are valves in my heart; there are valves in my car; if General Motors is unable to produce a valve guaranteed to last longer than one more year, what chance has random nature? I cannot help feeling sorry for myself. I cannot help feeling sorry for him). I felt sorry for him then (I feel sorry for him now); he was hanging around already with the vacant, colorless look of someone old and waning, denuded of wants and enthusiasm, like an invalid mother in

306

a nursing home who knows she has been put there to die. He hardly spoke. There was nothing he enjoyed, he seemed to lack even anything to hope for (God— he had given up so early!), except for that sweltering, muggy summer to end and school, which he feared, to begin and snatch him up again into its buzzing, fathomless drama of unknown conflicts and rewards. He had no spark or spirit. He was dull. He was always hanging around. Instead of catching fly balls and running around bases in games with friends, he tagged along with us to the boardwalk or beach and held himself apart, saying nearly nothing.

("When are we gonna go back?"

He didn't want to swim. Wherever he went with us, he was ill at ease and wanted to be somewhere else, usually back home, except in the dark at the movies.

"Do you have to go out again tonight?")

And sifted sand listlessly. (We did not want him with us.) Whenever my eyes fell upon his, he quivered and drew his neck in, as though he expected me to lunge toward him and begin browbeating him ruthlessly. He looked like someone sick. (People often inquired of us softly, to my intense discomfort, if he were not feeling well. At times I could not bear him.) I did everything I could think of to help.

"What would you like to do?" I offered.

"Where would you like to go?"

"What would you like to happen?"

"Do you want to go to the movies? Maybe we'll go with you. What do you want to see?"

"If you had one wish, what is it? Tell me. Maybe I can help make it come true. What do you wish for now more than anything else in the whole world?"

"Nothing."

"Nothing."

"Nothing."

"Nothing."

"Please stop."

I could have strangled him. I could have beaten him. (I think I wanted to.) All I got from him was nothing. He made no effort at all to help us make

307

things easier for him. I could not bear to see him always so idle and forlorn. He was always there. In the morning when we awoke. He never seemed to sleep. No matter how late my wife and I came in at night, he was always lying awake, his door open, to make certain we were back and that it was us, and not someone else, who had come in. He made no effort to talk to the baby-sitter we had got for him and Derek.

"Where are you going? What are you going to do?" he interrogated us closely each time it seemed to him that my wife and I were making ready to go out of the house together.

He trailed after us almost everywhere we let him. He began to get on my nerves. (I had to feel sorry for him too often. Why in the world did he happen to *me?* I began to feel about him then the way I feel about Derek now. But Derek, at least, I can disassociate myself from most of the time and escape from.) There was no escaping from him. He trailed us everywhere, a visible, public symptom of some odious family disease we would have preferred kept secret.

"I have nothing to do," he answered whenever we told him to go away from us and do something else.

We often felt grotesque. People saw him with us all the time. He had that lump in his throat. He would not speak to other lonely little boys we spotted for him and tried to introduce him to.

"Look, here is Dicky Dare. He is a nice boy and just about the same age as you. Why don't you go play with him?"

He would not want to.

"Why not?"

(He did not want to be associated with another kid who had no one else to play with. He admired the kid who had wanted to fight with him at play group and wished that other boy liked him enough in return to want to become his friend.)

When people we knew asked helpfully if he would like to meet someone to play with, we had to tell them no. We could never tell them why. We couldn't explain that he would not cooperate. (We had a lump in our throat.)

"I can't stand it," my wife would grieve, and be about to cry. "He looks like a ghost. He's so unhappy. I can't stand to see him this way. It breaks my heart."

"Me neither," I confessed.

The only good days I had that summer were the days I spent in the city at my office. It broke my heart too. He wouldn't roller skate or ride his bike. I began to lose my temper more easily. (I was ugly.)

"Go play," I ordered him curtly at the beach one day when I could control my temper no longer.

He blinked.

"Bob," my wife cautioned.

"Huh?" he asked.

"Are you deaf?"

"I didn't hear."

"Yes, you did. Go play."

"With who?"

"There's a kid sitting there near that fat lady."

"Daddy. Please."

"He looks your own age. He looks like he wants to meet somebody to play with."

"I'm playing here."

"With what?"

"Sand."

"Sand," I mimicked nastily, and pointed toward the shore. "Or I'll drag you over there by the arm and ask him for you." (Having made that threat, I had to mean it. There was an article in a women's magazine that month advising parents to be firm with balky children. There was an article in another women's magazine advising us to be sympathetic and indulgent. I didn't care about either magazine. I was mad. My wife was trying to warn me off with a look. I paid no attention. It was a matter of face now between myself and this poor, bewildered little boy.) "Would you like that?" I threatened.

His face was chalky. "I won't be able to speak."

"You're speaking now."

"I've got a lump in my throat. I want to vomit."

"You'll have a lump on your head," I could not

restrain myself from wisecracking. "Get going. You can vomit later."

He rose reluctantly and went with slow, wobbling steps to do as I had forced him.

"You see?" I whispered to my wife, fearfully and penitently, craving immediate absolution. "He's going."

"I think it's horrible."

"He's doing it."

He was speaking to the other boy, a wan, yellow-haired kid who shook his head without looking up and gave a labored, long reply. His mouth moved funny. I was sickened. The fat woman glared. My boy walked back to us with knees that seemed to bend with pain and he was almost in tears as he told us in a blocked, stammering voice that the other boy stuttered badly and had said no, he did not want to play.

"Well, I did what you wanted!" my boy spat out at me bitterly, giving me a quick, stabbing glance, and sat down in the sand again a good distance away. His eyes were steaming at me with anger.

I felt frustrated and enraged.

Everything was going wrong for me, one thing after another, even my wife's snatch (God dammit).

That summer my wife had a sensitive snatch, a recurring vaginal inflammation, and I (even she, until I tried) didn't even know if I would be able to get laid properly when I came out for those dragging, intolerable weekends. (I could have done much better staying in the city. I *was* doing better. I was getting all I wanted.) I did not have much else to do out there at the beach that I enjoyed, except make eyes at other wives and josh suggestively with very young girls. So I kept losing my temper with him and trying to help him. (I'd lose my temper when I'd see myself fail. I was filled with such depressing feelings of rejection and impotence at my inability to cheer him up, to alleviate his wretched agony and isolation, to have him succeed at doing something new.) I kept commanding him gruffly to attempt doing things that he did not want to do and was probably physically unable to do because of the rigid tension impairing his balance and coordination and because of the lump in his throat.

Because I felt he was afraid of the ocean, I made him go wading with me, and he almost drowned when a large wave broke suddenly and knocked us both down, tore him from my grasp, and sent him rolling and tumbling helplessly toward shore in the deep, swirling, tumultuous surf. When he stumbled to his feet finally (as I struggled feebly against the backwash in an effort to reach him and save him), he was holding his breath, and his eyes were clamped shut so tightly that both knuckled halves of his flushed face looked like clenched and crimson fists. He would not open them until I had taken his hand again and led him to shore. I have visions of that episode still.

"You know, Daddy," he said to me, "I was afraid to open my eyes. I didn't know where I was and I was afraid to open my eyes and look. I was afraid that when I opened my eyes I would be all the way out there, and I didn't want to look."

I was surprised he talked to me, surprised he still trusted me enough to confide in me. (He could have drowned or been battered to death or paralysis right then and there. He might have been swept away from me out to sea by a suction of rushing water in a matter of three or four seconds. Once I helped lifeguards save a baby in an inflated tube that had been carried out thirty yards from shore in an instant. I might never have seen him alive again. I have always been afraid of death by drowning. I might never have been able to forgive myself if I had lost him then. My wife might never have allowed me to. I would have had to divorce her, leaving her with a Derek who was destined by birth, we are told, to turn out mentally defective and my daughter, who has been of small aid and comfort, which might not be such a bad thing for me to do even now. I do think about divorce a lot and I always have. Even before I was married I was thinking of getting divorced. I can picture my next wife: she would be younger, prettier, dumb, and submissive. She would be blond, short, chubby, and cheerful and would be very eager to please me in the kitchen and the bedroom. In short order I would find it impossible to be with her for more than an hour or two at a time, and I would have to divorce her too. I'm glad he lived. Getting married was my idea. I enjoy fucking my wife. She lets me do it anyway I want. No Women's Liberation for her. Lots of male chauvinist pig. I couldn't bang her freely even when there was no soreness because he was always hanging around the house in the daytime and was apt to be lying awake at night. I often tried to chase him away from us just for that. If we locked him out of our bedroom we didn't know if he was camping discouragedly just outside the door, where he could hear. I was surly much of the time and did a lot of growling at everyone.)

I did such monstrous things to him. They seemed so necessary at the time. I did not know what else to do. I couldn't get rid of him, and he knew I wanted to. He did go bike riding one day and he fell against a wooden fence and bruised a knee so badly he had to walk with a limp for a week and got a long black splinter in his forearm that I had to poke at and dislodge with a sewing needle (and felt like vice personified doing so. I debated darkly with myself whether or not to take the two-week summer vacation I had coming to me. My wife made me; she said she would be unable to endure it any longer at the beach without me and that she would come back into the city. So I took it. And there were days on my vacation that I would have paid the company twice what I was getting just to be allowed to come in and work). I couldn't even get drunk anymore. I couldn't get high on martinis at cocktail time because he was always around somewhere listening and watching. (I got weary headaches over my eyes instead.) We couldn't tell dirty jokes, I couldn't be obscene, not even when we had people in. I couldn't flirt. He was there and would see me. (At least my daughter, God bless her benevolent heart, had been considerate enough to pack up her troubles in her old duffel bag and foot-locker and go off to camp to be miserable far away from us for the summer and pester us from afar.) He was right there. He was always right there. (I couldn't say or do anything I wouldn't want him to witness. There were so many ways I might upset him.) When

312

I turned around sometimes, he was underfoot and I would step on him, and we would both feel terrible and blurt clumsy, incoherent apologies. (I wanted to curse. I wanted to scream. I wanted to scream: "Get out of here!") I couldn't decide what to say. I didn't know how to handle it. Finally, I figured it out. I said:

"Get lost."

To make him realize he was capable of leaving us and finding his way around without getting lost, I made him go for a long walk alone; and, of course, he got lost.

"Get lost," I repeated more sharply, when he appeared not to understand.

"Huh?"

"I've got nothing to do," he had grumbled a moment before.

"Go someplace."

"Where?"

"Away. Take a walk."

"With who?"

"With yourself. Mommy and I want to be here on the beach alone for a while."

"I won't know how."

"Yes, you will."

"I won't get back."

"Yes, you will."

"Now?"

"When then?"

My wife stared away from him stonily. "You'd better go," she advised unsympathetically.

"Go down the beach to the amusement pier. Then turn around and come back. Just follow the water down the beach to the amusement pier. Then turn around and follow the water back."

"I want to stay here."

"I want you to go."

"I'll get lost."

"You'd have to be pretty damned smart to do that."

I was determined. He stood up, rubbing sand slowly from his palms, and walked off submissively in mute dejection without looking back. He was soon gone from sight behind the heads and torsos of other people jamming the shoreline. The amusement pier looked farther away than ever before, the beach more densely packed. I was afraid he'd get lost. (I was afraid *I'd* get lost if I had to do what I'd sent him to do.)

"Why did you do it?" my wife asked critically, already repenting her own passive cooperation.

"You wanted me to do it, didn't you?"

I kept craning my neck to keep slim flashes of him in view for as long as I could and grew worried and sorry also as soon as he was gone.

"I know," my wife admitted. She nodded absently. "I couldn't stand him hanging around here anymore."

"Me neither."

"He's always here. It breaks my heart."

"Mine too."

"He always looks so unhappy."

"That's one of the things I can't stand."

"Do you think he'll get lost?"

"He can't get lost. It's that damned play group, damn them. None of this would have happened if they'd kept closer watch of things. I want him to see that he can go from place to place alone without having something terrible happen to him."

"The beach is so crowded."

"He won't get lost."

He got lost.

(At least we thought he was lost.)

When twenty-five minutes passed and he did not return, we went surging after him in panic, my wife scurrying along the shore, myself trudging through deeper sand in the middle of the beach in the direction of the amusement pier. (I thought of homosexual perverts or of other kids from the play group spotting him, mocking him, ganging up on him.

"The sky is falling!" I wanted to shout in horror at groups of adults I hurried past with a thundering heart. "Have you seen a little kid? He's lost. He'll look worried.")

We found him standing by himself along the shore about two hundred yards away, floundering in one spot as though lost: he was not certain if he had overshot us already, and he did not know, therefore, in which direction to proceed. His cheeks were white, his eyes were distant, and his jaws were clamped shut. The tendons in his neck were taut, and he had a lump in his throat. The landmarks along the board-walk—all those familiar signs and structures—meant nothing to him.

My first impulse was to kill him.

"Were you lost?" I shouted to him.

"I don't know." He shrugged.

I wanted to kill him. I was enraged and disgusted with him for his helplessness and incompetence (standing there like that on the sidewalk in town that day as though all the bones in his ankles were broken. I was ashamed of him and wanted to disown him. I was sorry he was mine), then I wanted to clasp him to me lovingly and protectively and shed tears of misery and deepest compassion over him (because I had wanted to kill him. Imagine having a father that wanted to kill you. That's the part they all leave out of the Oedipus story. Poor Oedipus has been much maligned. He didn't want to kill his father. His father wanted to kill *him*). I don't know what I felt when I found him standing there like that, immense gratitude that he was unharmed and intense, depressing disappointment over everything else, a terrible rush of ungovernable, dissonant emotions in which landmarks made no sense to me, either. (I don't always know what I feel now.)

(I wish I were a chimpanzee.)

The next day my wife and I had a scathing quarrel in the house over money and sex that had nothing at all to do with him (although he could not know that). We snarled and snapped and sneered at each other like barking jackals. She yelled at me and I yelled back (we called each other bastard and bitch and told each other to go fuck ourselves), and when I stormed away into the kitchen to fling some ice cubes into my glass of whiskey, nearly shattering it in my hand with my violent force, I heard my boy move into the living room timidly and say, softly, to my wife:

315

"Should I go for a walk again? To the amusement pier?"

I heard myself sigh. I wanted to weep.

"Is that why Daddy's unhappy?"

I felt myself feel so utterly awful.

My wife came into the kitchen quietly.

"Did you hear him?" she murmured, her anger against me gone. (I said nothing.) "He wants to know if he should go for a walk again. He thinks that's why you're unhappy now."

"He did not," I denied finally, without spirit.

"You must have heard him. Go ask him."

"I don't believe you."

"You get crazy when you're this way," my wife lamented. "I can't talk to you. None of us can. You won't listen and you won't see. Go ask him. Go see what he looks like if you don't believe me."

I knew what I would see (and did not want to). I stepped around my wife without looking at her or touching her and walked into the living room. He was standing docile and repentant (as though he were to blame) near the door leading out to the porch, awaiting my directions. His skin was shaded blue. (He would do whatever I asked. He did not want me to be angry or unhappy because of him. His eyes were wide and serious. I have never before or since in all my life felt so totally cruel, so rotten, depraved, and inhuman. He was prepared to yield himself to any sacrifice I requested of him. I did not want him that way.) His look was expectant, grave, and resigned. I did not speak for a second. (I couldn't.) I had a lump in my throat.

"From now on," I told him gently, "at least until the end of the summer, you won't have to do anything you don't want to do. And you'll be allowed to do everything you do want to do. Will that be okay?" My tone was tender, apologetic.

His gaze was skeptical. "You mean it?"

"I promise."

"I love you, Daddy," he said, and rested his head against my belly to hug me peacefully. "You're the best daddy in the whole world."

I am the worst daddy in the whole world.

Yesterday, I helped a blind man across the street and was surprised that I did not feel revolted when I took his arm. (Actually, he took my arm. I started to grip his, but he told me:

"No, let me hold on to yours.")

I think I will do things like that more often (now that I see I can).

I broke my promise to him many times.

He continued to love me anyway.

I identify with him too closely, I think, and remember that once, when he was still an infant in diapers, kicking his legs away as he lay on the Bathinette, rocking it perilously and raising a violent clatter and spray of powder cans and safety pins, my wife yelled to me urgently to come into the room and showed me a fiery red blotch on the side of the head of his penis. (It must have been minuscule, had to be, but appeared a gigantic blister at the time.) And I doubled over with a keen, slicing pain in my own penis the instant I saw the rough (small), flaming-red patch and cupped my hands over all my genitals reflexively to preserve and soothe them. It hurt then. It hurts now when I remember. I don't have to look to make certain nothing's there. Once when I was small I felt a stinging itch at the tip and saw a brown ant come crawling out, but I no longer tell this to anyone because nobody believes me. I guess I really do love this little thing of mine still, although I'm not sure why. Where would I be without it? Neuter. It had led me into strange places. I have led it. Through these thrilled and limp, leaking tissues have come decades of exquisite and often intolerable pleasures and three big, fully formed children who were mammoth in camparison to it, from the day they were born, one of them defective. In a factory he would be a reject. He suffers less than normal. We make up the difference. By and large, I believe I really don't get all that much

317

pleasure out of it anymore, although I think I'd like to hold on to it a little longer, ha, ha. I don't always like putting it in, and I don't like taking it out. I wish there was something more to do with it than there is. Once in my early teens, I paid a younger cousin of mine, a girl, a dime to pull it for me and was terrified afterward that she would tell my mother or my brother or someone in her own family. I wonder if it warped her. It might have helped. She made me happy. For only a dime. I see her still as a dubious little girl, without a gleam of mischief or curiosity or sensuality of her own to enrich the experience for her. She was bored, and a little puzzled. I touched her gingerly. I molested a child. I was molested as a child. Everyone is molested. Maybe that's why I worry about my boy so much. I used to worry that way about my daughter. Now she is old enough to molest children on her own. I have paid much more than a dime many times since.

In my middle years, I have exchanged the position of the fetus for the position of a corpse. When I go to sleep now, it is no longer on my side with my knees tucked up securely against my abdomen, and my thumb near my mouth. I lie on my back with my hands clasped across my chest decorously like a cadaver and my face pointed straight up toward the ceiling. I hear and feel myself start to snore, on nights when I am lucky; a loose, membranous thing vibrates tantalizingly in back of my throat with a deep, delicious, tickling sensation, and I am assuaged also by the satisfying possibility that my snoring will annoy my wife and interfere with her sleep. I can't stand it when I am unable to sleep and my wife does; I sometimes want to begin beating her with the side of my fists. I like it when I am able to sleep and she can't. When I awake, though, it is usually on my side, and one of my hands is still always between my thighs, near my genitals. I guess I do want to hold on to them all for as long as I can. I knew I was getting old when I started to have dreams about peeing. I awake with a full bladder and the momentary, shame-filled horror that I have already wet the bed. And that everyone will soon find out.

I know at last what I want to be when I grow up.

When I grow up I want to be a little boy.

I'd like another chance. And then another. (And after that a couple of more. There were so many girls I could have laid when I was young and didn't because I didn't know I had the knack and could. I didn't know how easy it was. It never occurred to me then that they wanted to do it too. I didn't even have the urge. I fell in love instead. I'd like another crack. Ha, ha. I think I'd get the urge. When I grow up, I want to be someone dignified, tasteful, and important who does the things he does because he truly wants to and enjoys his work. I'd like to be William Shakespeare.) Maybe that's why I worry so much about my little boy (I identify with him too closely), why I grow somewhat frantic and exasperated whenever I see him bogged down, whenever I see him fail at something or even refuse to try. (Am I disappointed in him?) My daughter insists we are disappointed in her. I know I looked for something much different for all of us. I never became what I wanted to be, even though I got all the things I ever wanted, including two cars and two color TV sets. We are a two-car family in a Class A suburb in Connecticut. Advertising people and the U.S. Census Bureau prepare statistics that include us in categories of human beings enjoying the richest life. I wanted him carefree and confident, swashbuckling, able, successful, and dependent, so maybe I am disappointed in him, in everything but that last. Maybe that's why he's scared I want to take him someplace strange and dangerous and leave him there. Maybe I do. I have that same fear of something like that happening to him; I see him lost somewhere; and there is no hope he will ever be found. I know I fear for his safety more than I fear for my own, and this surprises me.

When he's scared, I'm scared, even though I'm not scared of what he's scared of. (I get rattled when things don't go right for him. I wish I could be guaranteed now that he will never do anything more to upset me. I can't hit back.)

When he quivers, I quake. My nose runs when he's got a cold; I sneeze too and my throat turns sore. When he has fever, my temples burn and throb and my joints and muscles turn stiff and sore. (I am all heart, ain't I?)

My boy is pretty much this same way. He identifies with other people in trouble too closely also. That's the reason he gives cookies and pennies away, I think, to people he feels want them—he knows what it is to long. (He longs along with them.) I remember the way he used to gape in disbelieving terror at deformed and mutilated people, at humpbacks, dwarfs, and people with missing or malformed arms or legs. I could read his mind: he did not know what had happened to them that could not happen to him, and it was not always easy to explain. (I could not assure him categorically that he would never be in a serious accident or fall fatally ill.) I note the way he avoids looking at them directly now. (He averts his eyes with a ripple of anger the way I avert mine. You are not supposed to look at them, you are not supposed to look away from them.) It used to be that his own arm or leg would lock momentarily in an unnatural position or knot up.

("Look!"

He would show me the rigid cramp of muscle or the fluttering spasms of fingers or feet, marveling at this telepathic phenomenon with as much curiosity as discomfort whenever he saw a cripple with arm or leg deformities and ask me why that happened.

"Mine does too.")

"I can tell you something else that's funny," he revealed to me recently. "Whenever I tickle somebody, I laugh."

"How come?" I exclaim. This strikes me funny an instant later and I begin to laugh.

"I don't know," he squeals in reply, laughing also. "Why are you laughing?"

"Because I think it's funny! Why are you laughing?"

"Because you're laughing!" he cries gleefully, and

laughs even louder, bubbling all about with delight and folding his arms around his sides as though his ecstasy is too much for his ribs and spirit to contain.

My boy likes to laugh and would be laughing and kidding jauntily all the time if there were not so many of us in the atmosphere surrounding him to inhibit and subjugate him. I have this constant fear something is going to happen to him. (He's the kid who gets stabbed to death in the park or falls victim to Hodgkin's disease or blastoma of the eyeballs. Every time I know he's gone swimming. Every time he's away from the house. Every time I know my daughter is driving in a car with older kids I expect to be told by telephone or policeman of the terrible automobile accident in which she has just been killed. There are times I wish they would both hurry up and get it over with already so I could relax and stop brooding about it in such recurring suspense. There are times I wish everyone I know would die and release me from these tender tensions I experience in my generous solicitude for them. I don't suffer these same acute anxieties about my wife, even though I know she drives about a great deal during the day after drinking. I hardly ever think about her death. Just about divorce. I don't like cars. Or swimming pools or the ocean.)

I think about death.

I think about it all the time. I dwell on it. I dread it. I don't really like it. Death runs in my family, it seems. People die from it, and I dream about death and weave ornate fantasies about death endlessly and ironically. (And I find—God help me—that I still do want to make that three-minute speech. I *really do* yearn to be promoted to Kagle's job. Last night in bed, I stopped dwelling on death for a while and began formulating plans for either of the two speeches I might be asked to make. I might be asked to make none, I found good phrases for both.) Last night in bed after fashioning my good phrases—or was it early this morning while journeying back uncrippled again from sleep?—I dreamed that our maid called me at the office while my wife was out drinking somewhere (or screwing somewhere, I have dreams about that too lately every once in a while and I don't like them at all) and told me, in her slurred southern accent, with her voice as deep as a colored man's:

"Mr. _____, your boy is lying on the floor of the living room and hasn't breathed for fifteen seconds."

That was precisely the way the words were floated to me in my dream or beclouded waking moments:

"Mr. _____, your boy is lying on the floor of the living room and hasn't breathed for fifteen seconds."

(No name. A gap, a portentous omission, an empty underlining—I don't know how.)

"What?" I gasped, turning freezing cold with prickling skin. (I was numb and powerless in the presence of that approaching tragedy that was at last about to occur.)

"Mr. _____, your boy is lying on the floor of the living room and hasn't breathed for fifteen seconds."

I had no name but knew who I was.

I could hear her clearly on the phone but had trouble understanding and believing her—I could see her woman's face; it was dark and full and impassive and I kept making her repeat what she was saying by asking "What?"—I could not think what else to do except stall desperately for time by hollering "What?"—and making her repeat her message—and the message from the maid was always the same:

"Mr. _____, your boy is lying on the floor of the living room and hasn't breathed for fifteen seconds."

(Time was rushing by, and it was still fifteen seconds.)

"Mr. _____, your boy is lying on the floor of the living room and hasn't breathed for fifteen seconds."

(I'm sure I dreamed it.) What would I do if something like that did happen, if I were sitting in my office in the city one uneventful day, like today, a day no different from any of the rest, and received a telephone message from my home that my boy had collapsed on the floor of the living room and seemed to be dying. I know just what I would do. I would telephone the police in Connecticut and let *them* handle it.

("My boy is lying on the floor of my living room

322

and hasn't breathed for fifteen seconds," I might have to tell them, and it would be just like my dream.)

Then I would sigh ponderously and feel very sorry for myself. I would have to cancel appointments, change plans, and make my way home in a hurry by very slow train. A taxicab all the way would be fastest, but I probably would not think of that until I was already in the railroad terminal waiting for the train to budge out. I would be nervous, frantic. But I would also know that I was not really in that much of a hurry anymore but merely pretending, that it was already over, that I would prefer to arrive after the emergency had been handled by other people and the outcome already determined, one way or the other, since it would be too late for me to be of use anyway. I would not want to tell any of my colleagues and employees in the office why I was leaving early that day because I would not want to subject myself to their looks and exclamations of sympathy and impassioned concern. I would not want to answer their questions when I saw them again. More than anything, I think I would feel inconvenienced. (I always feel inconvenienced when plans are changed.)

I was inconvenienced yesterday when a man my age was killed in a subway station nearby and caused a traffic jam that made me late for a cocktail party with salesmen at which I was expected to be early; his arm caught in the closing doors as he tried to push his way on, but the train started anyway while he was still outside, said the newspapers today, even though it was not supposed to, and dragged him along the station platform until he smashed against pillars and the stone and metal walls of the tunnel into which the subway train roared. His wife was already inside the car and watched the whole thing helplessly (I'll bet she even clutched his hand and held on, stupidly, in a vain and senseless effort to save him. It was like a dream, I bet. I'll bet she's even saying that right now:

"It was like a dream.")

Another man my age was shot to death in the park yesterday and no one knows why. (Men my age are starting to die of cancers, strokes, and heart at-

323

tacks now.) Last week, another man was shot to death in the park, and no one knows why. The week before that, another man was shot to death in the park, and no one knows why. Every week a man is shot to death in the park. No one knows why. A boy was stabbed on the subway. I don't go into the park. (In Jackson, Mississippi, every year or so, three colored college students are shot to death in cold blood by state police and everyone knows why, so none of the rest of us are afraid.) I'm even still afraid of doors. I'm afraid of closed doors and afraid of what I might spy or what might come in through open ones. I know I nearly died of fear from his tonsil operation that day in the hospital when the attendants rolled him back unconscious through the doorway still and pale, reeking of ether fumes that sickened me, and a crust of nearly black blood inching disgustingly before my eyes out through one of his motionless nostrils. (Only a miracle saved me.) My stomach turned. My head reeled. The room swam.

"What's the matter?" my wife shrieked at me in panic, looking at me. "What is wrong?"

(I don't know what she thought I saw or knew about him that she didn't or what she thought was happening to me that filled her with such alarm.)

I couldn't speak. I thought I'd vomit (but didn't feel healthy enough). My ears buzzed, my brain ached, the floor undulated insanely, and I really believe I might have fainted away right then and there (like a woman) if my wife had not jumped up from the bedside of my boy to grab me by the elbow, shocking me with the stinging points of her long fingernails and with her shrill, penetrating shrieks. She held me firmly, her eyes burning upon me as large as blazing lamps. She kept me from falling and helped me, like a feeble invalid, to a chair. (My wife is stronger than I am, and better too, but I must never let her find that out.) She poured a glass of cold water for me from a pitcher that had been set on the table near the bed for my boy. The doctor entered as I was sipping from it and asked if anything was wrong. I shook my head, faking.

"There's nothing wrong, is there?" I said. "Tell her. He's all right, isn't he?"

"Good as gold," he answered with a smile. "He's going to be fine. These are his. They used to belong to him. He may want to keep them."

We threw them away before my boy regained consciousness and knew about them.

I've never forgotten that tonsillectomy. (I've never forgotten my own.) I still relapse into acute symptom recurrences in which I gag on the sweet, suffocating odor of ether rising from him and remember that pale face and dried smudge of blood desecrating one nostril and recollect with inescapable pain how, back home and recovered, he began crawling obsessively and instinctively (for a little while he was like some living prehuman thing small and obsessed) through the low and musty darkness into our bedroom over and over again after calculating each time until he hoped we were both soundly asleep because it was impossible for him to remain alone at night in his own room. (We did not realize then that it was actually impossible. We thought he was just being smart. I think it was impossible for me to remain alone at night in my own room after my tonsillectomy. I think I remember being allowed to sleep in bed with my mother and father once, and I can't imagine why they would have let me unless I was ill and scared.) We would chase him out. Each evening, he would not even want to go inside his own room when we told him it was bedtime. We made him. (He was afraid, I think, that we were plotting to nail him in for good as soon as we tricked him into entering and permitting us to close the door. He would not let us close the door. We always had to leave it open at least an inch.) We did not lock him in. We locked him out. We locked ourselves inside our room because we could not stand him crawling back to us all night long with his gaily colored quilt, which he always dragged along with him (and found him huddled up outside against the door on the floor of the narrow, drafty hallway. We had to stifle screams in the morning when we opened our door and bumped him because, at first, we forgot he might be there. Later, we were almost unable to open our bedroom door because we sensed he was. Sometimes he was not; he was missing, and that was just as appalling until we found him where he was). It was a scary, nerve-wracking time for all of us (mostly, I guess, for him, although we tended to ignore that. I slept out someplace as often as I could. He got over it in a week. It took me longer). It was torture (and he was putting us through it). It was maddening and exasperating to have to lie in bed trying to sleep each night while waiting to hear him testing our doorknob again or scratching against our thick pile carpet as he came worming his way back inside our bedroom again, rousing us, frightening us, from sleep in sluggish protest and torment again, or to awake disgruntled in the morning and discover him lying prostrate on the floor at the foot of our bed or in some corner of the room, with his quilt, near the legs of a dresser or chair, his sticky, heavy-lidded eyes glued shut finally with exhaustion, his misshapen lips lax, swollen, and blubbery, his thumb lying lifeless near his mouth as though it had just fallen out. (What a terrible time that tonsillectomy of his was for me. It was worse than my own. I may never recover from it fully.)

"Stay in your room," I would command him sternly.

"You have to go back to your room," I would try to coax him gently in the darkness of our bedroom when some unexpected new reserve of kindness and pity would flow within me (pleading with him, really, to please let us alone). "You can leave the lights on if you want to. There's nothing to be afraid of."

"I'm not afraid."

"One of us will stay with you."

"Then you'll go."

"I can't stay in your room all night."

"Then why should I?"

"It's your room."

"I want to be in your room. I want to stay with you and Mommy."

"A doctor said you shouldn't. He said it would be bad for you."

"What doctor?"

"A doctor we saw."

"I don't believe him."

"Do you want to go see him?"

He was afraid of doctors then and has been afraid of doctors, nurses, and dentists ever since. (He doesn't ever want to have to have teeth drilled or pulled.) I don't think he will ever recover from that operation of his fully either. I fear he and my daughter too may never forgive me for permitting their tonsils to become so severely infected that it was necessary for them to be taken to a hospital to have them pulled out (or cut, if that's what they do. And his adenoids too. He isn't mad at me about his adenoids because he doesn't know what they are yet, and neither does anyone else, although those were taken away from him, too. They seem to be highly specialized organs growing inside a person's pharynx whose only natural function is to be taken out), and he keeps associating men he doesn't trust (not me, although he doesn't always trust me) with the anesthetist there, whose appearance he recalls only hazily.

"He gave me an enema," he alleges with abiding resentment and embarrassment during one of our disorganized discussions about everything that might be on his mind.

"No, he didn't," I correct him again. "That was an anesthetic. We gave you an enema at home the night before."

"He looked like Forgione."

"He was a Jap. You didn't even know Forgione then."

"Forgione is an Italian," he concedes abstractedly. "Forgione doesn't like me."

"Yes he does."

"No he doesn't."

"Yes he does. He does now."

"I don't like him."

"You don't have to. Just pretend."

"Miss Owens doesn't like me."

"Yes she does. She gives you good grades."

"She always hollers at me."

"She never does."

"I'm afraid she will if I don't do my work."

"Do your work."

"He says I can't climb ropes."

"Can you?"

"I hate Forgione."

"You don't have to."

"How come?"

"He likes you."

"Did you go see him again?"

"Did you want me to?"

"I'm afraid of Forgione."

"You don't have to be."

"How do you know?"

"He says you've got a good build and can run like a weasel. You don't try to learn. You're supposed to use your feet too when you climb ropes. Not your legs, your feet."

"What's a weasel?"

"A four-legged animal that runs like you."

"Will I have wisdom teeth?"

"Sure. When you grow up."

"Will they have to be pulled?"

"Are you going to start worrying about that?"

"Do you think I can help it?"

"If they're bad."

"You don't like me."

"Yes I do."

"You go away."

"Where?"

"To Puerto Rico."

"I have to."

"To Puerto Rico?"

"When?"

"Last year. You went away to Puerto Rico."

"I had to."

"Are you going again?"

"I have to."

"Soon?"

"In June."

"To Puerto Rico?"

"I'm on the committee. I help pick the place."

"Is that your new job?"

"I don't have it yet."

"To make a speech?"

"I hope so."

"They stole my bike when you were away."

"I bought you another one."

"I thought they were going to beat me up."

"They would have stolen it anyway, even if I was here. I would have been at the office."

"Don't go."

"I have to."

"Whenever you go away I'm afraid you won't come back."

"I know."

"How do you know?"

"You told me."

"Sometimes I cry."

"I'll come back."

"I don't want to be alone."

"You wouldn't be alone. You'd have Mommy."

"Mommy doesn't like me."

"Yes she does."

"She yells at me."

"*I* yell at you."

"*You* don't like me."

"You're full of bull. I'm always sorry afterward. You don't have to worry. I'll come back. I'm never going to leave you."

"When you die?"

His question catches me by surprise. "What made you think of that?"

"I don't want you to," he answers solemnly. "Maybe that's what made me think of it."

"Ever?"

"No."

"I'll try not to, then," I laugh. (My laugh sounds forced, hollow.) "For your sake. I don't want to, either."

"You have to," he speculates. "Won't you?"

"Someday, I guess. By that time, though, you might not care."

He looks up sharply. "How come?"

"You'll be all grown up by then, if you're lucky, and won't need me anymore. You'll be able to take care of yourself and won't want me around. You might even be glad. I'll finally stop yelling at you."

"Hey, slut, come here," he calls out excitedly to my daughter with a grin of incredulous wonderment. His eyes gleam. "Do you know what Daddy just said?" His eyes gleam. "He said that when he dies we might not even care because all of us will be all grown up and able to take care of ourselves. We might even be glad."

My daughter's mood is dour and unresponsive (and I feel already that she will soon be deep in deadening drugs, if she isn't using them already).

"What about Derek?" she demands with inspired malice, and her eyes grow bright and cold. I frown. (She is proud of this thrust.)

"I wasn't thinking about him."

"You forgot about Derek."

I forgot about Derek. I wish I could forget about him more often. It's hard to forget about him for long (while he's still here in the house with us, although I always try. When he's out of sight, he's usually out of my mind. We should send him away someplace and have him out of our house and minds for good. What a relief that will be. It would be upsetting. My daughter wants me to. My boy doesn't. It's no use seeing doctors anymore). Like my boy, I am afraid of doctors, nurses, and dentists (although I pretend not to be), and I guess I always have been. I'm afraid they might be right. (In the army, I would look directly at the needle when I got my immunization shots because I wanted so strongly to turn my head away. I am no longer a blood donor: I no longer give blood to my company blood bank when the Personnel and Medical Departments set up facilities annually to take blood from hardier employees than myself who volunteer and get thinned orange juice back in exchange. I do not set a good example for the people who work for me.) I am empathizing already with my boy's wisdom teeth. He has never mentioned them before (or I would have been empathizing with them sooner. I hope they're not impacted. How will I ever be able to get him to a dentist if he knows they are going to be pulled? Maybe he'll be different by then. And maybe he won't. I am not looking forward to having my own teeth pulled. I rarely get new cavities now, but old fillings fall away and teeth do have to be cleaned, and I don't like having my soft gums pricked by those hard, sharp dental instruments until they're sore from back to front and awash with blood. I don't like having my palate tickled when the backs of the uppers are polished. I am afraid to visit my dentist twice a year. I need periodontal work and have to go once a week). I am afraid of Forgione too (and would not want to have to climb ropes for him. He sneaks into my dreams occasionally too, along with niggers and other menacing strangers, steals through shadows in the background and slips away before I can find out what he is doing in them), although I do not associate him with the anesthetist at the tonsillectomy (who did not threaten me at all, although he did, quite cheerfully, give my boy a liquid anesthetic through a pink rubber tube as we watched. Is that an enema? Maybe he's right). No, I know I will never forget that tonsillectomy of his, or my own, or my daughter's, or the sequence of repetitious medical messages in hushed tones from doctors who told me to my face that my mother had probably suffered another small brain spasm or stroke and was degenerating simultaneously from progressive arthritis, so it was sometimes hard to be sure (for all of these were morbid and revolting experiences and I am unable to repress the memory of them), and I know I will also remember and dislike that last prospering young doctor with the pinstripe suit and exaggerated good posture (he was younger than I was and makes more money) as he stepped out onto the patio (I will never forget him) after examining Derek that pearly spring day (I will never forgive him), the screen door banging closed behind him, to tell us, with something of an unconscious quirk of a smile on his otherwise smug and emotionless face (I think I will always remember his smile):

"He will never speak."

That bastard.

All my life, it seems, I've been sandwiched between people who will not speak. My mother couldn't speak at the end. My youngest child Derek couldn't speak from the beginning. My sister and I almost never speak. (We exchange greeting cards.) I don't speak to cousins. (*I* may never speak. In dreams I often have trouble speaking. My tongue feels dead and dry and swollen enough to choke my mouth. Its coat is coarse. It will not move when I want it to, and I am in danger and feel terror because I cannot speak or scream.) I wish I didn't have to leave my family and go to Puerto Rico. (I worry when I have to go away. I worry about all of us. I worry what would happen to them if I did not return.)

Derek is pleasant enough most of the time (for a kid that cannot speak) and toilet trained now. He hardly ever causes a disturbance anymore when we take him out in public and usually does not act strange. But he will achieve a mental age of not much more than five, and arrive at that slowly, and turbulent emotional changes are expected with adolescence and full physical sexual maturity. (If he lives that long. I have heard that certain kinds of retardates—that's another thing we call him now—have a life expectancy shorter than average, and that's another thing I catch myself counting on.) He has a dreamy, staring, uncomprehending gaze at times that makes him appear preoccupied and distant, but apart from that, his face is not especially distinctive. (He does not embarrass us unless he tries to speak. We tell him not to.

"Shhhh," we whisper.)

"Will he ever speak?" my boy asks.

"No."

"Will you send him away?"

"We'll do what's best."

"Would you send me away if I couldn't speak?"

"You can speak."

"If I couldn't?"

"You can."

"But if I couldn't. If something happened to me."

"We would do what was best."

"For who?" sneers my daughter.

"For all of us. We aren't sending him away just because he can't speak."

"Please don't give him away," begs my boy, who is unable even to look at him without drawing back.

"Then why don't you help us with him?" I demand. "You never want to play with him. Neither of you."

"Neither do you," sneers my daughter.

I do not reply.

My boy is silent.

In the family in which I live there are four people of whom I am afraid. Three of these four people are afraid of me, and each of these three is also afraid of the other two. Only one member of the family is not afraid of any of the others, and that one is an idiot.

It is not true

————o————

It is not true that retarded (brain-damaged, idiot, feeble-minded, emotionally disturbed, autistic) children are the necessary favorites of their parents or that they are always uncommonly beautiful and lovable, for Derek, our youngest child, is not especially good-looking, and we do not love him at all. (We would prefer not to think about him. We don't want to talk about him.)

All of us live now—we are very well off—in luxury with him and his nurse in a gorgeous two-story wood colonial house with white shutters on a choice country acre in Connecticut off a winding, picturesque asphalt road called Peapod Lane—and I hate it. There are rose bushes, zinnias, and chrysanthemums rooted all about, and I hate them too. I have sycamores and chestnut trees in my glade and my glen, and pots of glue in my garage. I have an electric drill with sixteen attachments I never use. Grass grows under my feet in back and in front and flowers come into bloom when they're supposed to. (Spring in our countryside smells of insect spray and horseshit.) Families with horses for pets do live nearby, and I hate them too, the families *and* the horses. (This is a Class A suburb in Connecticut, God dammit, not the wild and woolly West, and those pricks have horses.) I hate my neighbor, and he hates me.

And I have plenty more I could let myself hate

(if I were the type to complain and run off at the mouth, ha, ha, or yield contemptibly to impulses of self-pity, ha, ha, ha). I can even hate myself—me—generous, tolerant, lovable old Bob Slocum (in a kindly and indulgent way, of course)—for staying married to the same wife so long when I've had such doubts that I wanted to, molesting my little girl cousin once in the summertime when no mothers were looking and feeling depraved and disgusted with myself immediately and forever afterward (as I knew, before I did, I would—I didn't enjoy it. I can still recall her vacant, oblivious little girl's stare. I didn't hurt her or frighten her. I only touched her underpants a moment between the legs, and then I touched her there again. I gave her a dime and was sorry afterward when I realized she might mention that. Nobody said anything. I still keep thinking they will. I didn't get my dime's worth. She was a dull, plain child. I wonder what became of her. Nothing. She is still a dull, plain child in my archives. That's the way she stops. The branches of my family have grown apart—I can kick myself for fumbling all those priceless chances I had with Virginia at the office for more than half a year, and with a couple of Girl Scout sisters I knew from high school earlier. I thought they were only kidding in their giggling insinuations. And they were having genuine sex parties with older boys from tougher neighborhoods who would crash parties in our neighborhood they had not been invited to and break them up. It was rumored they raped girls), seeing my big brother with his fly open on the floor of that shadowy coal shed beside our brick apartment house with a kid named Billy Foster's skinny kid sister, who was in my own class in grade school but not as smart (my big brother wasn't even that big then), had nipples you could notice but no breasts, but was doing it anyway (Geraldine was not as smart as I was in geography, history, or math but was going all the way already with guys as old and big as my big brother. While *I* wasn't even jerking off yet!), abusing and browbeating my children (I have seen them turn dumbfounded and aghast when they thought I was annoyed, observed how insurmountable their plight in trying

335

to talk normally. Their heart clogs their mouth. I see them trembling in such debilitating anxiety and want to hit them for being so weak. Later, I condemn myself, and I am even angrier at them), dishonoring my wife (I no longer want to tyrannize her and I try not to make passes at anyone who knows her), capitulating in craven weakness and camouflaged shame so often in the past to my possessive, domineering mother-in-law (who bossed me around a lot in the beginning) (while I had to make believe she didn't) and my shrewish, domineering sister-in-law (who is pinched and nasty now and whose face is drying up into lines as hard and deep as those on a peach pit), for surrendering so totally, despairingly, fatalistically to broad and overbearing unforgettable Mrs. Yerger in the automobile casualty insurance company, who towered over me then, it seemed (and comes to mind always now when I'm fuming over Derek's nurse—I don't know why we call her a nurse. She does no nursing. She's a caretaker. She takes care of my mentally retarded son), when she hove into view like a smirking battleship, moving out of one indistinct department of the company to take command of the file room—I knew on sight with a chill in my blood and bones and a feeling of frost on my fingertips that she would fire me soon if I didn't quit sooner—and again and again for fumbling it so thoroughly with luscious, busty Virginia back there in the office I worked in as a dumb, shy, frightened, and idiotically ingenuous virgin little boy, who felt like a waif, and sometimes worse.

What a dope I was.

"Do you remember Mrs. Yerger?"

There will be no one I know in this whole world who will have an inkling of what I am talking about. Virginia might understand, but Virginia will not be in earshot when I lose control of my reason in senility or delirium and begin pressing upon strangers such puzzles of ancient, germinal importance to me as:

"Do you remember Mrs. Yerger?"

(I remember Mrs. Yerger, and I remember Virginia is dead too now and would be a peeling water bag of emphysema and phlebitis if she were not. What a feeble-minded idiot: I could have had her then. She was hot. I was petrified. What in hell was inhibiting me so long, strangulating me? No wonder when I finally tore free it was with a vengeance.)

The company is still there. (She isn't.) It hasn't grown. Nobody ever hears of it. And life has pretty much been one damned sterile office desk after another for me ever since, apart from those few good years I spent away from home in the army.

What a deal I blew. (I was a moron. I have laid my wife on the desk of my study more than once and on the desk in my office in the city one Sunday afternoon while the kids were off on their own watching the holiday show at the Radio City Music Hall. They thought *that* was corny.) What good tits I could have been nibbling on all those months, instead of those soggy canned salmon and tomato or baloney and mustard sandwiches my mother made for me to take to the city for lunch to save money. I enjoyed those sandwiches too. I'd lick her lips and large breasts now with my salmon-and-tomato tongue. No, I wouldn't; everything would be the same; if I had her now and I was the one who was older, I would probably be calculating my ass off trying to keep free of her, squirm loose unscarred with a fairly clear conscience, as I find myself doing habitually with all my Pattys and Judys, Karens, Cathys, and Pennys, and even with my slim, smiling, tall, supple very young Jane, a kid, my refreshing new temptation in the Art Department, who would be putty in my hands. (But how long can you remain entranced with putty?) I break dates with girls with the same proud feelings of accomplishment I enjoy when I make them. (It is easier to break dates than keep them and takes up less time. All we really have is time. What we don't have is what to do with it. So I make dates.) Most of my girls have been very good to me. (That's what I feel girls are for.) But I don't want to see any of them frequently and can't bear being with them long. They want to talk afterward, get close, and I want to sleep or go home. I tell lies. (I like to date working girls for lunch in Red Parker's apartment because I know they'll have to leave shortly to get back to their jobs.) I procrastinate. I procrastinate with Jane (take three steps forward and three steps back); I hedge; I know beforehand what I will not like about Jane later (she'll be too thin, of course. And immature. They're'll be blades of bone everywhere. What will I find to talk to her about? Love? Her painting? She'll think we've been intimate. How awful. How will I ever get my emotions unmixed?); I move closest to Jane when there is no chance of moving closer; I never joke with her about meeting after work unless I know it's impossible. There is method to my madness. I am only rash when I'm safe. I throw caution to the wind when there isn't a breeze. I know I'll be sorry someday about all of my discarded ladies, the way I'm so sorry now about Virginia and even about Marie Jencks. I'm sorry about them already.

"Do it to me like you did to Marie," Virginia sang.

I did it to neither.

I'm always sorry about all of them, whichever way I move. Sorrow is my skin condition. Otherwise, I'm healthy and feel and look pretty good, although I've gotten a little paunchy and carry a bit of a sack beneath my jaw. I can lose the weight in a month if I really try. I think I may have been one of those pretty, young boys some of my girl friends brag about picking up now on bored or reckless afternoons or evenings. (They brag about picking up fags, spades, or each other, too. I don't care. I do care. But that makes it easier for me to dump them finally when I judge I want to. I like a girl who's going with someone else.) Virginia told me often I was handsome, cute, sexy, and smart, and guaranteed I would be able to get all the girls I wanted when I grew up.

She was wrong. I haven't gotten *all* I wanted. And have gotten a number I didn't.

"Take it in your hand, Mrs. Murphy," I sang back at her, gushing with joy, basking innocently in her sweet compliments and the affectionate warmth of her friendship.

Virginia was wide open for me then and I didn't know it. Virginia was wide open for me then and I *did* know it. That's probably the reason I always shrank back from her in such solemn ineptitude whenever she seemed to be sweeping me past a point I felt able to go. (As soon as I realized I could do whatever I wanted with Virginia, I lost my power to do anything at all. I could not say what was necessary. It came down to a matter of words, and I could not speak the right ones.) I would lose my power of speech (as I lost it with Mrs. Yerger—I never once believed I could ever say anything that would make Mrs. Yerger smile—and as my children, I think, and my wife, lose it with me). I don't know why it hit me that way. Kids today are doing it all over town with older girls and women (if you can believe the kids, or believe the older women). Truthful girls boast about seducing pretty or grimy young boys on summer weekends in places like Martha's Vineyard or Fire Island (it's Arabs, Greeks, and Slavs on vacations in Europe), or picking them up on city streets afternoons when they have nothing to do. They are sexually liberated (they say). They have no compunctions (they claim). They are slaves to no social or psychological restrictions. Anything goes. Then why are they anxious, hysterical, tense, and dejected? They are lonely. They have nothing to do.

"I have nothing to do," my boy says.

"I wish I had something to do," my daughter says.

"Can't you think of something to do?" my wife says. "Isn't there anyone we can go see?"

Sundays are deadly.

Spare time is ruinous.

Women my wife's age with broken marriages take up robustly with fellows much younger than themselves, sometimes boys, and their husbands don't like that part of it at all. (It's a means they have of really sticking it to us. The husbands can do without the money and kids. But they can't abide their wives' humping a younger dick and letting everyone know.) Our dicks are so pathetic. (I felt that way early and was close to a truth. I felt need, not power. I felt yearning. I never thought of it as an instrument of domination.) They can always find a hardier one for special occasions. (A girl can always find a man to lay her at least once.) I think they feel safer with teen-agers and young college kids or carpenter's helpers in vacation spots they visit and leave, grabbing the initiative with their tense, sharpened fingertips (if they haven't been chewing their fingernails down blunt, as more and more of us seem to be doing) and keeping control. Everybody wants to keep control. (I want to keep control. Penny makes me lose control, and often my wife does too. Penny diminishes me into a gargling, blabbering imbecile every time, and I love it.) I've got one girl who goes way out of control every time she has an orgasm and hates me and everybody else in the whole world bitterly and ferociously for five or ten minutes afterward (until she regains control of herself), until her scrambled senses start to reorganize. (Then she sucks her thumb.) She is humbled, vanquished, resentful, subdued. She is ashamed. She curls herself up away from me like a catatonic child and will not let me pet her, unless my touch and whispers are consoling. She'd rather not experience it (unless she's by herself, with her vibrator or her finger); she resists response; she'd rather just give them; she sees herself as the laughingstock of whoever watches her. I watch her. I'd just as soon not have to give them. (She and I are compatible that way. But I do taste what power over another human being is when I succeed in doing that to her. I do feel potent. We take leave of our character and are transformed into something else.) Were it not for the element of status, I really would rather not give orgasms to any of them but my wife, and there's even an element of sadistic cruelty (not consideration, not understanding) in that. Some of them change so grotesquely. They *ought* to be ashamed. There really is something disillusioning and degenerate, something alarming and obscene, in the gaudy, uncovered, involuntary way they contort. It's difficult not to think lots less of them for a while afterward, sometimes twenty years. At least we go in horny and bestial from the start; we want it, like lusting apes, and we let them know. Many of them start out that way too now, and I'm not all that comfortable with those (even though I know it's a sure thing. Maybe getting laid should never be so sure a thing. It isn't with

340

this girl I know, or even with my wife. She gets aches, upset stomachs, and fatigue. It is with Penny. I don't see Penny as often as I used to). I don't like women who are that decisive and commanding.

"Okay, let's have it," they seem to be ordering. "You've been using it your way long enough."

Those assertive bitches. Generally speaking, I prefer to make *them* do all the doing and giving; that way, I feel I *have* done something to them: I've gotten away with something. Many of them prefer that too. They blow their young boys. That must seem easier to them. They don't have to undress and show themselves. They don't have to be able to come or pretend to. They don't have to be "good." They don't have to go through motions. (Everybody wants to feel safe, not just me. Older, rancorous, divorced ones, though, do want to get laid, insist on it, demand it. I prefer my women with milder insecurities. I feed on submissive feminine loneliness like a vulpine predator. I'm drawn by the scent. My ravenous snout is insatiably passionate, for an evening or two. Bellicose women whose husbands have been philanderers will hatchet you for it: they are affronted if you do not wish to fuck them.) Then they throw them out.

"What the fuck would I have to talk to *him* about?" one of them told me about an eighteen-year-old she picked up in a record shop, brought home, and threw out before morning.

No wonder so many of our virile young men have trouble getting it up nowadays. (It serves them right.) I would too. I did. Virginia was certainly safe with me because I couldn't feel at all safe with her. (I certainly couldn't seize control. I had not the confidence or the know-how.) And Virginia, in her turn, could not ever feel safe again with the adjuster who threatened to throw her out of his car (or with Ben Zack either, for that matter, who tried to rape her in his car, despite his crutches, canes, wheelchair, and all) on the deserted street near the cemetery in Queens alongside which they were parked if she didn't put out for him.

"That's just the way he said it too," she complained

341

to me in a tone of petulant protest that was not typical of her. Her poise was shaken each time she spoke of it. "He just took it right out without even asking. I thought he was crazy. I just looked down and it was there. I was sure insulted, I'll tell you. I wonder what Ben Zack told him about me."

I didn't have the confidence and know-how to go too far with her even in my *sex reveries* without losing heart unexpectedly (and much more). Just like that, my little, rigid, dime-sized prick would dissipate into thinnest air. She scared me (the thought of her all naked scared me. I could never conjure up pictures of her that way). Pretty as she was, she could turn as grisly to me all at once as that separated head of Medusa, that evil, hairy, peristaltic nest of countless crawling adders and vipers arching out to fang me for no good reason.

"Let's do it all the way today," she'd say.

And convert me into lead, wood, or stone every time she appeared to be trying to skate me closer than I wanted to go (into what used to be called *sexual intercourse*. Today it's called *fucking*). I'd feel dehumanized and castrated; things would feel gone. There'd be a thumping blow in my chest, and my heart would stop. I would feel ill. With tendons and muscles fluttering weakly, I would long to sneak out of sight for a while, in order to creep back later and begin all over again with her from a distant and more secure footing, inching back cautiously. (I think I enjoyed just *flirting* with her more than anything else: flirting was an end in itself and still often is. I'm still not always sure I really want to get laid.) I would lose my urge, go numb; I would have a lump in my throat instead of my pants. I lost my cock and balls; they'd go away. They lost their sensitivity. I would have to squeeze or hold or look to be positive those limp and wrinkled sausage casings were still sticking there, still mine. I felt absence; no density or weight. I feel no density or weight there now. What an odd and derogatory thing to have to say about our masculine genitalia.

It is our weakest reed.

I can feel my feet in my shoes when I pause to

concentrate on them, and I can feel my thigh bone connected to my ass bone on this wooden chair. I can feel this hand and forearm of mine lying on my brown desk blotter. I can feel my other hand resting overturned on my thigh against the worsted fabric of my trousers and can feel my back turned and angled uncomfortably, the lower part (sacrum) aching steadily but tolerably, but I cannot, for the very life and dignity of me, feel anything inside my undershorts where my exterior sexual organs are supposed to be (and probably are). All I can feel, without touching, is something like sandpaper in one spot where my undershorts are pulled too tight. I try to force a stir and can't. I know I had something there a little while ago. I know they belonged to me. I think I'm entitled to them. I know I will have to open my pants and look if I wish to make certain that what is hanging there is hanging there. I do. It is; they are. What a minor relief. Where else would they go if they went away from me? They feel lost now (I've been robbed!), even as I *watch*, like sloughed-off skin from a blister or sunburn or the cellophane wrapping from a crumpled, discarded cigarette pack, as though they already have gone away from me to work for somebody better and left only these flaccid parings behind to jeer at me. Until I scratch slowly, rub, tickle, and then —ah!—take a hearty grip. *Now* I've got him, now I know I've got him back, sturdy, upright, alert, obedient, eager, loyal, ambitious. (I think I'll hire him right now for my department. Such attributes of prickiness are much esteemed in companies and governmental organizations.) That's because its natural state is always so very, very small, negligible, puny, slothful, not just mine, all, unless one's growing somewhere on some kind of human zoological freak, and even then it's large only in comparison with others, unless that human freak is a full-grown horse. There are big heads, bellies, and backsides, I suppose, and God knows there are tremendous, full breasts (although I find I am losing my taste for those and already prefer the smaller, shapelier ones of my wife, Penny, Mary, Betty, and Laura, all of whom wish they had bigger ones), even a brain weighs at least

a whole pound or two, I think, but I guess there really
is no such thing as a big human dick.

(*Women* don't suffer from penis envy. *Men* do.)

They are such fractional parts of the total construction they might easily be overlooked if we did not
dwell on them. They are arrogant and absurd in their
haughty, sniffing, pushy, egotistical pretensions. (We
let them get away with an awful lot.) They can't
even hold their lordly pose for half a day a week.
What a feeble weapon indeed for establishing male
supremacy, a flabby, collapsing channel for a universal
power drive ejaculated now and then in sporadic
spoonfuls. No wonder we have to make fists and
raise our voices at the kitchen table.

Mine would pop right up dependably in the days
of my youth every time I stopped (or even thought
of stopping) to resume joking salaciously with Virginia
at her desk beneath the big circular office clock whose
slender, pointy minute hand (symbolizing a long,
phallic sword or lance for me in those days and a
lancet or proctoscope now) sliced ahead with a twitch
every sixty seconds. It would project embarrassingly.
(I could not even dance with schoolgirl friends in
those molten pubic days without launching haplessly
into an instantaneous erection that had nothing at
all to do with me or with them—I might just as well
have shrugged my shoulders and claimed:

"It's not mine. There's nothing I can do about
it."

And walked off the dance floor and left it floating
there—in midair, disowned—and would have to draw
back a bit at the waist in an attempt to conceal it.
Now I shove it forward to let them see it's there.
That is, I have found, an effective gambit with mature
women who have let you know they want it.) I kept
myself covered with accident folders I made certain
to bring with me whenever I went to Virginia's desk
to pretend to search for others as we bantered lewdly.

"Meet me outside."

If she agreed—she always would if she could—she'd
smile and dip her face almost imperceptibly. I would
go out of the office into the hallway alone. My pulse
would race, my hands were sweaty, and I would want

to run past the bank of elevators down to the staircase landing between floors, even though I knew I would have to wait. Virginia was more discreet than I; she took her time. I was consumed with haste. I couldn't stand still as I waited. It never failed me then. It never let me, or itself, down when she joined me finally, hurrying also, and I began kissing her clumsily on the nose, cheekbone, and mouth, crashing teeth with hers so hard I thought my own must break, and squeezing and grabbing her in different places, pressing and rubbing it against her so savagely it hurt—she was panting too, but laughing as well—for the four or five seconds or one-eighth of a minute she'd allow me before she'd lie:

"Someone's coming."

Those were swift, incredible trysts we enjoyed sometimes every two or three hours a day on the landing between floors of the office of living people working above and the cramped, dingy, unoccupied storeroom below filled with cabinets of dead records that must have seemed important to somebody sometime in the past, or they would not have been kept. Hardly anybody ever looked at them anymore. They were accidents, old, forgotten casualties in blanched folders with blue or purple data on the outside and sheets of various types of legal and medical information inside. From folder to folder the facts were similarly old and uninteresting. (I soon stopped snooping into them.) They were settled cases of people who were closed.

"Somebody's coming," she would exclaim to me with a panic-stricken gasp when she decided my time was up, and be out of my hands and gone, even though nobody ever was.

I always wanted much more of her then, right there on the staircase, when I knew I couldn't have it. (I have gotten laid in bizarre and illogical places since —my wife goes for that kind of adventure too—but never, sad to say, on a staircase. We have a good staircase in our home in Connecticut now, but my wife's back condition might be aggravated, and I would chip my knees.) I always felt satisfied afterward, though. And very pleased with myself. Those were my first

345

good feels of grown-up woman; she was twenty-one, after all, nearly twenty-two when I saw her for the last time. I would crowd myself upon her from head to toe and try to seize or shove against her everywhere: if I had gone slower and been less gluttonous, I think now, she might have let me have more. In the store-room once she instructed me:

"Slower. Slower." Her voice was cooing, soothing. "That's better, darling. You scare me."

I was flushed and perspiring like a feverish baby. I wanted to lie on my back, gurgle cherubically, and kick my feet. I had never been called *darling* by anyone before.

"Darling."

(It goes a long way still.)

I was usually hindered in these frenzied assaults by those damned accident folders I'd brought, for I'd invariably forgot to put them down. I'd have to slide them behind her shoulders and brace her against the wall as I kissed and licked, snorted and groped; they would fall to the floor and spill open when she wrung herself away from me. I can still remember the cool, slick feel of her panties each time I touched them, my sense of miraculous astonishment that I was able to touch them at all.

"Somebody's coming," she'd repeat in a growl.

(In another two seconds it would have been me.)

I would have to let her go, for she herself would suddenly turn wild with fright. There was boiling lunacy around us. The glint in her eyes was penetrating and slightly insane as she tugged her skirt down and made ready to run off, endeavoring to smile. I think she was more greatly aroused by my touch beneath her skirt than she had expected. And I was too rough. (She could have been wide open for me then if I knew how.) She is closed now. Virginia is closed now, like those people in the storeroom whose cases had been settled in one way or another. So am I. And lying among them like flaked stains now in that dreary storeroom for dead records are my own used-up chances for attaining sexual maturity early, for getting laid young (or what *we* considered young). I could have had her there. I could have done it to her right on the desk top or floor of the storeroom (she all but asked me to. But I didn't know what to say) or in one of her friends' apartments or in a hotel room while still a gawking, young, moronic, skinny teen-age kid bringing momma's soggy sandwiches into the city to eat for lunch almost every working day of the week while I pored over the sports section, comics, and sex stories in the New York *Mirror,* which is out of business now—everything is going away. (The old order changeth. There is no new.) There is nothing new and good under the sun. Everything you buy has to be brought back for repairs or exchanged at least once. All of us tell lies. We call that *initiative*—although I remember it accurately (as though fearful to forget. If I forget thee, O New York *Mirror,* where will you be? And all those industrious hours of intent diversion I spent with that shitty tabloid) and the New York *Daily News.* I worked for sixty cents an hour. I earn more now. Ask the people who work for me. Ask my kids. (One of them won't answer.) I wolfed down two of those sandwiches every day on seeded rolls, then three. I could have eaten four. I could have lost my cherry in her juicy box at age seventeen right there on that same desk top between *Property Damage–1929* and *Personal Injury–1930.* I could have done it to her lying down and sitting up, frontwards or backwards, sideways frontwards and sideways backwards too, the way I'm able to do now with girls who are slim and agile and don't get cramps (if I don't put on more weight. And I hope I don't lose more hair, or I soon might not be able to do it any way with anyone but my wife. I used to be praised for my lush wavy hair. Now curls are the thing, and I don't have any), several times a day most days of the week—and had my sandwiches and *Mirror* on the desk top there too—with my leather shoes propped firmly against the *Personal Injury–1929* file cabinets for greater drive and mobility and my folded elbows cushioning our heads against a smash into *Property Damage–1930.* That image of us fornicating on that old desk comes back

347

to me often. We have our clothes on. Her makeup's smeared, her face is lax and lopsided, her clothes are always in disarray, torn, pulled open, up, down, brushed aside. We are not nude. It's deformed, distorted, a desecrated sketch in colored chalk and wax. Some of those people in the Personal Injury files had been killed. It was hard to believe that cars had been colliding in the Property Damage files as far back as 1929. It was hard to believe that there were even cars. No, I couldn't. I could not have done anything different. I did what I could. It would be the same. It would be no different if I were that same hesitant, backward teen-age file clerk still bringing momma's sandwiches with him to work for lunch. Then it did let me down. It went away, thawed, resolved itself into an unfeeling flap of a foreskin and receded timorously whenever she rode me smack up to that immediate next step of registering at a hotel—I didn't even know how to register at a God-damned hotel. I was only seventeen and a half—or going to her friend's apartment with her after work, whenever I could not wisecrack and postpone any longer but had to look straight at her and say *Yes* to that bewildering and truly repelling situation in which I would have to be alone with her, get undressed beside her, take it out, and try to stick it in before it went soft. (I knew it would go soft before I even got it out.) I couldn't do it. I did not want it. I would get headaches. All *I* wanted to do was joke with her, listen to her tell stories of sex experiences with other people, and feel her up a few times a day a few seconds at a time. I was too young. I would lose my bravado, personality, ambition, wit. I had no sense of humor. I would lose my will to say *Yes*. I would lose all energy and soul and be left with almost no substance I could feel. That lump would come to my throat—*that's* what I'd be left with, a lump in my throat instead of my pants—and I would lose my power to speak and be unable even to confess to her and plead:

"I'm afraid, Virginia. I must go slowly, darling. Let me call you darling. You must help me see where I am."

I felt nausea instead of desire, and immense, mortal

348

desolation. I think she knew it and pitied me, and I hated her and hoped she'd be crippled and die. Tom with the flowery, affected handwriting was sticking it routinely into big, blond, gruff, bossy, and horsey Marie Jencks on demand three or four times a week on the desk in the storeroom (and sometimes she made him do it to her standing up against a wall, he told me later, or against the walls in a corner, where it was easier). And I was scared stiff of gentle, short Virginia. I didn't want to see it. I still don't really enjoy having to look at it. They still set me back for a moment or two. I have to steel myself, make ready (unless I'm rollicking drunk and bobbing along on a tide of ebullient self-confidence that might carry me right through into it without pause). I wasn't scared stiff: I was scared soft (ha, ha). But Tom was older than I was, and when I was his age, I was doing it too, and they still astound me. The sight. They are distinct. No two are the same. No one is the same way twice. If I live to be a hundred and fifty years old (and if it please God, I will), I don't think I will be used to the sight of a naked girl, unless I become a physician. I still steal peeks at my wife. It's more likely I'll become a peeping Tom. Snatches vary. I am always tense and somewhat disbelieving as they undress. No two are alike. (Why are they doing this for me?) There is always still at least one second of awe, of raw curiosity in which I am breathless at the possibilities of what is about to be disclosed and offered me. I have to accept it, whether I like it or not. (While I counterfeit nonchalance all the while and appear to be gazing elsewhere at something infinitely more engrossing. Like my trousers folded over a chair, the grille of an air conditioner, or my woolen socks, with my garters still attached, lying in my shoes.) I wonder if we are as interesting and peculiar a spectacle to them. I think we are. I get compliments for cleanliness and symmetry, and for the cute pliability of my foreskin (which more and more girls in recent years are finding as novel a decoration as my garters. They don't see many of either anymore. I'm damned if I'll cut it off now. I'll give up garters. I may look a little bit Jewish to some people, and think Jewish a great deal of the time, but it's proof I'm not if I ever want to use it against someone like Green, who is. That same elusive imp dodging around so artfully inside me somewhere that urges me at times to kick Kagle in his leg, or my daughter in her ankle, also often gives me a throbbing, delectable wish in my upper palate, along with a tickling yen in one nostril to—the wish and that exhilarating tickle join forces virtually to exhort: "Go ahead. Do it, sweetheart. See how good it feels"—to—how shall I say it?—Jew-bait). Moles, birthmarks, pimples, crimped scars, and untended dark hair in filaments or clumps in unexpected places on women sicken me with disappointment and leave me morose and queasy unless I take a Spartan grip on myself at the start and go right at these things as though with an uncontrollable desire. (I must make myself seem to adore with the passion of a fetish what I find so repugnant. Else I might quit entirely. I don't want to hurt their feelings. Or mine.) I hope for silken perfection every time and am relentlessly unforgiving of blemishes. (I feel swindled, injured.) I must make myself look past them at the whole picture. Some have hair growing down the sides so long it curls out of their bathing suits. They don't seem to notice or mind. I do. I don't know where to look away from. (They must know it's there.) You can't just say:

"Pardon me, Mrs. I think your hair is showing."

Because you might get back:

"So what?"

Or:

"Don't you think I know it?"

Or:

"Don't look, if you don't like it so much."

Slightly more judicious, and less risky, would be:

"Pardon me, madam. But do you know your hair is showing?"

Unless you want to go after it, and then you can make whatever clever gutter gambit you want to. I don't usually like that kind (although I have had to welcome them with manufactured enthusiasm on many occasions when it turned out to be the kind I'd been dating and sucking around after). I don't like excess black face or body hair on anyone, men or women, even when it's been shaved. It seems aberrant to me, infernal, revolting. (It's there to revile me.) My wife has black hair. By now, though, I know where it all is. No coiled, fuzzy surprises from her. (I have stumbled over hairs in my time that I could dissertate about for hours if I were the type to dwell compulsively upon past failures. Mrs. Yerger had a wen. Betty Stewart had a cast in her eye, but I continued to copulate with her weekly anyway for several months until she met a younger man she thought she might want to marry. My mother started sprouting bristly, dark gray hairs on her face when she was no longer able to tweeze them out herself. Her pores turned gaping and coarse. I looked past the hairs at her face, when I forced myself to look at her face at all. I could not say to her:

"Mother, I think you have some hairs growing on your face."

By then, she might not have heard or understood, and I would have had to say, more loudly and crabbedly:

"Hey, Ma. Gee whiz. You got hair on your face."

Not ever. How could you ever say that to your own sick mother? On the Rorschach test I took to get this job, it was observed that I was able to look at the whole picture and did not digress to delve wastefully into unrelated details. The probability was that I'd succeed, and I have.) In the early years of our marriage, my wife did not like me to see her naked unless she was in the bathtub, did not want to watch me stare at her while she undressed. (She still does not want me to see her on the toilet, and I'm not keen anymore about seeing her there, either. Once or twice a year is enough.) But now she enjoys having me watch her, strips like a teaser and flops down in bed and lies there like Goya's duchess. I enjoy it and laugh with her. I'd enjoy it more if she hadn't been tippling all day and was still not partially drunk. (She could have been killed while driving, or killed someone else. She could be stripping with just as much giddy and inebriated anticipation for somebody else.) My wife and I do enjoy ourselves together much more than I tend to remember. We often have fun. I'm not sure that things can get better for me. She had a technique for changing clothes that never exposed her bottom parts. Nightgown over panties or girdle, panties or girdle pulled on under nightgown. One caught glimpses only. That heartless, unfeeling bitch. In bed, she'd take it off anyway as soon as I asked. She'd even dress and undress inside the closet. No wonder I won't wake her from her bad dreams. Let her die in them or be mangled into a thousand bloody pieces by the illusion she's going to be. If my wife dreams of a prowler approaching her bed is it the same prowler I'm dreaming of?

"What were you dreaming about?"

"It was awful," she answers in the morning, still shaken. "Something terrible was happening to you."

"Horseshit."

"I swear."

"People don't dream about other people. They only dream about themselves."

"Something happened to you, and I couldn't stop it and was afraid."

"You were dreaming about yourself."

She must have been taught to dress and disrobe that way at summer camp, where males could peek between the bunk boards, or by her mother or divorced jealous-faced sister who got knocked up as a college kid before that became fashionable and grew up frigid and ill-natured. She lives by herself now with her liver-hued freckles in a small house nearby and advertises she would not have it otherwise. I believe her. (I also believe that nothing would please her more than for me or the husband of some other woman to fall in love with her. We would fail. She would spurn us. She would love that chance to.) I also believe she will always want to live nearby. I think she hates me, is envious of my wife, and contaminates my wife's trusting, abject nature with doses of guileful animosity. She spouts bigotry and reactionary political comment. She is childless. Her first husband has married again and has children. She has a store. There is much in the world of which she disapproves. She wishes my wife would be more like her and chides her because she is not. She criticizes our children and volunteers advice to my wife on how to turn me into a more submissive husband.

"I wouldn't let him get away with it. That's why I threw Don out."

She is glad that John Kennedy and Robert Kennedy were killed and that the girls in the family have crooked teeth. She wants my wife to agree with her. She wants me to put in a swimming pool. I feel rivalry between us. (I used to feel rivalry with her mother.) I didn't let my wife know how much it pained me to see her undress that way. (How often I cursed her and swore to get even. I do get even. We Slocums have our family honor.) It was a matter of high principle (as well as of low prurience. I cherished seeing her in ungraceful positions. Still do). She never guessed the effect it had on me (she is not mean), and I was too sensitive and proud to complain. (I did not want to beg. While she did not even know what was going on.)

"Don't you ever dream I'm dead?" she likes to ask.

"Did you dream I was dead?"

"I think so. I think that's what was happening."

"Thanks."

"I was sorry."

"I don't remember. My dreams are about me, and you're not me."

"I dream about you."

"You're in my dreams. Do you want me to return the favor? To promise?"

"You couldn't keep it."

"Then why bring it up?"

I'm grateful she doesn't ask me if:

I ever dream about her and another man, because I do, and that dream is about me also. (They are coming together in sexual union for the sole purpose of denigrating me.) And I don't like it. I don't want my wife to commit adultery. I don't think she wants to, either, ribald and vulgar as she sometimes gets at large parties now (although she may think she wants romance. I'd like some too. Where do you get it?); more likely, she is reacting against being the kind of old-fashioned person who doesn't want to (while so many other women we hear of do want to and are). She would have to be drunk and more stupefied than she's ever been (that I know of) and fall into very bad, greedy hands. She would have to be led away without knowing it to someplace remote and be overcome in silence by somebody wicked and unmerciful. (Conversation would eliminate his chances. She'd recognize he wasn't me.) I hate that man (all of them who've ever calculated their chances with her) and want to kill him, especially with this foreknowledge I have that she would probably enjoy it more with him than she ever has with me.

"Oh, darling," she exclaims to him over and over again in sighing adoration. "I never knew it could be this way. I will do everything you ask."

She would have no real need for me after that except to pay certain bills. (She does not like to write checks for things like insurance premiums and mortgage payments.) I hang within earshot at parties (unless I am off on my own taking soundings of somebody else's drunken wife. I prefer them comelier and better-tempered than my own) to lead her away before an insult or assignation becomes inevitable.

("Come along, dear. Come on now. This way, dear. There's an elegant man here who wants to meet you."

"Who?"

"Me."

In these dreams of mine in which she abandons me for somebody else, I seem to dissolve while dreaming them and am left with nothing but my eyes and a puddle of tears.)

Divorce, however, is a different matter. We *like* to try each other on that.

"Do you want a divorce?" she will ask.

"Do you?"

(I've thought about it. What happily married man of any mettle hasn't?)

"What would I do?" she speculates with a long face. "I couldn't find another man. Who would want me?"

"Don't be too sure."

"I'm too old."

"Nah. I'm older."

"It's different for you."

"Yes, you could."

"It's too late."

"No, it isn't."

"You're eager, aren't you?"

"You're the one who brought it up."

"You're the one who's always thinking about it. I can tell. You get so happy every time a marriage breaks up. Why don't you come right out and say so?"

"Why don't you?"

"You're the one who's unhappy."

"Who says so?"

"I know how you feel."

"Aren't you? You do a lot of complaining. You're complaining right now."

"Don't you want a divorce? You can tell me if you do."

"No, I can't."

"You can."

"I can't even tell you if I don't."

Almost from the first week of our marriage we have been jostling each other this way over divorce. (Almost from the first week of our marriage I have found these squabbles sexually arousing, and I am in haste to hump her and reconcile. She always gives in.

"Say you're sorry."

"I'm sorry.")

She would like me to say:

"I love you."

I won't.

I can't.

I shouldn't. This is a matter of principle (and manhood) too. (I can say it easily enough to other girls if I have to, when it does not mean I will have to give up anything. It means I will get, not give.) I couldn't even say *Sure* to Virginia when it would have gotten me a great deal; instead, I would twist away from her sideways, recoiling lamely with some

355

face-saving wisecrack, and slink out of sight miserably like an exiled dog.

"Come outside," I could say.

Or:

"Meet me downstairs," I could propose like a carefree buccaneer (when I knew we would not have much time).

But never:

"Yes."

When she said:

"Get a room."

And always when I began inching back to her tremulously (that's the perfect word) I did not know if she would let me back into her voluptuous and smutty good graces. (I would have felt penniless without them.) She always did. She could have cut me off at the knees with a single, slicing sentence (she could have told people about me); and I might have remained like that forever, no legs, just stumps. (Somebody would have had to move me about, lift me up from one spot, like a chess piece or checker, and place me down in another.) She liked me. She was not impressed by Tom.

"You're better," she told me.

"Then why doesn't she do it to me?"

"Do it to me like you did to Marie on Saturday night, Saturday night."

Tom had no sense of humor. (What he did have was a handwriting I wanted and took from him.) He was getting laid, but I could make Virginia laugh. (Ha, ha.) I was pleased with myself when I did. (I told stories about her to teen-age friends back in my neighborhood.) We teased each other lubriciously all day long. I leaked (lubriciously. *Lubricious* is a lubricious word). Nobody teases me now. They say Yes if they come along at all and are out of their clothes before I can even get my shoelaces unknotted.

"That was good," they sigh afterward.

"I really needed that," they declare.

As if I believe them. Or even care. All I'm thinking about is when I ought to leave or how I'll be able to get them out of Red Parker's apartment in time to take a nap before returning to the office or catching my train. They're as obtuse as my wife in her naïve good moods, still trying to work out ground rules for a happier marriage, while I am wondering how much longer I will have to remain with her before I pack my bags and get my divorce. That sanguine stupidity of hers (that utter lack of connection with my deeper feelings) is maddening.

"I'd like to know," she'll sometimes say, "what you're really thinking."

(No, she wouldn't.)

"About my speech."

"I mean all the time."

"My speech. I may have to make a much different one if I get the promotion."

"All of us think you're angry when you get so quiet. We try to guess what it is."

Virginia would tilt her head backwards and to the side, eyeing me lewdly with a knowing, taunting look, a festive leer, her powerful breasts (girls with big breasts sometimes wore very tight bras then too) elevated like artillery pieces on weapons carriers and thrust out brashly just for me. *She* knew what I was thinking.

"These," she'd announce proudly, "are what Mr. Lewis likes about me." The tip of her tongue would glide for an instant between the edges of her shiny teeth as she watched me stare. "You do, too."

"Come outside."

"Come inside."

"You're a tease."

"*You're* a tease. You keep a girl all hot and bothered all day long and then won't even take her to a hotel."

"I don't know how."

"I'll tell you."

"You do it."

"They'd lock me up. They'd lock me up as a prostitute. We'll do it together. Register as Mr. and Mrs. Bang."

Today, twenty-one is too young for me, childish, pesty. I wouldn't lay one like that on a bet now if she worked in the same office. The whole company would know. (They talk about you now to their

357

friends. They talk about you to their parents!) I don't even like them working for me that young or hearing their strident gibberish (with defective pronunciations that give their neighborhoods and working-class background away). They lack refinement. Most of those that don't wear bras have pendulous breasts that look awful. I don't often envy youth. I detest it. Kids don't hear noise. They make so much. I wish they'd all keep their mouths shut in public and turn down their phonographs and transistor radios. My daughter will soon be the same age as Virginia. She looks older now, because she's taller, when she stands up straight. I wish she'd realize that and wear more than just a nightgown when she comes out of her room. I wish my wife would tell her. It's hard for me to say anything about it to either one. (I don't think I will ever be able to sleep in a double bed again with a male. I would choose the floor or a chair. And that would be equally suspect.) I am not a fanny patter. There are times I don't even want to handle my wife. I just want to put it in and get it over with. Or I don't want sex at all. I make excuses. There is a barrier of repugnance. It's shelter. It dissolves when I want it to. They've got nothing there but something missing. I think filthy. That's shelter too. (Other times I want it and my wife doesn't, and it's like receiving a blow across the forehead, eyes, and the bridge of my nose.) Virginia was twenty-one and *older* than I was (and that's the way I will have to keep thinking about her if I want to be able to keep thinking about her with romantic nostalgia and devotion).

She would have lapped me up, turned me topsy-turvy (as Penny can do), spilled me head over heels into a sea of winy, rippling vibrations, whirled me backwards quivering into a hailstorm of palpitating infancy and insanity, sent me scrambling up the walls with sensation and rocketing through the ceiling like a surface-to-heaven missile with the flaming tip of her crimson, naughty tongue. I would have begged for mercy as soon as I recollected who I was and found myself able to speak again. (I do that with Penny now. I do it with my wife.) And she would have looked lovingly at me with sated sweetness afterward, resting on her knees between my own, satisfied herself by how beautifully she had done, how prodigiously she had pleased me. I'd like that now.

"Isn't he jealous?" I had to ask. "He can see us right now."

"He wants to leave his wife and marry me. We go to empty restaurants and have drinks and dinner. He likes the way I kiss."

"So do I."

"So do I. It took a lot of practice for me to get it just right. You should try me when I'm all naked and really feel in the mood. I don't know what you're waiting for."

I lowered an accident folder over my groin (in case another one took place).

"Come outside."

"I see, said the blind man. Something's happening."

"Is this case yours?" I inquired boldly.

"I bet I know the cure."

"Meet me?"

"Did you ever go to bed with a stiff problem and wake up with the solution in your hands?"

"You made it hard for me but I can't hold it against you."

"Go first. I'll meet you."

"I'm coming, Virginia."

"Do it to me like he does to Marie," she sang back softly, as I moved past her out into the hallway.

I was Captain Blood the pirate on that staircase, a dauntless freebooter. I bore the accident folders before me prudently like a gallant shield. (I had something to hide.) I was carrying hot pellets.

I always yearned to take it out and ask her to hold it a little while. I didn't dare. Mrs. Yerger was in charge before I was able to, and I quit soon after. I practiced the words but couldn't say them; interchangeable first ones jammed in my larynx and pharynx; there was a multitude of syllables with which I might have begun:

"Will—"

"Take—"

"Would—"

"How about—"

"Don't be—"

"I—"

"Please."

I could not speak any of them. I did not know what pose to adopt. (I had no choice.) Now I know it would not have mattered. (She either would or wouldn't. The thing to have done was to whip it right out, mumbling anything. *Please* would have done fine.) How I wanted her to. It would have been laden with need almost beyond endurance, swollen to bursting with tenderness, gone lunging off rabidly like an epileptic relative I would soon attempt unsuccessfully to repudiate, self-centered, an embarrassment, a connection of some distance I might have to mutter an apology for. I don't get that hot anymore. Apathy, boredom, restlessness, free-floating, amorphous frustration, leisure, discontent at home or at my job—these are my aphrodisiacs now. I never got that far. It ended before I learned how. "All that's required is one or two years of specialized training," say the military recruiting posters. I got that specialized training in the armed forces. I came out of the army a handsome captain, and Virginia was dead. I was glad. (I was surprised I was glad, but that's what I was.) I tried to make a date with her from a telephone booth in Grand Central Station and failed. It's hard to succeed that way with someone who's dead. I liked hearing her tell me about sex. (It was like watching a dirty movie.) It was hard picturing someone as gentle, moderate, and considerate as Len Lewis being incited by her in a restaurant, movie, or automobile.

"I make him," she boasted. "I lead him on slowly. I know how."

"How?"

Her father had killed himself too. "We never knew why. We had lots of money. He was a quiet man. Like Mr. Lewis."

"What does he do to you?"

"Whatever I ask him to. Or show him. He isn't sure how far he can go with me yet. He can't believe

it," she praised herself with a grin. "He's very sweet.
I like to make him happy. He's easy. You're easy
too."

"I'm hard."

"Easy."

"See?"

"I see, said the blind man."

"You're making things very hard for me."

"Should I meet you?"

"Hurry up."

"I can only stay a second."

"Hurry up."

Her face wreathed in pink, blissful smiles of contentment whenever she saw me get an erection. (I think
I got more hard-ons from her in my twelve months
at that automobile casualty insurance company than
I've had in the twenty or thirty years since.) I wish
I had her smooth, round cheeks in my hands right
now. I would stroke them languidly with pinky and
thumb, stimulating her slowly, instead of grabbing
and racing. (I know how to do that now.) It would
be I who picked the mood and did the delectable
tantalizing.

"Cover up," she'd say.

"Come outside," I'd beg.

"You won't have time," she'd laugh. "Better shoot
to the men's room."

"Meet me there."

"I've got no key."

"I'll sneak you in."

"I've never done it in a men's room."

"You did it in a canoe once at Duke University."

"I did it in a men's dormitory once also at Duke
University. With five football players. They made
me. I was expelled. The one I liked so much brought
me there. They sent me home. I was afraid to go.
I never found out if they told my father."

"Did they rape you? Is that what happened?"

"No. They didn't have to. I didn't want to. But
they made me. They just held me down and kept
talking. I knew them all. But it was fun once we started
and I stopped worrying about it. I would have told
the other girls. I think I hoped we'd get caught. I

361

think I'd like to do something like that again sometime soon. It's exciting."

"It's exciting me right now."

"I see, said the blind man."

"Come outside."

"For a minute."

"On the staircase?"

Sometimes she'd give me about three and one third seconds.

"Someone's coming!" she'd hiss with vehemence, and tear herself away. "Let me go."

I should have guessed from her educational curriculum at Duke that she was a little bit nuts and would probably kill herself sooner or later. I am able to spot propensities like that in people now (and I keep my distance). A friend in need is no friend of mine.

I envied and abominated those five football players at Duke. They thought so little of her. They treated her like crap. And she did not mind. There were days I found myself detesting her on my long, drab subway rides back and forth. There were mornings I would not talk to her and could not force myself to look at her, she seemed so foul. (I was betrayed. She was trash, that fatal kind of trash that can make you want to die. I'm glad I didn't die. I'm glad I outlived her.) I felt—and knew I felt correctly—that she still would have preferred them to me.

I am gifted with insights like that and able to prophesy with conviction in certain morbid areas. I know already, for example, that my wife (as she foresees also) will probably die expensively of cancer (she'll need a private room, of course, and private nurse) if she doesn't outlive me and we do not divorce because of drunkenness or adultery (hers, of course). If we're apart, or if I'm already dead, who cares what she dies of? (I'll probably miss my boy every now and then for a little while if I do move out for a divorce. I like it so much when he smiles. I'll have to leave so many things behind. My golf clubs. How can I rationally make time and room for my golf clubs and new golf shoes when I am breaking away from home and family in an irrational rage?) Will I be happy when my wife is dying of cancer? No. Will I be sorry for her? Probably. (Will I be sorry for myself? Definitely.) Will I still be sorry for her after she's gone? Probably not.

I am especially good on suicides and breakdowns. I can see them coming years in advance. Kagle is close to his breakdown now; his God won't save him, but maybe his boozing and whores will (supplemented by fortifying compounds of vitamin B-12 and self-pity mixed with self-righteous claims of mistreatment. If nothing else, everybody will agree he has been a nice guy). Kagle won't kill himself; he'll enjoy his wronged status too much for anything like suicide (he'll enjoy smiling gamely, forgiving generously). I'll have to get rid of him. I try to help him now. He grins incorrigibly (and I want to kick him in his leg). I know something he doesn't know, while Green, Brown, Black, and others watch mistrustfully and theorize (I feel. I know I don't feel honest with them). I want Arthur Baron to note my efforts to aid Kagle. Kagle's job will be given to me; it's all but inevitable now. Kagle welcomes my criticism (and ignores it. It's the attention he welcomes. If I threw spitballs at him he'd be just as grateful). He thinks I am a doting parent fussing over an appealing child. It does not cross his mind that I am a zealous heir grown impatient to supplant him. (I'd like to spit in his face. Won't he be surprised?) Martha, the typist in our department, will go crazy eventually (probably in my presence. I'll get rid of her deftly and be the talk of the floor for a few days), and I won't lay Jane, although I'll continue to flirt with her (fluctuate and vacillate, hesitate and saturate) and ferry the prurient interest she stimulates in me home (like melting ice cream or cooling Chinese food) to my wife in Connecticut or uptown to old girl friend Penelope, my weathering, reliable Penny, who still studies music, singing, and dance diligently (while working as a cocktail waitress in one place or another) and still likes me better than any of the younger men she successively falls in love with for a few months three or four times a year. (She should like me better. I *am* better. They're jerks.) My wife loves doing it with me in Red Parker's apartment in the city, and I like doing it there with her too. It's different than at home. We go at each other full force. I have grim premonitions now for Penny, who traveled through her thirtieth birthday still unmarried (with much deeper emotional changes than she seems to recognize) and is not as jolly as she used to be. I've known and liked her now for nearly ten years. I don't know what will become of my daughter. I make no firm predictions for teen-age girls today. (The boys, I know, will all fail. They've failed already. I don't think they were given a fair chance.) She'll want to take driving lessons even before she reaches sixteen. Then she'll want a car. She'll have duplicate keys made and steal one of ours. I wish she were grown up and married already and lived in Arizona, Cape Kennedy, or Seattle, Washington. Someone older will advise her to steal our car keys and have an extra set made. She steals money now from my wife and me to chip in with friends for beer, wine, and drugs on weekends. I don't think she uses the drugs. I think she's afraid, and I'm glad. I'm glad they seem to be going out of fashion in our community, along with spade boyfriends. I'm glad she's afraid of Blacks too.

"If you'd give me my own car, I wouldn't have to steal it," she'll argue when we catch her, and believe she's right.

I'm in the dark:

(My lucid visions bleed together.)

Something terribly tragic is going to happen to my little boy (because I don't want it to) and nothing at all will happen to Derek. Police and ambulances will never come for him. I see no future for my boy (the veil won't lift, I don't get a glimmer, I see no future for him at all) and this is always a heart-stopping omen. When I look ahead, he isn't there. I can picture him easily the way he is today, perhaps tomorrow, but not much further. He is never older, never at work or study as a doctor, writer, or businessman, never married (the poor kid never even goes with a girl), never in college or even in high school; he is never even an adolescent with a changing voice, erupting skin, and sprouts of sweating hair discoloring his upper lip and jaws. I mourn for him (my spirit weeps. Where does he go?). He doesn't pass nine. He stops here. (This is where he must get off. Every day may be his last.) Either he has no future or my ability to imagine him present in mine is blunted. I view the empty space ahead without him dolorously. Silence hangs heavily. I miss him. I smell flowers. There are family dinners, and he is not present. What will I have to look forward to if I can't look forward to him? Golf. My wife's cancer? A hole in one. And after that? Another hole in one.

"I made a hole in one," I can repeat endlessly to people for years to come.

When obscurity and old age descend upon me like thickest night and shrivel me further into something small and unnoticeable, I can always remember:

"I made a hole in one."

On my deathbed in my nursing home, when visitors I don't recognize arrive to pay their respects with gifts of very sweet candy and aromatic slices of smoked, oily fish, I may still have it in my power to recall I made a hole in one when I was in my prime—I'm in my prime now and I haven't made one yet. It's something new to start working toward—and it may cause me to smile. A hole in one is a very good thing to have.

"Will you believe it?" I can say. "I once made a hole in one."

"Have another piece of smoked fish."

"A hole in one."

I don't know what else one can do with a hole in one except talk about it.

"I made a hole in one."

"Eat your fish."

"Hello, girls."

"Did you ever hear the one about the amputee without arms and legs outside the whorehouse door?"

"I rang the bell, didn't I?"

I can picture such scenes of myself in a nursing home easily enough. I can picture Derek out front easily too, slobbering, a thickset, clumsy, balding, dark-haired retarded adult male with an incriminating

365

resemblance to a secret me I know I have inside me and want nobody else ever to discover, an inner visage. (I think I sometimes see him in my dreams.) I bet Arthur Baron doesn't suspect he's there (that I have the potential for turning myself inside out into a barbarous idiot) or that I am stricken chronically with a horror—a horror so acute it's almost an exquisite appetite—of stuttering (or experiencing a homosexual want. Perhaps I already have) or having my tongue swell and stick to the roof of my mouth and be unable to talk at all. (No wonder I am terrified of being condemned behind closed doors, without my even knowing sentence has been passed. Perhaps it's already happened.) But not one day more of life can this fertile imagination of mine provide for my poor little boy.

(What work will he do? What clothes will he wear? Oh, God, I don't want to have to live without him.)

And Kagle's job will be proffered to me and I will accept it. By now, I want it. (By now, I no longer misrepresent to myself that I don't.) Kagle is an enemy: he is blocking my path, and I want him out of my way. I hate him. The need to kick him grows stronger every day, to yawp with contempt right in his hollowing, astounded face. (It would turn to a human skull. I would steam the flesh away in a second.) I'll never be able to do that. Civilization won't allow me to. But I might kick him in the leg if the temptation persists and my self-control flags. I will kick him before I can stop myself. I will be at an utter loss afterward to explain. I might want to die of embarrassment (and I'll feel like a caught little boy).

"Why did you do it?" people will demand.

I'll have to shrug and hang my head. I'll weigh eighty-four pounds.

"He kicked me in the leg," Kagle will protest to everybody.

"He kicked Kagle's leg."

"Did you see that?"

"He kicked Kagle in the leg."

There's nobody else whose leg I want to kick except my daughter's ankle at the dinner table at times when it would be easier for me to do that than reach out to smack her in the face. She flinches as though I already have as soon as I feel I want to and raise my voice. My wife makes me want to hurl her back a foot or two to give me room to cock my arm and punch her in the jaw at least twice with my fist. I shake my finger at my boy. Derek I smother with a huge hand over his mouth to stifle his inarticulate noises and hide his driveling eyes, nose, and mouth. (It is not to put him out of *his* misery that I do it; it is to put me out of mine.) He's a poor, pathetic, handicapped little human being, but I must not think about him as much as I could if I let myself, and I hate his nurse, whom I propel over the threshold —throw her out of my house—bracing her below with one arm to prevent her from falling to the ground and suing me. She falls anyway and sues me. The repulsive woman exudes an unpleasant odor of rancid grease mixed with dust and perfumed bath powder. She bathes mornings and evenings. Her hair is ghastly white. Her cleanliness is reproachful. I can't bear her intrusive familiarity. She treats me with no more solicitude than I get from my family, and she's a salaried employee.

I know what hostility is. (It gives me headaches and tortured sleep.) My id suppurates into my ego and makes me aggressive and disagreeable. Seepage is destroying my loved ones. If only one could vent one's hatreds fully, exhaust them, discharge them the way a lobster deposits his sperm with the female and ambles away into opaque darkness alone and unburdened. I've tried. They come back.

It's all Kagle's fault, I feel by now: I blame *him*. Minute imperfections of his have become insufferable. Irritability sizzles inside me like electric shock waves, saws against the bones of my head like a serrated blade. I can quiver out of my skin, gag, get instant, knifing headaches from the way he sucks on a tooth, drums his fingers, mispronounces certain words, says *byōō′tē fool* instead of *byōō′tə fəl* and *between you and I* instead of *between you and me,* and laughs when I correct him—I have an impulse to correct him every single time and have to stifle it. The words spear through my consciousness and slam to a stop against bone, the inside of my skull. I can restrain myself from saying them, but I cannot suppress the need to want to. I am incensed with him for provoking it. He bubbles saliva in the corner of his mouth and still wears the white smudge on his chapped lips of whatever antacid pill or solution he has been taking for his stomach distress.

"Heh-heh," he has fallen into the habit of saying, with lowered, escaping eyes.

"Heh-heh," I want to mock back.

I loathe Andy Kagle now because he has failed. I'd like to hit him across the face with the heavy brass lamp on his desk. I tell him.

"Andy," I tell him, "I'd like to hit you across the face with that lamp."

"Heh-heh," he says.

"Heh-heh," I reply.

I chuckle kindly when I see him, joke with him snidely about Green's vocabulary and well-tailored, showy clothes, help him dutifully in ways he can observe. I weighed one hundred and ninety-eight pounds this morning, down four and a half since Monday (when I decided to begin losing weight), and am nearly a whole foot taller than he'll ever be.

"Heh-heh," he wants to know. "How you getting along with that kid in the Art Department?"

"Fine."

"The one with those small titties."

"She's young enough to be my daughter."

"What's wrong with that? Heh-heh."

"Heh-heh. I've got these call reports for you from Johnny Brown."

"Didn't think I noticed, did you? Going to cut me in?"

"How would you like a kick in the leg?"

"My good one or my bad one? Heh-heh."

"Andy, this time I think you ought to look at them and make some comments before you pass them on."

"Clamming up? Heh-heh."

"Heh-heh."

"Heh-heh-heh. What good are they? Salesmen lie."

"Catch 'em. You'll make a good impression on Arthur Baron and Horace White."

He pays no attention. "Ever go two on one?"

"Two on one what,"

"I do that now in Las Vegas. I know the manager of a hotel. Two girls at the same time. I did it again last week. You ought to try it."

"I don't want to."

"Two coons?"

"How about these call reports?"

"You do that for me. You're better at it. What do you hear about me?"

"Don't travel."

"Do I need a haircut?"

"You need a kick in the ass."

"You're sure doing a lot of kicking today, aren't you?"

"Heh-heh."

"I'll let you in on something. Green is finished. How would you like his job?"

"Bullshit."

"I'll recommend you. They're cutting his budget."

"How much?"

"You won't get a raise. I will. I made a killing in Xerox last week."

"That's more bullshit. You're always making a killing in Xerox and always complaining about all the money you owe."

"Heh-heh."

All he's got is his home in Long Island and a house in the mountains, to which he sends his wife and two children every summer. He goes there some weekends. I inquire after Kagle's family as periodically as Arthur Baron inquires about mine.

"All fine, Art," I always reply. "Yours?"

(Green never asks. He isn't interested in my family and won't deign to pretend.)

I have dwelt wistfully more than once on the chances of his being killed in an automobile accident driving back or forth to work one lucky day. Kagle is careless in a car and usually sluggish or drunk when he leaves the city at night. Kagle is one of the very few upper-middle-echelon executives left in the country who still make their homes in Long Island, and this gaucherie too has scored against him, along with the white-tipped hairs growing out of his nostrils and the tufts in his ears. Nobody has hair growing out of nostrils or ears anymore. (He ought to see a barber now just for that.) This is something I've not been able to bring myself to mention to him. (I fear it would hurt him.) It has become difficult for me to look at him. He senses a change. I think that is why he heh-hehs me so much now. I pity him. (He does not know what to do about everything that is happening.)

"Heh-heh."

"Heh-heh."

"Heh-heh-heh. What's so funny?"

"Why are you wearing covert cloth, for Christ sakes?" I admonish him instead.

"What's that?" he asks in alarm.

"It went out of style thirty years ago."

"Covert cloth?"

"Switch to worsted."

"I've got a blue blazer now," he says proudly.

"It's double knit."

"How would I know?"

"It would look terrific in Erie, Pennsylvania. Have we got any big accounts in Erie, Pennsylvania?"

"I'm going to L.A. next week. From there I sneak into Las Vegas. Two on one," he explains with a wink.

"And it doesn't fit. It's loose and lopsided."

"I'm lopsided too, you know," he reminds me gravely, with the shade of a crafty and hypocritical smile I've seen on him before. "I was born this way, you know. It didn't just happen, you know. It was God's will. Don't laugh. It isn't funny. It isn't so funny, you know, being born with this deformed hip and leg."

"I know, Andy."

"It's nothing to laugh about."

"I wasn't laughing."

"This is the way He wanted me."

"Hallelujah," I think of replying cynically. "I wish He'd given as much thought to me as you feel He gave to you."

When Kagle draws upon his leg or God for deference and sympathy, he *becomes* those odious strands
and bushy tufts of hair in his nose and ears—intimate,
obscene, and revolting—and I have wished the poor
man dead many times lately just for filling me with
ire, shame, and disgust. Worsteds won't help him.
Everything is going wrong. I have wished other
unsuspecting human beings I know and like dead
also for most-trivial slights and inconveniences. Let
them all die. (I'm liberal: I really don't care how.)
I visit fatal curses on slow salesgirls and on strangers
who get in my way and delay me when I'm walking
hurriedly.

"Die," I think. "Pass away. Let me step over you."

I can find many men—they are always men—in public life I'd like to see assassinated (and I can't stand
bums anymore. I don't feel sorry for them), although
I'd never think (I haven't yet) of doing that kind
of work myself. I feel I understand why other people
beat, kick, and set fire to bums and panhandlers.
(We have too many of them.) I do not grieve at
the death of Presidents: (usually, I'm glad): they're
finally getting what they deserve. Not since F.D.R.,
I think, which was the last time in my life, if memory
is correct, I was able to raise a tear. I have to choke
back sobs now and then (usually at bad movies),
but my tears are bottled away somewhere deep inside
me. Nobody can tap them. That was a man, that
Franklin Delano Roosevelt, the last time I had a President I could look up to (the rest have not been mine),
or maybe I only thought so because I was gullible.
No—the whole country wept when he died. My mother
wept.

"One third of the nation," said he, "is ill-housed,
ill-clothed, and ill-fed."

By now, with our improved technology and humane
social and political reforms, it must be more than
half. When it hits a hundred percent (the millionaires
will have Swiss nationality by then and live in France),
trumpets will play, the heavens will open, and everybody will hear Handel's music free. Last night
I dreamed again my mother was alive, thin with age
but in perfect health, clothed attractively in a cool

print dress and thin white sweater, chatting naturally with me without a grudge at some cordial holiday festival in the nursing home. It was Christmas, Easter, or Thanksgiving. She beamed at me often, as she used to do when I was little. I was forgiven everything. I missed her like a forsaken child when I awoke in the morning—I had a sticky, crusted sensation of tears drying on my cheeks—emerging gratefully from sleep once more in my entirety, bringing my memory and all of my physical parts back with me successfully one more time from wherever it was I had been when I was not here.

"What were you dreaming about?" my wife always wonders.

"Me."

"You were groaning."

"My mother."

"Still?"

"You will too."

"I do already. Ever since she got arthritis. Her fingers curled. Won't it ever stop? The dreams?"

"It hasn't for me."

"Will I get arthritis too?"

"I will too."

"I hope I don't get it in the spine. I wouldn't want to curl up there."

"Fuck me."

"I'm not in the mood. The children are up."

I miss my mother again when I remember how poignantly I missed her when I woke this morning. I miss the forsaken child. He's me. But I'm not he. I think he may be hiding inside my head with all the others I know are there and cannot find, playing evil tricks on my moods and heartbeat also. I have a universe in my head. Families huddle there in secret, sheltered places. Civilizations reside. The laws of physics hold it together. The laws of chemistry keep it going. I have nothing to do with it. No one governs it. Foxy emissaries glide from alleys to archways on immoral, mysterious missions. No one's in charge. I am infiltrated and besieged, the unprotected target of sneaky attacks from within. Things stir, roll over slowly in my mind like black eels, and drop from consciousness into inky depths. Everything is smaller. It's neither warm nor cold. There is no moisture. Smirking faces go about their nasty deeds and pleasures surreptitiously without confiding in me. It gives me a pain. Victims weep. No one dies. There is noiseless wailing. I take aspirins and tranquilizers. I am infested with ghostlike figurines (now you see them, now you don't), with imps and little demons. They scratch and stick me. I'd like to be able to flush the whole lot of them out of my mind into the open once and for all and try to identify them, line them up against a wall in the milky glare of a blinding flashlight and demand:

"All right, who are you? What were you doing in there? What do you all want from me?"

They wouldn't reply. They'd be numberless. I'd find 1,000 me's. (I like to fuck my wife when she's not in the mood. I like to make her do it when she doesn't want to.) I'd like to be able to photograph all my dreams with a motion picture camera and nail the guilty bastards in them dead to rights. I'd have the evidence. I'd like to wiretap their thoughts. I'd like to photograph *their* dreams to find out what's going on in their minds while they are going around at liberty in mine. (A man's head is his castle.) I don't hear voices. (I sometimes wish I did.) I'm not crazy. I know people do talk about me behind closed doors but I don't imagine I hear what they are saying. Yesterday, a little boy was found dead in the cellar of an apartment building, sexually mutilated. The murderer is still at large. Another child was found dead in the airshaft of a different apartment house, thrown from the top. Nobody knows why. (A girl. The police have not yet determined if she was sexually abused.) Another child is missing from home after several days, and no one knows why. Family and neighbors wait for word in pessimistic suspense, lighting religious candles for the soul already in solemn expectation of the worst. I too believe she's been murdered (and I wonder why she has been. In Oklahoma today farmers decided not to deliver cotton at the price agreed to, because the price of cotton had doubled between the time the sales were made

373

and the time the contract forms were prepared. Buyers will take them to court. Bodies of other people's children are found in airshafts and stairwells all the time, and I'm not even sure what an airshaft or stairwell is). I wonder also what narrow, reedlike Horace White really feels about me. He's such an influential prick. (I hate that influential prick, and he means so much to me.)

"Well, well, well—here comes our company nail biter now," he'll say when I enter his office, and think it's funny. "How are you today?"

He's usually clipping, filing, or buffing his own translucent fingernails behind his enormous walnut desk whenever he summons me to request some kind of new work from me or discuss corrections. (He calls the changes he wants me to make *corrections*.)

"If you ever write a book," he has repeated to me, "put me in. I'll buy a lot of copies."

I'd like to wiretap *his* head too. I'd like to know if I range about impertinently in his dreams the way he roams about in mine (as though he owns them). I doubt I symbolize enough. Horace White strolls into my dreams often with his nearly featureless face, hangs around awhile, and turns into florid, fleshier Green, who fumes and glares scathingly at me as he starts to make a cutting remark and then clears out as rapidly as I'd like to as soon as the menacing, dark stranger enters and draws near with his knife I never see, either waking me up moaning in primordial fright or quitting the scene graciously to make way for someone like my wife's mother or sister, Forgione, or Mrs. Yerger. Or my daughter, boy, and/or Derek. Or someone else I haven't invited. What a pleasant interval it is when I can hump my wife or Penny in my dreams. I come a lot with Penny and wake up just in time. I come a lot with my wife. I'll fondle my wife sometimes after I awake until she turns over amorously and do it to her for real. (It was usually better in the dream.) Dreams of Virginia never move toward climax. I fiddle with her blouse and fumble with her thumb-smeared garter snaps. I have so many people to cope with at night. Many are made of varnished glass wax. There's no such thing. Ghouls are there, and midgets. Carcasses. I have my wife, mother, children, sister, dead brother, and even my dead father to bother about in my dreams (even though I don't know what he looks like. The photographs he left behind don't convince), all of them but my dead father petitioning me for some kind of relief that I cannot give them because I am in such helpless need myself. No wonder my dreams all seem to unreel in the same stuffy, choking atmosphere of a chapel in a funeral home. Only Arthur Baron provides some solace, but he is busy and never stays for long, and I'm not even sure it is my father or able to understand why he is so displeased. (I haven't done anything.) My staring, waiting nine-year-old boy becomes staring, speechless Derek. Both are motionless. I was speechless once. I did not know what would become of me. Now I've derived some idea. I have only to sit down to holiday dinner with the full family and have something arise that recalls my dead father or older brother and my dying, wordless mother and I can see myself all mapped out inanimately in stages around that dining room table, from mute beginning (Derek) to mute, fatal, bovine end (Mother), passive and submissive as a cow, and even beyond through my missing father (Dad). I am an illustrated flow chart. I have my wife, my daughter, and my son for reference: I am all their ages. They are me. (But I'm not them. They'll run through sequences obligingly for me as many times as I want to view them.) The tableau is a dream. The scene is a frieze.

"Freeze."

None of them moves. All of them sit like stuffed dolls. And I can perceive:

"This is how I am when I was then."

And:

"That was how I will feel when."

Now they can move.

I think I know how it must feel for my wife to be married to a philandering executive like me to whom she can no longer make much difference unless she gets cancer or commits adultery. (Suicide won't do.) It must feel cold. Shifting my eyes left or right, I can transfer myself into my mother's, brother's, sister's past to see my present and my future. I shift my glance into the future of my children and can see my past. I am what I have been. I incorporate already what I am going to become. They inform me like highway markers. And here is another dream I imagine as I see myself hunched over the smoking, roasted turkey with my bone-handled carving knife, poised for severing, after separating the second joints, that first dramatic slice of white meat from the breast while they all watch and wait silently in high-backed chairs like skeptical shadows, unbreathing: they're mine. I own them. They belong to me. I'm in command (and hope the white meat will be toothsome and the dark meat juicy). Now we are frozen again and do not move. (Get the picture?) We cannot move. I stand over my turkey; they sit rigid. And I feel weirdly in that arrested dumb show in which we are all momentarily statues that even if I'd never had them, had never married, sired children, had parents, I would have had them with me anyway. Given this circle, no part could be different. Given these parts, the circle was inevitable. Only Derek deviated, and that was an accident, somebody else's. (We played our parts.) Now he is fixed in place with the rest of us. They have been in my head for as long as I've had one (the stork didn't bring them) and I cannot remember myself without them. (So much of me would be missing.) They bump against brain and give me headaches. Occasionally, they make me laugh. They're in my plasm. Now we can move. They don't. They wait like stumps. They sit like ruins in a coffin in their high-backed chairs. The turkey's carved; white meat, dark meat, second joints, wings, and legs lie laid out neatly like tools on a dentist's tray or surgical instruments of an ear-nose-and-throat man about to remove tonsils. But the platter's not been passed. There are spiced apples, chilled cranberry molds, and imported currant jams. It's a gelid feast, a scene of domesticity chiseled on cold and rotting stone. I'm in control, but there's not much I can do. (I can pass the platter of meat to my wife.) My mother's there with hair that's white as soap. My father's else-where. She'll die. I know she will because she already has. (I was so offended by my father when he died that I did not want to go to his funeral. I wanted to teach him a lesson. I taught him a lesson.) My wife is the only wife I could have had till now (I had no choice) till death, divorce, or adultery do us part. My children were the only ones permissible. (Other people's belong to them.) No dimpled, freckle-faced smiles, no cheerleaders, gladhanders, backslappers, or starlike overachievers were ever in the cards, for them or for me. They became what they were; if I had to imagine them better they would be no different. It was not within my scrotum to father a child who would ever be invited to the White House to pose for a picture with the President exemplifying all that's shimmering and wholesome in national life. Soon they will have to invite a porcelain bowl of strawberries and cream. The people have started to look accursed. (The strawberries will be tinted redder with synthetic coloring. The cream will be adulterated with something whiter. The porcelain bowl will be made of painted rubber.) All but Derek, who sits with us—we give his nurses family holidays off and hope to God they take them. I can imagine him otherwise. I could not conceive of him this way. Now we can move. I can pass the platter of turkey meat to my wife and offer the others some sweet potato pie, which is made of yams. There are no sweet potatoes anymore. (They're gone too. I don't know *what* became of them.) I don't know *why* my father comes into these dreams of mine in which I cannot speak or move but only stay and hear, since I hardly know the man, except to turn into someone fearsome as a nigger or Horace White, who, in my dreams, uncovers a scarlet underside of erotic cruelty to the insipid outerface I know. Horace White owns stock. I wonder if I miss a memory of having been spanked at least once on the bottom by a father. I don't own one. There is a closeness in that, a stable understanding, a promise for the past and assurance for the future. Perhaps I ought to start spanking both my sons every fortnight for their own good. My daughter is too old. My wife isn't, and I do. She likes to scratch with her fingers and toes or bite mildly. We let each other.

377

It's more fun for both of us now if we sting at least a little. I wonder if I'm the only middle-aged man in the whole world who still contains within himself his distant childhood fear of homosexual rape? Is that why that man invades my dreams?

"Get out!" I order clearly.

But what comes out are croaking grunts of pain that alarm my wife.

"What's the matter?"

"It's okay."

"You were screaming."

"What?"

"I don't know. Sounds."

"I was only groaning. I'm all right now."

My wife and children are never in danger then. They aren't even home. There's only me. He's coming after me. I've got no one I can ask about this but my family religious adviser or my psychiatrist. My psychiatrist enlightens me on this question by replying:

"Why do you ask that?"

"Because—"

"You bite your fingernails," he guesses.

"—I'm afraid. I have dreams and thoughts that trouble me, even when they're pleasant. I get headaches. I'm dissatisfied. I believe I suffer from thought disorders. I don't hear voices—"

"Ah," he observes in a long sigh.

"—and I never have hallucinations."

"What would you call this?"

"I smell excrement often."

"Ah?"

"But there is always dog shit on my shoe."

"You will have to learn," he says, "to walk more carefully."

I don't have a psychiatrist (the company takes a disapproving view of executives who are not happy) and my family religious adviser belongs to my wife. (He takes a disapproving view of people who are.)

I know I will have to stop biting my fingernails soon if I ever want to go much higher in the company than Kagle's job or grow up to be President of the United States of America someday when the job falls vacant and no one else wants it. I know I was sorry when John F. Kennedy was killed because he was shot in the head when neither he nor I expected him to be and because of the magazine and newspaper photos. They were gruesome. (They could have sold a million of them as souvenirs if they had thought of it.) Poor man. I hope that I am never shot in the head. He's scaled much smaller now in my imagination (but he's there. It's him. I'll take care of him for as long as I can); it's necessary he be reduced to miniature to fit inside my thoughts and move about in memories, whimsies, and night dreams and do unnoticed things on his own when I'm too busy with other duplicates and shades to bring him out and play with him. Other people might have him on half dollars; I've got him saved in my head. He's clean, glazed, handsome, grinning. His hair is glossy. I like him now. My wife's sister doesn't. His kid brother didn't live as long as he did. It isn't generally appreciated that Lyndon Baines Johnson was only forty-six and still a U.S. senator when he had the first of his heart attacks. It was all over for him right then. He never amounted to much after that. Eisenhower got better after his. His golf game improved. (So will mine.) Harry Truman died too. I knew he would. My own head hurts a good deal these days, and I haven't even been shot there. I get pains in the back of my neck too, very close to the top of my spine. Aspirins help. My wife's tranquilizers help me sleep. Three layers of tissue envelop my brain and spinal cord and are called, collectively, *meninges*. I was delighted to find out I had three. I didn't know I had any. Meningitis, then, is an inflammation of the head. Infectious meningitis is an infectious inflammation of the head. Meningitis appears frequently on military installations. Civilians get encephalitis, which is an inflammation of the substance of the brain and is often mistaken for sleeping sickness. People doze off into paralysis. It is another good cure for insomnia. I have grown too old now to worry foolishly about something like meningitis. I don't have chest pains yet. I have exchanged my infantile fears of meningitis for more adult infantile fears. I never give meningitis a thought anymore. (Ha, ha.) Meningitis kills. So do bullets in the head. Martin Luther King got one: several months after he died, our alert FBI stopped tapping his telephone (and started tapping mine). Meningitis ravages the nervous system, leaves one deaf, dumb, blind, paralyzed, and dead. I was even sorrier when Bobby Kennedy was killed because he was younger than John and the photos of him on the floor of that hotel kitchen were worse. He looked so weak and confused with his immense eyeballs adrift in their sockets and his outflung arms and legs lying angular and spindly. His shoes were still on. He was dressed in black for the occasion. He is covered with glaze now too. He will never sneeze. He is in my head now also. I have him tucked away. I will keep him warm. And there he will lie, until I die—or the day comes when I forget to remember him again. I don't know what will happen to him after that. He'll have to fend for himself. I don't know how he'll survive when I'm no longer able to take care of him. Or where. It used to be when I was hot for a girl there was torrid heat. Now I'm only horny. There's just an erection. My wife's sister does not approve of violence, she says, but was pleased when the Kennedys were killed, seeing grim justice prevail.

"They only got what they deserved," she said. "In a way, they'd really been asking for it."

My wife was sorry for the children.

I must remember not to smile too much. I must maintain a façade. I must remember to continue acting correctly subservient and clearly grateful to people in the company and at the university and country clubs I'm invited to who expect to find me feeling humble, eager, lucky, and afraid. I travel less, come home more. (I'm keeping myself close to home base, which isn't home, of course, but the company.) My wife is pleased to have me around, even though we quarrel. My daughter suspects I'm checking on her. We suspect she's been using one of the cars when we're out—she has older friends with junior driving licenses—and that she's been threatening my boy with disfigurement and blindness if he tells. (I think I might kill her if I found out she's been threatening him with death or mutilation.) Derek can't say anything. I wonder what impressions flow through his mind (he does have one, I must force myself to remember, and ears and eyes that see and hear) and what sense he is able to make of any of them. I would not care to wiretap *his* head. I would hear much crackling, I think. I think of him as receiving stimuli linearly in unregulated currents of sights and sounds streaming into one side of his head and going out the other into the air as though like radio signals through a turnip or through some finely tuned, capstan-shaped, intricate, and highly sensitive instrument of ceramic, tungsten, and glass that does everything but work. I can't call it a terminal, because nothing ends there. I think of my own thoughts as circular, spherical, orbicular, a wheel turning like the world in a basin of sediment into which so much of what I forget to think about separates and drops away into the bottom layers of murk and sludge. (I even forget the things I want to try to remember.) Like a vacuum tube, he can peak suddenly into fiery heat. Like a transistor, he is affected invisibly by jarring and by variations in humidity and temperature. I have a son with a turnip in his head. I think there must be static and other kinds of interference there, and possibly then is when he has his tantrums. (I have static in my own that leads to cranky outbursts at home and wish my head would break open and let the crackling pressure escape.) He does have a sweet face. All my children do, and my wife is more attractive for her age than any other woman her age I know. I wonder what architectural connections stand unfinished in his brain. Is he too ignorant to apprehend yet that he is an idiot and will grow up to be an imbecile? Does he know he's supposed to be wishing me dead and reacting with fear I'll murder or castrate him for experiencing that hope? He'd better learn to keep his filthy designs on my wife to himself. He is blameless. I dream he's dead also and am inconsolable when I awake because I'm sorry for him and know I'm dreaming of me and don't entirely want him gone.

"What were you dreaming about last night?" my wife wants to know as she fixes breakfast.

"Derek."

"You were laughing."

"You. I dreamed you were fucking another man."

"You were laughing."

"You were funny. A big black spade. You grabbed me by the prick. I like girls who grab my prick."

"Should I grab it now?"

"I have to get to work. Make dinner tonight."

"I had a horrible dream."

"You were crying."

"In your dream?"

"In yours."

"Why didn't you wake me up? I dreamt I was crying and couldn't stop."

"I was busy in my dream. Maybe it was the same dream. Did you dream you were fucking a big black nigger last night?"

"I don't have to. I get all I want from you."

"I think the bitch *is* stealing one of our cars. He started to say something at dinner last night and she gave him a look."

"I'll ask her."

"I'll trap her. Make dinner tonight. I like trapping her."

"You're sure coming home a lot these days."

"So what?"

"I didn't mean anything. I'm glad."

"Neither did I."

"And you don't have to yell."

"And I'm not yelling. I don't see why I can't raise my voice around here once in a while without being accused of yelling. Everyone else does. You do. I don't know what you're so edgy about."

"You're the one who's edgy this morning. I'm glad when you come home. You even whistle. Maybe you're starting to enjoy being here with us."

"Of course I do."

"Is everything all right?"

"Everything's fine. And would be even better if you stopped asking me if everything's all right."

"I knew it wouldn't last until you got out of the kitchen."

"No wonder I can't wait to get to work."

"If anything's wrong at the office I wish you'd tell me."

"Everything is fine."

"What's wrong?" Green demands of me bluntly as soon as I get to work.

"Wrong?"

"I said it loudly enough." (Oh, Christ—he's in a mood also, and he's taken me unawares.)

"Nothing."

"Don't lie to me."

His exophthalmic eyes are glaring at me with moist and sadistic petulance, and his sensual face is hot and beady around the brows and mouth. Green will normally not allow himself to perspire where other people can see him. (I wonder if he is bothered more this morning by his thyroid deficiency or his enlarged prostate.) He is wearing a large, soft, box-plaid camel suit with notched, wide lapels and a gray vertical weave and fine violet lines, and can get away with it. The rest of us have to wait for festivals and expositions, although box-plaid slacks are okay on weekends at barbecues, marinas, and country clubs. Green is a flamboyant presence with an overwhelming vocabulary that keeps most of his superiors in the company aloof and ill at ease. Horace White shuns him like the plague. Green courts Horace White; White flees from him toward Black, who despises Green and vilifies him openly; Green retreats, nursing his wounds.

"Black is an animal," Green has complained to me. "An ape. There's no point talking to him."

Black is an anti-Semite. Green waits and regards me truculently from behind his desk as though I were to blame for his thyroid, prostate, colitis, or Black.

"I don't know what you're talking about."

"Don't lie to me unconvincingly," he begins almost before I finish, as though he can anticipate my replies. "It's all right to lie if I don't suspect you. I'm your boss. Don't lie to anyone around here unconvincingly if you want to keep working for me. I don't want anyone working for me to be held in contempt by anyone but me."

"My fucking wife."

"Don't use that word with me."

"You asked me, didn't you?"

"I'm not Andy Kagle."

"I wouldn't tell that to Andy Kagle."

"I like your wife."

"No, you don't, Jack. So do I. What's wrong?"

"I've had four wives and you've never heard me say anything uncomplimentary about any one of them, even though I've hated them all."

"She's not so crazy about you."

"Don't tattle."

"She thinks you're a bastard because you wouldn't let me speak at the convention."

"Stop using her."

"Oh, come on, Jack. You don't like her that much."

"I don't like her at all, if you want to stay on that subject. Would you like me to tell you why?"

"No."

"She drinks too much at some parties and not enough at others. She's stiff and uncomfortable and makes other people that way. She gives off clouds of social uneasiness at company affairs the way other people give off smells."

"I said I didn't want you to."

"She isn't much. She isn't rich and she isn't famous or social and she won't help you and she won't help me."

"You asked me what was wrong, didn't you?"

"And you're using your wife to avoid telling me."

"I'm not. What are you in such a bad mood about?"

"Why are you in a good mood?"

"I'm not, now."

"You're sulking, now," he retorts, grimacing, in a cadence of echoing ridicule, and I surmise that he too may be vulnerable to that squirting impulse to mimic hatefully someone who is vexing him unbearably.

It's called echolalia.

It's called echolalia (the uncontrollable and immediate repetition of words spoken by another person. I looked it up. Ha, ha).

Ha, ha.

Ha, ha.

(It can go on forever.)

It can go on forever.

"Shouldn't I be?" I ask.

"Shouldn't you be?" he asks.

"What's up, Jack?"

"What's up, Jack?" I expect to hear him reply to me in my own voice, as in a nightmare (as I often hear myself lashing back at my wife or daughter in their own voices when I am too riled up and discombobulated to think of a more mature way of hurting).

"Have you been out somewhere sniffing around after a better job?" I hear him inquire instead.

"Better job?"

"You won't find one without my help."

"Should I be?"

"You wouldn't even know where to look."

"What's wrong with my position here?"

I feel myself beginning to perspire.

"You're starting to sweat," he says.

"I'm not."

"It's on your face and coming through your shirt. Why do you give me asinine denials? You know I wasn't asking you what was wrong before when I asked you what was wrong. I didn't mean wrong. I was asking you what was right. I was being sarcastic. You've been acting funny. And I don't mean funny when I say funny. I mean strange. And I don't mean strange, either. I mean buoyant. You've been doing a lot of whistling around here lately."

"I didn't realize."

"And you don't stay on key. You must think you're the only one in the company who ever heard of Mozart. You've been making yourself pleasant to a lot of people here I don't like. Kagle, Horace White, Arthur Baron. Lester Black. Even Johnny Brown, and you make more money than he does."

"It's my job. I do work for them."

"Fawning? Let me handle all the fawning for the department. I'm better at it than you. They enjoy watching me fawn. Nobody cares about you."

"Kagle?"

"Kagle's through," he snaps impatiently with a glow of satisfaction. "He spits when he talks and

385

walks with a limp. I could have his job. I probably could. I wouldn't take it. I don't want to sell. Peddling is demeaning. Peddling yourself is most demeaning. I know. I've been trying to peddle myself into a vice-presidency and haven't been able to, and that's most demeaning of all, when you peddle yourself and fail. If you tell anyone I said that, I'll deny it and fire you. The company won't fire you, but I will. I will, you know. Red Parker."

"What about him?"

"Steer clear of him. He's been going downhill ever since his wife was killed in that automobile crash."

"I feel sorry for him."

"I don't. He wasn't that fond of her when she was alive. He drinks too much and does no work. Steer clear of people going downhill. The company values that. The company values rats that know when to desert a sinking ship. You've been using his apartment."

"I wash up. I bring my wife there too."

"You've been acting like a simpering college fool with that young girl in the Art Department."

"No, I haven't," I reply defensively. (Now my pride is stung.) "Jack, that's only kidding." (I can feel my eyes welling with tears. They must be moist as his own.)

"She isn't pretty enough. Her salary's small."

"You flirt."

"I have a reputation for arrogance and eccentricity to protect me. You haven't. You're only what you're doing. I have rose fever. If I look like crying, it's allergenic. What's so funny?"

"I wish I could use a word like that."

"You can't. Not while I'm around to use a better one. You can't think as quickly as I can, either. You don't have style enough to be as eloquent and glib as I am, so don't even try. That girl won't help you. Go for wealthy divorcees, other men's wives, and attractive widows."

"Widows aren't that plentiful to come by."

"Read the obituary pages. You're smiling again."

"You're funny."

"But you aren't supposed to be laughing now.

Slocum, you're in trouble and you don't seem to know it. And I don't like that."

"Why am I in trouble?"

"Because you work for me. And you've been too 'fucking' cheerful for my taste."

"I thought you didn't want that word."

"You don't seem as much afraid of me as you used to be."

"I am, right now."

"I don't mean, right now."

"Why should I be afraid?"

"And I don't like that. It makes *me* afraid. The last thing this Jack Green wants is someone secure enough in his job with me to walk around whistling Mozart's *Great Mass in C Minor*—I looked it up. Don't grin. You're as easy to impress as the rest of them. What baffles me is how *you* know it."

"I know a girl who—"

"*I* can be that pretentious here. You can't. I don't want whistlers working for me. I want drunkards, ulcers, migraines, and high blood pressure. I want people who are afraid. I'm the boss and I'm supposed to get what I want. Do you know what I want?"

"Good work."

"I want spastic colitis and nervous exhaustion. You've been losing weight too, haven't you? I've got spastic colitis. Why shouldn't you? I take these pills. I want *you* to take them. Want one?"

"No."

"You will, if you want to keep working for me and ever make a speech at the convention. God dammit, I want the people working for me to be worse off than I am, not better. That's the reason I pay you so well. I want to see you right on the verge. I want it right out in the open. I want to be able to hear it in a stuttering, flustered, tongue-tied voice. Bob, I like you best of all when you can't get a word out because you don't know what that word should be. I'm not going to let you speak at the convention this year either. But you won't know that, even though I'm telling you. You won't be sure. Because I'm going to change my mind and let you prepare and rehearse another three-minute speech on the chance I might not change my mind

387

again. But I will. Don't trust me. I don't trust flattery, loyalty, and sociability. I don't trust deference, respect, and cooperation. I trust fear. Now, that's a fluent demonstration of articulation and eloquence, isn't it? You could never do something like that, could you?"

"What's wrong, Jack?" I repeat lamely, almost whining, with a weakness that makes me abject. "Why are you doing this?"

"I have the best paid department in the company. You're stuck here."

"I know that."

"I get criticism for the high salaries I pay."

"I know that."

"Unless I decide to fire you. I'm stuck here too. Do you know that also? I want inferior people with superior minds who feel in their bones their lives would be over if they lost their jobs with me. And I want that to be true. *Now* it's visible, *now* it's coming right out in the open where I want it. *Now* you're afraid. Yes. Go ahead, Bob, relax—hide your hands in your pockets. They're trembling."

(I would kill him if I dared.) "Why do you want me to be afraid?"

"You work for me! I can fire you, you damned idiot. And so can two hundred other people neither one of us even knows about. Do you doubt it?"

"Christ, no."

"Isn't that reason enough? I can bully and degrade you anytime I want."

Oh, Christ, yes—he's got the whammy on me still. He *can't* fire me; but every cell inside me is convinced he can and bursts open in panic. (My mind has a brain. My glands don't.)

And I do not trust myself to reply without stuttering disgracefully, effeminately, a sissy. I do not feel I can unblock my mouth, unlock my tongue, and unlimber all my cheek and lip muscles to try a single word until I have sorted through all possible sounds and selected what that first word should be. And at least the one behind it, which might guide me safely to the next. (If I keep my sentence short, I might get out a complete one. I must begin with a one-syllable word. All possible sounds go clumping about in my mind like a jumble of lettered wooden blocks in a noiseless children's classroom.) Otherwise, there might merely come from me an unintelligible gabble or shriek. I feel like a slice of scorching toast ablaze in a toaster, and then my pores gush open in a massive flow of sweltering perspiration before I even have time to recollect that they don't have to. I don't *need* to be afraid of Jack Green anymore. I merely have to pretend.

But I am.

(And I fear I always will be.)

I hate him so and wish him dead as Kagle. I wish he had cancer of the thyroid, prostate, and colon. He hasn't. Him I probably would visit in the hospital just to hear him speechless and see him wasting away. I'll probably be in a hospital before he will, and he will not stoop to visit me. (Perhaps he will—just because he'll know I'll think he won't.) I wish I could be like him. I envy and idealize him, even now as he gazes away from me with a look of studied indifference that approaches boredom. He will not even give me the satisfaction of gloating victoriously. (I am not that important to him. How marvelous.) I wish I could do that. Maybe someday, if I practice regularly (when he is not around to observe with excoriating contempt that it is *he* I am training myself to emulate), I'll be able to carry off similar things with other people with the same disdainful composure.

Green is not going to fire me now—he merely wants to abuse. He is having one of his tantrums. (He has static in his head.) But my fear blows hot and my fear blows cold. And I sometimes think I am losing my mind. The fear (and the mind I am losing) does not even seem to be mine (they seem to be his)—broiling on my insides one moment like a blast furnace, chilling my whole skin like foggy winter wind the next, alternating out of control against me from within and without inside the sagging pavilion of my tapered, made-to-measure, Swiss voile, powder-blue shirt, the very finest shirt fabric there is, Green has told me. It's almost funny. I could have worn a dark broadcloth or heavier oxford weave to work today that would have contained without blotches the flows of telltale sweat spreading beneath my arms and trickling down my chest and belly from my breastbone.

"Try wearing a sweater next time," I can almost hear Green saying, reading my mind. "Cashmere. A cardigan. Like mine. That's why I wear one," I can hear him add, reading his.

It's almost uncanny the way he's still got the whammy on me. I wish he would die. But this one, I feel with some basis, I might eventually be able to lick. I have age, Arthur Baron, and spastic colitis on my side.

But not as easily as I'd hoped.

I'd like to shoot him in the head.

I wish I could make a face at him and stick my tongue out. (I wish I could have a hot sweet potato again or a good ear of corn.)

"Do you want to fire me?" I ask awkwardly instead.

"I can humiliate you."

"You are."

"I can be a son of a bitch."

"Why should you want to fire me?"

"Without even giving you a reason."

"You'd have to replace me with somebody else."

"To make you remember I can. You're not a free citizen as long as you're working for me. You sometimes seem to forget."

"Not anymore."

"Neither am I. To let you feel what true subjugation is. You wouldn't be able to get a better job without my help, and you wouldn't be able to take it if you did. You'd have to give up your pension and profit sharing here and start wondering all over again if they like you there as much as we do here. You'd spend three years and still not be sure. You're dependent on me."

"I know that."

"And I'm not sure you always know that. *I* always want to know you are. I always want to be sure you know you have to grovel every time I want you to. You're a grown-up man, a mature, talented, middle-level, mediocre executive, aren't you? You don't have to stand there sweating like that and take this from me, do you? You do have to stand there and take it, don't you? Well?"

"I'm not going to answer that."

"Or I can give you another big raise and humiliate you that way."

"I'll take the raise."

"I can make you wear solid suits and shirts and striped ties."

"I do."

"I've noticed," he answers tartly. "You're also playing golf."

"I've always played golf."

"You haven't been."

"I play in the tournament at the convention every year"

"With a big handicap. You're in there as a joke, along with those other drunken charlatans from the sales offices. And that's another thing I don't like. You don't belong to the Sales Department."

"I have to work for them."

"Would you rather belong to Kagle?"

"You."

"Why?"

"You're better."

"At what?"

"What do you want from me?"

"Who do you work for, me or Kagle?"

"You."

"Who's nicer?"

"He is."

"Who's a better person?"

"He is."

"Who do you like better?"

"You."

"Now we're talking intelligently. You shouldn't be thinking of a better job now, Bob." His pace slows, his voice softens. He is almost friendly, contrite. "I really don't think you could find one outside the company."

"I'm not, Jack. Why should I want to?"

"Me."

"You're not so bad."

"Even now?" His eyes lift to look at me again, and he smiles faintly.

"You do things well."

"Everything?"

"Not everything. Some things, Jack, you do terribly. I even like the way you've been talking to me now. I wish I could be rude like that."

"It's easy . . . with someone like you. You see how easy it is? With someone like you." He sighs, a bit ruefully, sardonically. "I'm not going to fire you. I don't know why I even started. I get scared sometimes when I think about what would become of me if I ever had to leave the company. Do you know what's happening to the price of meat?"

"It's high, isn't it?"

"I don't, either. But I worry what would happen to me if I did have to know. They've cut my budget."

"How much?"

"That's not your business yet."

"Kagle said they were going to."

"You're thick with Kagle."

"It might help."

"Thicker than with me?"

"He needs me more."

"I don't need you at all."

"You'd have to replace me, wouldn't you?"

"No. As far as the company is concerned, no one needs anyone. It goes on by itself. It doesn't need us. We need it."

"Should I talk to Kagle?"

"Kagle's a damned fool. It doesn't help him to downgrade us. You'll get your raise, if I get mine."

"I'll talk to him."

"I'm not begging you to."

"I'll cut the leg out from under him."

"That isn't funny," Green retorts.

"I know."

My smirk feels alien and bizarre, as though someone else had smirked for me and stuck it on.

"You're supposed to be his friend."

"It just came out," I apologize in confusion. "I didn't even know I was saying it. I'll go talk to him."

"I haven't asked you to. I don't know why I even

care. None of us are going anywhere far. Kagle limps. I'm Jewish. Nobody's sure what you are."

"I'm nothing. My wife's a devoted Congregationalist."

"Devotion isn't good enough. She'd have to be a celebrity or very rich. You've got a crippled child of some kind you don't talk about much, haven't you?"

"Brain damaged."

"Serious?"

"Hopeless."

"Don't be too sure. I've heard—"

"So have I."

"I know a doctor—"

"I've seen him."

"Why—"

"Cut it out, Jack. I mean it."

"I've been wondering if you had limits," Green replies. "I just found out." He looks sorry, reflective. Green has problems with his children, but none like Derek, which gives me an effective advantage over him I might want to use again. (The kid comes in handy after all, doesn't he?) "You'll get your raise," Green tells me finally, "and I'll probably get mine. I might even let you make your speech this year."

"I don't believe it."

"You shouldn't."

"I won't believe it until I do it."

"It's part of my strategy. You wouldn't be able to handle this job if they decide to give me Kagle's. I could do better. Better than him. I might be able to make vice-president that way."

"Kagle's not."

"Kagle limps and has hair in his nose and ears. Nobody with a limp or a retarded child is ever going to be president."

"Roosevelt limped."

"I mean of the company. The company is more particular than the country. They cut my budget. That's what I'm sore about. And I don't trust you. I'll get it back. But I'll have to fight for it. I'll have to grovel. That's the way I have to fight, and that's the part I hate. That's the reason I wouldn't recommend you to replace me. You're not qualified. You can't grovel."

"I grovel."

"You grovel, but not gracefully. It's like your fawning."

"I could learn how."

"I know how. See Green, Green says. See Green grovel, Green jokes. That's the reason they cut my budget. They like the way I grovel. They cut it every year. Just to see me grovel."

I will cut it even more, for I know how much of the expensive and truly urgent work we produce is not needed or used. I must remember to seem humble and unexcited and trustworthy. Green is right. Nothing any of us does affects matters much. (We can only affect each other.) It's a honeycomb; we drone. Directors die; they're replaced. I'll retire Ed Phelps. I must look innocent and act reserved. If I feel like kicking my heels, I must kick them in my study at home or in Red Parker's apartment in the city. I must stop using Red Parker's apartment. It shows. What will I do with Red Parker? He's younger than Ed Phelps. I must be nice to everybody. (I must act dumb.)

"What the hell are *you* so God-damned peppy about these days?" Johnny Brown demands, with one of his light, big-fisted pokes in the arm.

(It isn't difficult to imagine that fist in my face.)

"You," I jolly him back. "You're giving me call reports."

"Have you checked them against the sales figures?"

"These are what count."

"They're full of shit."

"As long as they sound good."

"Don't count on it," Johnny Brown answers. "There are better ways the salesmen could spend their time than making up lies like this. I'd know how to handle them. I'd make sure the bastards were out on sales calls all day long. I'd take the chairs out of their offices. They hate writing up these."

"Arthur Baron wants them for Horace White and Lester Black."

"Ask him why."

"The computer breaks down and cries if it doesn't get good news."

"You're a card."

I grovel gracefully with Johnny Brown and get the call reports I want for Arthur Baron. I'll get a raise. (My wife and children will have more money.) What will happen to me if Arthur Baron has a stroke soon? (He *is* overweight and smokes cigarettes, and I don't know a damn thing about his blood pressure, blood lipids, or cholesterol count. I don't even know what blood lipids are, or what they're supposed to do.) Who would look after me if Arthur Baron died? (Who would get his job?) Horace White? I'd hate to have to rely on that stingerless wasp for protection while sleek, Semitic Green with envy was burrowing away at me from below with his quicker mind and brilliant vocabulary and Johnny Brown was bunching his fist to punch me in the jaw. I hope he doesn't. A punch in the jaw would just about ruin me: it would damage not only my face but my reputation for efficiency and authority. It would be much worse for me than kicking Kagle in the leg. I could, conceivably, kick Kagle in the leg and pretend it was a joke or do it when just the two of us were together in his office and not many people would have to know. But everyone in the company would know if Johnny Brown punched me in the jaw. (I wish *I* were the one who was strong and courageous and *he* was puny and craven. He makes me feel two feet shorter than I am, and sexually impotent.) How would top management feel about someone in middle management who'd been punched in the jaw and felt sexually impotent? Not good, I think. My wife would lose respect for me. I wouldn't want my children, my neighbors, or even Derek's nurse to find out. No one with a limp, a retarded child, or a punch in the jaw will ever be president of the company or of the world. If someone had punched Richard Nixon in the jaw, he would never have made it to President. Nobody wants a man who's been punched in the jaw. It's hard to put much faith in the intelligence of someone who's been punched in the jaw. It would do *me* no good if Brown were fired afterward; it wouldn't *un*-punch my jaw.

What will I do if he does? (How will I handle it?)
I know what I will do. I'll fall down. But suppose,
to my wonderment, I didn't fall down? I'd have to
try to punch him back. Which would be worse? I
know which would be worse.

Both.

I have sudden failures of confidence that leave
me without energy, will, or hope. It happens when
I'm alone or driving back from somewhere with my
wife and she is at the wheel. (I just want to stop,
give up.) It often follows elation. Everything drains
away, leaving me with the apathetic outlook that I
have arrived at my true level and it is low. There
are times now when I have trouble maintaining my
erections. They don't always get and stay as hard
as they used to. I worry. And sometimes they do—it
all charges back vigorously—and makes me feel like
the heavyweight champion of the world. That's a
good sensation. There are times when I'd not be afraid
to fuck anybody, when there is not even the thinnest
curtain of doubt to weave myself through in order
to start doing the job. I don't even think of it as a
job. It's a pleasure. I will not hesitate to make Ed
Phelps retire.

"Oh, boy," says my wife, impressed. "Where is
it all coming from? You're like a young boy again."

"What do *you* know about young boys?" I banter,
smarting a little in jealous recoil from the comparison.

"I know more than you think I do. Come on."

"I think you do."

"You're even younger now than you were when
you were younger," she says with a reveling laugh.

"So are you."

"Any complaints?"

"Of course not."

"Come on. Why do you always like to wait?"

"Again?" Penny asks, with an exclamation of flattered delight. (She is so honored and appreciative
when I want her.) "How come you have so much
time for me lately? Wait," she laughs, in the throaty
voice of a sensuous contralto. "Wait, baby. You don't
give a young girl a chance."

Penny is thirty-two now and I have been going with her for nearly ten years. She is no longer in love with me. I was never that way about her.

Penny and my wife are just about the only two left with whom I feel completely at ease (and also the two I find least intriguing). With every other girl I can call (I have a coded list of twenty-three names and numbers in my billfold, my office, and in a bedside drawer in Red Parker's apartment, and I might get a *Yes* from any one of them on any given evening or afternoon) each time is like the first time all over again (a strain. It's a job. I'll have to do well. I liked it better when they thought they were doing us a favor. I'm sorry they ever found out they could have orgasms too. I wonder who told them).

I know I can make a good impression on Arthur Baron by forcing Ed Phelps to retire. And unlike Kagle, I've had no close relationship with the kindly, prattling old man who's been with the company more than forty years and whose duties are now reduced to obtaining plane and hotel reservations through the Travel Department for anyone who wants to use him, and following up on shipping, transportation, and room arrangements for the convention. He has to make certain enough cars have been rented and enough whiskey ordered. His salary is good, although his raises the past ten years or so (ever since he grew obsolete and became superfluous and expendable) have been nominal.

"It will be in Puerto Rico again, I'm sure," he repeats incessantly, and whispers, "Lester Black's wife's family owns a piece of the hotel there. As soon as they hurry up and make it official, I can begin. I wish they would."

I have ducked around file cabinets to avoid hearing him say that to me again. He could retire with a fortune in pension and profit-sharing benefits: he doesn't want to go. I'll make him. But what about Red Parker, who's just about my own age and isn't old enough to retire? How will I get rid of him? He has indeed been going downhill fast since his wife was killed in that automobile crash—the girls he goes with now are not nearly as pretty as the ones he went with when she was alive—but he might not crack up in time to do me any good. The announcement will have to be made soon.

"How are you, Bob?" Arthur Baron asks every time now when we pass in the hallway.

"Fine, Art. You?"

"That's good."

Otherwise, the changes will dominate attention at the convention. I must remember to be modest, bland, and congenial to one and all for the time being. I sometimes feel I have Arthur Baron over a barrel. This is known as a *delusion of grandeur*. (He could change his mind and keep Kagle for years and nothing consequential would result. Or someone else could fire Arthur Baron and me together without an instant's notice and there would not be a ripple in the total operation of the company. It would not falter.) And I don't entertain this thought seriously. But who *will* replace Arthur Baron when he does fall ill, dies, retires, is promoted, or runs out of ability and is eased away to the side? It won't be me. (Maybe it will.) I don't think they think I ever could replace Arthur Baron, just as Arthur Baron could never become Horace White when Horace White falls ill (it will be of a much different kind of disease from the ones that will put Arthur Baron, Green, Kagle, and me away—I sense that already—it will be something lingering and tediously progressive. Horace White is not the outgoing, wholesome type to fall ill and die rapidly. He will come creaking into the office on aluminum-alloy canes and wheelchairs for years after he is disabled, smiling, chortling dryly, looking ghastly, and alluding to old times familiarly, oppressing us all despotically right to the end, for he will still own stock), dies, or retires. (Horace White already has been eased aside.) Horace White can go no further in the company because there is nothing more he can do than be Horace White. He can be named to prestigious government commissions that issue reports on matters of grave national importance that are methodically ignored. (Arthur Baron and I can't do that.) His name looks good in the newspapers and on certain letterheads, for he is not merely Horace White but Horace White

398

III, and his wife—she is his third; one died of cancer of the lymph and the second was crippled in a sporting accident—and his mother—she is now in the very high eighties (like the company's common stock again, ha, ha, after the most recent two-for-one split)—come out looking good enough in photographs of people who raise dogs or sponsor charity balls and prominent benefit performances of musical comedies, operas, and ballets. Arthur Baron can move up *past* Horace White (and so, in theory, might I), for the company does, in its own biologically deterministic and unpitying way, elevate ability over ownership, but he can never become Horace White (and neither, in practice, can I). Only another Horace White, a brother, cousin, son, nephew, or husband of an undistinguished sister, could move right into the corporate structure and meet all the requirements of being another Horace White. (Every company needs one.) He is such a small-minded, oblivious prick, a self-satisfied simpleton (I wonder why I do have such haunting dreams about him in which his thin features turn despotic and carnal and he seems so viciously out of character); he buys puzzles, perpetual-motion gimmicks, and other novelties in Brentano's book store and has his secretary send for me and other employees of the company to show them off (as though we could not afford to buy them ourselves if we wanted them. He wore a red blazer of nappy wool at the convention one night last year and took us all by surprise. It looked good. This year there will be other red blazers).

"Look at this," he will command, beaming, as though he had just chanced upon something of vast benefit to all mankind. "Isn't it something? Just stand still there and look at it. It will never stop as long as you keep doing this. Each one is always different."

"That's really something," I have to respond, and have to remain standing still until he grows tired of having me in his office and sends me back.

I hate to have to stand still.

I have had to stand still for the longest time now, it seems, for nearly all of my life. Nearly every time I search back I come upon myself standing

399

still inside some memory, sculpted there, or lying flattened as though by strokes from the brush of an illustrator or in transparent blue or purple chemical stains on the glass slide of a microscope or on the single frame of a strip of colored motion picture film. Even when the film moves, I am able to view the action only in arrested moments on single frames. And yet I must have moved from where I was to where I've come, even while standing still. Was I brought here? I have this full country acre in Connecticut. I think I was. Who did it? Only in the army do I think I had more freedom of choice, more room in which to move about. At least I *felt* I did. I did. I was outside my family, had no wife, job, parent, children, met no one I cared for. I had no ties. I had no one anywhere I cared for. I got laid a lot. Overseas I went with prostitutes and enjoyed that too. I had fun. I enjoyed being away (at least it was something to do. If you sat home alone Saturday night, at least you were sitting home in a barracks, which was better than sitting alone in your own home on a Saturday night. One New Year's Eve in the army I had nothing to do and didn't care. We take weekend drives now to people I don't want to be with and can't wait to leave. A long weekend will break up my family one day. I stroke my dick. I stroked it often then too. I was often lonely and wished I had someone I *could* care for. I would have liked a pen pal, a pin-up girl in a cashmere sweater and chaste pleated skirt, a sweetheart I adored who photographed beautifully and mailed me snapshots. I still would. I felt cheated, underprivileged. I wanted to be the nice boy in the Hollywood movie the nice girl was crazy about, that fellow in the love songs the girls were all singing to on the radio. I wasn't); and I know already that I'll be standing still again after I've been moved one giant step forward into Andy Kagle's position and have nailed down the job. I'll make my speech. I'll have important new work to do (nailing down the job), but I'll do it standing still. (And after I've done it and know I'm not in danger of being kicked out for a while, my interest will abate and my work will grow monotonous again.

I will not want what I have and will be in fear of losing it. I will not ever be convinced my illegal thoughts and dreams are not apparent to the authorities in the company, and I will still slither numbly into dismay at sight of a closed office door of a higher executive from behind which something small as a mouse might emerge that will bear my secrets out into the open and leave me worse off than dead. For everyone to see.) Everything dead lies still unless winds ruffle the feathers, fur, or hair. (I have the feeling now that I have already been everywhere it has been possible for me to go.) The sight of a dead dog on a highway is enough to turn my stomach and wrench my heart with pity. It reminds me of a dead child. And I never even had a dog. Children and dead dogs evoke sympathy. Neither can speak. No one else. Two dead dogs on a highway seconds apart lead me to think my sanity is finally going and that it is no longer possible for me to separate what I see from what I remember or what I don't want to see. In flickers of disorientation I often glimpse in silhouette from the rear or side people I did not know well and have not seen or thought about in decades (total strangers take on the identity for a second of kids I remember from elementary or high school or people I was acquainted with briefly in other jobs or brushed against uneventfully in the army. I was once beaten up by an enlisted man who didn't know I was an officer). They are always people I was not close to and do not want to see again. (I don't catch unreal glimpses of people I do want to see.) Real and imagined events overrun each other in my mind in hazy indistinction. I sometimes find it hard to be certain whether I have done something I intended to or only thought of doing it but didn't. I have answered letters twice. I have no system. Others I don't answer at all because I remember wanting to promptly and think I have. There's much I think of doing and saying I know I'd better not. I'd lose my job or go to jail. I am growing forgetful. My eyesight is deteriorating: I wear reading glasses now and require a stronger prescription every year. Periodontal work will save my teeth only for a while. I know I repeat myself at home with

401

my children and my wife (my children point that out with unkindness): soon I'll be repeating myself with everyone everywhere and be shunned as a prattling old fool. In southern Louisiana, I learned recently (on a business trip to New Orleans, where, because I found myself alone in a strange, big city, I picked up a chunky, Negro whore in a bar and asked her to follow me to my hotel room. I figured if she could make her way through the hotel lobby into my room, I could make my way into her. I get so lonesome in glamorous cities in which I have nobody I can call. Everybody else, I feel, is having a good time. I get the blues when it rains. The blues I can't lose when it rains. I've never learned how to make friends in strange cities. Men who strike up conversations with me appear homosexual and drive me off.

"I've got to go now. I have this friend I have to meet."

"Take care."

All I know how to do in a strange city is read the local newspapers. Late at night, I'm good at that in bed. I'm good at eating candy bars in bed too. I get the feeling when I'm alone in strange American cities that I have no inner resources and no cock. She was just under thirty. She said she was a mixture of French, Chinese, and Mexican parentage and could therefore do sweet things to me in bed no one had ever done before. She said it only half seriously in a husky southern drawl. I knew she was Black. I haven't been with Black girls much in this country, only twice before, but I knew that much. I've been afraid of them, first for my dignity, now for my life.

"I don't dig," I said, "French, Chinese, and Mexican girls." I was kidding back with her in the bar. "I want someone Black."

"I'm a little of that too," she chuckled heartily.

She was simple, good-natured, guileless, and I felt myself in charge. She asked for fifty dollars, grinning. I got her to agree to twenty. Then I threw in ten dollars more to inspire her by my generosity and make her like me and really do sweet things to me no one had ever done before.

"I can show you a good time," she vowed.

By the time I returned to my hotel room I no longer wanted her and hoped she wouldn't follow. I had all the evening newspapers for New Orleans and Baton Rouge and was raring to take my clothes off and get to work on them. I have this clinging fear of catching a venereal disease somewhere and bringing it home to my wife. How would I get out of that one when she found out she was infected? Easily. Lie and deny. She did. She paid off the desk clerk, she said. She rapped softly on the door and came in smiling, and I had to stare at her as she undressed in order to get interested again. She wasn't pretty.

"Do it slowly," I requested. "Take them off slow. And shimmy a little."

"Sure."

I don't like girls who get out of their clothes too quickly. I get the feeling they've been getting out of those same few clothes all day long for other men before they came to me.

"Okay."

"Sure. Some men—"

"Not now."

"Huh?"

"Come here. Shhhh."

"Sure."

She was still grinning. She had nothing different to offer. In San Francisco not long ago a stunning, willowy blonde who looked like royalty whispered the same alluring promise and turned out to be lying also. She made me give her a hundred dollars. Whores in Naples, Rome, and Nice after the war had uttered the same exotic guarantees and had been no more successful in filling them. I guess there's really not that much variety around for normal degenerates like me. It was flat, and over quickly.

"Where's all those sweet new tricks of yours?" I taunted, and was pleased I was justified in doing so.

She was hurt and looked a little frightened, and that was gratifying to me also. "I did what you asked, hon," she apologized hesitantly. "Didn't I?"

"You're supposed to do things I don't ask. It's okay."

"Didn't I?"

"You were fine."

"Did I show you a good time?"

"Really. You can go now if you want."

"I thought you wanted me the whole night."

"So did I." I forced a laugh. "But I can't go that distance anymore. I must be getting old. I thought I could when I was looking you over in that bar. Those are some knockers you have. Mmmm. And some big ass."

"You like it?"

"And how. I like them big on a short girl."

"I'm short, all right." She was pleased as punch with my compliments. "You want some more?"

"But I can't. I guess my eyes are bigger than my dick."

She was relieved I wasn't angry.

"You're all right down there too," she complimented me.

"I know. You can keep the money. I enjoyed it."

"Did I show you a good time? Was I really good?"

"As good as the best. And I've been to Paris."

"Really?"

"I've even been to Bologna."

"I don't know about that."

"That's where they really know how to slice it."

"You sure you don't want me to stay till morning, mister? You're nice. I got no place I have to go."

"I've got an early plane."

"I could stay in the other bed until you want me. I don't even snore. I'll bet you'll want some in the morning." She giggled. "I'll do what you want. I do everything."

"You should put your legs up higher."

"It hurts. I get cramps here."

"And you really don't do anything new."

"I did what you wanted. You got to ask, hon."

"I am not bizarre."

"I don't know about that."

"I'm never sure what I want." I felt positively regal using a word like *bizarre* with her. "You're supposed to help me find out what I want. I'm not

404

saying that because I'm unhappy. It will help you with other men."

"Some men beat me up."

And I have no compelling fetishes, although certain silken undergarments get me hot and are more attractive to me than the parts they cover. Big tits in bras and jersey can get me hot. Small ones make me romantic. Small asses on slim girls are starting to draw appreciating gazes from me. Many of these are on very young girls, and this is something new. The only woman I've ever wanted to beat up was my wife, and that—to my shame—was over money. She insinuates I give too little but won't take more. I felt most content as I watched her dress to leave, lofty. She looked comical and naïve stuffed into flowered bikini underpants. I thought a moment of flipping her over my knees and paddling her smooth muscular bottom but remembered she'd be heavy. That's the trouble with so many of our damned picturesque sex fantasies: they hurt. I've pampered myself before with the temptation of spanking a nice ass someday but never got one beautiful enough. Maybe there are no beautiful ones outside of magazines. I'm in love with a four-color magazine page. She still smiled; I was sorry for her, in a patronizing, uncommitted way. I wonder what happens to squat, homely Black and Puerto Rican whores with one missing molar when they grow too old—who takes care of them—and ugly to attract handsome, pinstriped libertines like me. I know what happens. They attract me anyway if I'm alone in New Orleans where everyone else seems to be having a good time. I ought to know by now that hardly anyone over the age of four ever has a good time anymore. Women do, at weddings and movies. It was a waste. The hundred-dollar beauty in San Francisco was a waste. She didn't look like an aristocrat once I had her. She looked like a skinny girl in need of sunshine or more red corpuscles. I'm glad I never had to see either of them again. I wonder what happens to homely white whores when they grow older and lose their figures and lose their teeth. They become public drunkards with gravelly, masculine voices who quarrel with each other loudly on sidewalks in warm weather. I still had all my news-papers after my little Black beauty left—thank God —and I ate three sticky candy bars and drank two cans of soda from a vending machine in the hall as I read them. I would have felt self-conscious going down into the lobby again that night. I went to sleep with caramel and nut crumbs in my mouth. I had what might have been the start of a homosexual dream, stopped it in time, and switched reels into the middle of a different dream I barely remembered in which I was a failing history student at the University of Bologna striving to find my way out of the yellow rock tangle of school buildings in time to catch a plane back home to my wife. There was a hatchet-faced, bleached-blond, scrawny actress I was trying to flee who kept sliding along the opposite sides of the stone walls in stealthy pursuit. She carried an icon of some kind cradled in her hands that was smaller than herself and could have been a human figure carved out of a penis—feces?—or a stick of African sculpture. I seemed able to identify all and wanted none, and that's why I was running from her. Her face was Horace White's. The next day I worried intermittently on the plane going back about carrying syphilis, gonorrhea, or crabs home to my wife from New Orleans. In the dream, I was failing in Bologna because I had been unable to find my way to any of the classrooms all year, although I had tried repeatedly. I itched. I scratched. I always itch afterward. Guilefully, I would deny to my wife I'd even had it and accuse *her* of having given it to me. Both statements could not be true, of course, but she would be intimidated by my yelling and unable to grasp that, and I would yell in sancti-monious outrage and convince her. There are no con-venient army prophylactic stations around anymore dispensing soapy absolution by the pint for our sins of the flesh. They're gone too. So is sin. Most of my favorite restaurants are closing. There is only crime. I often don't enjoy it. My climaxes often aren't. Other times there's this gigantic, spurting leap. The difference is me. It's got nothing to do with them. They all do pretty much the same things by now. So do we. Sometimes it really dances. Other times it only stirs as much as necessary to get the ridiculous ritual over with. In Italy after the war, girls from Bologna stated they were the best in all Europe and wheedled for premium fees; they were no different from lower-class girls in Naples and Rome. They did the same things. They were interchangeable. They still are.

I can't fall in love. That's probably what holds my marriage together. If I didn't have this wife, I would have another. It's lots of trouble to leave. I don't like to be alone. Red Parker needs a wife and ought to marry one fast before I have to fire him. I guess there's really not much more one can do easily with a human dick than what we have been doing. Everything else stinks or hurts. So much of the quality of response seems a matter of chance. In the army, I would rent my girls by the hour and go three-and-a-half times in those sixty minutes—I got bargains leasing them that way—that final half time signaling a valorous raising of my standard as I made ready to ride off. I'd win applause, even from blondes from Bologna, for my virile performances and for my good looks and lean, firm, sun-tanned body. I used to be lean, and hungry. I had appetites. I used to have a full head of hair. I had strong teeth. I once had tonsils. We scarcely need them at all. I know I've had wet dreams that were more delicious and satisfying than anything I've experienced at complicated orgies I've attended in London, Las Vegas, and Los Angeles, and much less trouble. My wife would like me to take her along on business trips to Los Angeles, Las Vegas, Chicago, San Francisco, and New Orleans. She thinks I get laid there. I usually do; I feel the country, the company, and society expect me to. I usually don't enjoy it. I enjoy the local newspapers more. I remember wondering when I was finally able to do it the first time, even as I was doing it, if that's all there was to it. There was more, I learned the second time, and still is, there is enough to launch me into unrestrainable fervors all over again—even now I'll rape my wife, *only* my wife, force her at times when she doesn't want to and I feel I *have* to have it from her *at once;* but there's no sublime

407

relationship, no reciprocal contact; like a mad chemist, I knew I was carrying the whole magical process and potential along with me like a pair of bubbling retorts inside my head and my vesicles. If my balls ever exploded, I knew it would not be because of a female; the mixtures inside me would have made up their own independent mind to detonate. They would not consult even me.

Bang! They would decide to go.

They do look queer to me still, hairier than me, many of them. Some look like Van Dykes, and these I'm tempted to tug. Others have sideburns and shock me a moment like card number eight on the Rorschach test again. I was struck speechless when that damned color shock card appeared. I was stupefied. Others vegetate profusely with more rotund and corpulent growths of wiry foliage and look like Karl Marx, Sigmund Freud, or Joseph Conrad. They affect me too. I sometimes want to quail. Will my wife turn white? She'll have to. So will I. We have adenoids and vesicles and never get to see them while they're alive. I think a good ear-nose-and-throat man today doesn't dirty his fingers much with them either. His skill lies in popping his head into the hospital room afterward to tell us everything went well—that's all he does and leaves the whole gory, grisly, repelling procedure to his Oriental anesthetist and ambitious apprentices. Why should *he* be disgusted? By now I'm used to the way my wife looks.

"How was New Orleans?"

"Dull."

"You should have brought me along."

"There was nothing to do."

"I'd have given you things to do. You know how hot I get in a place like that. What'd you bring me back?"

"Clap."

"Good."

My wife is usually much better for me than most. Only Penny does it with a consistent, keen, unbearable beauty every single time and has me begging her helplessly to stop, my eyes blind and my mouth glutting incoherently with babbles, giggles, gasps, and spasms.

Penny knows where to hit and strikes like an eagle. She knows exactly how much longer it's safe to go on after I feel positively I will die in pieces if she continues at all. And I'm glad she goes on. Penny makes it dance like an angel and sprint like a whippet every single time. I comprehend then why owners and whole cultures have worshiped it. It's an ironic master-servant association: I am the master; she serves me by reducing me to a writhing, pleading blob of chaotic, giggling blackness and a single burning nerve that cuts like a blade. I think I whimper with hilarity. I'm not sure what noises I make as I wait for my vision to recover and my power to speak to reassemble. I would not want anybody else in the world to see me that way, in the collapsed state of what is called *ecstasy*. I would not want to be photographed. She gives me scotch and makes hot coffee for me afterward. Penny has a hazel muff, with no scraggly hairs migrating and never any surprises or disappointments. I do not phone her much anymore), motorists driving at high speed swerve out of their way deliberately to kill nutrias dazed by their headlights standing hypnotized in the service lanes at the sides of the highway. In the morning, there are too many furry, dead bodies to count lying along the road from Hammond into New Orleans. Seen quickly from certain angles they look like cozy muffs. Seen from others, they look like crushed wild animals with bloody beaks and talons. During the morning, I suppose, local fur trappers arrive in pickup trucks to remove the bodies for their valuable pelts. This is called *hunting*. (Other people, I think, might veer away to avoid killing an animal, even a sleeping frog.)

(Man is a carnivore, a swift, accurate, rapacious hunter, and he ought never try to compete with the electric vibrator. It tires you out, and there isn't a chance of winning. Ask a girl who owns one.)

Green was right about Jane too.

I have stopped flirting with Jane (what *would* I do with her afterward?) and started flirting platonically with Laura, Arthur Baron's secretary (which makes a much better impression). Laura is older and unhappily married. She is highly regarded by everyone but her husband, who is three years younger than she and perhaps homosexual, and my attentions are clearly friendly and humanitarian (although she does have a thick ass I think now and then I might like to toss over onto my lap and paddle bare with stinging, tingling noises. It's good I don't try, for I forget how heavy she'd be, and I would risk a hernia or slipped spinal disk. If I did that once to someone, I might want to do it always—and then I would be a pervert. Girls would talk about me unfavorably to their friends. I think I feel that way too about stuttering. I think I may *want* to stutter. What a liberating release it might be from the lifelong, rigorous discipline of speaking correctly. I'd feel tongue-tied and free. I might spank and stutter at the same time. I feel I might never want to stop once I started and would let my tongue wobble as it wanted to for the rest of my life and never have to say anything intelligible to anyone again. I would lose my job. I would lose my wife and friends. I don't have close friends anymore. I have friends, but I don't feel close to them. Some feel close to me. Red Parker is my friend, and I don't feel close to him). I really don't know *how* I would have disposed of Jane after taking her to bed with me in Red Parker's apartment early one evening probably after cocktails. She's only twenty-four. I can't imagine what in the world I would want to talk to her about once we no longer had to talk about going to bed. She's probably too young to understand there'd be nothing personal in the enmity and disgust I'd feel toward her afterward and in my never wanting to see or speak to her again. That's happened to me before. She'd probably conclude it had something to do with her. I'd have her lovely blue eyes fastened upon me in wondering, repentant apology. I could not say to her outright—I like her too much for:

"Nothing—nothing—nothing, dammit. You didn't do *anything* wrong. It has nothing at all to do with you. You aren't important enough to affect me. Don't you see?"

That might hurt her feelings too.

I would have to overcompensate with pleasantries

and consideration: I might even have to lay her again, just because I'm a real nice guy. That's happened before too. (Or I might tell her my wife is undergoing tests for cancer and win some pity for myself that way. I've done that before also.) It's why I don't like to get involved with girls in the same office anymore. They're there. (If only she worked somewhere else. I could use her often these days. But then I might not have her.) She would have Red Parker to contend with. (I've already told him I was thinking of laying her. He's already told me he's thinking of following me.) He hurts his women sometimes; he hits them now. He'll get in trouble. The funniest part is that he really did not like his wife while she was alive and expected she would throw him out and ask for a divorce. He did not expect her to die in an automobile accident and leave him with three temperamental children. He tries to keep them away in boarding school. One or the other is always coming home. He doesn't know what else to do with them except send them away to boarding school in the winter and to his wife's relatives, camp, or on group journeys in the summer. Parker's got money too, and so does his wife's family. He used to have stronger connections in the company. He goes with prostitutes too now. I've caught him in bed with two at one time (two on one with him also? Is *everyone* but me doing it?), one of them white and one of them dark.

"Come on in buddy," he invited convivially, and started to move from the bed. "I'll go eat."

Both naked girls waited for me with blank, phlegmatic smiles. The white one had a sore on her jaw that looked bleached with calamine lotion.

I left.

I have stopped using Red Parker's apartment in the city and no longer go to his noisy cocktail parties there on the chance of striking it lucky with one of the large number of girls he is still able to persuade to attend. (I have made out well more times than I can remember with girls I've met through Red. I met Penny through Red and still have her. And soon I will have to fire him or design some gentler means

411

of getting rid of him. Like an antiquated building with white X's on the front, he must be demolished shortly. He has a naturally disrespectful way with women I've always envied. It's effective. They mean nothing to him; they mean dramatic things to me. It's really hard to be indifferent laying somebody new the first time. His girls have gotten older, though, blowsy, thicker about the waist and chin. But so, for that matter, have he and I. His wizened cheeks are veinous jowls now, and his lips are blistered. He chortles as much as ever, as though his wife were not dead and his job not in jeopardy. He heh-heh-hehs a lot now too. He's been warned by Kagle. The apartment is garish and sleazy. Furniture is stained and needs cleaning and upholstering. Will it be with someone like him that my wife decides to cheat on me? I hope not. I would like it at least to be with someone I can look up to, a man to whom she'll mean a little more than just another married piece of ass. I'd hate her to do it with that arrogant, obstreperous, bad-mannered, flamboyant type. I am that type. I would not like them to think I am married to just another piece of ass.) The last time in town I took my wife to a big room at an expensive hotel. My wife loves it in expensive hotels. So do I. There's something about my own wife in a luxurious hotel that beats everything else in the world.

"I'll fuck like a racehorse in a room like this," she glories, a vibrant strumpet lying eager for more as soon as I'm ready to supply it. "Don't I?"

"Ride, racehorse."

"You jockey me."

"Or I'll whip you some more."

"Do what you want, darling."

"Stop talking so much."

"Put me in a bed in a hotel like this and I feel I can fuck the whole world."

"Put your knees up."

"Oh, good. God. Goodness gracious, deary me."

My damned dumb wife still can't remember to put her knees up after all these years—and she feels she is ready to fuck the whole world.

I wonder what I *would* feel like if my wife ever

did come home smelling of another man's semen. I think I would die a sudden, shriveling death inside. (Would it excite me?) I would wither and curl up inside my skin and spend the rest of my dull, spiritless life hiding my dead, small self inside a head and torso now many sizes too large. I would pray my wife and children would let me keep it secret. (I'm not sure what other men's semen smells like, unless it smells like my own. I'd guess it smells of sweat and hair. I've caught the scent of sweat and hair on my wife a hundred times when she's not had time to wash and change before I plant my perfunctory kiss on her cheek, but it's only sweat and hair, I think.) She does not guess what I'm thinking as my eyes examine her critically these days. (It would not excite me.) It would fill me with saddest resignation and lifelong self-disgust. Judgment will have been rendered against me by her and someone else behind another closed door I did not know was even there, and the judgment will be irreversible. I hope it will not be with someone crass and repellent like Andy Kagle or Red Parker. I would not want their hands or fluids on her. (Someone like Green might be better for me.) Sometimes on my train ride home from work —I even have trouble sleeping when commuting—I have the clairvoyant certainty I am going to catch her that very day within the next forty-five minutes, and just that way: by a stain. She'll hurry into the house after I do, dinner will be late reaching the table, and there it will be, that smudge, that stain on her slip, her belly, her skirt. The details of sequence are disorderly —but they won't matter. I will not be able to say anything in the dining room because of the children. Later, I will not be able to say anything anyway. I will not want her to know I know (and hope she doesn't make a point of telling me. I would have to *do* something if she knows I found out, and there'd be nothing I'd really want to. I would even have to fake the anger and unhappiness I was experiencing. I could not let it emerge so vulnerably. It would be easier for me to rot and decompose in hidden torment for the rest of my life than to let her see how cruelly she hurt me and how easily she could do it again

413

every time she chose. I do not want her to). I must never let her see I care.

"I love my wife, but, oh, you kid."

I am not as big a shot as she and the children think I am (but must not let them find that out). I have horrendous visions of her being felt up greedily on packed subway trains, and enjoying it, and my wife doesn't even have to ride the subway trains. Penny does. A man came on her dress in the rush hour during the summer. She didn't know it until she was off the train and the fingers holding her pocketbook brushed against the sticky substance on the back of her hip. *I* began in a random glob shot like that and will end, if I'm lucky, decaying like Red Parker with white-washed X's splashed across my eyes and a sign on my chest or forehead reading: COMING DOWN SOON. FORGIONE DEMOLITION CO. While Negro junkies, winos, and dealers in stolen wallets, cameras, and wristwatches hang out in my squalid, dimly lit hallways.)

"I knew it was either that or phlegm," Penny told me with a snorting laugh she has I often find grating. "And no one was doing any coughing. Was I ever embarrassed. Imagine the nerve."

I can't.

I miss my mother, sister, and brother more and more often lately and regret we did not remain closer as a family when we were all still together. On balmy evenings in spring and summer, my mother would send down to the drugstore for a container of bulk ice cream, and we would eat it together. She let me get it when I grew big enough to go. We liked strawberry best of all, and it was good. Sometimes we had strawberry mixed with vanilla.

I don't think I have ever had a homosexual experience that counted. I was molested twice as a child, once by an older boy, but I don't think that counted. The other time was by an older girl in the same apartment house who pretended to wrestle with me but was really intent on giving me an erection and feeling it bounce against her. That does count because it felt so nice. I was lucky. I was eager to have her do it to me again and lurked around her optimistically.

414

She didn't. Poor me. It's hard to believe one can experience such acute sensitivity and still be unable to come. How does it end? We can't remember. It peters out. Penny never has to be reminded to put her legs up and keeps them up for the longest time without complaining of aches or strains. She's good. She takes dancing lessons still (which might help), along with her singing lessons and exercise classes. At age thirty-two, she still wants to be Shirley Temple. For a little while last spring I had a nice-looking, slightly nutty, twenty-six-year-old, tall, ex-college kid from Ann Arbor, Michigan, I met at an office Christmas party who would start to come as soon as we began and raise her legs from feet to hips straight up toward the ceiling for as long as it took. I liked that: I liked her quick response and that feel of ass against my knees; it let me think I was getting away with something extra. She made shrill noises and I would have to muffle her mouth. (It was soon very tiresome listening to her. I do not think of it as doing something together and don't believe anyone else really does, either.) She got to be a nuisance and a bore. She had spare time. She's the one that made fun of my garters. I could not brook such churlish insolence to the Slocum name from such a woozy upstart (she did take drugs, which made her even more vapid still), and I began to snub and neglect her. I played on her ignorance and provincialism. (She really knew almost nothing.) She thought it was beautiful.

"Isn't it beautiful?" she would say.

Anyone could please her, and she left me in the warm weather for younger men in beach houses with less money who played volleyball in the sand but had more time to spend with her. I tried to get her back but failed. She jilted me. (I had to face the fact *I* bored *her,* too.) She outgrew me, saw through me. *There* was degradation—oh, boy—turned down by *her*. She had never *seen* men's garters before or noticed them in fashion ads, and she had never heard of Camus, Copernicus, or Søren Kierkegaard (the three big *K*'s, ha, ha), either. She found my garters quaint and curious; she never actually ridiculed them, but her amusement was insult enough. I guess men's garters do look funny. I had to employ some technique, though, for keeping my socks up during important business meetings. I've switched to full-length stretch socks now—always dark, except in summer at the country or shore or on weekends at somebody's club. (I won't join a club until I've got the new job and know I can keep it.) They look funny too. Stretch socks choke. I shove them down around my ankles whenever I can in order to release my calves from their abrasive grip. With my dark socks down, my ankles remind me of shifty, slimy men I used to see in dirty movies, the kind of unshaven, evil sneak who'd sidle close and feel my wife or daughter up on crowded trains or come on Penny's pretty skirt and make a mental note (perhaps even jot it down industriously on a small record pad) that his day as a molester was off to a shooting start. I bet these people organize their work week around their sly, depraved perversions. (I've got *them* ghosting around inside the narrow passageways of my brain also, with this difference. They aren't ghosts. I feel it when they walk about.) They try to take what doesn't belong to them. What do they do on vacations? I wonder how the poor creatures got along before there were buses and subways. What effect will growing investments in mass transportation have upon their activities, particularly in respect to productivity and competition? Will the liberated woman feel back? Will the homosexual liberated woman on crowded buses and trains start feeling my wife and daughter up also? Maybe people will begin riding the subway trains *just* to be felt up. They could sell tickets, raise the fare. I see a panoramic mural. (My wife thinks I have a dirty mind.) Imagine the trainloads of smiling faces. No one would want a seat. Every hour a rush hour, every rush a crush hour. That could be a partial solution to the energy crisis. (A lot of energy would be discharged.) After all, the opportunities for being felt up in one's own automobile aren't that promising, unless you're my daughter or one of her teen-age friends, or a college kid, although I've done some hearty automobile groping myself from time to time,

416

most recently while being driven home from a party by the heavyset wife of one of our millionaire corporation executives. She wore heavy perfume I didn't like and took me by surprise.

"Do you have to go right home?" she asked unexpectedly. "Or aren't you afraid of your big, mean wifey?"

"No to both," I responded with terse bravado. "What do you have in mind?"

"Lover's lane," she announced, then tittered a moment. "Do you know where lover's lane is?" she asked. "Right here," she answered with another laugh, and touched herself.

She was a millionaire's frolicsome wife with a double chin and acrid perfume I didn't like, and I had always had to respect her (because she was a millionaire's wife. I was afraid of her husband). She was four years older than I was and had a hearty, predatory vivaciousness about her. She made fun of my shy caution and was entertained by my ignorance and naïveté.

"I've got a reputation as big as this whole county, baby. Oh, have you got a lot to learn. Didn't you know that?"

I felt like a yokel. "Does Bill know?"

"A lot I care. I'm a free spirit, puddy poo. I do what I want."

"Will Bill know about me when he finds you dropped me off?"

"Don't be such a worry wart," she chided with a squeaky titter.

My skin prickled, and I thought for a moment she might pinch my cheek or tweak my nose. She tore her stockings at the knees on the floorboard of her car and stuffed them in her purse before she started driving again.

"I can't walk in with these, can I? I'll call you in the city. I come in every Wednesday to see my mother."

"I have an apartment."

"We own a co-op."

"Will Bill know?"

"Don't be such a worry wart."

"Don't use that phrase. It makes my skin prickle."

"Your skin prickles easily, I've noticed."

"It isn't fitting for a woman of your position."

"I'll show you some new ones. Bill and I have an understanding."

"What does that mean?"

"I do what I want. And he can go to hell if he doesn't like it."

"That's some way to talk about a millionaire."

"Puddy poo."

When she called on Wednesday, I didn't want to see her again and told her I had a meeting. (I was afraid of Bill, and I didn't think I ever wanted to see again someone who had called me *puddy poo*.)

"I'm at the hair dresser," she said on Thursday the week after.

"I was expecting you yesterday," I lied again.

"You'll have to take me when you can get me. Let's have lunch."

"It can't be done."

"I'll pay."

"It's not that."

"You think I'm homely?"

"No. I think you're sexy as hell."

"So does he, puddy poo."

"Who?"

"The guy I'll meet instead. You're not the only fish in the sea, baby. We'll talk about you."

"Does he know me?"

"We'll have a big laugh."

"Who is it?"

"That's for me to know and you to find out."

(I began to feel she had the whammy on me.) I began to believe she would come up to the office unannounced at any time just to make a fool of me in front of the others there.

"You're afraid of me, puddy poo, aren't you?" she taunted prankishly the next time we met at a party, and she did indeed—while my wife and *her* husband observed from different parts of the house —tweak my nose. "Isn't he, Mrs. Slocum?"

"I wish he were afraid of me," my wife yelled back.

418

"Call me Wednesday," I ordered her curtly. "And I'll show you how afraid I am."

"I'm at the Plaza," she said when she called.

"I think I've got the flu," I apologized with a snuffle.

"I thought you might, baby," she chirruped pleasantly, "so I brought along a list. And I do mean baby. You come on much better at parties. You're not the only fish in the sea."

I wish I had her on her knees again right here right now. Alongside Virginia. I've done it with my wife here in my study many times. My wife and I go on honeymoon sprees still, lashing all about the house and grounds in frothing spasms. We need liquor. We've done it in all the rooms by now except the children's and Derek's nurse's. We've done it in our attached garage at night when we did not want to risk waking up anybody inside, and we've done it outside in the darkness on soaking wet grass. (If we had a swimming pool, I'm sure we'd try it in there at least once.) We've done it on our redwood patio furniture. I whiff her dense perfume again (and turn around to look). Of course her husband knew. I wonder how he stood it. I know it vexes me almost beyond toleration—I could bang bricks against my head with both hands—to recall I was called *puddy poo* not long ago and tweaked on the nose in public by someone tasteless and vulgar like her and that my garters were the source of innane merriment to that uninteresting Ann Arbor dropout who wore denim jeans and jackets and never seemed clean. I do not want such people to enjoy even a moment's advantage over me. I wish I had them both magnetized on computer tape and could bring them back to start all over again. It would be the same. One would tweak my nose, the other would smile and quiz me presumptuously about my garters. I called her once two months later to make a date and had to call her again to break it. I did want to see her.

"This time it's true," I explained. "I have to be out of town. Let me call you when I get back."

She sounded unexcited both times, as though all the tittering had run out of her. She didn't seem to care.

"It's all right," she said. "You're okay. My looks are gone. I lost them overnight."

She and her husband split up, and both have moved away. The children were all at college. The house stands empty and no one knows if it's for sale. I suppose my wife and I will have to split up finally too when the children are away at college. I hope it doesn't have to happen sooner while I'm changing jobs at the company or while my daughter is still mired indecisively in adolescence and high school and my boy stands rooted numbly in terror of Forgione and rope climbing and gives no sure indication yet of whether he will make his way up or down. She has nothing to do.

"I have nothing to do."

She has nothing to do but align herself unpassionately with the new women liberationists (although all that blatant discussion about orgasm, masturbation, and female homosexuality makes her uneasy).

"That's only because," I inform her, "you've been conditioned to react that way by a male-dominated society."

She is not certain whether I am siding with her or not.

"Why should you," she wonders dejectedly, "have all the advantages?"

"Do I seem to you," I answer mildly, "a person with all the advantages?"

"You've got a job."

"Get a job."

She shakes her head with a soft snicker. "I don't want to work." (She does have a sense of humor.)

"Do you want more money?"

"It's not money. You always think it's money. I've got nothing to do."

"Have love affairs. Commit adultery."

"Is that what you want?"

"It's not what I want. I can give you more money, if it will make you happier. I'll be able to."

"That's not what I want. There isn't anything I *can* do."

"Cure cancer. Money isn't shit, you know."

"Please don't get mad at me tonight."

"Money is love, baby, and that's no shit. I'm not getting mad."

"I'm feeling so bad."

"Don't drink whiskey after wine, and maybe you won't feel so bad."

"I may be getting my period. You even look younger than I do. And that's not fair."

"You'll live longer. Women do."

"But I'll look older."

"What do you expect, if you live longer? At least you're alive."

"I was kidding," she says. "You don't even know when I'm kidding. It's getting harder and harder to talk to you."

My own good joke about Freud, money, and excrement went right by her, and I suppose I *will* have to leave her for something like that someday (she has never heard of Copernicus or Kierkegaard either, although she may have heard of Camus because he was killed in an expensive sports car), although I would not want to do it while my little boy still appears in such precarious need of me. (I am not sure he needs me at all.) I do not feel he'd last if I died suddenly or moved out. (He would not know what hit him if I were gone. My daughter's wish to steal our automobile may be a wholesome development: it gives her a goal to work toward.) When he grows up and gets away from me, I will get away from him. My daughter will be away too and there'll be only Derek, if we still have him. I wouldn't want to move away and stick my wife with a retarded child. Actually, I *would* like to stick her with Derek. She stuck me with him. (And he won't even be a child then.) But everyone would be on her side, unless I left her for another woman, which would change everything, because that would be romantic. I think I'd elope. There'd be lots of:

"Why did he leave his wife? They have a retarded child, don't they?"

"He fell in love with another girl and ran off with her."

"Oh."

But change that to:

"Why did he leave his wife with a retarded child?"

"He didn't want to be married anymore."

And there'd be plenty of:

"He was only thinking of himself, wasn't he?"

And:

"How selfish. That poor woman. She left her alone with a retarded child just because he didn't want to be married to her. What will the poor woman do?"

I can hear those choruses of opprobrium reverberating to the four corners of the company. Not that I'm much help to her now when it comes to him. I don't have the strength. I'd rather slink off or look away. Someone will have to make the decision for me: *she* will, without even realizing she is doing it, or a doctor will have to aid us with an unambiguous recommendation based on anything but our own selfishness. (Our conscience must be clear.)

"He'll be much better off there, safer. They have good ones now. It's best for all of you, the other children too. It hasn't been fair to them. You deserve a rest. You've both been marvelous. I know it will be hard to give him up."

Or an illness or accident will have to occur.

Till then, I'm powerless. (I don't have the guts even to want to talk about it. I've got no answers to the unspoken criticism I imagine I'll hear. I do not want to listen for the rest of my life to my wife's second thoughts. I could forgive myself in a second for putting him away. She would not forgive either of us.) I am not the pillar of support she wants. I keep my mouth shut and my sentiments suppressed, and I adamantly refuse to merge my feelings with hers. (I won't share my sorrows. I don't want her to have a part in them. They're all mine.) I wish I had no dependents. It does not make me feel important to know that people are dependent on me for many things. It's such a steady burden, and my resentment is larger each time I have to wait for her to stop crying and clinging to me and resume placing the silverware in the dishwasher or doing her isometric hip and thigh exercises. (I can't stand a woman who cries at anything but funerals. I feel used.)

"For God sakes, what do you want from *me* of

422

all people, Jesus Christ?" I roar at her. "They're my children, too. Do you really expect me to feel sorry for *you?*"

"I need someone to talk to. I wasn't asking you to feel sorry for me. Can't I even say how I feel?"

"Call your sister. You know damn well I can't stand crying anymore." I don't want to hear how she feels. I don't want to have to talk to anyone about Derek. I don't want to have to hear anyone talk about his own troubles. (I find it harder and harder to feel sorry for anyone but myself.) "I can't help you with this. I don't know how. I didn't order it this way and I don't know what to do, either."

And I saw it happening before anyone. Someone cursed us. I am ashes and stale air inside when it comes to him, have the fortitude and fiber of dried mushrooms and wet fallen leaves. I am cold. I could have prophesied. When pediatricians said he was slow, I saw he was clumsy. His knees and feet and fingers seemed angled slightly out of kilter. I discerned he could not seem to hold his head up straight for long. I had a feeling of disaster about him even before he was born (but I had that anxious feeling about the others too). I expected a Mongoloid. I would have settled readily beforehand for a harelip or cleft palate and trusted to surgery—with all three—although I can't visualize either my boy or my daughter wading through life even this far with any kind of serious birth defect. They've had trouble enough without it. I can't see how my wife really expects me to feel sorry for her when I have so many good reasons for feeling sorry for myself. Among them, her.

I want to get free of her before her health fails. I see an ailing wife in my future. There are eloquent forerunners now of chronic invalidism. (She's sure she has, is getting, will get cancer, and maybe she will.) I know her health will degenerate before mine does. She's better at it. I don't want to be tied to her by sickness (hers, that is). I will. I'll get battered by continuing hurricane warnings of bursitis, arthritis, rheumatism, diabetes, varicose veins, dizziness, nausea, tumors, cysts, angina, polyps, the whole fucking shebang of physical dissolution. (I can do without

423

everyone else's but my own.) I'll be caught on that barb. And my grown-up children will keep me there.

"Dad, how can you even think of leaving her, when she's feeling so bad?" they'll say to me in reproof.

"But how can I ever leave her, when she never feels better?"

They'll get away from it all quickly enough (the self-centered fuckers).

"I don't feel well," my wife wakes up whimpering some mornings in a little girl's voice (when she feels someone wants something from her).

As if I care.

("I was watching you sleep," a girl will tell you while she's still in love with you. "You were snoring."

When she's not in love with you, it's revolting, and she will not want to see you again unless she's lonely or needs your money.)

My wife snores now sometimes, and occasionally her breath is bad in the morning. But, so is mine, and so do I, so we are already in a headlong race toward decrepitude. The children join in with sniveling complaints of their own.

My daughter gets sore throats and stomach pains. My boy pleads tiredness and nausea and will sleep past noon some days if we let him. I use headaches. So does my wife. I've got chest pains I can draw upon, for everybody has great respect for a heart attack, and a liver up my sleeve I can play in a clutch. My wife can counter with cancer scares, and it's even-Stephen down to the wire in the shadow of the valley of Blue Cross major medical benefits. Wouldn't it be a laugh if my wife died of chest pains and I was the one who got cancer? When my wife is depressed and my daughter drops innuendoes of suicide, I can plunge into thick, sepulchral silences for days and feign such absorbed distraction that every remark to me has to be repeated—I can out-ail any of them at anything but hysterectomies if I want to make the effort, any of them but Derek, who begins with certain congenital handicaps that are impossible for me to overcome. (Ha, ha.) All of us boast of insomnia, not always truthfully. Were we taken at our word, not one member of the family has ever enjoyed a good night's sleep. Except, perhaps, Derek, who just can't bring himself to complain. (Ha, ha.) I wonder what's done with them in homes when they reach sexual maturity and discover they might just as well masturbate as do anything else. I'm glad he's not a girl. Castration's inhuman. So they cut off their arms. I wonder how they control attendants. How do they keep them away from the idiot boys and girls? My thoughts go haywire when I try to think of him. Tell me he'll not progress to a mental age past five: and I find myself thinking again if people at five know how to clean themselves properly after defecating. Of course not. My boy of nine still leaves stains on his undershorts, and so do I. (So does everyone, probably, so why must I single out us?) I see him now so lovely, touching, and pitiful I can't bear to look. I see him next at thirty moving toward sixty, and he is appalling. I am dazed, horrified, stricken dumb. Dark hair is growing on his face and on the backs of his hands, and his eyebrows are bushy. Will he look like me? He'll be balding. His suit won't fit. No one will groom him. His dandruff falls like fish scales. I color his sweaters and jackets dark and his face pale. He is slack-jawed and flabby as they steer him about, he is repulsive, lame, and monstrous. He still won't be able to speak. He will not know how to diet or play tennis, squash, or golf, and his build and muscle tone will be sickly. He'll be ungainly. People would stare with hostility if he were anywhere else. They'll forget to clip his fingernails. People will want to kill him. They'll call him Benjy. I will not want to visit him. I hope I can't remember him. I hope I don't find out my wife is committing adultery, even though she probably should.

"Do it," I'd advise, if she were someone else's.

"Okay. I will."

It might do wonders for her morale, if she didn't expect too much. It's also time she struck back. Wouldn't it be funny if my boy is the one who turns out to be homosexual and I do not? It would be tragic. I, at least, have inhibitions of steel. It would be worse than tragic for me: it would be socially embarrassing. A suicide, a fag, and an idiot, the Slocum offspring from the Slocum loins. And an alcoholic, neurasthenic, adulterous wife. God bless the girl— she'd come in handy. I'd blame the children on her. Until someone as astute as I am pointed an accusatory finger at me and inquired:

"Hey, wait a minute, buddy. Buddy, wait a minute. Was she always this way?"

"I don't know. All of this takes time to mature and emerge. You'll have to ask some reliable, revolutionary, evolutionary, psychological historian, an experienced botanist of the psyche. Was I this way?"

"You made me this way."

"You made me make you."

"You made me make you make me. Why can't I talk to you?"

"Call your sister."

"I need a sympathetic ear."

"You drink too much."

"You make me."

"Call your sister and complain to her."

"I hate my sister. You know it."

"She has a sympathetic ear."

"You bastard," she blurts out. "You just can't wait to get away from me, can you? I know what you're thinking. I can tell by the way you look."

More and more often lately, I find myself looking her over critically evenings for stains and bite marks of illicit sexuality. I feel cheated when I don't find any.

"What'd you do today?" I'm the one who's likely to ask.

"Nothing."

"Shopping."

"Went to the beauty parlor."

"Saw my sister."

"Saw some friends. Why?"

"Just curious."

"What'd you do?"

"Worked. Nothing."

"Anything happen?"

"It's moving along, I think. I don't want to talk about it."

"Jinx?"

"That's talking about it."

"I'll knock wood."

There are even mornings now when I catch myself scrutinizing her for stains and blemishes obsessively with the same aggressive and scavenging suspicions, and this, I know, is irrational, for she has spent the night in bed with me. I don't want to go crazy. I like to keep tight rein on my reason, thoughts, and actions, and to know always which is which. I don't want to lose my inhibitions. I might hit people if I did (strangers, friends, and loved ones), commit murder, spout hatred and bigotry, scratch eyeballs, molest teen-age girls and younger ones with trim figures, come on crowded subway trains against the side of a hefty buttock on someone like my wife or Penny. Dreams are merciless; they come upon you when you're asleep.

I might start stuttering.

Waking up is such a peculiar and extraordinary process that I'm surprised we are able to manage it successfully so many times while we are still half asleep.

I think I might get used to the idea of my wife's copulating with other men, but never to the specifics, the mechanics, to all that probing and liquid, all those grunts and strenuous bendings. Everything gets wet. Places are raw or bruised afterward. I don't like to picture my wife ever doing with another male the things she does with me. Or my daughter. (Will he put—of course. Will she—why not?) Everything does get so wet and smelly, and this is called *making love*. Beasts do it. It has no connection with *love, q.v., op. cit.* (But better wet and smelly, for my taste, than dry and perfumed. I hate those artificial, candy-store scents. I want to embrace human flesh with musky, natural odors, not a bar of soap.) Even business handshakes these days have turned wet and smelly. Show me a young man with a dry, pumping handshake today and I'll show you an unscrupulous young man on the make. I wish my daughter would stop leaving her bra around where I can see it and stop leaving her nightgown hanging on the door of the bathroom. She's developed fast and knows it. I see the way she dresses sometimes to go out, and I am furious. (She has bigger breasts now than my wife.) I can barely look at her as she pauses in front of me to wait for the money she says she needs. (There isn't anything *I* can say that wouldn't be derogatory and crushing to her self-esteem at a moment when she might be feeling good about herself. I wish she'd always *wear* her bra instead of leaving it tossed around. She'll wear blue denim jeans and doesn't always look clean. She reminds me of Ann Arbor. Every girl I meet these days reminds me of a different one I've known.)

"No wonder they say dirty things to you when you walk past. You're asking for it. If you get raped you deserve it."

She'd break down immediately into sobbing hysteria.

"You always do that," she'd accuse shrilly (while my boy watches from a corner in apprehensive deliberation, and I am already sorry I started). "You always say something to spoil everything."

"I *have* spoken to her," my wife replies in wilted exasperation. "She thinks I'm mean and jealous. She thinks I'm envious because I've got no tits."

"You've got tits."

If anything does happen to my daughter these days, it will probably happen with that college graduate she's mentioned who works on a land-fill truck and has offered to give her driving lessons evenings and weekends if we let them have one of our cars.

"No."

My wife nods in agreement. "You have to be sixteen."

"I can get a little head start. Everyone else does. You want me to pass, don't you?"

I want her to pass geometry, English, French, social studies, and science—not driver education. And I want her to get at least a B average so she'll be able to go off to college when she's through. (I won't want her here.) I don't see how I'll ever be able to make conversation with a simpering, clever son-in-law much younger than I who I know is humping my daughter quietly in another part of the house when they come to visit us weekends. My wife will bake cakes for them and look forward to grandchildren. (*She's* the one with the dirty mind.) They'll want things from us and lie to me.

"Maybe she won't. Maybe she'll be different. Maybe she'll grow up by the time she's married."

"We didn't."

"What do you mean?"

My wife doesn't understand me.

I don't think she ever thinks I'm thinking she might be out screwing another man or that I am inspecting her belly, hair, thighs, neck, chest, panties, slips, and blouses systematically and belligerently for semen stains that aren't mine. (My wife has one of those light and softly sloping bellies you often see in photographs of attractive, long-waisted girls.) Often when I'm inspecting her hair and belly closely my antagonism turns into passion (to antagonistic passion, of course, otherwise known as *lust,* and I will want to make love). I'll have to leave her if I find one. I have something more potent than an ordinary hypocritical, male chauvinist double standard to give me the strength and determination to walk out: I have insecurity.

I have forgotten all about brain tumors, the thirteenth largest killer of undivorced men my age in Connecticut with three children, two cars, and an opportunity for promotion to a better job. No wonder I have to yell a lot at home to make my identity felt. (I don't really want to be feared; I want to be nursed and coddled. I don't get the love and sympathy from my family that I used to get as a child from my mother and certain women teachers. God dammit—I want to be treated like a baby sometimes by my wife and kids. I've got a right. I need that feeling of security. I'm not one of these parents that expect to be taken care of by their children in their old age: I want my children to take care of me now.) My wife believes I enjoy being home with her these days; she cannot detect that I can hardly wait to get out of the house to the office to be near Arthur Baron (with whom I am exchanging glances these days, I think, that are of more than ordinary significance).

The convention's in Puerto Rico again (to do rightful honor to Lester Black's wife's family), and Kagle's away in Toledo. My wife will find it hard to forgive me for firing Andy Kagle (until I tell her unequivocally it's him or me. Then she'll look over my shoulder into a distance and not wish to know anything more about it). My wife feels sorry for Kagle's leg, wife, and two children. My wife empathizes easily with all religious families, except Black ones, and except Jewish ones, whose foreign language ("It isn't even Latin.") and incomprehensible praying seem crude and offensive to her. (She thinks they are praying about *us*.) Even their holidays fall on different days. (They are a perverse and stiff-necked people. She does not want our daughter to marry one, although she'd prefer that to a Puerto Rican or Negro.) Kagle won't improve. He still goes to church with his family when he's home on a Sunday and to places like Toledo on business for a week and to low-class whores in the late afternoon. He is still a bigot and won't hire a Jew or fuck a Black girl, unless he's away at some business meeting on an island in the Caribbean. Then he likes them young; he's had them fifteen and would take them thirteen and eleven, I think, but would feel abnormal. I *have* to fire him; I've been to whores with him and can't forgive him or forget. He'll hover. He'll bump shoulders with me, snigger indecorously.

"Aw, come on, Bob. Cut it out. I know you. Remember when . . ."

"It never happened. And if it did, I don't remember and you have to pay."

I will shift his hard-drinking cronies in out-of-town offices around to new positions in different cities and hope they quit. Arthur Baron and I do not talk much about matters like this when we meet by chance in corridors, but there is a diplomatic understanding now, I feel, in the small talk he makes.

"How are you, Bob?" he'll always stop me now to say.

"Fine, Art. You?"

"That's good. Horace White tells me he gets a big kick out of you."

"I like Horace White a lot, Art. He's a fine man."

430

(My facts are wrong but my answer is right.)

Horace White approves. Does Lester Black? John-ny Brown will go growling to him in dissension when he learns I'm his boss. Black probably won't care. It's out of his area, and Black is ready to retire anyway and spends much time out of the office sailing.

I did my best to dissuade Kagle from going to Toledo (and knew, of course, I would fail. My con-science is almost clear.

"Stay in town, Andy. You know Arthur Baron wants you here."

"I'll tie it in with a supermarket promotion," he responds with one of his conspiratorial winks. "Heh-heh. You'll see.").

"Kagle in Chicago, Bob?"

"Toledo."

"There? He told Laura Chicago. What's there?"

"He might come back with a supermarket promo-tion."

"He shouldn't be the one to do that."

"He phones in every day. I know where I can reach him. He asked me to cover the office."

"Good, Bob. We'll have to start making our prepara-tions for the convention. I'd like it to go very smoothly this year."

"I think it will, Art."

"So do I. Horace White gets back to town next week and he and I'll start setting up our meetings upstairs. Are you ready to make some enemies?"

"If I have to."

"You'll have some friends."

I'll have some speeches, too. I'll need Kagle for the convention. He'll do that well, claiming credit for having engineered the changes himself and pro-fessing gladness at having shed administrative re-sponsibilities he did not want and being free at last to do the type of work he really enjoys. No one will believe him. But that won't matter. After that, I won't want him around.

"What will you want to do about Andy Kagle?" Arthur Baron will ask.

"I think I'd want him to open the convention."

"I think that's good."

"I think he'll do that well. He'll smile enough without being told."

"And afterward?"

"I don't want him around."

"Would you want to keep him on as a consultant or use him on special projects?"

"No, Art."

"He could be useful."

"But not here. I think it might be a bad idea to have him around."

"I think you're right, Bob."

"Thanks, Art."

Of course, I can't fire Kagle. (If I could fire people, I would fire Green, and I would fire the typist Martha, who is still going crazy slowly but not fast enough to suit me.) I can merely indicate that I don't want him around and the company will move him somewhere else. I wish somebody else would fire her before I have to make Green do it.

"Art," I might say. "Have you got a minute?"

"How are you, Bob?"

"Fine, Art. You?"

"That's good, Bob."

"There's a girl in Green's department with a serious mental problem. She's going crazy. I think she talks to herself in imaginary conversations. She laughs to herself. It doesn't really help the appearance of the department to have her there."

"Is she happy?" he might ask.

"Only when she laughs," I answer. "But she stops typing then and her productivity suffers."

"Tell Green to get rid of her."

If he says that, it will signify he wants me to start issuing instructions to Green and take dominion over his department. If he says:

"I'll talk to Green."

That means he wishes us to maintain our departments separately (and I will not be downcast, for there's an advantage in having Green's department to shift blame to).

If, with an expression of sobriety, he asks:

"What would you do?"

"She probably has a fair amount of sick leave

coming to her," I'll answer. "And after that her major medical hospitalization insurance can take over, if she wants to use it. People who go on voluntary sick leave for mental disorders almost never try to come back."

"That's good, Bob. It sounds like the kindest way for her."

"The jobs aren't held open. We can tell her that, if she reapplies. One of the nurses can tell her she needs a rest."

"But I'm happy here. I smile and laugh all day."

"It's just for a little while, dear. We—they—have to cut down."

(Sick leave is what I am holding in reserve for Red Parker.)

(He'll think I'm slipping him a favor.)

(Wait till he tries to come back.)

(I'm so smart I ought to be President.)

I might even start using Red Parker's apartment again when he's no longer with the company. It will not dawn on him for a while that he's not with the company but outside it, and there will be major medical benefits for me in his major medical insurance policy. His job will be filled. (He will be filed.) The opening he left will be closed if he tries to come back. (He probably won't. He'll get used to doing nothing and jumping about aimlessly on reckless vacations.)

People who go on voluntary extended sick leave for anything but surgery or serious accidents almost never try to come back. They don't feel up to it. (Even people who've been out awhile with hepatitis or mononucleosis have a hard time making their way back. They lack pep.) (Long after they've left, somebody who enjoys keeping track of people (in the army, it was our public relations officer) drops by to tell us they're dead (or suffered a "cerebral vascular accident," and then we know they really are gone for good. Or bad, ha, ha).

"Did you hear about Red Parker? Or Andy Kagle? Or Jack Green?" someone like Ed Phelps will stop by to say, if Ed Phelps isn't dead by then too. Ed Phelps will be dropping in often after he's retired (like Horace White with his wheelchair and metal canes after he falls ill, or pushed into the office on a stretcher on wheels, waving hello limply as he rolls past, by an inscrutable Black chauffeur in meticulous gray livery. How will I look when I'm eighty and toothless? I'll have no teeth—periodontal work will not preserve my deteriorating jawbone forever—and my ankles and arches grow worse. My nose will be closed, and I'll breathe through an open mouth. My fingers will roll pills. I've met me already in hospitals and photographs. How will I smell? I know how I will smell. I smell that smell now and don't like it) because he will have no place else to go. It would not surprise me if Ed Phelps began showing up at my army reunions (in place of me. I've never gone) as another surplus survivor. (We really have no need for that many survivors anymore.) "I'm not sure what it was," he'll keep repeating about Red Parker. "I wonder who'll take care of the children. How many did he have?"

No one will know or care. With everyone else at the company these days I try to maintain an artless and iridescent neutrality. Jane knows I've stopped flirting with her.

"What's the matter, big boy?" I hear her on the verge of baiting me. "Get cold feet? Afraid your mean little wifey might find out? Or maybe you're just afraid you can't get it up often enough for a young girl."

Jane is not a person to say anything like that, or even think it, but I witness the scene anyway and wonder how I can get out of it. Outside the office, I have begun training myself assiduously and realistically for the higher responsibilities that lie ahead: I am organizing speeches and I am playing golf. I am outlining the speeches I will need for the convention (mine and Kagle's) and for the corridors at the company.

"Gee whiz," goes one. "*You're* surprised? How do you think *I* felt? You could have knocked me over with a feather."

(I wrote that one in a minute.)

And I have got myself new golf clubs and clothes. My daughter thinks I look good in my whites and pastels and in my peaked caps. (My daughter is most pleased with me when I look handsome.) My wife is perplexed. She thinks I've gone back to golf because I want to flirt with college girls at the different clubs I'm invited to. I don't know how to flirt with college girls anymore and wouldn't want to if I did. They're kids. (And none seem to be sending out signals to me or any other golfer my age. They send them out to good tennis players. I have decided not to flirt at parties or anywhere else if my wife is with me and might be embarrassed, and I wish *she* would stop flirting when drunk and stop embarrassing me.) I'll give her more money. I take private lessons secretly on public courses weekends and accept invitations I get to private clubs. My wife won't take up golf again because she knows she won't excel at it, and she hates going to a club for lunch or dinner because of the people she finds there. All of them are divorcing. Everyone everywhere seems to be coming to an end. I'll buy another house. My wife wants that. It will please my daughter, who is keenly sensitive to friends in families with more money and not mindful at all of those with less, like the college graduate on the land-fill truck who says he wants to get her into a car at night in order to give her driving lessons. (I know the kind of lessons he wants to give her. I'd like to kick him in his stomach and jaw with my knee. How dare he deal in dirty thoughts about my buxom sixteen-year-old? How can she know so many people and still be lonely?) We'll have to buy a bigger house because the kitchen table in this one is too small.

"Golf?" says my boy, in squinting confusion.

"It's a game."

"He's playing again," my wife says.

My boy looks hurt, my wife is crabby. He isn't used to seeing me all dolled up and raring to get away from home so early on a Sunday morning.

"If I wasn't going," I say to him, "is there anything you would want me to do with you?"

He shakes his head pensively. "You can go. Swimming, maybe."

"It won't be hot enough. Mommy can drive you to the beach club."

435

"I don't like it there."

"Do you have anything else to do?"

"Watch television. I saw some golf on television."

"You hit a ball in a hole."

"Like pool?" he ventures hopefully.

"Pocket pool," I joke.

"Don't start," warns my wife.

"What's pocket pool?"

"Not on Sunday. Not at breakfast."

"The Lord's day," my daughter intones in mocking solemnity.

"I'll tell you Monday."

"I know," my daughter brags.

"I'll bet you do."

"Are you getting angry?" she asks me with surprise.

"Of course not," I answer, dissembling a bit. It doesn't please me that she knows. (And I remember again that I saw her the night before riding around town in the back of a car with boys. I'm just not able to talk to her long these days without wanting to say something stinging. There is latent animosity between us always. I don't know why.)

"I'll leave the table if you are."

"Don't be silly."

"I am," my wife declares.

"I've made my date. I can't help you today. I'll go to church with you next week."

"We're away next week."

"Do you like it?" my boy asks.

"Church?"

"Golf."

"No."

"He hates it," my daughter tells him.

"You got it," I praise her. "I even hate the people I play with."

"Why do you go?" His face furrows with puzzlement.

"It's good for me."

"For your health?"

"For his business," my daughter guesses correctly, mimicking me with comical accuracy.

"You got it again, daughter," I praise her again. "It gets me better jobs. It helps me make money, for all of you honeys."

"Will you buy me my own car, since you're making so much money?"

"When I lower my handicap. This table's too small. I don't see why we can't eat in the dining room."

"I didn't know we'd all get here at the same time. Usually I have to eat breakfast alone, along with everything else."

"You sound bitchy."

"I don't see why you have to play on Sunday morning."

"It's when I'm invited."

"You go for lessons."

"It's when I can. Go alone, can't you?"

"I don't want to go alone. I have a family, haven't I?"

"You're going with God, remember?"

"Don't make jokes about it."

"Go with them."

"They won't go either unless you go. You influence them."

"You'll go with her, won't you?"

"Don't make them."

"Don't be a hypocrite, Dad."

"We'll all go on Mother's Day."

"And that will make it Father's Day."

"We hate the people we have to pray with," my daughter wisecracks brightly, and my boy giggles.

"That's good," I compliment her, laughing also. "I'm proud of you for that."

"I love it," my wife says, "when the three of you find me so funny. They get that from you. They think they can be funny about anything."

"They can." (She is starting to ruin my whole day.) It's been close to a very delightful family meal for everyone but my wife, and I wish I were through with it and out of there. "You know, I don't get any of this at the office."

"I don't get it at the beauty parlor."

"Good."

"You aren't married to people at the office."

"I got it the first time. Why must you repeat everything?"

"You really do stink."

437

"We're only kidding, kids. You do this every week."

"Have some eggs," she answers in a low voice.

"You're ruining my whole day."

"You're ruining mine."

"I'll have some juice. You do this every week, don't you? Every time I have a day off."

It isn't true, but she doesn't answer. Her face is set in lines of stubborn silence. Her hand is quivering on the handle of the large glass pitcher. We'll have fresh orange juice when I take the trouble to make it, from a cold glass pitcher instead of the lighter gummy plastic one she and the maid find easier to use. The children sit as still as replicas in a store, hiding inside their own faces as they wait to see what will happen. And my day had begun so auspiciously: I had made love to her at night when I'd wanted to and had avoided doing so in the morning when I didn't by scooting downstairs and starting to prepare breakfast while she was in the bathroom. (She had given me signals I didn't want.) I will find it difficult to forgive her for spoiling my morning. Even fresh oranges taste fraudulent today. Oranges aren't good anymore. It may be something in the soap we use to clean glasses or something in the water. Soda fountains serve ice cream sodas now in paper cups or clouded plastic glasses that don't get cold and don't give back flavor. Nothing stands up. London Bridge is falling down and was shipped to Arizona as a tourist attraction. I make better eggs and bacon than anyone because I take more trouble than anyone else does. I make garlic toast the way my mother used to, and it's just as good. That's easy. Everyone likes it. Nothing's pure anymore. Not even people. I decide to use jokes.

"Be honest now, honey," I begin to cajole her.

"They'll go if you go," she breaks in curtly.

My boy shakes his head.

"I won't," announces my daughter.

"You told me not to make them."

"I feel all alone in the whole world."

"Will I have to?" complains my boy.

"Be honest, honey," I begin again, touching her

438

arm. (I'll have to leave her, if only for making me do that.) "Would you rather be poor and go to heaven, or rich and go to hell?"

"That isn't the question," my wife argues.

"It's my question."

"How poor?" my daughter quips tentatively.

"I don't care as much about money as you think I do."

"I do," croons my daughter. "I like to have all I can get."

"You want a new house, don't you?"

"What's criminal about that?"

"Nothing. Would you rather be poor and go to heaven or rich and—go to hell."

She smiles resignedly. "Go to hell," she tells me, picking up my cue.

And I sense that the storm has passed and I might yet succeed in sailing away from them all unscathed. I feel like celebrating.

"That's my girl," I exclaim affectionately to my wife.

"I'm tired anyway," she admits without a grudge.

"Go alone."

"I don't like to. I'll stay in bed and read the papers. I'll watch Gilbert and Sullivan. Sounds exciting. Doesn't it?"

"I love money," my daughter declares in a manner of robust cheer. "I think I really do."

"Do all poor people," my boy asks seriously, "go to heaven?"

"Do you believe in heaven?"

"No."

"Then how can they go there?"

"Very funny," he observes wryly, frowning. "If I did believe in heaven, would all poor people go there?"

"They haven't a chance."

"No. Really."

"They haven't a chance in hell. What kind of place would heaven be if all those poor people were around?"

"Are we poor?" he wants to know.

"No."

439

"Then why can't you buy her a car?"

"That's the boy."

"I can. Let her learn how to drive."

"I'm almost sixteen."

"Then we'll talk about it. I've got the money. So don't worry about being poor. And I'll soon have more."

"I think I love money," my daughter brags daringly, "more than anything else in the world. I love it more than ice cream."

"Someone, my daughter, might think that ungracious."

"I don't care. I love it like the last spoon of ice cream on a plate."

"Money really talks, young lady, doesn't it?"

"It sure does."

"How come?"

"Because money, young man, is everything."

"What about health?" says my wife.

"It won't buy money. And that's why you shouldn't give your dimes and nickels away."

"I don't anymore."

"I would never give it away," my daughter asserts self-righteously.

"I don't think, daughter dear, that you ever have, heh-heh. Money makes the world go round, young man, and money makes history too."

"How come?"

"You take history, don't you?"

"It's called social studies."

"Money makes social studies. Without money there would be no social studies."

"How come?"

"What Dad means," explains my daughter, "is that the love of money and the quest for gold and riches in the past is what caused most of the events we read about today in all our history books. Right, Dad?"

"Right indeed, my darling daughter. You got it again. I'm glad to see you're learning something more in school than pocket pool and rolling drugs, and how to walk around the house without any clothes on."

I am more startled than she is when I see her gasp and turn white. (I don't know why I said that then. I swear to Christ I don't know where those words came from. I know they didn't come from me.) Her voice is a whispered plea.

"Did you have to say that?"

I murmur no. "I didn't."

"Yes, you did," she charges. "You always do, don't you?"

"I'm sorry."

"You always spoil things. You ruin things for everybody. Doesn't he?"

My wife looks like she's going to cry.

"You knew I was kidding."

"Should I go?"

"No. We both were. But I've told you before not to walk around the house without a robe on."

"May I please leave the table?"

"No, stay. I'll go." (I feel inept, clumsy.) "Can't we make up? I have to go anyway. Heh-heh."

She's ruining my whole day too (even though it's all my fault. And it isn't even ten o'clock). That octopus of aversion had been there in bed with me and my wife again this morning when she awoke me with languorous mumbles and by snuggling close, that meaty, viscous, muscular, vascular barrier of sexual repugnance that rises at times (when she takes the initiative. It may be that I prefer to do the wanting). I eluded it spryly: before my wife knew what was happening, I was downstairs in the kitchen halving oranges, making coffee, and breaking eggs. I don't know where it comes from or why it does (and I don't ever want to find out). It seems to come from the brain, the heart, and the small intestines in a coordinated assault. (Men with heart attacks, I know, use them to avoid having sexual relations with their wives, though not with their girl friends, unless they are tiring of them. I make coffee and break eggs. I get a feeling of tremendous personal satisfaction whenever I hear that someone I know has left his wife. It serves the bitches right. Yesterday in a gourmet store I overheard one woman tell another that some man I didn't even know had left his wife, and my

441

mood soared. I feel despondent afterward, sorry for myself, left out of things again.

"What are you looking so pleased about?" I could hear my wife saying, as I returned to the car.

"The price of artichokes," I offer in reply, or better still:

"A man left his wife.")

The wall of aversion was there again in my head and my breast even as I came awake (and would not go away), and I did not want her to touch me or have to touch her. (It has nothing to do with her.) I felt I might crumble to something dry and moldy where she pressed, I was soft dough or clay and would be deformed by indentations where her hands and knees pushed. I would stay that way. It is invisible and unyielding. It is heavy. It is living and it is dead. I am living and I am dead. There is grainy paralysis. It is hollow and dense. It is airless, making breath seem doubtful, arousing head pains, nausea, and sickening reminiscences of disagreeable, musty smells. It isn't fun. I have no will to overcome it. I can't confess it to her.

"I don't feel well," I'll whine. "I think it's my stomach."

"Is your chest all right?"

"I think so."

"You work too much. We never take a real vacation."

"You go away every summer."

"I don't call that a vacation. Why can't the two of us just go to Mexico? I've never been."

I would rather surrender to it and lie docile and enslaved. I would rather succumb. I would rather bide my time and wait for it to relent and recede like some risen demon returning to an underground lair somewhere inside my glands than engage it in battle or try to squeeze my way through an opening with batrachian strivings of my feet. I am a tail-less amphibian again. I have warts, but they are small, because I am small. I see myself struggling to squeeze my way through head first like a miniature white swimmer or frogman in black rubber, and the free-floating aches in my temples filter into throbbing pains in the occipital regions behind. I might never be able to come back if I ever forced my way through an opening of revulsion that pressed closed behind me. To where? There might be no here to come back to if I were there. I have wormed my way through aversion before and it has disappeared without hurting me, as though it were not even there. I imagine conversations. I wish I never had to experience it.

"C'mon, tell me," I coax my daughter. "Heh-heh. You can talk. Are you using drugs or doing dirty things with lots of boys and girls? I'll understand."

"If you really understand," my daughter reproaches me in a calm monotone, "you'd understand that you wouldn't have to ask me if I wanted you to know."

"That's smart. I'm proud of you."

"Do I have to be smart? Would you still be proud?"

"Of course."

"Of what?"

Maybe that's why her father killed himself. (She ruined his whole day.) He was probably a modest, introverted man no taller than Len Lewis who had sent the apple of his eye away to a very good southern university from which she had been kicked out for fucking football players en masse and in formation.

"En masse and in formation," she said to me with lilting gaiety, her dark eyes twinkling. "They made me do it," she went on, with flaunting radiance (so that I was never certain if she was telling the truth. She knew I loved to hear her talk about her dirty experiences. I was stirred to question her by an irresistible and ambivalent fascination. Rape enthralls). "They held me down at the beginning. But then I began to enjoy it. I showed him."

"Were you scared?"

"No. I was really crazy about that quarterback. Was *he* conceited. We did it once in a canoe. Did you ever do it in a canoe?"

"Weren't you mad?"

"Of course not. But he was. At me. He didn't think I'd enjoy it, but I showed him. He was the biggest thing on campus, and I had him for a while. I think

I was the only Jew there. He wouldn't see me after that."

"Show me."

"I bet you'd faint."

"I bet I wouldn't."

"I bet they still remember it at Duke. They should put up a statue. I gave them a winning season."

It did not please me entirely to hear her talk about it all that way (I missed at least a shadow of repentance), and I would have rebuked and punished her severely if I had the right and the means. I would have slapped her face. (There was jealousy.) My wife and I started to try it once in a rowboat after we were married, but she turned shy and made me row her to an island.

I'd recognize now that she was slightly crazy and likely to kill herself too when the brazen euphoria ran out. (She would not know how to subsist without it.) I'd also understand she was moody and that much of her exuberance was forced. I think Penny might kill herself without much fuss a few years from now if something engrossing and lasting doesn't happen to her soon—I can't help much. She knows now I won't marry her if my wife dies or if I get a divorce. I don't get close to her anymore. I come and go, ha, ha—and I think my wife will probably kill herself also when the children grow up and move away if I've left also. Maybe Derek will keep her going if we haven't sent him away by then. (The kid might come in handy for me that way too. He'll be older, though, and won't be a kid.) I wish we could do that soon. (I won't want him when he's older.) When I go, I won't look back for a second. I won't even want them to have my phone number. I'd like to change cities. Except my boy, and maybe not even him. He'll change. I'm not sure how much longer I'll want him to talk to me. If I am ever in a hospital, I will not want any of them to pay me visits and add to my distress (and I have told them so. Except my boy. I may miss him and worry he's worrying too much about me. I will be lying there dying or recuperating with a tube in my nose like a tortured political prisoner, and they will want *me* to make *them* feel better. I will not want her sister. I will not be able to keep her sister out. My small secretary will send a get-well card. And I will have to thank her). I should have known she was crazy just from that football game she played at Duke and her swift, sullen emotional changes when we had been going at each other for a minute or two like shaggy bears with clothes on against a wall of the staircase landing between floors or in the storeroom downstairs, from the frenzied terror that erupted without warning and swept over her like a storm. We met there so many times. I did want to take it out and rest it in her hand. I outlined different plans for months.

"There's something I want to do. Please let me," I said to her in a choked voice many times on the crowded subway train riding back and forth from my home to the office. (It was not always clear in my mind which was my home and which my office: I often felt more at home at the office.) "I want to put it in your hand."

(My heart was heavy and I was not able to joke.)

I imagined it soft but swelling when I took it out and felt it hardening fast in her fingers.

Things always sped right by that point of negotiation. We met on the staircase landing and plunged right in. We began without words: no deals could be struck, no more subtle stratagems executed by me than to wedge my accident folders in behind her ass or back to prevent their falling. And:

"Someone's coming."

And it was too late again. She'd wrench herself from my hands with little growls and mewing whimpers that seemed to originate in her mind instead of her throat, shaking free as though I were trying to restrain her. (I wasn't.) With flushed bewilderment, her bosom heaving, her breath rasping and whistling in her mouth and nose, she would glare at me in savage outrage as though I were someone new who was trying to cheat her, as though she did not know how she'd got there with me. It was panic or orgasm. (I'll compromise.) I think she dreaded the start of the inrush toward orgasm there on the staircase or even in the storeroom downstairs. I think she wanted a bed or

445

a car. (I knew a young college girl once who told me she used to do it against the bedpost in her room before she was old enough to go away from home. I know other girls now with vibrators and rape fantasies.) She did not have to fight me so. I was a lamb. Her eyes were sharp and damning, her face accusing, her mouth poison. She hated in hectic irrationality. She would have hit me with a dagger. (It's a face I would throw away today. If that's the way she was affected, I would not want her.) She wanted me passive (as a bedpost or vibrator). She seemed unaware I was touching her inside her skirt until I had been doing it awhile. Then she was thunderstruck; she was tricked, seduced, and violated. That part of her panties still feels slick and puckered to me when I slide my thumb over my fingertips. (I have fun with it now.)

"Someone's coming," she would blurt out tearfully in a frantic, pleading whisper, grimacing at me cruelly, wishing to smash and kill, smoothing herself for a second or two, and hastening away. In the mirror of a small, round compact she brought with her she'd be checking and shaping her lipstick as she vanished in desperate flight.

I keep forgetting she was only twenty-one.

I wasn't going to harm her. I was only seventeen and a half and adored her. There would be no smile for me again until she was back in the office in her swivel chair behind the desk under that large, twitching, black and white Western Union clock, a mirthful, composed, sophisticated, experienced sex queen again. (Western Union has cut down drastically on telegram service and makes its money doing something else.) I think I was jealous and unforgiving of those hulking, primitive football players at Duke who were able to have intercourse with her in front of each other that way (make love, *q. v., op. cit., ibidibibidi*) and think so little of her afterward (while I thought so much. That was worse than unkind. Did they realize how mean they were being to me?).

She was cuckoo. She sometimes wore a girdle and panties both, and I still have not been able to figure out why. She was a short, kind of roly-poly pretty

446

girl in shiny stockings and smooth, tight skirts, and I think I am still in love with her (and glad she is dead, because otherwise I might not be, and then I would have no one). She sought trouble—the rape in the storeroom was all her idea. (I use *rape* loosely and boldly to relieve my fear of it. Rape intrigues and excites me slightly in a sinister way that also makes me feel a little bit ill. Girls I've met are titillated by the phenomenon of rape also and have been since their teens. Stories of rape in newspapers hold my attention hypnotically if they do not involve children or beatings. I enjoy them and continue staring at the paragraphs of type after I've stopped reading. Stories of orgies are as delightful as livestock reports. What can be rare once everything is permitted? I have never wanted to rape. I have wanted to stroke, follow the contours of flesh and female clothing on strange women with my hand. The girls I find myself eyeing grow younger and younger and someday I'm afraid I might want to do what I'm afraid I might want to do.) She brought it up and led all three of us on. She did not even like one of the other two: she told me he was homely, dumb, and coarse.

"I could handle you all. I could show you a good time. I could show you what it's really all about," she taunted pertly with a speculative smile. "If you weren't all so afraid."

It was lunchtime. The other two weren't afraid, and when she came to her feet with gripping, rigid, insensible arms to begin by kissing me (for them. I remember elbows like angle irons), showing off (for them. I knew it was as far as she wanted to go. It was an awful, corrupt, inane performance on her part—I was being used like a bedpost or stage prop, while she showed off for *them*—unworthy of her, an unemotional, almost malign procedure speeded up for the occasion like an old movie film into a grotesque and sterile parody of muddled, bumping, fumbling motions. A marble, nonhuman tongue was knocking about my mouth and the fingers scratching wildly at my head and neck were brittle and cold. She ground her face against mine; perhaps that looked good to them. I grabbed her breast because I did

447

not know what else I was expected to do), they went at her from the rear and sides and were under her skirt with their dozens of hands and infinity of mechanized fingernails before she knew what was happening. They were at her buttons, snaps, and elastic waistbands. They were forcing her knees in from behind and trying to press her to the floor. They had her down for a moment nearly into a squatting position. She struggled back up.

"You tore my stocking."

Her face looked frantic. They kept kidding ruthlessly with hard smiles, muttering inaudible remarks incessantly to sustain the pretense it was all only a pleasant bit of horseplay that ought not to be misunderstood. (I learned for the future how to execute variations on the same masquerade from them.) I saw flashes of pale flesh and eggshell lingerie. I saw no twat or bush. I looked and was disappointed (although I did not want to). I imagined it huge, thick, and snarled. I imagine it now. The tough, gruff one she didn't like left off for a moment with one hand to go for his zipper—I flinched and tried to shut my eyes and turn away. I did not want to see his oily tube flop out. My feeling now is that it would have been soft. I knew it would be long: I'd urinated with him in the men's room. (I didn't want *her* to have to see it. Not in front of me.) Where was passion? Why were all of us doing it? There was not even a genuine sex drive at work—but grabbed her again when she nearly squirmed free.

"No."

Feet were scuffling on the floor and heels were kicking against the legs of chairs and the bottoms of file cabinets.

"Sure."

"Come on."

Clusters of little frightened cries and groans were sounding in her as she tried with all her might to keep her feet and maintain a smiling face. Everyone but me, it seemed, was trying to smile. Images flashed and persisted, returning under layers of each other like double exposures: glimpses of garter snaps, thighs, and stretched eggshell underthings, a masculine, crawling hand with weeds of curling, black hair on the knuckles moving briefly for a zipper, then covering her lower belly, the pinky hiking her skirt up by the hem.

"Let me go now. I mean it. Please."

"Uh-uh."

"I'm coming, Virginia."

"You've got to do it."

"You said you would."

"You know that."

"Not until you do it."

"No. I won't. Stop now. Please."

"No."

"No."

"No. Not until you do it. You've got to do it with one of us."

"You've got to do it with one of us."

"Do what?"

"You know."

"Anything."

"Just one."

"Which one?"

"You pick."

"Just one?"

"Then me. You said you could handle us all, Ginny. Prove it. Why not?"

"You're lying."

"You'll see."

"Where's that good time?"

"Be a sport."

"Be a big sport."

"Don't forget that life is short."

"It's only human nature after all."

"When a fellow gets a girl against the wall."

"Stop that. You'll break it."

"Did you ever take it into your head to make money?"

"Just one," she agreed dubiously. Her nostrils and bloodless lips were flaring and shaking skeptically and pugnaciously. "Remember."

"Just one."

"I mean it. I'll scream. I'll tell the police."

"Horseshit. There's no need to do that."

449

"Pick."

She picked me.

"Him."

She looked at me for help with plaintive eyes. I thought my knees would buckle.

"Him?"

"Help me," she said.

Hands pushed me toward her.

"Let her go," I cried.

"She wants you."

"We'll watch."

"Go outside," she bargained. "Not while you're here."

"No, sir. We want to make sure."

"It's a free show."

"We may have to show him how."

"You'll lock us out."

They were still touching her all over with greedy hands, taking things that did not belong to them.

"Let her go!" I screamed threateningly, in a voice that cracked and must have quavered with hopeless cowardice and resignation. "I mean it."

(I was her hero.)

My fists were clenched in adolescent fury (and my heart was fluttering in adolescent dismay). They could have beaten me up easily, either one (taken an arm and twisted it, broken it in its socket). I felt faint with misgivings. They stared at me with amazement and scorn. She slipped free of them. I hardly noticed her leave. When I heard the door click closed, I loosened my fists and waited. I did not want to fight. I did not want them to beat me up. I don't think I would have fought to defend myself. (I would have preferred to succumb. I was like my boy in the play group. I don't think I've ever wanted to fight with anyone except my wife, my daughter, my boy, and Derek, and with Derek's nurses.) I waited to see if they would beat me up.

"You prick," they said (and I was relieved when I saw they were not going to beat me up. I was being set free). "We could have had her."

"We'll get her without him."

That thought struck pathos into my soul. I was

not allowed to feel like her hero for long. By the time I returned upstairs, she was at her desk chatting with both of them over what had happened, flirting brashly with them again, especially with the tough, coarse, sinewy one she hadn't liked (mending her torn silk stocking with colorless nail polish, lifting her breasts for him as she had always done for me, tilting her head and tempting him with her ruby, saucy smile. He was a tough, swarthy Italian, like Forgione, and I felt he had just shoved me out of the way again, as he had downstairs. I hated her. My feelings were hurt. I felt she would have fucked for him from that time on sooner than she ever would for me, if he was smart enough to pose and wait—"I'm on my back, he's in my crack," was part of another bawdy song she liked to sing to me—even though she still liked me better), and I felt pangs of jealousy. (What good did it amount to, being liked, if she wanted to fuck for people she didn't like?)

"You were jealous," she said. "Weren't you?"

I must have been gazing at her moon-eyed with all the pain of my broken heart flooding into my expression. I have never been able to cope with jealousy. (I wish someone would teach me how.) It leaves me weak and at a loss for honest words. I can't make jokes. My eyes water and I want to cry. (Marie Jencks would accuse me of staring at her like a mooncalf. Perhaps I did, especially after I found out about her and Tom in the storeroom. I wanted to be absorbed into her embraces also. I didn't like feeling left outside. I still do stare at girls who are attractive, and look away quickly if they stare back. Today, I chuck brassy, overpowering women of twenty-eight like Marie Jencks under the chin nimbly and pass them by with a half-hearted falsehood. Today, girls of twenty-eight don't try to boss me around. Derek's nurses do.) Other men go berserk with jealousy and fly into Herculean rages. I produce tears.

I was never jealous of her and Len Lewis. (I felt he should be jealous of me.)

"He wants to leave his wife," she confided about him. "He used to think I was too young. By now I've showed him I'm old enough. I like him, he's so shy. I like older men. I like younger men too. It's the ones in between I have trouble with. I don't like football players anymore. Maybe I do. Now I can teach *them* a few things."

"Teach me."

"Get a room."

"I've got no money."

"I'll chip in."

"Where do you go?"

They went to empty restaurants for dinner one evening a week, sometimes two, and then sat in his car awhile and talked and petted. He lived far out in Queens and had to start back early. He didn't drink. She was teaching him how.

"He enjoys it. I make him feel young."

"How?"

"I kiss him very softly and slowly like this . . . all over his face for a long time. Then I do it harder and faster. I breathe hard. He thinks I can't control myself. I like doing that to him. He says nobody ever kissed him the way I do."

"I'll bet he's right."

"I'll bet nobody ever kissed you the way I can."

"Do it now."

"His wife wouldn't know how. He's never had a modern girl friend. I slip my hands inside his shirt and rub my fingers against his chest. His hair is soft and curly. Like a kitten. Nobody ever did that to him before. He's fifty-five years old. I tickle him with my tongue. Soon I'll let him touch these."

"Come outside."

"He doesn't know I'll let him if he wants to. I talk a little dirty to him. He likes it. So do you. Don't you like my nipples? If you'd go slow once in a while, you'd see how pointy and hard they get. I like to talk dirty too. I love to say words like nipples, pointy, and hard. And tongue."

I had my hard-on again.

"Come outside."

"Well, hello, dear," she greeted, winking at it. "Good to see you again."

I reached for an accident folder with one hand

and slid the other into the side pocket of my trousers. I blushed with pleasure.

She grinned, pleased with her prowess, widening her eyes with mock astonishment and pursing her lips into an open pink circle of admiration and surprise. I know now what that open circle was intended to suggest. (I've seen it since on gorgeous faces of photographers' models in the best fashion magazines.) I didn't believe then that girls really did such things (although I'd seen comic-strip drawings). Now I know they do and I'm glad. I love it more than ice cream. (I am anaclitic, I guess, when I'm not sadistically aggressive. When the telephone rings at home, I want someone else to answer it.) You can't get good ice cream anymore. (Everything is getting worse or going away. *The Woman's Home Companion* is gone, and so is *The Saturday Evening Post,* and *Look* and *Life,* and soon even *Time* may run out for all of us as well. Colleges are going into bankruptcy. Restaurants I like are closing.) It tastes like gum and chalk. Virginia was peaches, strawberries, and cream with touches of rouge on her ripe, lustrous cheeks. She shaped her lipstick often by pressing her mouth together. Her legs were smooth and glistening in unruffling silk stockings, and even her somewhat chubby feet seemed rich and sweet as butter compressed into her shiny tight shoes with their high spiked heels. Women wore shiny black pumps with high spiked heels when I was young, and evil-looking, skinny men were unshaven and wore loose black socks in the dirty movies I saw. (Penny and other girls make me take my socks off for just that reason. My wife never saw any of these movies and doesn't. I often leave them on with her as a ruse. I am an evil-looking, skinny man in an old dirty movie, and I am defiling her. My wife has no idea that she is a character actress in a dirty movie of mine. She may, however, for all I know, be the leading performer in one of her own.)

Dirty movies have gotten better, I'm told. Smut and weaponry are two areas in which we've improved. Everything else has gotten worse. The world is winding down. You can't get good bread anymore even in good restaurants (you get commercial rolls), and there are fewer good restaurants. Melons don't ripen, grapes are sour. They dump sugar into chocolate candy bars because sugar is cheaper than milk. Butter tastes like the printed paper it's wrapped in. Whipped cream comes in aerosol bombs and isn't whipped and isn't cream. People serve it, people eat it. Two hundred and fifty million educated Americans will go to their graves and never know the difference. (I wish I could get my hands on a good charlotte russe again.) That's what Paradise is—never knowing the difference. Even fancy bakeries now use a substitute for whipped cream that looks more like whipped cream than whipped cream does, keeps its color and texture longer, doesn't spoil, and costs much less, yielding larger profits.

"It tastes like shit."

It tastes like shit. Nobody cares but me. From sea to shining sea the country is filling with slag, shale, and used-up automobile tires. The fruited plain is coated with insecticide and chemical fertilizers. Even pure horseshit is hard to come by these days. They add preservatives. You don't find fish in lakes and rivers anymore. You have to catch them in cans. Towns die. Oil spills. Money talks. God listens. God is good, a real team player. "America the Beautiful" isn't: it was all over the day the first white man set foot on the continent to live. The Fuggers were all right as long as they stayed in Germany: then they sent their mothers here. Depreciating motels, junked automobiles, and quick-food joints grow like amber waves of grain. The faces of the rich and the poor age from nativity into the same cramped, desiccated lines of meanness and discontent. Women look like their husbands. God had no computer. He had to use clay, which was hard to work with, and a human rib, which was a little easier. God was just and fairly ambitious, but in a rudimentary way. He had to use the flood once (He couldn't think of smog or nerve gas) and fire and brimstone. People between rich and poor radiate uneasiness. They don't know where they belong. I hear America singing fuck off.

The peregrine falcon is just about gone (done in

454

by DDT. The shells of the eggs laid by the female, of course, grew too thin to survive incubation without cracking). The hot dog is going too. Soon there'll be no more whales; my wife and I will just have to make do without them. The good old American hot dog is filled with water, chicken innards, and cereal (the same cereal they divert from bread and rolls and replace with synthetics and additives). Mom's apple pie is frozen. Mom went public several years ago. There is no Pa. She did it with gas.

"He did it with gas," she told me about her father, when I could bring myself to ask. "The rest of us were away in the country for the summer. He did it all alone in the garage in his car. I'll never forget it. I didn't want to go to the funeral. I heard somebody say he turned all red. My mother made me. I've always hated my mother for the way she treated him. 'Look what he did to me,' she kept wailing all week long to whoever would listen. I don't like to talk about her."

She did it with gas also, in the kitchen of her mother's house in New Jersey, which was most inconsiderate of her, since we had better ways of killing ourselves by then. We had plastic bags. (Last night, my wife had another one of her bad dreams. I didn't wake her. Afterward, after all the smothered moaning and spastic shuddering, she began to snore lightly, and I did wake her, to tell her she was snoring and complain she was not letting me sleep. She apologized penitently in a drowsy, cranky voice and turned over on her side while I looked at her ass. I smiled and slept well.) She was no longer at the office when I telephoned on my first furlough home after returning from overseas. Ben Zack told me. She was no longer on the premises. (Neither was I. Ben Zack didn't know who I was. I keep the old codger guessing.) She was no longer on the payroll. Whoever was at the switchboard had never heard of her (has still not, probably, heard of me) and gave me Ben Zack, who *was* still on the payroll in the Personal Injury Department as an assistant to Len Lewis, who was still there then too.

"Virginia Markowitz?" Ben Zack repeated in a

tone of bemused surprise. "Oh, yeah. Didn't you know?"

"What?"

I didn't tell him who I was but felt he could see me anyway. I told him I was an old college friend of hers from Duke University, a football player, and wanted to get in touch with her. That last part was true. I was an officer. I had wings, and I wanted her to see them. I wanted to station myself erect before her in my uniform and suntan and exclaim:

"Hey, Virginia. Virginia Markowitz—look! I'm all grown up now. I'm twenty-two years old and a real smart aleck, and I get lots of good hard-ons. Let me show you."

But she wasn't there.

(She was no longer employed by the company because she was dead, you know.)

"Oh, no," Ben Zack explained with patient good humor, as though pleased to have someone to talk to about her. "She's not employed here anymore. She's dead, you know, poor kid. She killed herself about a year and a half ago."

"Was she sick?"

"Nobody knows why."

"How?"

"She did it with gas."

"Did she turn all red?" I was tempted to ask in an outburst of caustic bitterness the next time I dialed the switchboard and asked to speak to her.

"I'm afraid I don't know," I could hear him reply in the manner of serious courtesy he was developing. "I wasn't able to attend the funeral. I don't get around too easily, you see."

"Then she's really out of a job now, isn't she?" I thought of observing irreverently.

(And am not positive if I did. I sometimes think of saying something and am not certain afterward if I did. Even in conversations I know are imaginary, I'm not always sure I remember what I've imagined.)

"She doesn't work here anymore, if that's what you mean," he might have replied tartly. "I'm not sure I understand."

She was out of a job, one of the unemployed; she

had been let go for committing suicide and would probably have difficulty finding a suitable position anywhere (in her new condition and without favorable references) else but in one of the file cabinets downstairs where I would have laid her if I could while she was still alive and kicking (I bet she would kick, until she got cramps) and should have done it to her right there on the desk if I only knew how. If there was room enough on that desk for titanic Marie Jencks and Tom, there was room enough for tiny us.

That was the time to have done it (if I'd wanted to). We signaled salacious caresses to each other all day long with coded phrases and patches of melody from ribald songs we shared.

"I asked for number one. She said let's have some fun. Ba-ba, ba-ba, ba-ba, ba-ba, ba-ba."

I would color a lot and feel my happiness bubble up into tingling ripples of joy and warmth. I have never been so pleased by intimacy with anyone since. She would smile and color a lot with merriment too, dimpling. She was always pleasant with me, even when she was having her period (I wish my wife was) and imagining that her face was breaking out into ugly boils and craters. (It wasn't.)

"Look what she did to me."

She killed herself before she was twenty-five, doing it with gas, as her father had done before her (and maybe his father before him—she didn't say—deserting me without two weeks' notice) and leaving me feeling destitute again in a phone booth in a train terminal. After a moment of utter shock, I found myself feeling like a foundling again, abandoned heartlessly in a soiled telephone booth in Grand Central Station (through tears, I saw banner headlines and front-page photographs in the next day's editions of the New York *Daily News* and *Mirror,* which is gone now too. O, weep for the peregrine falcon and the New York *Mirror:* ARMY OFFICER FOUND ABANDONED IN TERMINAL PHONE BOOTH. *No Clue to Identity*) in my Mediterranean, bronze suntan (which was turning yellow) and natty military officer's uniform (spotless dry-cleaned pink gabardine trousers and forest-green regulation tunic with ribbons above the breast pocket, or both pockets—I forget things like that. I had done well in the service. I was a twenty-two-year-old success) with a malodorous, black telephone instrument in my hand announcing her death. Things stank. I thought I smelled my armpits, neck, and feet stinking.

And then the air cleared (a breeze, a breath of fresh air) and I was glad—glad, God dammit—*glad* she was gone and dead and that I would never have to see her again. (I would not have to screw her.) And glad that I was the one who was still alive.

I had not realized how much hidden tension I was under (I had jokes massed on my lips to conceal and ameliorate it) until I watched the sweat flowing in torrents from the hand holding the telephone. I was released from my obligations. I did not have to say hello, make a sociable wisecrack (and hope she'd remember and want to see me. She could have been married, engaged, going steady, and I would have believed none of it. I would have believed she had lost interest in a seventeen-year-old file clerk like me and was going with older married men and gangsters). She was a challenge, and I did not have to meet it. I did not have to make a date, show up early, sip whiskey, look her over (while she looked me over), sound her out to see if she was still the same, move her into some kind of bedroom, undress with her (until we were both naked), and then get right down to the sheets with her and look it squarely in the eye once and for all. I had no idea what I would find, what she would look like. (And I was still afraid.) I still didn't want it from her. (And I didn't want to see. All I still wanted, I think, was to lay it in her hand and have her lead me around with it like a domesticated pet.) I would have preferred malted milk. I have cravings for food. I have a weakness for dairy products and never liked baseball. I could have handled it all with a dashing display of confidence and technique, but I was so glad I didn't have to (she was dead, God dammit. And she was also nearly twenty-six). I had a rich chocolate malted milk in a tall, cold glass at a lunch counter in the train station and called another girl who'd been crazy about me the last time I was in, but she had moved out west to marry a sheet-metal worker in an airplane factory who was making a big salary. I called another girl I'd laid once a year and a half before who didn't remember me by name and sounded so absurd in her tinny and stand-offish mistrust that I laughed and made no effort to remind her. (She was putting on airs.) I had no one else to call. I had no close friends around. Before the week was out, I went back to the air base a few days earlier than I had to. I felt more at home in the army than I did in my house. (I feel more at home in my office now than I do at home, and I don't feel at home there. I get along better with the people there.) I don't think I ever had a good time at home on a furlough. I don't think I've ever had a good time on a vacation (I'm not sure I've ever had a good time anywhere); I find myself waiting for them to end. We have too many holidays. Birthdays and anniversaries come around too often. I'm always buying presents or writing out checks. The years are too short, the days are too long. I called Ben Zack again before I went back and pretended to be somebody else. (I did that twice. I couldn't help it.)

"I asked for number two.
She showed me what to do."

"How odd," he said.

I inquired innocently about Virginia as though I had not done so before. I told him I was a former eastern intercollegiate boxing champion from Duke University.

"It's really very strange," he said.

Calling Ben Zack again like that was a malicious trick, a practical joke. It did not feel like a joke. It felt like a willful, destructive crime, a despicable act of obscene perversion. It felt thrilling and debasing. It felt like it used to feel that time I was telephoning hospitals for a while to inquire about the condition, my very words: "I am calling to inquire about the condition . . ." of people I knew who had just died. "I'm sorry. Mr. _____ is no longer listed as a patient," they'd say.

I was always in fear of being discovered (have

459

always felt myself on the very brink of imminent public exposure.

"Look, there he is! That's the one. That's who he really is," someone, a woman, will shout, pointing at me from a crowd in an open place, and all the rest will nod in accord, and everything will be over for me.

It surprises me still that they could not read my mind over the telephone, could not see my clammy sweat).

You have to call quick. Once the autopsy's over and the funeral parlor's got them they give you nothing; they say:

"We have no record of any such patient."

I could write a manual. (I think I know what a morbid compulsion is.) I had to gird myself to speak to Ben Zack, even when I did not identify myself to him the first time. (I did not want him to know who I was.) I had to disguise my voice. I was certain Ben Zack would uncover my deception, snap angrily at me from his wheelchair, demand to know what type of demented prank I thought I was playing (I've never been wholly comfortable with telephones or banks. All my life I've had this fundamental fear of being chastised over the telephone by someone who does not know who I am.)

"How odd," Ben Zack said. "I can't get over it. Somebody else called to ask about her just last week. Then somebody else yesterday. And now you. I guess all the boys must be coming home from the war."

"Could you tell me how I can reach her?"

"I'm afraid that will be impossible," he reported to me again in that same dropped octave of ceremonial awkwardness and lament. "She doesn't work here anymore, you know. She's dead, you see. She committed suicide some time ago."

"How?"

"She did it with gas."

"Her father did it that way too. Didn't he?"

"Did he?"

"Did she turn all red?"

"I'm afraid I don't know. I wasn't able to attend

the funeral. I'm afraid I'm not able to get around too easily. I have to drive a special car."

"Then she's really out of a job now, isn't she?"

"She doesn't work here anymore, if that's what you mean," he snapped in a troubled voice. "Everybody keeps asking that, and I'm afraid I don't understand."

He thought I was somebody else. (I think he was probably right.) I told him I was a former wrestling champion from Duke University. (But somebody else than whom? Nameless I came and nameless I go. I am not Bob Slocum just because my parents decided to call me that. If there is such a person, I don't know who he is. I don't even feel my name is mine, let alone my handwriting. I don't even know who I'm not. Maybe I'll ask Ben Zack the next time I call.)

I have called Ben Zack since.

"I asked for number three.

She told me it was free."

"Who is this? I don't understand."

"Don't you know?"

"No."

"Then I must be somebody else," I said and hung right up.

He keeps thinking I am somebody else. (And I keep thinking he's right. I get the wheelchair and metal canes and crutches I give to Horace White from him.) He is the only one left now. Len Lewis retired years ago. (He is my personal dead record file. He had infantile paralysis in his teens and came and went in a wheelchair even then. He drove a special car and had a special permit from the police department that allowed him to park anywhere. He was a handicapped person. He had an animal's sex drive and went to whorehouses.) Sometimes I tell him I was a national intercollegiate weightlifting champion at Duke University who was once engaged to her. Sometimes I tell him I am somebody else. He is easy to lure into conversation. (I have the feeling that when I am not talking to him, no one else is. He has grown garrulous with the years. He has been grotesquely fitted all his life for work in the Personal Injury Depart-

461

ment and will remain in that opening until his wheelchair stops rolling or until the police department takes away his special parking permit. Then he will have to park himself elsewhere. Without permission to park, you are not allowed to park.) Len Lewis left a long time ago after a serious case of influenza from which he never bounced back.

"He never really bounced back."

I knew he was dead before he told me. I can add: Len Lewis was fifty-five when I was there and that was thirty years ago.

"Then his wife passed away about a month after he did. It's odd, really odd, the way people remember and keep calling up after so many years. I'm sorry I don't remember you, but you say you only worked here a very short time, didn't you?"

Len Lewis never left his wife. He didn't really want to. Virginia didn't want him to. He was too old. She was too young. Then she was dead. And I was alive in a phone booth. I called Len Lewis once shortly after I was married when I was feeling terribly lonely and despondent (and didn't know why. Oh, that abominable *cafard*. I was over thirty years old before I even knew what to call that permeating, uninvited sorrow dwelling inside me somewhere like an elusive burglar that will not be cornered and exorcised).

"Won't you come up and say hello?" he invited in his reticent, soft-spoken way. "There are still a few of us left."

"I want to get in touch with Virginia," I said. "I think I'd like to keep in touch with Virginia Markowitz if I can."

"She did it with gas . . ."

"How terrible."

". . . in the kitchen of her mother's home. I was very fond of her. She was always very fond of you."

(A woman's place is in the kitchen. A man's is in the garage. If I catch my wife and leave her, it won't be out of jealousy. It will be out of spite. If she leaves me, it would be shattering. I will turn into someone nervous. I might never be able to meet anyone's eyes. I would lack confidence and lose my job.)

462

I called Ben Zack a month ago late one afternoon when I felt I could not make myself go home one more time to my wife and children on my country acre in Connecticut if my very existence depended on it. I do indeed know what morbid compulsion feels like. Fungus, erosion, disease. The taste of flannel in your mouth. The smell of asbestos in your brain. A rock. A sinking heart, silence, taut limbs, a festering invasion from within, seeping subversion, and a dull pressure on the brow, and in the back regions of the skull. It starts like a fleeting whim, an airy, frivolous notion, but it doesn't go; it stays; it sticks; it enlarges in space and force like a somber, inhuman form from whatever lightless pit inside you it abides in; it fills you up, spreading steadily throughout you like lava or a persistent miasmic cloud, an obscure, untouchable, implacable, domineering, vile presence disguising itself treacherously in your own identity, a double agent—it is debilitating and sickening. It foreshadows no joy—and takes charge, and you might just as well hang your head and drop your eyes and give right in. You might just as well surrender at the start and steal that money, strike that match, (masturbate), eat that whole quart of ice cream, grovel, dial that number, or search that forbidden drawer or closet once again to handle the things you're not supposed to know are there. You might just as well go right off in whatever direction your madness lies and do that unwise, unpleasant, immoral thing you don't want to that you know beforehand will leave you dejected and demoralized afterward. Go along glumly like an exhausted prisoner of war and get the melancholy deed over with. I have spells in spare time when it turns physically impossible for me to remain standing erect one second longer or to sit without slumping. They pass. I used to steal coins from my sister and my mother—I couldn't stop. I didn't even want the money. I think I just wanted to take something from them. I was mesmerized. I was haunted. I wanted to scream for help. I had only to consider for an instant the possibility of taking a penny or a nickel again from a satin purse in a pocketbook belonging to my mother or sister and it was all over: I would have to do it. I was possessed by the need to do it. I would plod home through snow a mile if necessary in order to get it then. I had to have it then. I took dimes and quarters too. I didn't enjoy it, before or afterward. I felt lousy. I didn't even enjoy the things I bought or did. I gambled much of it away on pinball machines at the corner candy store (and felt a bit easier in my mind after it was lost). I didn't feel good about a single part of it, except getting it over with—it was an ordeal—and recovering. After a while the seizures ended and I stopped. (The same thing happened with masturbation, and I gave that up also after fifteen or twenty years.)

I called Ben Zack again yesterday.

She was still not there.

"I asked for number four.

She said she wanted more."

"Although I remember her very well, of course, of course. Then you don't know what happened to her, do you?"

I told Ben Zack my name was Horace White. He didn't think he remembered me.

"I asked for number five."

I asked for Mrs. Yerger and was so glad when he said he didn't think he remembered her either.

"I felt it come alive."

"She was that very big, broad woman who was put in charge of the file room from someplace else and said she was going to fire all of us if we didn't shape up soon."

"Perhaps she didn't stay long, Horace," Ben Zack apologized. "It was all so long ago. Somebody else called up a few weeks ago to ask about Virginia Markowitz also. Isn't it odd? Isn't it odd that there are still people who call up for her after so many years?"

I asked for Tom.

"Tom who?"

"Thumb."

"Thumb?"

"Johnson. He worked in the file room too when

464

Virginia and Mr. Lewis and you were there. He left to go into the army."

"He isn't here now. There's hardly anybody here now."

Tom Terrific, of course, who had given me the handwriting I use and who was able to stick it to Marie Jencks whenever she wanted him to in a way I wished I could and knew I could not. I couldn't even do it to Virginia, and I wasn't really afraid of her. (Just of that.)

I asked for me.

I was not there either.

(I had never done that before.)

It made me sad to hear that.

"But I'm pretty sure I remember who you mean, Horace," he said. "He was that nice-looking, polite boy with a good sense of humor, wasn't he? No, I don't know what ever became of him."

Neither do I. (I don't feel even distantly connected to him.)

It would have made me glad to hear I was still working there in the file room as a nice-looking, polite, seventeen-year-old boy with a good sense of humor (at least I'd know where that part of me was while I scrounge around looking for the others), cracking jokes as I carried my accident folders back and forth past Virginia's desk, humming "Take it in your hand, Mrs. Murphy," or warming and coloring with contentment (I had everything in life I wanted) as I whistled:

"Johnny, come tickle me.
You know just where.
Under my petticoat,
You'll find a bush of hair.
If you don't tickle me.
In the right place,
I'll lift up my petticoat.
And pee right in your face."

We had other dirty songs we loved too.

I could find that right place now and wish I had a chance to prove it. I wish I had her on her back right now (and that I was the one who was older. She is twenty-one. I am twenty-eight). There'd be more than just bone with her. I wouldn't be afraid. (I don't think I'd be afraid.) There is just bone with so many of them now. (I get black and blue marks instead of ecstasy. I might still be afraid of Marie Jencks. I was enamored of her size and flashy good looks. After I found out about her and Tom, I was afraid. Her yellow hair seemed cold and crackly, her skin looked rough, and I often dreamed of the things growing in the cluttered junctures of her thighs as mossy crustacean claws, dark and barnacled as uncooked lobsters, if indeed they were hers. The smeared rectangular smile of vivid lipstick on the face they bore along beyond them was hers as the pincers advanced to seize, engulf, and consume me. Poor Tom. I often feared for him in that cavernous burlap wilderness that fascinated and repelled me. Maybe that's what happened to him. I envied him.) Virginia, at least, was soft and kind. More and more often lately I find myself wishing I had remained on closer terms with my sister and her family, and with my brother's wife and her children and even with her second husband. She married again and had at least one more child. She sent a card. They are nieces and nephews and might even enjoy a visit from me for a few minutes. Some people don't mind their uncles. I wish I were part of a large family circle and enjoyed it. I would like to fit in. I wish I believed in God. I liked shelled walnuts and raisins at home when I was a child and cracked the walnuts and mixed them all up with the raisins in a dish before I began eating. My mother sent out for ice cream often in the spring and summer. In the fall we had good charlotte russes. I would spin tops. I remember the faces of street cleaners.

I was so distracted to hear from Ben Zack that I was not in the file room anymore that I left work early to drink alone in Red Parker's apartment. I began making phone calls.

I called an airline stewardess I'd met who was out of town. Her roommate had a date. I tried a model I met at a photographer's party last week who said she was desperate for help in finding some kind of temporary work, but I wasn't sure of her last name or even that she was really a model, and I was unable to locate her in the phone book or obtain a number on what I thought was her street from directory assistance. (Telephone companies are putting more and more announcements on records that are no more efficient than people.) I called an actress I've known for several years and got her answering service. I called a woman I know who's divorced from a man I knew; her son told me she had driven to the shore that day to try to sell their summer house. I called a soft hooker I know who's always glad of the chance to pick up a dinner and fifty dollars, but she was already busy for dinner (or said she was) and was leaving the next morning for a week in Barbados with a man who was older than I was and had much more money. (By then I should have gone home and fucked my wife—I thought of that. She would have been a pushover, unless she hadn't sobered up graciously from the day's imbibing. Wine gives her headaches. Whiskey makes her sick. I have my problems.

"I don't feel well," I could hear her bleat. "Can't you understand?")

So I called a widow with two children in private school instead who sounded doomed: she told me in a flat, barren voice that she was going to try getting by alone from now on rather than waste any more time going out with men like me who had no intention of ever marrying her. (She didn't enjoy sex anyway.) It was getting her nowhere. I called Jane. She was out (I was relieved). Her roommate sounded younger than my daughter and dumber than my secretary and seemed squeaky and disappointed, as though I had interrupted her timetable for putting her hair up in large pink rollers. I didn't leave my name. (I would have been ashamed to.)

"Did I interrupt you? I'm sorry."

"I thought you were somebody else."

"Were you very busy?"

"I was doing something."

"Were you putting your hair up in pink rollers?"

"That's for me to know and you to find out."

I called Penny, who had just come in from another one of her singing lessons and exercise classes and begged me to give her an hour and a half to wash up and straighten the apartment. I was there in fifty minutes. She was still damp and fragrant from her bath.

"Please, baby," she requested gently. I had opened her robe. "Go a little slow. I still get scared when I see you start so fast."

Penny has an alabaster body that never fails to astonish me with its sturdy beauty every time I see it again. I think I must gasp loudly and glare voraciously. Her white neck flushes. I came three times with her (and think I could have gone four. It was just like the army again) and was back in Red Parker's apartment with the newspapers before midnight. (It was an unqualified success.)

I really don't like spending the whole night with anybody but my wife, not even Penny. (That's one reason I never take girls with me on overnight business trips and am surprised by men that do.) I guess I'm used to my wife. I like waking up with her. I like it better than waking alone. I *had* to use Red Parker's apartment again because I had nowhere else to go. I did not want to go home. I may have to get a small apartment of my own. I will have to lie to my wife about it. I lied to Penny, who thought I was on the last train back to Connecticut. I made her come once, the second time (when I could take my time and work on her as scientifically as she likes—it *is* work), and that is all she wants. Her neck and pale face flushed. The third one was all for me. She made me coffee afterward and hinted I could stay the night. (I felt so much at home I didn't want to.) Someone like Amazonian Marie Jencks would have suctioned me right back up into the womb with a single siphoning contraction, and then puffed me out on a flat trajectory into the spongy, red catacombs of a testicle belonging to a man riding the subway trains in search of a curvy backside to splash me back out against. That's what I call dismemberment. *That's* regression. (It wasn't so bad living in my old man's scrotum, as far as I can recall. It was warm and humid, and there was lots of companionship. I had a ball.)

(*That* was a good one.)

Maybe I do love my wife. I think I would have been stricken sightless and mute and turned into a dangling form of dingy cement or sodden papier-mâché from the top of my head down if I'd ever been forced to mate with Marie's. (She was so large and domineering.)

"I asked for number six."

I asked for Marie Jencks.

"Oh, yes," Ben Zack remembered immediately. "I'll always remember Marie."

"The sperm began to mix."

"Her husband passed away from heart trouble at a very early age. They didn't have heart surgery in those days. She married again soon after and moved with her husband to Florida to cash in on the land boom."

I was not ready for Marie Jencks then. I was not ready for Virginia. My wife has brown nipples as lovely as any I've ever seen in the movies or still photographs and a nest of curly black hair I can rest my head on snugly. I feel safe with her. I feel safe with Penny. (I wonder why I always think of Penny last.) I don't think a human twat has teeth and don't believe I ever did. I've got this idiot child of mine I don't want and don't know what to do with. He belongs to me. Little Derek. (He doesn't even know what he is.) He is small, heartrending. He is unbearable. (He cannot be borne.) What threats he will pose for me later. What hazards he poses for me now. What will they do to him? Who will take care of him if I don't? How will he survive? What will become of the poor little thing if he doesn't die soon?

There's no getting away from it

────────○────────

I've got to get rid of him. There's no getting away from it. (He is so sweet. People who meet him tell us how sweet he is. They are being sweet when they say so.)

I've got to get rid of him and don't know how. And there's no one I can ask. There's no one I can tell I even want to, not even my wife, who wants to get rid of him also (but doesn't dare say so to me). Especially not my wife. We blame each other for him, when we aren't blaming ourselves, and that's another thing we haven't been able to say to each other yet.

"It's your fault, not mine."

We have to try to make believe he was nobody's fault, that he was a circumstantial twist of nature, a fluke. (A fluke is a fish.) All of us want to get rid of him, but only my daughter is honest enough to say so (and is set upon like a pariah by one or the other of us).

"Is he going to have to be with us forever?" she'll complain in a temper.

"What do you care?" I'll lash back at her, as though she had said that just to wound me. "You'll be away at college."

(She might stay home, just to torture me. I sometimes feel that if not for Derek we would never quarrel with each other. I know it's a lie.)

He does not seem to be mine. He may be my wife's.

There is no idiocy in my family that I know of (or in hers). My wife has begged me not to use that word (which may be why I do. She winces every time).

"How would you like me to describe it?" I inquire, with a lordly air of inexhaustible tolerance. "Do you think it would help him much if I called it genius?"

"It's heartless." She shudders, pale and close to tears. "Mean. I get so frightened when I see you so cold."

It is ungodly the way I am able to forget about him for long periods of time, even when he is close by. (I blot him out and try to keep him out.) I think of myself as having just two children. One says:

"What would you do if I came home with a Black boyfriend? And wanted to marry him."

The other asks:

"What would you do with me if I couldn't speak?"

"But you can," I've answered.

"If I fell down the ropes one day in the gymnasium when I was trying to climb them and hurt my head and Mr. Forgione had to carry me home and I couldn't speak anymore, either?"

"I used to be afraid of rope climbing and falling down too," I try to explain encouragingly. "And of swimming naked in the pool in the high school also."

"I never said anything about swimming naked in a pool," he protests firmly (as though that fear had not yet taken root in him, and I had just implanted it). "Did I?" he demands.

I am embarrassed.

"Suppose I had an extra set of car keys made after I got my license," says my daughter, "and used the car when you were away. You couldn't stop me, could you? What would you do, have me arrested?"

The third one doesn't speak to me at all.

I have conversations that do not seem to be mine.

I feel afloat (legless). Legless, I walk around with headaches that do not seem to be mine (on feet that do. Arches ache and seem to be crumbling, I have a spur on one heel, middle toes are hammered, others are gnarled and require Band-Aids or corn plasters frequently, the tender pads of flesh on the bottom of my toes chafe and inflame if I do not switch pairs of socks and shoes, the soles itch dryly in cold weather, the tissue between the gnarled end toes splits and peels and I have to pour talcum powder in. There is no limit to the ills I could describe). I do not always feel securely connected to my legs or to my own past. The cable of continuity is not unbroken; it is not thick and strong; it wavers and fades, wears away in places to slender, frayed strands, breaks. Much of what I remember about me does not seem to be mine. Mountainous segments of my history appear to be missing. There are yawning gulfs into which large chunks of me may have fallen. I do not always know where I am at present. I sit in my office and think I am at home. I sit in my study and think I am at my office firing Johnny Brown or retiring Ed Phelps, in Penny's or some other girl's underthings, rolling them off, or in a bank, hotel lobby, or police station searching my pockets for some form of evidence or identification required of me. It may be that I talk to myself already without being aware of it. How debasing. No one has said so, but I don't think I do it when I'm with someone who might. I think I do it only when I think I'm alone. Maybe I am senile already and people are too kind to tell me. People are not kind and would tell me. (Maybe people have told me, and I'm too senile to remember. Ha, ha.)

"What? Did you say something?" one or the other of the members of my family has shot at me when I assumed I was alone and unobserved in my study or in some other room in my house, deep in thought.

"What? Nothing," I reply, startled and shame-faced. "I was just thinking."

Or:

"I was just reading the paper."

(Probably I was deep in thought imagining myself orchestrating rhythmic, polysyllabic replies to Green's thrusts without tripping over a single vowel or consonant.)

"You were laughing in your sleep again last night," my wife will say.

And I won't know if she's toying with me or not. It's the sort of lie I might make up for her, if I had thought of it first. I can never remember what it was I was laughing about when she tells me I laugh in my sleep. I wish I could. I could use a big laugh on days when I have these headaches that do not seem to be mine.

I get the willies in my spare time; I don't normally sleep well (although my wife tells me I do); I get the blues I can't lose; *they* decide when to leave (I either talk to myself or believe I might); I get depressed and don't know why; I mourn for something and don't know what; (legless) I walk around with jitters, headaches, and sadnesses ballooning and squiggling about inside me that seem to belong to somebody else. Is this schizophrenia, or merely a normal, natural, typical, wholesome, logical, universal schizoid formation? (I could plead temporary insanity. They would call it a mercy killing. There would be testimony under oath that it was done to put him out of his misery. He isn't miserable.)

I have these perfectly controlled conversations with Arthur Baron about Andy Kagle and with Andy Kagle about Arthur Baron, and I find myself wondering even while they are taking place, just what the fuck I am doing in them. (Is that really me there talking and listening?) I'll float away outside them a few yards to watch and eavesdrop and begin to feel I am looking down upon a pornographic puppet show of stuffed dolls in which someone I recognize who vaguely resembles me is one of the performers, and I have no more idea of why I am taking part in them, even as this separated spectator, than I do of these weird melancholies, tensions, and arid impressions of desolation that come upon me when they choose in my spare time.

"I have nothing to do," I whimper also in my spare time.

I have too much spare time. The same thing often happens with sex. I like to try to move outside our bodies and watch me. I go blind. I allow myself to be obliterated and am resurrected so slowly it takes a while to remember who I think I am and resume the role effectively. (It's all so silly it can't really be me.) I used to be able to watch me all the way

473

through. That was nice too. Am I demented already, in what I genuinely feel to be the prime of my life? Or maybe I am that somebody else Ben Zack keeps declaring I am.

I feel strange.

"You look strange," my wife says, trying guardedly to draw me out.

"No, I'm not."

"Funny."

"*You* are."

"You've got that funny look on your face I can never figure out."

"Why aren't you laughing?"

"You look depressed."

"I'm not."

"Is anything wrong?"

"No."

"I'd love to know what you're really thinking," she hazards with a frowning smile.

No, you wouldn't.

(I'm thinking of death and divorce.)

Today at lunchtime a man fell dead in the lobby of my office building as he was coming toward me. He was a large, portly, elderly man with woolly white hair and a gray pinstripe suit, and he was carrying a slim, black umbrella in one hand and a brown attaché case in the other. He was a majestic, attractive figure who looked great enough to be president of General Motors until his face hit the floor. He was too old to be me.

I don't think I feel different now than I've ever felt. She's the one who seems to be changing: she fidgets more noticeably when I'm silent and she thinks I am angry or dissatisfied. (Am I silent more often? She is afraid of me.) She is rattled when I'm feeling too good. (She thinks I harbor secrets. I do.) I'm glad I've got golf to turn away to now. I want a hole in one someday so I can talk about it forever. I don't want to go to movies or plays, and my wife concludes I don't love her anymore. I don't even want to go to parties. We see the same people. I wish I had an interesting friend. My wife is bored too. My wife likes variety and movement and would prefer to mix around her different kinds of boredom. I'm content with the boredom I have. (If I kill my wife, who will take care of the children? If I kill my children, my wife can take care of herself. A prudent family man must plan ahead toward possibilities like that in order to provide for his loved ones.) I almost wish my wife *would* go ahead and commit adultery already so I can get my divorce.

(I'm not sure I can do it without her.)

My wife is at that stage now where she probably *should* commit adultery—and would, if she had more character. It might do her much good. I remember the first time I committed adultery. (It wasn't much good.)

"Now I am committing adultery," I thought.

It was not much different from the first time I laid my wife after we were married:

"Now I am laying my wife," I thought.

It would mean much more to her (I think), for I went into my marriage knowing I would commit adultery the earliest chance I had (it was a goal; committing adultery, in fact, was one of the reasons *for* getting married), while she did not (and probably has not really thought of it yet. It may be that I do all the thinking about it for her). I did not even give up banging the other girl I'd been sleeping with fairly regularly until some months afterward. I hit four or five other girls up at least once those first two years also just to see for myself that I really could.

I think I might really feel like killing my wife, though, if she did it with someone I know in the company. My wife has red lines around her waist and chest when she takes her clothes off and baggy pouches around the sides and bottom of her behind, and I would not want anyone I deal with in the company to find that out. (I would want them to see her only at her best. Without those red marks.)

My wife is not as wanton and debauched as most of the young girls and women we're apt to find ourselves with today (and I would not want any of the men I work with to know *that* about her, either. I don't want anyone I know in the company to be able to blab to anyone else I know that my wife has red marks on her body and just might not be the most versatile piece of ass in the world), although I like that about her—I would not want her the other way —and repay her virtue and restraint with frequent overflows of affection and esteem and frequent acts of kindness. (I'll take her to church.)

Sober, my wife is a lady (and makes me proud). Especially when we entertain. She does that beautifully. (We had Arthur Baron and his wife to dinner once last year and she was superb. Everyone there had a good time.) We do not entertain as much anymore because of Derek. (He produces strain. We have to pretend he doesn't.) I used to like him when I still thought he was normal. I was fond of him and had fun. I joked with him. I used to call him Dirk, and Kiddo, Steamshovel, Dinky Boy, and Dicky Dare. Till I found out what he was. Now it's always formal: Derek. (You prick.)

(Why won't you leave us alone?)

My wife is happiest of all when I'm simply relaxed and kind, and responds to my acts of consideration with lively gratitude and astonished gaiety. It is so easy to make my wife happy it's really a crime we don't do it more often. (She's even prettier when she's feeling good, her face lights up. She doesn't hide it.) I try. When I can. (It isn't always easy to want to.) I'll make the children come along with us to church when I go, and we'll generally have a joyful time. (It isn't always easy to want to be kind and make her happy when I'm thinking of death, murder, adultery, and divorce.)

I feel tense, poor, bleak, listless, depressed (and she calls that strange). I have jagged, wracking inner conflicts filing, slicing, hacking, and sawing away inside me mercilessly like instruments of bone, stone, glass, or rusty, blunted iron butchering their own irreducible muscular mass, and so does she (but won't acknowledge it) almost everywhere we go now but church, which is one reason she might be so eager to go. (The world just doesn't work. It's an idea whose time has gone.)

My wife is a cheerful Congregationalist now (when she isn't getting drunk and crude at parties or humping me on floors or against the butcher-block table in the kitchen or outside at night on our redwood patio furniture). My wife is a devout and cheerful Congregationalist now because the building is airy and the people friendlier than the Methodists, Baptists, Presbyterians, and Episcopalians she has gotten to know since we moved from the city to Connecticut.

"Episcopalians," she has told me, "are the ones who go *shush* in movies."

And I laughed.

(My wife can often make me laugh.) She will bake for cake sales. She will even stop drinking in the daytime well in advance of church socials, and she will grow more reserved in bed. (I can almost always tell when some spectacular social gala is in the offing at church by the waning initiative in her sex drive.)

I am a registered Republican (who nearly always votes Democratic sneakily) and believe I am nearer to God than she.

"The Lord is my Shepherd, I shall not want," says the new minister, who has been with us just about a year and seems to want a good deal more than he has in the way of social contact and community influence. (He strikes me as a man with his eye out for a better job in a growth industry.)

No registered Republican would go quite that far. We'll let the Lord be our shepherd readily enough, but there's *plenty* we'll want, no matter how much we've already got. Otherwise we'll fire Him, retire Him, or ease Him aside.

I'll let my wife drive us to church some Sundays when I'm feeling especially benign and charitable (the children exchange cryptic, supercilious signals during the service but do so inconspicuously, because they do not want to embarrass my wife) and then, often, feel like breaking her neck afterward for making me go and ruining my whole day. (I could have slept late, or phoned around for golf invitations. After all, how many years' worth of Sundays do I have left? Thirty? Two?)

"That new minister of yours," I might announce sonorously on the way back, pausing to make certain the two children in the rear of the open convertible are brought in as accomplices, "gives me a sharp pain in the ass."

The children crane forward delightedly.

My wife purses her lips with a sidelong smile and decides to pretend to whistle. It will take more than a little routine baiting this fine sunny morning to crinkle the state of euphoria she's in as a result of having shown up in church with her husband and children. At moments like this, we are suddenly very close. (They don't last.) My wife even had the hope not long ago of walking unashamedly into church one day with Derek too. I killed that one quick.

"What say, Dad?" inquires my daughter, to help things along, when she sees my wife intends to remain silent.

"I really don't think," chastises my wife amiably, going along with the game against us in a manner of placid contemplation, "you ought to say things like that in front of the children."

"Like what?" I am all contrived innocence.

"If you don't know."

"Minister?"

"No."

"What then?"

"You know."

"I've no idea."

"What?" demands my boy, bouncing on his haunches in anticipation as the three of us close in on her.

"Donkey," exclaims my wife in triumph, evading his snare nimbly.

"No fair. He didn't say donkey."

"I know, dear."

"He said ass," says my daughter.

"I know, darling. And I think he's depraved."

"And I'm inclined to agree," I second immediately. "And his English is terrible. And I don't think it's healthy to bring the children to church to listen to a depraved minister."

"I'm not talking about him!"

"His vocabulary's pretentious and his syntax is frequently wrong."

"I'm talking about you. I'm not talking about his language. I'm talking about yours."

"Well, it is."

"And yours?"

"All right," I yield, with a gesture of liberal acquiescence. "I'll change the subject. What do you think of the rectum as a whole?"

"That's even worse!"

"I don't get it."

"Don't you get it?"

"Now I get it."

"Pretty shitty, huh?"

"I thought we agreed," says my wife, with an exaggerated politeness that sometimes gets my goat, "to try not to disagree anymore in front of the children."

"A-men," says my daughter sarcastically, and claps her hands.

"That's the kind of remark," I reply good-naturedly, because I really do not want to upset her, "that can only lead to a disagreement. But, I surrender. I yield. That new minister of yours *doesn't* give me a pain in the ass."

The children explode with laughter.

"You show me one doctor," says my wife, when she can be heard, "who'll say it's healthy to use such language in front of your own son and daughter."

"Name one we've seen who'd say it isn't."

"I thought you agreed," interjects my daughter cynically, "not to fight in front of us anymore."

"We aren't fighting," my wife responds automatically.

"I know," scoffs my daughter. "You were *discussing.*"

"With *emphasis,*" adds my son in friendly mockery.

All of us smile but my wife, who nibbles on her lip in distracted gloom. She is extremely uneasy.

"What's wrong?" I inquire softly.

She is silent a moment, seems burdened with a knowledge almost too enormous to express. "He's coming to the house," she blurts out sheepishly.

"Who?"

"Him."

"When?"

On the part of the rest of us, there is massive shock.

"Today."

"Today?"

"I invited him for lunch."

"You're crazy!"

"I'm getting out!"

"I don't want him."

"And *I,*" announces my wife in an expansive bellow of glowing self-congratulation, turning pointedly to gloat at each of us, "was making that up! Do you think," she continues in her rare flight of exultation, "I would expose a respectable man of the cloth to a gang of idiots like you?"

"Oh, Mom!" My daughter flings her arm around my wife's neck and hugs her from behind. "Mom, Mom, Mom. I just love her when she kids like that. Don't you?"

"And so do I."

But it doesn't last, not on a Saturday, Sunday, or holiday, unless all of us have already made plans, for Derek is waiting at home.

He is still there. He grows older every day.

"Can't she take him out some place?" my daughter objects. "He's always home."

And so is his quacking, ill-visaged, overweight nurse with her rinsed white hair and offensive scent of bath powder, whom I've ordered my wife to get rid of once and for all, even if we have to take care of him ourselves for a little while. (It might do us some good.) And the maid can go too, for all I care. (I can't feel at home when she's tiptoeing around.)

"Get a German, for Christ sakes," I barked at my wife. "Import a Dane."

"Where will I get them?"

"How the hell should I know? Other people do."

"I get embarrassed when my friends come over."

(So do we.)

"There's no need to," I tell my daughter gently.

"I knew you'd say that," she sulks in disapproval. "I knew you wouldn't understand."

"You ought to be ashamed of yourself for saying anything like that," my wife says to her in reproof.

"Leave her alone."

"She ought to be glad she's not that way."

"She is."

"You always take her part," my wife accuses. "The doctors said you shouldn't do that."

"She thinks I take yours."

"Why does she always have to bring him in?" my daughter protests. "Can't she keep him in his own room when my friends are here?"

(We wish she would keep him out of sight also when our friends are here and have told her so. She parades him through anyway, gabbling loudly at him and pointing to our guests to show him off, or to inflict a penance on us.)

"You shouldn't mind it that much," I counsel.

"You do too."

"He isn't that bad."

"He makes us uncomfortable."

(He makes me uncomfortable too.)

"You shouldn't be," I tell her. "It wasn't the fault of any of us. It could have happened in any family."

But it happened in mine.

"We have another child also," I have been forced to reveal time and time again in ordinary social conversation to people I barely knew, "who's somewhat brain damaged. It was congenital," I add. "He's retarded."

"We also have a child who's retarded or very seriously emotionally disturbed," couples who knew about us have sought me out to reveal (as though we had something I wanted to share).

It's a club I don't want to join, and I find those clannish parents repellent. (Their suggestive intimacy makes my flesh creep and I want to shake them away from me as I would flies. I detest clannishness of every kind. It boxes me in claustrophobically. Or shuts me out. I don't like to feel boxed in.)

I saw it happening to Derek long before anyone else did (boxing me in) and said nothing about it to anyone. (Later, when others began to notice things and make hesitant, fearful observations, I denied them with *emphasis*. I didn't want it to be true. I had nightmarish warnings. I saw the realities assembling themselves ahead of me in mapped-out phases. I still do. I felt if no one talked about it, it would not be true. I was wrong.) He sat late, stood late, walked late, ran late. Even to a father's doting eye, his coordination was poor. We thought him clumsy and cute as a newborn puppy or foal as he staggered, stumbled, and fell. There is not harmony in his movements now. He makes no effort to open his jaws wide when he tries to speak—he does not seem to associate mouth with speech. He looks like lockjaw when he tries to talk. (Tendons stretch and bulge and I wish he'd stop.) He can open his mouth wide enough, though, when he eats or laughs or just wants to make noise. Though what he's got to laugh about I don't know, except when I offer him things in play and snatch them back, and then he's just as apt to cry.

(You can't even play normal infant's games with him anymore. I feel worthless when I try to play with him and he cries. I slink away in rejection. I am furious with myself and with him. The least he can do, it seems to me, is be decent enough to laugh when I try to play with him.)

"Is having Derek for a brother," my daughter wants to know, in a manner that is somewhat demanding and somewhat abject, "going to make it harder for me to find a husband?"

"No, of course not," we lie.

"Why should it?" my wife flashes at her belligerently. She is shocked and outraged by the directness of the question. (And now it is *I* who must shield my little girl against her.)

"Leave her alone," I request softly.

My daughter turns to me for the truth. "Is it?"

"Are you thinking of getting married?" I gamble in a pleasant rejoinder.

"See how he tries not to answer me?"

"You should be ashamed of yourself," my wife says to her, "for even thinking like that."

"Leave her alone," I repeat.

"Will people think my own children will turn out the same way?" my daughter persists.

My wife gasps. "That's a terrible thing to say!" she rebukes her with emotion. "He's your own brother."

"That's why I worry about it. Can't I ask?"

"Leave her alone, for Christ sakes," I shout, and whirl upon my wife to glare at her. "I worry about the same thing."

"She's the one who should be ashamed."

"And you worry about it too. For Christ sakes, stop blaming her for him."

"Stop blaming me. You're always taking her part. The doctors said you shouldn't do that."

"I'm not."

"He's nothing to be ashamed of."

"If he's nothing to be ashamed of, why the hell are we always ashamed of him?"

"We're not."

"We are."

"You're always blaming me for him."

"I'm not. Like hell I am."

"Don't yell at me," my wife says unexpectedly, with an air of indignant calm and refinement that is utterly astounding.

I turn away from her in disgust. "Oh, Christ," I mutter. "You make me laugh."

"And don't swear at me, either," she reacts mechanically. "I've told you that before. Especially in front of the children. I think you must enjoy humiliating me. I really think you do."

I am incredulous. And I find myself wondering again just what in hell I am doing married to a woman like this. Even if I had no other reason for wanting a divorce, this idiot child she gave me would be enough.

I want a divorce.

I need a divorce. I long for it. I crave a divorce. I pray for divorce.

Divorces seem impossible. They're so much work. It's hard to believe so many really take place. It's enough to stab the heart with envy, turn eyes dewy with pining and sentiment. People less proficient than I am manage to breeze right through their divorces without breaking stride, while I can't even get a foot out the door.

I want one too.

I have always wanted one. I dream of divorce. All my life I've wanted a divorce. Even before I was married I wanted a divorce. I don't think there has been a six-month period in all the years of my marriage—a six-*week* period—when I have not wanted to end it by divorce. I was never sure I wanted to get married. But I always knew I wanted a divorce.

"If it doesn't work out," I kept assuring myself right up to the day of the ceremony, "I can always get a divorce."

I *can't* always get a divorce.

I don't know how it's done.

Maybe I attach too much importance to a shirt.

I'll have undershorts at the laundry. Will she let me come for them? Or will she burn them, hide them? Will she tell me my little boy is upset when he isn't? That she cannot live without me when she can? I know she'll tell me she's thinking of killing herself. The obstacles appear insurmountable. In the summer my winter clothes are in mothballs; in the winter, my summer suits are hanging somewhere else and my sneakers are packed away. How will I ever get them all together? I'd need weeks. I don't have time to get a divorce. There's so much packing to be done (she won't help), so much talk to go through. (How does anyone *ever* get it finished?) There'll be fights, discussions, more fights. (Will it never end?) Bank statements will already be in the mail. A letter will be due any day, a pinstripe suit I like has just been sent to the cleaner's. There'll be books to be boxed in corrugated food cartons from the supermarket, the smaller the lighter, the lighter the better. No wonder I keep finding reasons for postponing the action: the welfare of the children (a fat lot of good it's done any of *them* to have *us* stick together so long), the money, the office, my wife's health, a dinner party for the following week or a date for the theater with another couple that will have to be broken. Neither one of us will want to call; we'd rather stay married. It's so much easier to ride things out until my mood changes and I kid myself into thinking I will never really want to leave her.

I just don't know how it's done.

Weaklings do it. Will she forward my mail? Or will I have to telephone and talk to her about that and other things. I guess it helps to have a wife who falls in love with another man and wants a divorce first. But mine is so lacking in initiative of that kind she might never come around to it. I would still have all that packing to do. I have shelves of books from college days with handwritten notes I scribbled in the margins. I probably will never look at them again. Yet I would want to take them with me. I would have to find an apartment, furnish the apartment, make my own dinner most evenings or eat out, get some girl friends I could stand, and sooner or later get married to one of them so that I could start looking forward to a divorce again.

I wish there were someone I could hire by the hour to go through the whole wearying procedure for me from beginning to end, even to experiencing those ritualistic qualms of guilt, concern, and remorse without which a conscience can never feel antiseptically pure again.

I remember a pledge: when Derek reached five, I promised myself, I would go. What irony! (All I did was fuck her once, and now I am saddled with him.) It isn't his fault. Even without him, I'd still be unable to go; and even if he were normal, I would want to. I will always want to.

I yearn to.

I do have dreams about divorce. I want to leave my home but I'm unable to. Even when they let me. (They always let me. I don't go. I don't want them to let me.) I'm unable to get anywhere. I want to speak but I'm unable to. People leave messages for me and I am unable to get back to them. I have to take a test and I am unprepared. All term long I have been unable to find my way into the correct classroom. The lessons have proceeded without me. The term is ending. I have trouble finding my way to the correct examination room. Every building I enter is wrong. Time is passing. I will fail.

I would not even know how to begin if I had to begin with a straight face. I don't think I'd be able to make all those necessary pompous statements without cracking a smile. I think I might actually burst out laughing. I think a man like me would have to fly way off the handle into the wildest emotional state to get it done, go mad, utterly berserk, for an hour or two and give no thought at all to mail, children, books, underwear, and pinstripe suits. Man can live without a pinstripe suit, if he has to. All it would take is enough rage to throw together a small suitcase, checkbook, passport, credit cards. Even then, there would be no guarantee.

Not for me.

Suppose, for example, one of the children, even Derek (perhaps especially Derek), came to the doorway to watch while I was packing. How could I go on?

Or suppose my wife, whom I've known so many years now, simply walked into the room when I was almost finished and said:

"Please don't go."

I don't think I could (I would probably miss her.) She wants me to tell her I love her. I won't. A reason I won't is that I know she wants me to. This is one advantage I have over her that I am still able to hang on to.

She used to make me say it. It seems a silly, awkward thing for a sapient human being to have to say—especially if it's true. It might make some sense on occasion when it's a lie. Now she cannot make me say it, and I have my revenge. She doesn't ask me to anymore. And between us now there is this continual underground struggle over something trivial and nebulous that won't abate and has lasted nearly as long as the two of us have known each other.

"I love you."

What funny words ever to have to say. (They become more flexible if you're allowed to add a couple of others fore and aft to round them off with some frills of humor or sarcasm that pervert the meaning. Something like:

"Gee, baby, I sure do love you a lot when _____."

486

Complete the above statement in fifteen words or less.)

I have not told my wife I love her, I think, since shortly after Arthur Baron first proposed Andy Kagle's job for me, and that was at night in bed and the meaning was sexual (which is not what she means. My wife does not know yet that it will be Andy Kagle's job I'm taking). It gnaws at my wife's self-esteem, tears at her pride and vanity that I do not say:

"I love you."

I relish that. I have it on her. It has nothing at all to do with love. It has more to do with hate. We hoard pillows. We have big, fluffy, soft ones now, and she steals mine when I'm asleep. Also, she sleeps better than I do, which arouses so much wrath in me that I can hardly sleep at all, and then she maintains she's been awake all night with heartburn, headache, and humanitarian concern over the well-being of others. (I'm the one who's been awake. She won't stay in her part of the house, as my son and daughter prefer to do now. She won't answer the telephone, even though the calls are mostly for her. When one does come for me, she'll wait until I've been talking for thirty seconds and then pick up the extension breathlessly to shout: "Hello?" We run out of light bulbs.) There is face to be saved in this tug-of-war, and I want to save mine. This is one victory she cannot pluck away from me. I have the advantage, because I don't care if she never says it to me (although I might begin to care if I felt she didn't).

She wants me to say it precisely that way:

"I love you."

I prefer to sidle into it through methods of my own.

"Oh, Mom!" my daughter exclaimed in the car, pulling close to her in a hug. "I just love her when she kids around this way."

"So do I," I said, edging it in.

There it was. But that isn't good enough. It doesn't do the trick.

(I meant it when I did.)

I've said it to her also the way she wants me to and will again; but I refuse to say it when she is trying to make me. I balk. I have my masculinity and self-esteem to protect against this indecent attack. I resist.

Call it spite. Call it petty spite. But call it highly sensual and gratifying spite.

"Would I be here with you if I didn't?" I have answered.

"Then why don't you ever say so?"

"I love you—there! I did."

"You never tell me."

"I just did."

"But I had to ask you—no, don't smile, don't say anything, don't make a joke out of it," she laments (just as I am about to make a joke out of it). "I guess I expect too much."

My wife not only *wants* me to say:

"I love you."

She wants me to *want* to say it!

"I love you."

"Do you?"

"I just said so, didn't I?"

"I had to ask you. I always have to make you say it."

And I might consent to let her make me, out of the hospitable goodness of my heart, if I did not know there was this contest between us that I don't want to lose. I might make a deal with her on it anyway if she'd get me the pillows I want and stop snoring or breathing away indifferently in such slumbering, nasal contentment while I'm still lying awake trying to sleep.

"Get more pillows, for God sakes. We've got more cars and television sets than we have pillows."

We've got four pillows for our king-size bed (which is something of a mocking joke. We could move around it for years and never come in contact with each other if we didn't want to. We do not sleep entwined). And I want her to get at least four more, maybe five. She forgets. I want there to be enough for me, which means at least one or two more than there are for her. (When we do buy light bulbs, we put them in places we can't find when we need one. We run out of toilet paper. The ladies run out of sanitary napkins. The world is running out of good maids and qualified laundresses, cobblers, and tailors. The wheels are falling off this gyroscoping toy. It hasn't stood the test of time. I can't get a maid to remember to put fresh towels in my bathrooms after she removes the old ones. I can't get my wife to serve dinner on time unless there's company.) It is very important to me where I sleep in relationship to her. I want more pillows under my head than she has so that I will be above her. I sleep almost against the headboard so that she will be below me. It is very important to me that my wife seem small. She isn't. We are nearly the same height, unless she kicks her shoes off. That was uncomfortable when we used to dance, still is when we want to kiss (we bunk foreheads and noses); and I still cannot walk with my arm around her shoulders without experiencing twinges of tendonitis. My wife just doesn't seem to fit. I want my wife's face on a line with my shoulder or lower when we sleep, make love, walk, or eat; I do not want it confronting me on a level equal to my own. (When we're out in public, though, I'm glad she's straight and handsome. She cuts a stately figure when she's all dressed up and makes a dazzling impression for me if she isn't drunk and obnoxious.) She is starting to snap her chewing gum again when she sits beside me in the car or movies. She goes back to chewing gum when she's trying to stop drinking. It drives me up the wall, nearly out of my mind with pent-up rage, some nights to see and hear her sleeping soundly in futile battles against worry, hurt, grievance, and overstimulation. (There are nights after drinking a as an innocent child while I am lying wide awake lot or thinking very hard about matters at the office that I am unable to turn off my mind for hours or even slow to a governable tempo the free-flight of disjointed ideas from all sources that go racing through my brain. I never think of anything good. I sometimes think of something good.) I want to pummel her. I want to hiss vitriol. It is there in the darkness of sleep, when no one is looking, not even ourselves, that our true rudimentary spirits emerge. Like furled and eyeless embryos, we wage war murderously over areas of quilt and corners of pillow; bumps of knee and hip are the weapons we use; mewing grunts and moans are the curses and battle cries. (We are babies, although we probably did not feel this way when we were babies.) It infuriates me that she does not even know I'm awake. I feel martyred by neglect. (Some nights I can sleep and she can't: it registers upon me that she is leaving the bed repeatedly in some state of agitation, and I doze off again more blissfully as a result of this knowledge.) I am in a turmoil of tragic insomnia, and she is lying inches away from me in a mellow stupor of oblivious tranquillity. How *dare* she be so insensitive to my wretchedness and distress, especially when it's all probably her fault. And I want to shake her awake roughly.

"Get up, you, dammit you! Why should you be able to sleep when I can't? And it's all your fault."

She wouldn't know what I was talking about and might think I'd gone mad.

"Do you love me?" she might ask.

She doesn't ask it anymore. She knows we are in a struggle also and has too much pride to fly a white flag of ignominious defeat. (I'm glad she doesn't. I would have to make concessions. I wish it were over.)

I think I know when it will end, how I will be able to disengage us from this stalemate and resolve the conflict in a way rewarding to both: on her deathbed.

"Don't die," I can say then. "I love you."

I will have my honor. She will be appeased. I will be a hundred and eight years old. She will be a few years younger. I will have to start doing my own shopping in supermarkets and groceries to make certain there is coffee and juice in the house for me. I will have to sell the house and move to an apartment. (And then I will miss her.)

She hasn't asked in years. Age and self-respect, I think, have stilled the question every time she wanted to ask:

"Do you still love me?"

It is in her mind, though. I can see it as a verbal sculpture. She fishes, hints. I decline to oblige. Or perhaps she believes I don't love her any longer and fears that if she were to ask:

"Do you love me?"

I would answer:

"No."

And then we would have to do something. (And wouldn't know what.)

I'm glad she doesn't, although I frequently feel her on the brink. It would be demeaning to have to deal with. I don't want to have fights with her about this. I don't know how I would answer now if she were to ask:

"Do you love me?"

Unresponsively, facetiously, evasively. I would not want to lie and I would not want to tell the truth (no matter how I felt). If she were to ask while we were savaging each other in sex, the answer would be easy.

"Turn over, and I'll show you."

But that would not be what she wanted, and both of us would know. And I am so pleased she doesn't ask, feel so grateful and deeply indebted to her at times, that I want to throw wide my arms in relief and proclaim:

"I love you!"

And after I made that mistake, I might never be able to get my divorce. (I believe I understand now why I get along so well with women when I want to and have so much trouble getting along with my children. I treat my girlfriends like children and expect my children to behave like grown-ups.) Arthur Baron wouldn't want me to.

"Well?" he's asked. His smile was a trace broader than ever before and there was a stronger cordiality in his expression.

"I really have no choice," I surrender with a smile, "have I?"

"You do."

"Not really. I want Kagle's job."

"That's good, Bob. Congratulations."

"Thanks, Art."

"We'll tell him early next week. You know him pretty well. How would you guess he'll take it?"

"Bad. But he'll do everything to hide it. He may ask to be the one to tell me."

"We'll let him."

"He'll want to take credit. He may even want to be allowed to issue the announcement."

"That will make things easier. You'll have much to put in order."

"I've made a list."

"I'll probably want to add to it, Bob."

"That's okay with me, Art." I laugh lightly (before tendering my gentle wisecrack) and bow my head in a gesture of self-effacement. "I'm not one of these officials who'll resent advice from his superiors."

"Ha, ha. I didn't think so, Bob. You'll run the convention."

"I've begun making plans. I think I know how."

"There's one more thing we've found out about Kagle, Bob," Arthur Baron tells me. "He goes to prostitutes in the afternoon."

"I've gone with him."

"You'll stop, though. Won't you?"

"I already have."

"That's good, Bob. I was sure you would. By the way," he adds, pressing my elbow with a conspiratorial wink and chuckling. "They're much better in the evening."

"Ha, ha."

Almost imperceptibly, my relationship with Arthur Baron has altered already in the direction of a closer conversational familiarity. Shrewdly, discreetly, diplomatically, I make no comment to indicate I've noticed the improvement. I've had a talent, thus far, this footman's talent, for being able to decipher what Arthur Baron and others of my betters (Green is my superior, not my better. Kagle is neither) expect of me and the subtle theatrical instinct for letting them observe they are getting it. (I have the footman's fear of losing it and being turned out of my job for betraying a spaniel's eagerness to please. Holloway in my department is that way again now, stopping people, dogging footsteps, fawning aggressively, extorting attention, demanding praise or benign admonishments. He'll break down again soon. They always break down again. I don't know why they even bother to try to come back. Holloway cannot be trusted with important business responsibilities: he lacks the fine genius for servility that I have.) I know that Arthur Baron doesn't want us to invite him back again. My wife doesn't.

"I'm sure she must be counting," my wife has repeated worriedly. "They've had us there twice since we had them here. Three times, if you count that cocktail party they gave for Horace White. I never expected to be invited to that."

"He doesn't."

"I'd be so embarrassed if I ran into them."

"I'm sure."

"I'm glad. I would like to give another nice dinner party soon. I'm glad I don't have to."

Arthur Baron lives not far away in a much better house in a much richer part of Connecticut than I do, although the part of Connecticut we do live in is far from bad. He has more land. (I own one acre, he owns four.) Most of the people around me seem to make more money than I do. Where I live now is perfectly adequate: and when I get my raise and move, it will again be among people who make more money than I do. This is known as *upward mobility,* a momentous force in contemporary American urban life, along with *downward mobility,* which is another momentous force in contemporary American urban life. They keep things stirring. We rise and fall like Frisbees, if we get off the ground at all, or pop flies, except we rise slower, drop faster. I am on the way up, Kagle's on the way down. He moves faster. Only in America is it possible to do both at the same time. Look at me. I ascend like a condor, while falling to pieces. Maybe the same thing happens in Russia, but I don't live there. Every river in the world, without exception, flows from north to south as it empties into the sea. Except those that don't, and the laws of the conservation of energy and matter stipulate harshly and impartially that energy and matter can either (sic) be created nor (sic) destroyed.

A lot that has to do with me. My dentist scraping at one tooth in my socket is more painful to me than my wife's cancer will be if she ever gets one. I get corns in the same spot on the little toe of my right foot, no matter what shoes I wear.

Arthur Baron has had us to his home for dinner half a dozen times the past two and a half years (and never serves enough food. We are hungry when we reach home). And we have had him to our house once. We have a good time. He usually will have just one other person from the company, whom I may or may not have met before, and three other amiable couples with occupations unrelated to our own. There is room for just twelve at his dining room table. The evenings are quiet and end before midnight. The subject of Derek has never come up at his house and we tend to feel we could gloss by it without discomfort there if it did. Nothing unpleasant ever comes up; no one's misfortunes are ever mentioned. The fact that they do not serve enough is a prickly trait for us to absorb, for we like both Arthur Baron and his wife and enjoy going there, even though we are uncomfortable. His wife is an unassuming woman with whom we almost feel at ease.

We had Arthur Baron and his wife to our house for dinner just about a year ago (time does fly). And we served too much food. People tend to eat more than they want to at our house. We like to offer guests a choice of meats and desserts. We also like to show we are people of lusty appetite who know how to entertain generously. My wife was troubled awhile that they might take it as a criticism.

"Do it your way, honey," I encouraged her. "Not the way someone else would."

The evening went marvelously. Intuition told me it was the proper time to invite him. (Once we invited Green. He told me he didn't want to come to my house for dinner, and we were relieved. There is an insulting honesty about Green that is refreshing afterward.) Wisely, I did not organize the evening around Arthur Baron. (We would have had the dinner anyway.)

"Yes, Bob?"

"Hello, Art. We're going to have some people over to dinner the third or fourth Saturday from now.

494

We thought it would be nice if you and Lucille could come."

"Love to, Bob. I'll have to check."

"Fine, Art."

Before noon that same day his wife phoned mine to say they were free either weekend and were pleased we had thought of asking them.

They stayed late, and ate and drank more than we would have supposed. (I still wonder with some perplexity about the small amounts of food they prepare when they entertain. I guess they must be hungry too by the time we reach home.) I mixed tangy martinis that everyone drank, and the mood was lightened from the start. I thought of myself as courtly as I stirred and poured. I caught glimpses of myself in the mirror: I *was* utterly courtly. I wore a courtly smile. (I am vain as a peacock.) I had no one there from the company. I had a copyright lawyer, a television writer, an associate professor of marketing, a computer expert, the owner of a small public relations firm, and an engaging specialist in arbitrage with a leading brokerage, about whose work none of us knew much and all of us were curious (for a while). The wives were all pretty and vivacious. The conversation was lively. There was boisterous laughter. My wife gave recipe tips when asked. The Barons were nearly the last to leave.

"Thanks, Bob. We really enjoyed it."

"Thanks, Art, I'm glad you could come."

My wife and I were aglow and enchanted with our success and made love. The evening went marvelously indeed, but it was written in the atmosphere—and my wily sixth-sense tells me it is still there—that we were not to invite him again for a long time, although it was much more than just okay to have done so then. My wife, a churchgoing Congregationalist, doesn't understand; she is instructed by a minister of God in matters of duty and hospitality. As a registered Republican, though, I know more about protocol.

"Why not?" she wants to know, and there is a tinge of eagerness in her perseverance. "Aren't you getting along with him?"

"We're getting along fine."

"Don't you think they'll want to come?"

"It isn't time."

"I don't know what you're talking about."

"It's written in the atmosphere. Give a dinner party without them if you want to give one."

My wife falters. Derek's a heavy presence in the home now and changes things. (Enthusiasm dwindles rapidly into lassitude and stillborn wishes. Long-range plans for joy turn dreary in contemplation of their fulfillment. Then she has nothing to do.) Then we have my daughter to cope with as well if she doesn't have a date of her own for that evening and decides to stay home to watch. Either she mingles with our guests more intimately than we want her to or passes through in silence with a countenance of rude displeasure that everyone can see, responding with the barest cold nod to the salutations of anyone there who knows her (and passes through again like that an hour later, every hour on the hour, until my wife mutters, "I'll kill her if she does that again" and goes to tell her off). The time may soon come when I'll have to order her acidly to keep out of sight completely whenever we have company, like Derek. (I don't like children hanging around when I visit other people, either.) Derek creates disturbing problems also in our relationship with our other children because of the attention we have had to concentrate on him and the large amount of money he costs. (Soon, I will have to start putting money aside for his future.)

"How are the kids?" people feel obliged to inquire whenever they come to our house, or we go to theirs.

It's a question I've learned to fear.

"Fine, all fine," I feel obliged to reply with too much alacrity (in order to get off that subject as speedily as possible). "And yours?"

Derek is a heavy presence outside the home as well, for my wife and I still nurture that special terror of walking into a frolicsome party at somebody else's house one evening and meeting socially one of the score of doctors and psychologists we've gone to in the past who know all about him, and all about us. It hasn't happened yet. We prefer large, noisy gatherings, at which public conversation is impossible; we are on guard at smaller, formal groups in which the discussion at any time might take an unpredictable turn to zero in on us. Then we must react hastily to divert it or sacrifice ourselves for a minute or so to talk evasively about something we don't want to talk about at all. (We have to admit it quickly. Admitting it may be good for other families. It isn't good for us. *Everybody* in the room turns uncomfortable suddenly.) Even at large parties, I have been taken aside often by someone who feels closer to me than I do to him and asked confidentially in a hawking undertone:

"That youngest boy of yours. How is he?"

"Fine, fine," I respond. "Much better than we would have hoped."

By now, my wife and I have had our fill—are sick and glutted to the teeth—of psychologists, psychiatrists, neurologists, neurosurgeons, speech therapists, psychiatric social workers, and any of all the others we've been to that I may have left out, with their inability to help and their lofty, patronizing platitudes that we are not to blame, ought not to let ourselves feel guilty, and have nothing to be ashamed of. All young doctors, I'm convinced, strive to be beetle-browed, and all older ones have succeeded.

"Prick!" I have wanted to scream at them like an animal. "Prick! Prick! Prick! Prick! Prick! Prick!" I have wanted to shriek at all of them like a screech owl (whatever that is, including the two I went to see briefly in secret about myself). Why can't the simpleminded fools understand that we *want* to feel guilty, *must* feel guilty if we're to do the things we have to?

Unperturbed, they would answer equably that my screaming at them was a way of trying to relieve myself of blame and call the repetition *perseveration*.

And they would be right.

And they would be wrong.

I could tell stories. An outsider wouldn't believe the number of conflicting opinions the different doctors gave us and the backbiting judgments they made of each other, but we did. We believed them all, the good and the bad. And disbelieved as well (we had no choice) and had no choice but to search for others, like wandering supplicants.

"It's organic."

"It's functional."

"It's largely organic with functional complications now."

"He isn't deaf but may not be able to hear."

"At least he's alive."

"The prognosis is good."

"For what?"

"The prognosis is bad."

"It would not be possible to offer a prognosis at this time."

Not one of them ever had the candor, the courage, the common sense, the character to say:

"Jesus—I really don't know."

It began with:

"You're making too much of it."

And moved to:

"He will never speak."

"He probably will not surpass a mental age of five, if he attains that. His coordination and muscular control will never be good. It will require tremendous patience."

We hate them all, the ones who were wrong and the ones who were right. After awhile, that made no difference. The cause didn't matter. The prognosis was absolute. The cause did matter. It was organic (ceramic. The transistors are there). It just doesn't work the way others do. (A radio will not work like a television set.) There was no malfunction. It worked the way it was built to (worked perfectly, if looked at their way). The architecture's finished. The circuits can't be changed. Nothing is broken; there's nothing they can find to be fixed.

"Why can't they do it with surgery?" my wife's asked me.

"They wouldn't know where to cut and stitch."

He's a simulacrum.

"If only we hadn't had him," my wife used to lament. "He'd be so much better off if he'd never been born."

"Let's kill the kid," I used to joke jauntily when I thought he was just innately fractious (I used to carry color snapshots of all three of my children in my wallet. Now I carry none), before I began to guess there might be something drastically wrong.

I don't say that anymore.

(Poor damaged little tyke. No one's on your side.)

He is a product of my imagination. I swear to Christ I imagined him into existence.

We do feel guilty. We do blame ourselves. We're sorry we have him. We're sorry people know we do. We feel we have plenty to be ashamed of. We have him.

My head is a cauldron.

My mind is an independent metropolis teeming with flashes, shadows, and figures, with tiny playlets and dapper gnomes, day and night. My days are more lucid. I never think of Derek in danger; I only think of my boy or myself.

I have melodrama in my noodle, soap operas, recurring legends of lost little children trying wretchedly to catch up with themselves, or someone else, the day before. They stare. They are too sad to move. They are too motionless to cry. There are blurred histories of myself inside requiring translation and legibility. There is pain—there is so much liquid pain. It never grows less. It stores itself up. Unlike heat or energy, it does not dissipate. It all always remains. There's always more than before. There's always enough near the surface to fuel a tantrum or saturate a recollection. Tiny, barely noted things—a sound, a smell, a taste, a crumpled candy wrapper—can mysteriously set off thrumming vibrations deep within. It's mine. I have more than enough to share with everyone I know. I have enough for a lifetime, and someday soon when I am fifty, sixty, seventy, eighty, or ninety, I will overhear someone speak the word *birthday, brother, father, mother, sister, son, little boy, doggie, frankfurter,* or *lollipop* and my eyes will dissolve into tears and I will throb inside with evocations of ancient, unresolved tragedies in which I took part replayed in darkness behind curtains that have come down. That will happen. It happens to me now. *Frankfurter*. A poignant nostalgia befalls me. *Merry-go-round*. I want to cry. *Cotton candy*. My heart breaks. I feel I can't go on.

I want to keep my dreams.

Ball-bearing roller skates. I melt.

I want to keep my dreams, even bad ones, because without them, I might have nothing all night long.

I miss my father, they told me. As if I didn't know. (I miss my boy now too. He is pulling away from me. He does his homework in his room without my help and doesn't talk to me anymore about what is happening to him at school. I don't know if he's more unhappy or less.) They didn't tell me anything I didn't know. They couldn't help. They said I was perfectly normal—which was the most deplorable thing I have ever been told! With time and much treatment, that condition might be remedied. They envied my sex life. (So do I.) The pity, we agreed, is that I don't enjoy it more.

(The company takes a strong view against psychotherapy for executives because it denotes unhappiness, and unhappiness is a disgraceful social disease for which there is no excuse or forgiveness. Cancer, pernicious anemia, and diabetes are just fine, and even people with multiple sclerosis and Parkinson's disease may continue to go far in the company until they are no longer allowed to go on at all. But unhappiness is fatal. If my daughter or son were to commit suicide, that would be overlooked, because children do things like that, and that's the way kids are. But if my wife were to jump to her death without a prior record of psychiatric disturbance, did it only because she was unhappy, my chances for further advancement would be over. I'd be ruined.)

I have acrimony, they told me (which is also normal. I have more pain than acrimony. My mind is a storehouse of pain, a vast, invisible reservoir of sorrows as deep as I am old, waiting always to be tapped and set flowing by memory. I can discharge acrimony. I can only experience pain).

There are times when I am attacked from within by such acrimonious enmity toward people I like who have suffered serious personal tragedies or business failure that if something (or someone else) inside me were to give voice to the infamous words that leap to mind, I would be put away and reviled, with no possibility ever of absolution or apology. (The tragedies of people who are not close to me move me distantly, if at all.)

"Good for you! It serves you right!" I want to sneer.

(I want to spit.)

I'm afraid sometimes I might. (I have sat at tables with men I've known a long time and have wanted to touch their hand.)

It's not I who wants to kick Kagle in the leg. New people are hatching inside my head always, whether I want them to or not, and become permanent residents the moment I take note of them. We are often at cross purposes. They have time. They have time to work without interruption at whatever it is they came there to do, and they saunter away with great self-possession into darknesses I've not been able to penetrate. They weave back and forth in droves through a labyrinth whose tunnels I've never seen. I have a small cemetery there lying on a diagonal with orderly rows of identical headstones, an image left by a photograph, perhaps, or the reduction of one actually seen long ago. People may be buried there. Every once in a while startled three-dimensional thoughts, fancies, or series of new old recollections go flying across my mind like flocks of sparrows and disappear in unlit underground holes. I can summon them back when I want to if I can remember to make the effort, but only one at a time. The man who wants to make me kick Kagle in the leg is a worldly, relaxed fellow with black silk socks and a gray pinstripe suit. He's a man about my own age with neatly trimmed white hair. He is little, of course; he has to be to fit inside. (Even all those sinister and gigantic ogres who've been menacing me in my nightmares all my life have been small; it's just that I am so much smaller.) He seems to know his way about the stone passageways of my brain much better than I do, for he reappears in different settings, often reading a newspaper with one ankle crossed comfortably over his knee, biding his time. He thinks he's got more time than I have. (He hasn't.) I think there's a sauna, for many of the more affluent, better-bred occupants of my thoughts seem the type that likes to scorch itself leisurely after playing squash. I suspect there's a homosexual haunt located somewhere secret. Tiny shops are all about at which wicked contraband is exchanged by grimy, unshaven men who know how. Grimy, unshaven men expose themselves to me and to children of both sexes and go unpunished. All crimes go unpunished.

Vile these evil, sordid, miniature human beings who populate my brain, like living fingers with faces and souls. Some wear hats. People suffer. I suffer. Children wander. Women weep. Mothers lie on death-beds. I am afraid—I have been afraid—a screaming, wailing, or sobbing might start at any instant inside my ears, be taken up by other tortured voices from within, and never stop. I would not know if I was imagining it. It would not matter. I would hear it. Minikins move, and I can feel them, and dirty, cynical old men with sharp crutches and pointy beards pass with insinuating glints in their cruel, unscrupulous eyes. They hurt. Ugolino eats a head: mine (that son of a bitch).

No one will help. (Only my wife's sister verges close enough to that delicate nerve of truth we want unbared, but her front is callous, her motives unkind, and I want to hit her.)

"Give the kid away," she as much as commands with taunting relish in her rasping, obtrusive way, attacking, pressing her advantage, and we must unite to resist her and beat her back.

"Good for you! It serves you right," is what I hear her snarling invidiously at us in my own voice and words. "I'm glad it happened. Ha, ha. I'm glad it happened to you because I know you, instead of to people I don't know who live far away."

I want to hit her because I feel she sees inside me and steals my thoughts, compelling me to repudiate them.

We want to get rid of him. We want to give him away. And need people in positions of respectable authority to tell us. We haven't nerve to do it alone. What will people we know think of us?

Unfeeling.

Inhuman.

We want to give him away and are afraid.

(Other people we hear about in Connecticut, New York, Long Island, and New Jersey intend to keep theirs. Why?)

"Don't," my wife's sister has warned consistently almost from the first day there was no longer any doubt (which was too soon). "Do it fast. Don't be hypocrites. The longer you wait, the worse it's going to be for everybody."

That suggestion was monstrous. (Hypocrisy was easier.)

"Don't say that again!" my wife flares up at her that last time. "I don't ever want to hear you say anything about it again to us, or I won't let you come here. I mean that."

"I've had it," I roar at my wife afterward. "I don't ever want to hear her talk about him again. Or about any of the other kids either. I'll throw her out if she does. If you won't tell her I will."

"I did tell her. You heard me. Did you think that was easy?"

"You're only reacting that way because you know I'm right," her sister had responded self-righteously.

"She was only trying to be helpful," my wife continues repentently. "Now I'm sorry I yelled at her."

"No, she wasn't. Do you think she was trying to be helpful? I wish she'd move to Arizona with your mother."

"Her store is here."

She is a seamy, murky inner lining of my wife's character that my wife has never been able to look at without retreating immediately into remorse. She is another underside of my own (that I am able to show often at home to my family and reveal to myself in daydreams with vindictive jubilation) just as Derek also is, in my occasional wish to be speechless and powerless again and wholly dependent once more on parents and big brothers and sisters. (Except that I would not want to be sent away to a home.) Everyone around me now reminds me of me. Even Kagle reminds me of me. (Green doesn't. I admire Green. Arthur Baron doesn't; I find I don't identify as readily with my betters or with people who have more attractive qualities than my own. Only with people who are worse.) Arthur Baron never mentions Derek to me. Andy Kagle does, and I hate him for it. (I could have killed him when he showed up at the house Sunday without invitation to tell me, unctuously and pretentiously, that it was God's will. I wanted to hit him too.) I resent it blazingly when anyone talks to me about him (and want to kill them), although I also hope that everyone in the world will join together soon at the identical moment to tell me:

"Give the kid away."

That isn't going to happen.

I don't have to poll the members of my family to find out what we want. Even my fair-haired, lovable, good-hearted, sensitive boy, who is appalled by the alternatives, really doesn't mean it when he pleads:

"Don't."

He means:

"Please."

"But please whisk him away too swiftly for the eye to see or the mind to record and remember."

Kagle called from the filling station in town with the lie he just happened to be driving through and would like to say hello to the family. He looked haggard. There were sleepless shadows under his eyes and it was all he could do to force even a nervous smile.

"You hear things," he confided. "This time I'm really worried. Has anyone said anything about me?"

"I hear you've been to Toledo again."

"They aren't even talking to me about the convention. By now they usually give me a theme."

"Maybe they don't have one."

"I have to meet with Horace White. With him and Arthur Baron. I never have anything to do with Horace White."

"Maybe he's got some ideas."

"Two on one," Kagle chirps at me with a wink, as soon as my wife starts back into the house again.

"Coons?"

504

He misses my irony.

"Not for me. Not in Toledo. I've got good connections there. You ought to tag along sometime. I'll take good care of you."

"Should I ask him to stay for dinner?" my wife asks.

"Don't."

"He looks so unhappy."

"He wants to drive around."

"I don't even care," Kagle says, wiping the back of his hand over his mouth, drying his lips. "I'm getting tired of doing the same thing anyway. Where's the kids? I'd like to say hello to them before I go."

"Out playing."

"What about the little one? The one with the brain damage?"

"He's resting. He has to."

"You know, you shouldn't blame yourself about your boy," Kagle tells me, twisting himself back into his car. "I don't blame myself about my leg. It was God's will."

"Sure, Andy," I reply with a nasty smile, gritting my teeth. "And you don't worry about your job. If you lose it, it's God's will."

"Heh-heh," he comments hollowly.

"Heh-heh."

"Why didn't you let him stay?" my wife asks.

"I didn't want him."

It is God's will.

I've got Kagle's job.

"You were with Andy Kagle today," my wife says.

"How can you tell?"

"You're walking with a limp. Is his leg getting worse?"

"No, why?"

"His limp is worse than ever. You're almost staggering."

I straighten myself from a position characteristic of one of Kagle's and lean in a slouch of my own

505

against the newel post of the staircase leading to the second floor.

"No. He's the same."

She looks at me askance. She's been drinking wine again while helping the maid prepare dinner. Her bleary eyes are tense and patient. (I cannot meet them.) She senses something, and moves ahead carefully with mixed curiosity.

"Then you must have been with him a long time."

"I got his job."

"Did you?"

"I was promoted today."

"To what?"

"Kagle's job."

"Kagle's?"

"It finally went through."

"Was that the job?"

"Congratulate me."

"Did you know it was his job?"

"No."

"Yes, you did."

"I had a hunch."

"What happened to him?"

"Nothing."

"What will? I saw the way he looked."

"He was fired."

"My God."

"I fired him today. He doesn't know that yet. But I think he does."

"You fired him?"

"I had to, God dammit. He won't be fired. He'll be transferred somewhere else until he quits or retires. I can't keep him around. I couldn't use him after he's been in charge. He's embarrassing. He's sloppy. He'll run my work down."

"He's got two children."

"So have I."

"You've got three."

"So?"

"You're forgetting Derek again."

"So?"

"You're always forgetting Derek."

"So?"

"So's your old man." She is drunk and she is defiant.

"What the hell else am I supposed to do?"

"I'm better than you," she tells me.

"You want a new house, don't you? You liked the idea that I was getting a better job, didn't you?"

"I used to think I wasn't," she continues. "But I am. You like to think you're better than me. But you're not. I'm the one who's better."

"Yeah? And you'd be even better still if you'd lay off the wine in the afternoon."

"Your mother was right."

"Leave her out of it."

"You're just no good."

"I told you to leave her out of it."

"I never thought I was."

"You're always bothering me about money, aren't you?"

"No, I don't."

"The hell you don't."

"And neither do they. We don't bother you about money that much."

"And you wonder why I don't tell you I love you, don't you?"

"I never thought I was good at anything." There is undisguised scorn, calm, measured contempt that I've never seen in her before. "You don't help much there."

"Kagle isn't sore at me. Why are you?"

"Isn't he?"

"No. In fact, he's the one who recommended me to replace him."

"No, he didn't," she jeers, with a curling lip and a belittling shake of her head. "You knew months ago. He just found out."

"You're getting good at this."

"You taught me."

"At least you got something."

"But now I know I'm better than you are, aren't I?"

"Amn't I. There's no such construction as 'aren't I.'"

"Puddy poo."

"What'd you say?"

"Puddy poo."

"Where'd you get that from?"

"From you. You say it in your sleep."

"I'm going upstairs. I can't take this."

"Puddy poo. What about dinner?"

"Count me out. I'll celebrate upstairs alone. I've got to start working on my speech."

"What speech?"

"The big speech I'm going to have to make to open the convention. I'm head of the department now. That might not mean much at home but it means a hell of a lot there. I run the whole show. I can do what I want."

"Can you get Andy Kagle his job back?"

"Fuck you," I tell her.

"You're just no good, are you?"

"I told you. I warned you. I don't want you ever to say that to me again."

"I'll say anything I want," she shouts back at me heatedly. "I'm not afraid of you."

"Yes, you say that to me often," I remind her. "And then you sober up, and discover that you are."

She shatters. "You bastard." The tears form quickly and are streaming down her face. "You won another argument, didn't you?"

I don't feel I've won. I feel I've lost as I mount the stairs wearily. It's been a harrowing day at the office. The meetings were concluded at five to allow the rumors to spread and percolate through the company overnight. Kagle lingers later than the rest of us to confirm them appreciatively.

"I want you to know I had a big hand in it," he tells me. "I fought for you with Arthur Baron when he asked me to recommend someone who I thought could really handle it. They were thinking of someone like Johnny Brown or one of the branch managers. I told them you knew more about it than any of them. Now I'll be free to do the kind of troubleshooting work I like. Don't be afraid of any of it. I'll be around to help you all I can."

No, he won't.

"Thanks, Andy. What's that you've got there?"

"It's a perpetual-motion machine Horace White gave me. I'll bet you'd never be able to figure out how it works if you didn't know where the battery was hidden."

(Batteries run down. He'll have about ten days after the convention and then he'll have to take a leave of absence for a few weeks and move. Or retire. I have a plan.)

"What about me?" I maintain to Johnny Brown, who blocks my path skeptically with smoldering belligerence, his muscled jaws knotted for combat (and I wonder, perhaps, if he might not mercifully end my suspense by giving me my punch in the jaw right at the start). "You could have knocked me over with a feather when they told me, I was so surprised."

"I heard the good news the little birdies are chirping," Ed Phelps chortles to me softly by way of offering congratulations.

I elude Green. I don't see Red. I feel tense and exhausted on the train ride home. I could use one of my wife's tranquilizers. Even before I walk in the house I am feeling sorry for myself and don't know why. I go to our bathroom for a tranquilizer before I enter my study and close the door.

"What's wrong with Daddy?" I hope the children are murmuring downstairs in grave consternation, along with Derek's nurse, and that Derek too can perceive in some way that I am upstairs in my study with the door closed.

"He isn't feeling well," I hope my wife replies with sharp compunction.

I would like to feel that the closed door of my study or office produces the same ominous, excluding effect on others that the closed doors of certain people still create in me. (I am still affronted that my daughter always keeps the door to her room shut when she's inside. My boy does that too, now.)

I'm sorry I ever told my wife what I think my mother said to me before she died. (I'm also sorry I said "puddy poo" in my sleep. Now she'll have *that* on me, also.) I don't know what ever made me feel I could trust her. (A man must make a resolution *never* to reveal anything personal to his wife.) I was not even sure my mother said it. I wasn't sure she recognized me for more than an instant the last few times I went to visit her in the nursing home or remembered I was there as I sat at her bedside without talking for the twelve, then ten, minutes I stayed. I brought no more gifts of spicy meats and fish and honeyed candies; she couldn't eat. I gave her no gossip. She couldn't hear. I was not even certain most times that she was able to see anyone sitting there when her eyes were upon me.

"You're no good," she said. There was no voice. It was more a shaping of the words with her lips and a faint rustle of breath. I was surprised, and I bent forward over the cavity of her mouth that I was no longer able to look at straightly and asked her to repeat what she had said. "You're just no good."

Those were the last words I think I heard her speak to me. If I live to be a hundred and ninety years old, I will never hear any more from her. If the world lasts three billion more, there will be no others.

Those are some last words for a dying mother to tell a child, aren't they? Even a grown-up family man with a wife and three children. I felt sorrier for myself when I heard them than I did for her. She was dying anyway.

But I had to go on.

I don't know what made me think it was safe to confide in my wife. A long time passed before I did. I was feeling so sad. The world was a rusty tin can. We used to curl ourselves up inside discarded old automobile tires and try to roll down slanting streets. We never could. We made pushmobile scooters out of ball-bearing roller skates. It was easier to walk. Mommy caught me when I fell, kissed the place to make it well.

I should never have told the bitch. The bitches remember things like that.

The linings of the brain. (The linings of my brain, they give me such a pain.) The linings of my brain are three in number and called collectively the *meninges*. They surround it on the outside. The innermost is called the pia mater. It is a delicate, fibrous, and highly vascular membrane (gorged with veins and capillaries, I suppose). I feel pressure against it from inside. Things bubble and shove against it as though they might explode. It reminds me at times of a cheese fondue. The pia mater, reinforced by the two supporting layers, the arachnoid and the dura mater, holds fast against the outward expanding pressure of my brain, pushes back. At times, there is pain. The name pia mater derives from an imperfect translation into Latin of Arabic words that meant (ha, ha) *tender mother*.

My boy has
stopped talking
to me

———— o ————

My boy has stopped talking to me, and I don't think
I can stand it. (He doesn't seem to like me.) He no
longer confides in me.

There are times he rebuffs me and I want to cry.
I remember the rebuff and it tears at my heart. Why
should he want to stop talking to me? I want to be
his best friend. Doesn't he know I probably love him
more than anyone else in the world? He used to have
dreams, he said, in which the door to our room was
closed and he could not get in to see us. Now I have
dreams that the door to his room is closed and I
cannot get in to see him.

He goes to bed without even saying good night
to me, closing his door.

My head spins, my emotions reel downward into
whirlpools. He no longer comes to me for information
as often as he used to, and I have no way of knowing
anymore what he's thinking, who his friends are, what
games he enjoys most, how much trouble he's having
at school and with his homework. I hang on news
of Forgione. He acts angry with me. It is impossible
to get more from him than he wants to tell without
offending him or finding out about him surreptitiously
by asking someone else. (I wonder if he feels I'm
spying on him.)

"I climbed the rope in school today," he announces
one evening when he comes home late for dinner
after dark, with his eyes shining warmly and his cheeks

and lips colored a healthy, handsome crimson with exercise and excitement. "I made it almost all the way up to the top. Dammit. I bet I could have touched the ceiling if I'd only had the nerve to let go and try."

"Did you touch the ceiling yet?" I ask him.

"Why do you keep asking me that?" he blurts out at me resentfully, and goes into his room.

He is moving away from me and I don't want him to. He is shutting me out. I see the doors closed to his and my daughter's rooms and think of the closed doors at the company and am reminded squeamishly of all those closed cupboard and closet doors I had to open each morning and evening back in the apartment in the city with those baited spring traps concealed behind them when we were trying to catch or kill those mice. Those were not the good old days.

"Remember," I reminisce with my wife, "those mice back in the city? That one time we had them?"

"They weren't mice," says my wife. "They were roaches."

"We had those too."

"We never had mice."

"And I was afraid I would have to kill one with a magazine?"

"And you were afraid to kill them. You didn't like to step on them. You didn't like the way they squashed. I had to do it most of the time with one of my house slippers. And neither did I."

She may be wrong.

My memory does get faulty of late, merges indistinguishably with imagination, and I must make efforts to shake them apart. I remember waking up as a child, howling from a dream my bed was crawling with roaches and I continued to see them scurrying away into invisibility all over the room for minutes after the lights blazed on and I was wide awake. It was my brother who had come to console me (who once threw a lump of coal at me), and he sat with me tenderly until I was able to stop quailing. Now I have no big brother. One of my children—I forget which one—had a bad dream years ago about snapping

513

fishes swimming in the bed, and I remembered instantly I had suffered those too.

"There were fishes in my bed," I sobbed, shivering. "Swimming around on the blankets."

"They aren't there now," my brother comforted me patiently. "Keep looking and you'll see."

"They weren't there before," I exclaimed, still sobbing. "But I saw them anyway."

I see things that aren't there. I used to lie awake listening to people coming to steal me away. I was afraid of the dark. I heard drugged moaning and sobbing from a different part of the apartment. When I crept from my room, it stopped. When I returned to my room it started again and continued at irregular intervals until I was stolen away into sleep. My boy used to be afraid of the dark but isn't anymore. (I'm not sure I didn't like him better when he was. I think I was happier with him when he needed me more.) He'll stay out now after dark, sometimes until I worry, and won't tell us where he's been or with whom unless we ask. I don't want him to shut me out.

"In open school week this year," I begin to scheme with my wife, "I'm going to try to sneak away to speak to Forgione and the principal and find out all I can about him."

"He doesn't want you to come this year. And he doesn't want me to stay more than an hour."

"Why didn't he tell me?"

"He told me."

And my daughter stole the car with one of her friends by telling my wife I'd given them permission to take it and alibiing to me that my wife had misunderstood. She started to cry when we trapped her between us. She said we were always picking on her. She said I was nicer to my boy than I was to her. She said she couldn't wait to graduate from high school and go to college, just to get away from us. She said she could tell we didn't want her living there.

"If you'd buy me my own car," she said through her sniffles, "I wouldn't have to tell lies to get one."

I suppose I'll have to, sooner or later (for my sake more than hers). She'll wear me down. I'm glad the price of gasoline is going up so that poor working people won't have any and there'll be more than enough for people like my daughter and me.

"At least she's not seeing that boy anymore," my wife says. "And she doesn't take drugs."

"You think I believe her?"

"She drives with her friends. She's home early. She doesn't go out as much on weekends anymore. Haven't you noticed?" She lowers her head in dismay, hesitating sadly. "I wish she would. She has nothing to do."

I feel locked inside a hopeless struggle. Forecasts are coming true. I am better off these days at the office. I feel safer, even when at home (I don't feel safe at home. I feel things are going inexorably out of control. Things are not out of control at the company), if I can concentrate all my attention on the office, where the tasks are discernible, the obligations all cut and dried. I know what I must do: for the time being, I must be cordial and close to everyone here, even those who are disposable, and cool and distant to everyone under me in all the out-of-town offices. No one must feel secure. Everyone must be kept in suspense about new decisions that might emerge from meetings behind closed doors in which I am now a participant. (I am a kingmaker.) Plans for the convention are moving ahead efficiently because no one entrusted with executing any of them feels secure. I am regarded with envy, hope, fear, ambition, suspicion, and disappointment. My small secretary congratulates me and hopes I will take her with me. I won't. I tell her she is too valuable where she is. I'll have better safeguards with Kagle's girl, who's more persuasive at lying and more adroit at covering things up. In my former department, I have Schwoll the wise guy and Holloway the weak guy, a new, bright young fellow who isn't going to stay and an elderly plodder who isn't going to go, along with three other underlings who do what they're told to industriously enough, and I leave them all behind with pleasure on moving day. My new, temporary office is a windowless one across from Kagle's. Kagle's been told by Arthur Baron and Horace White that he'll be allowed to remain in his spacious executive office for as long as he stays. (He hasn't been told how short a time he'll be allowed to stay.) Green will have to replace me. I wonder with who (whom). I haven't decided yet how to handle Green. (He isn't as afraid of me yet as I feel he should be.)

"Have you anyone in mind you can recommend to take your place?" he asks me pleasantly enough on moving day, but with a taint in his manner that puts me on guard. "I'd like someone better than you," he adds with breezy malice the moment I nod.

"You'll have to pay him much more," I joke.

"I'll be happy to," he scores. "He'll be worth it."

Green is not afraid of me at all yet, and I may have to handle him, for a while, by groveling.

"What about Kagle?" he inquires sweetly. "Do you think he'd be good enough to take your place?"

"He wouldn't want to. I'm afraid he'd interpret it as a big step down."

"Not from where you're planning to put him."

"Special projects?"

"For you?"

"Of course."

"After working for you he'd interpret it as a big step up."

"Jack," I entreat him in a conciliatory tone, "you're supposed to be afraid of me now. At least a little."

"You knew about this when I was threatening you last time. Didn't you?"

"It had to be quiet."

"And you were afraid of me anyway."

"I wasn't afraid."

"My judgment may be bad but my eye isn't. I couldn't be that wrong about you."

"You had the whammy on me then."

"There was all that sweat. And you're afraid of me now. Right now."

I grin submissively. "You've got the whammy on me still."

"And you always will be."

"I'm not sure about that. I won't have to go to meetings with you alone. I can criticize you to others. I can kill your projects and reject your work."

"Would you?"

"I'd rather not. I'd rather have your help. Just don't make a fool of me."

"It will be hard to resist, with someone like you."

"I know. You're tempted right now. Fly into somebody else's face if you want to be squashed. Try Lester Black. He'll do it quickly enough."

Green is not able to keep the flush of anger from climbing into his cheeks. "If I did," he retorts hotly, "I'd probably find you in the way, anointing his cheeks."

And for a moment, I am the one with superior poise. "You're starting," I chide gently.

"It's hard not to."

"Now you're starting again."

"It gets harder. How will you treat me?"

"With deference. Better than Kagle did. With fear—I don't want to fight with you yet, not this year. I'll be very nice to you with everyone, if you don't make me look ridiculous for being so."

"You'll be nice? That's a humiliation for me right there."

"That's a part I'll enjoy," I agree affably. "I'm smiling now because I know it's true. Not because I'm enjoying it yet. Jack, there's been a big change. I don't work for you anymore. You have to be afraid of me now," I remind him. "You know that."

"I'm afraid I can't be."

And Green still has the whammy on me! I can stomp all over him, spit in his eye, beat him down into nervous collapse, send him, clutching his bowels, into a hospital bed with his spastic colitis; I am younger, stronger, bigger, and in better health than he is and can punch him in the jaw as easily as Johnny Brown can give me my punch in the jaw—and he still has the whammy on me. I am still afraid of him and perspiring copiously under the arms again. No wonder I am more and more prey to weird visions and experiences. (Some tickle my fancy. Some do not.)

The day before yesterday, I walked into a luncheonette for a rare roast beef sandwich on a seeded roll and thought I found my barber working behind the counter.

"What are you doing in a luncheonette?" I asked.

"I'm not your barber," he answered.

I was afraid I was losing my mind.

A week ago I looked out a taxi window and saw Jack Green begging in the street in the rain, dressed in a long wet overcoat and ragged shoes. He was a head taller, thinner, pale, and gaunt. It wasn't him. But that's what I saw.

I was afraid I was losing my wits.

Yesterday I looked out the window of a bus and thought I saw Charlie Chaplin strolling along the avenue and believed I knew him. It wasn't Charlie Chaplin and I didn't know him.

My memory may be starting to fail me. I have trouble with names now and with keeping in correct order the digits of telephone numbers that have long been familiar to me. Pairs of digits from other telephone numbers push their way in. After all these years, I am not always certain anymore whether the seven-seven belongs in the first segment of Penny's phone number and the eight-seven in the latter or vice versa. I don't know every time if Red Parker's phone number is two-eight-o-two or two-o-eight-two. I do know Penny is pregnant again—not by me. I have given her money for the abortion. She will insist on paying me back when she's saved enough from the money she receives monthly from her parents in Wilmington. It used to be that every cocktail waitress I ran into had one divorce and two children who lived outside the city with the girl's mother. Now they've had two abortions. College students and young models, secretaries, stewardesses, and acting students have had one. Graduate students may have two, depending on their field of study. Jane is gone, along with the entire Art Department. (It was unprofitable.)

"Call me," I asked her. "As soon as you're settled. Or even before."

She did. When she called, I said I was busy and would call her back. I haven't. Sometimes when I'm asleep, I try to wake up and can't. Sleep has me in its grip, and that is my dream.

I am trying to get my affairs in order. I have written a list.

"Listen," I say to my wife one day in a quietly decisive manner. "We're going to have to sit down together soon and do some serious thinking about Derek. We're not going to be able to keep him forever, you know."

"I don't want to talk about it."

Neither do I.

I think I'm in terrible trouble. I think I've committed a crime. The victims have always been children.

"Are you angry with me?" I inquire of my boy with an appraising smile, in a voice I keep as bland as possible.

"No. I'm not angry."

A flicker of some kind has crossed his face. My question is disturbing him. I'm almost afraid to go on.

"You don't talk to me much anymore."

"I talk." He shrugs. "I'm talking now." He wiggles with unease, a downcast mood darkening his features. He will not look at me.

"Not as much as you used to. You're always in your room."

He shrugs again. "I like it there."

"You don't like me to ask you questions, do you?"

"Sometimes."

"What do you do in there?"

"Read. Watch television. I do my homework. Think."

"Alone?"

"I like it."

"You didn't use to."

"Now I do."

"Are you always able to do all of your homework without me?"

"Not always."

"What do you do?"

"It's all right if it's wrong."

"Wouldn't it be better, though, if it were always correct?"

"The teachers don't care. Can I go now?"

"Where?"

He smiles apologetically, anticipating the humor of his reply. "To my room."

"Sure," I consent genially, with a heartiness that is false. "I just wanted to make sure you weren't angry with me."

"You stay in your room a lot," he pauses near the staircase to argue over his shoulder defensively. "Mommy stays in her room. You don't think there's something wrong with me, do you?"

"But I always let you come into mine."

Oh, God—here he is, a sensitive, candid, alert little boy, no larger now, it seems, than he was as a toddler; and I am quarreling with him, near tears (and with a lump in my throat), as though I were a rejected suitor, fencing with him selfishly as I would with my wife or my daughter.

How shall I die? Let me count the ways. (No, I won't.) I've been through that juvenile exercise before and won't waste time. None is good. I'm unable to eradicate from my mind the image of that vigorous, prosperous, large, handsome man who fell dead in the lobby of my office building a few weeks ago as we were nearly abreast of each other. I saw him clearly as he fell forward. Even as he was doubling over and crumpling he looked the epitome of radiant and robust indestructibility until his face hit the floor with a soggy whack and blood from the impact shot out of his mouth. I continued walking past him without a hitch in my stride. I made believe I didn't see. When I got back from lunch, he wasn't there. He had been taken away. I was disappointed. Someone had distorted reality for the sake of neatness. (I have things organized very neatly now upstairs.) I still catch myself looking for him in the spot where he fell. I still remember him falling. This morning on my way to work I saw an unconscious derelict lying on the steps of Saint Patrick's Cathedral, staining the stone platforms with a fluid that could have been urine or whiskey. Policemen were there and had the situation in hand. They didn't need my help.

It's a good thing they didn't.

Woe, woe, alas, and alack. My wife is unhappy too again. We have arrived at a reasonable understanding: it isn't all my fault and there's not much I can do to improve things (even though I still won't tell her I love her and she refuses pointedly to ask). She makes no difference to anyone.

"I wish I had a career at something exciting."

"It isn't too late."

She lifts her eyes to study me in steadfast gaze. "It is too late."

"Of course it is."

She accepts the fact that Kagle was fated to go no matter what I did, and that if I had not gone in to replace him, I would never have been allowed to go anywhere else.

"You'd get a housekeeper, wouldn't you?" she says dreamily. "And put Derek in a home. Or you'd send the children away to boarding school and move into the city."

"If what?"

"If I committed suicide or died of cancer or just moved away alone or with some other man."

"Are you thinking of any of those?" I ask with healing indulgence.

"And I wouldn't blame you. I just don't make a difference to anyone."

"Neither do I," I have to confess intimately. "Except to you and the children. Not even Derek."

"I'd be satisfied with that. No, don't lie to me about it," she adds with dignity and a very small, regretful smile. "I wouldn't believe you."

My wife feels she makes no difference to anyone anymore and she is probably right.

There is so much torment around, even for her. I have to make a speech. My boy will probably perish without me (or I without him. I think I may always have felt that way about him). Oh, my God—we go into torment long before we even know what suffering is. We are saddled with it before we can even see. There is so much inner fright. I was born, I was told, with a mashed face and red and blue forcep bruises on my shoulders and arms but felt not one message of pain because I had no nervous system yet that could register any. But I knew what loneliness was. I was already afraid of the dark. Or the light. If I

521

knew what cold and sleet were I would have been afraid of those too. (Are we afraid of what we can't see or of what we will see when we do?) I was afraid I would open my eyes and it would still be dark. (It was that way in that hospital the night they took my tonsils out.) I am afraid of that happening now. And no one would come. Fear. Loss of love, loss of the loved one, loss of love of the loved one. Separation. We don't want to go, we don't want them to go, we can't wait for them to leave, we wish they'd return. There seem to be conflicts. I was in need of whatever nipple succored me and whatever arms lifted me. I didn't know names. I loved the food that fed me—that's all I knew—and the arms that held and hugged and turned me and gave me to understand, at least for those periods, that I was not alone and someone else knew I was there. Without them, I would have been alone. I am afraid of the dark now. I have nightmares in strange beds, and in my own. I have apparitions underneath my bed waiting to stream out. I have spirits in my bedroom closets. I am anxious as a four-year-old child. I am afraid of the light. I am afraid I will open my eyes someday and it will still be dark. And no one will come. (I woke up without tonsils and adenoids in the hospital one thousand times that night and it was always dark, and I thought there would never be light again. And no one came.) What will I have to look forward to if morning comes one day and there is no light? What will I be like when I am senile? Will I molest children, break wind, defecate on living room floors, say nigger, bait Jews? I say nigger now occasionally; it slips out. I could bait Green. I think I know expressly how to cope with Green.

"Jack," I could begin, with an air of disarming joviality, "I think I'd like to hire a Jew. Do you know of any? I'd want a smart one."

"I'm afraid that would be impossible," he might reply, with the same pretense of amiability.

"Aren't there any smart ones left?" I could follow up, tauntingly.

"Oh, yes," he would answer. "But a smart one

wouldn't work for you. And if you're going to hire the other kind, you'd might as well stick with a Protestant. They'd make a better appearance, for you."

And I'd discover once more that I'd still not been able to cope with him at all. I'll bet I'm probably one of the very few people in the entire world who know (not *knows*) that *livid* means blue and *lurid* means pale. A lot of good that knowledge has done me. (Green may be one of the others who know, and it's done him even less.) My boy's complexion is pale again, and his eyes are blue and deep. I wish I could look all the way inside them to see what is going on in his mind.

"Why are you staring at me?" he asks uncomfortably.

"I'm not staring."

"You were."

"I'm sorry. I was thinking." He intends to remain silent. "And if you asked me what I was thinking about, do you know what I'd say?"

"What?" he asks, to oblige me.

"I was thinking about when you were going to ask me why I was staring at you."

He grins with a small noise of appreciation as a token of acknowledgment, and goes into his room, closing the door.

I don't want him to go. My memory's failing, my bladder is weak, my arches are falling, my tonsils and adenoids are gone, and my jawbone is rotting, and now my little boy wants to cast me away and leave me behind for reasons he won't give me. What else will I have? My job? When I am fifty-five, I will have nothing more to look forward to than Arthur Baron's job and reaching sixty-five. When I am sixty-five, I will have nothing more to look forward to than reaching seventy-five, or dying before then. And when I am seventy-five, I will have nothing more to look forward to than dying before eighty-five, or geriatric care in a nursing home. I will have to take enemas. (Will I have to be dressed in double-layer, waterproof undershorts designed especially for incontinent gentlemen?) I will be incontinent. I don't want to live longer than eighty-five, and I don't want to die sooner than a hundred and eighty-six.

Oh, my father—why have you done this to me?

I want him back.

I want my little boy back too.

I don't want to lose him.

I do.

"Something happened!" a youth in his early teens calls excitedly to a friend and goes running ahead to look.

A crowd is collecting at the shopping center. A car has gone out of control and mounted the sidewalk. A plate glass window has been smashed. My boy is lying on the ground. (He has not been decapitated.) He is screaming in agony and horror, with legs and arms twisted brokenly and streams of blood spurting from holes in his face and head and pouring down over one hand from inside a sleeve. He spies me with a start and extends an arm. He is panic-stricken. So am I.

"Daddy!"

He is dying. A terror, a pallid, pathetic shock more dreadful than any I have ever been able to imagine, has leaped into his face I can't stand it. He can't stand it. He hugs me. He looks beggingly at me for help. His screams are piercing. I can't bear to see him suffering such agony and fright. I have to do something. I hug his face deeper into the crook of my shoulder. I hug him tightly with both my arms. I squeeze.

"Death," says the doctor, "was due to asphyxiation. The boy was smothered. He had superficial lacerations of the scalp and face, a bruised hip, a deep cut on his arm. That was all. Even his spleen was intact."

The nurses and policemen are all very considerate to me as I weep. They wait in respectful silence.

"Would you like to be alone?" one murmurs.

I'm afraid to be alone. I would rather have them

all there with me now, to see me weeping in such crushing grief and shame. I cry a long time. When I feel I am able to speak, finally, I lift my eyes slowly a little bit and say:

"Don't tell my wife."

Nobody knows
what I've done

———◦———

Nobody knows what I've done. Everybody is impressed with how bravely I've been able to move into Kagle's position and carry on with the work of organizing the convention. No one understands that carrying on bravely was the easiest thing to do.

I get to make my speech, finally. It is a solid success (and nobody cares. Nobody, I learn, remembers shortly afterward what it was even about. I had entertained the hope that one of the officials, in commending me, would suggest that mimeographed copies be made and distributed by Public Relations to executives in other divisions of the company, trade publications, and Chambers of Commerce. None do). My speech, at Arthur Baron's suggestion, was kept short. I spoke for exactly three minutes. Kagle, who opened the convention, introduced me lavishly in a speech lasting fifteen. Green spoke for twenty-seven minutes, arrogating to himself the entire time I had budgeted for his department, and was glittering and boring.

"I enjoyed your speech, Jack," I complimented him.

"Would you like a copy?" he responded. "I've had it mimeographed."

"I was going to ask."

"Be sure you credit me if you ever quote any of it. I'm thinking of having it published."

His eyes are hunting behind me already for bigger game. (I am still not important enough for him—this year.) He deserts me for Horace White, who jettisons him by moving to Lester Black, who is listening attentively to baleful mutterings about me from Johnny Brown, with whom I am going to have to talk strongly soon, and of whom I am afraid. People seem dazzled by the swift competence with which I appear to be taking things under control.

Systematically, I am putting my affairs in order. I tick them off my list.

I have told my wife I love her.

We have decided to keep Derek longer (he may get better. They may be wrong. They're finding new things out every day) and have found a nurse for him who may work out (the first two replacements wouldn't stay, and this one has body odor).

I have given my daughter a car of her own. Her spirits seem to be picking up. (I bought my wife a new convertible she likes, sent her shopping for the new house we need. It's not a career, but it will have to be furnished. My wife won't take a vacation without me. We are now a three-car family.) My daughter promises she will pass her high school courses this year and tells us she wants to go to college. She says she's stopped telling lies. (She may be telling the truth.)

I have retired Ed Phelps and fired Red Parker. (Red Parker doesn't know that yet. He mails warmest greetings from St. Thomas every time he flies down there with some other female whack.) I get call reports every Friday now, and they are accurate.

"Well, at least there's one good thing," Brown conceded to me grudgingly when we got back to the office. "We can stop wasting time on these stupid call reports."

I made myself ready for the worst, stood up, and confronted him squarely. "No, you can't. I'll want them all on my desk by the close of business every Friday."

"You're a pisser."

"And I don't want you to say I'm a pisser."

Our eyes locked. There was hatred between us. I saw his large fists clench and was trembling inside. I thought he was going to give me my punch in the jaw right then—until I suddenly realized the blood was draining from *his* face too, faster, probably, than from mine. He was afraid also. He was dissolving: sick little tremors were playing like maggots around his mouth and sinewy jaw. All his truculent bravery was vanishing, and I saw him slipping away from me someplace from which I knew I would never see him return.

"Johnny!" I wanted to cry. "Johnny Brown! Where are you going?"

"Okay," he mumbled, looking down.

But he was already gone, transubstantiating himself like witchcraft into someone obsequious, cringing to hold on to a job he would no longer be able to do. I have had him transferred to another division of the company and replaced by an Italian graduate from a business school who wants to make good, and who is afraid of me.

I play more golf. (Swish!) And am getting quite good.

Kagle's off the payroll with his pension and profit-sharing benefits and has a two-year contract with the company as a part-time consultant whom no one will ever use.

But I've still not been able to hire a Jew. We are an Equal Opportunity Employer and Advertiser and I don't know where to find one. (Green found one to replace me and is paying him more money than he was paying me. I hope he's not pushy.)

Martha the typist is gone. (In every office in which I've ever worked, though, there was always at least one person who was going crazy slowly, and I am waiting to see how long it will take Personnel and Providence to send along the next one.)

A man named Gray has joined the company from a high government post and will fit right in between Black and White. We have no primary colors left, I believe, although we probably have some reds, ha, ha, most of us feel blue, ha, ha, and all of us are yellow.

Whenever I have a really good bowel movement, my lonely hemorrhoid begins to bleed. Maybe I ought to get it a friend.

Now that I have taken charge of my responsibilities, I do hear voices. I hear:

"You're a good administrator, Slocum."

"You've done a good job, Slocum."

"I liked the way you stepped right in and took over."

"You've got the department really humming, Slocum."

"You got Kagle out pretty smoothly, didn't you, Slocum? Ha, ha."

"I've never seen them working so hard, Slocum."

"I like the way you've taken control."

"I'm glad to see you're fitting in."

(I am fitting in.)

"Who's that?"

"Slocum."

"I'd like you to meet Bob Slocum," Arthur Baron and Horace White introduce me now. "He's one of our best men."

I meet a much higher class of executive at Arthur Baron's now when he has us to dinner. I play golf with a much better class of people. (Swish.) I have played golf at Round Hill twice already as a guest of Horace White, once with his undistinguished sister and her husband. She made eyes at me. (Swish.) I have a hitch in my swing. I have played at Burning Tree in Washington as the guest of a buyer and heard a deputy cabinet official tell an old joke poorly. I laughed. (Swish.) I laughed rambunctiously.

"Slocum's the name. Bob Slocum."

"Look me up the next time you're in town."

I have played at White Sulphur Springs in West Virginia as the company's representative to a national business conference. Maybe someday, if my game and my job continue to improve, I might even play St. Andrews in Scotland. (Swish.) I miss my boy. Martha the typist went crazy for me finally at just the right time in a way I was able to handle suavely. I took charge like a ballet master.

"Call Medical," I directed with an authority that was almost musical. "Call Personnel. Get Security. Call Travel and tell them to hire a chauffeured limousine immediately."

Martha sits in her typist's chair like an obdurate statue and will not move or speak. She is deaf to entreaty, shakes helping hands off violently, gives signs she might shriek. I wait nearby with an expression of aplomb. Her look turns dazed and panicky when anyone comes close. The nurses from Medical are quickly there.

"How are you, dear?" the eldest asks soothingly.

We have a good-sized audience now, and I am the supervisor. Martha rises compliantly, smiling, with a hint of diabolical satisfaction, I see, at the wary attention she has succeeded in extorting from so many people who are solicitous and alarmed.

"There, there, dear."

"Come along, dear."

"That's nice, dear."

"Take your purse, dear. And your book."

"Do you want to rest, dear?"

"Do you have a roommate, dear? Someone we can call?"

"Would you like to lie down, dear? While we're waiting for the car?"

"That's fine, dear."

"Good-bye, Martha."

"Good-bye, Martha dear."

"Bye, bye, dear."

"Did you leave anything behind?"

"Don't worry, dear. We'll send it along."

"Be gentle with her," I adjure. "She's a wonderful girl."

I hear applause when she's gone for the way I handled it.

No one was embarrassed.

Everyone seems pleased with the way I've taken command.

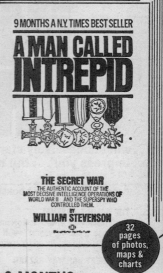